BURNING LOVE
Hell Yeah!
Cajun Style

By
SABLE HUNTER

This is a work of fiction. Names, characters, places and incidents are either the product of the author's imagination or used fictitiously, and any resemblance to actual persons, living or dead, business establishments, events or locales is entirely coincidental.

Beau's passion burns hot for Harley Montoya. When he discovers that the woman who has enflamed his libido is the girl he fell in love with so long ago in a runaway shelter, he is overcome with joy. But Harley - or Nada as he knew her - has been burned by tragedy. They both live lives full of adventure. He builds custom weaponry and owns a reptile preserve, and she is an EOD expert - Harley defuses bombs for a living. But nothing is more explosive than the love they share.

eau is determined to show Harley that he is worthy of her trust and that he is willing to protect her from anything that would cause her harm. But Harley has a mad-man on her trail and she can't walk away from her responsibilities. Bombs, alligators, haunted plantations and Louisiana lore spice up their life, and danger and ghosts from their past threatens to tear them apart - but nothing can put out the white-hot flames of their Burning Love.

**Warning: Intended for Adult audiences 18+. Contains: graphic scenes and sexual content.

Six brothers. One Dynasty—
TEBOW RANCH.
Meet the McCoy brothers and their friends
Texas men who love as hard as they play.
Texas Cowboys and Hot Cajuns – nothing better.
HELL YEAH!

Prologue

Brownwood Children's Home – New Orleans – Sixteen Years Ago

"Don't be afraid. I won't let him hurt you." Beau held his arms open and Nada ran into them. He just prayed he could keep his promise. She was so little and so very brave.

"He hurt you, too. I saw him." She whispered into his chest, her arms clasping him tight around the middle. Nada didn't know what she'd do without Beau. Pell was getting more and more demanding. Just today, she had barely eluded the police. Mardi Gras was usually an easy time for pickpockets, but the cops were cracking down. Sometimes, Nada thought it would be easier if she were arrested. How much worse could juvee be than Brownwood?

He ran a hand over her neck and noticed it was wet. Damn! "You're bleeding! He's already whipped you, hasn't he?" At her slight nod, he grabbed her hand and pulled her toward the sink in the small room. "Let's get that blood off and I'll put some medicine on you." Turning on the tap to let the water heat up, he went and put a chair underneath the doorknob. That small amount of security wouldn't stop Pell, but it would slow him down and deter any of the other kids from intruding on their privacy. Brownwood housed twenty-five unfortunate orphans or runaways and it existed because Pell could afford the bribes to keep the authorities at bay.

Taking a raggedy washcloth, he wet it and stood there awkwardly, trying to determine the best way to proceed. Finally, he said, "take your shirt off, I won't look."

Nada slid her T-shirt up and off. She had no bra – not that she needed one. Still, she was embarrassed. Holding

5

the scrap of cotton over her chest, she turned her back to Beau. "I only got two wallets and a few credit cards, not enough to make him happy." The drag of the rag on her skin stung a little. "Sharon is missing."

"I know." God, her little back was striped. Bastard. "We've got to figure a way out of this mess, or one of us will go missing, too." He knew the score, and usually he stole enough to pacify Pell, but it went against everything in him. Beau wasn't a thief and being forced to steal made him sick. He didn't like to take hard earned money from innocent people, no matter how drunk they were.

"Beau, can I stay in here with you tonight? Pell comes into my room at night and I try to pretend I'm asleep. He just stands there in the shadows, watching me. I'm afraid of him." Nada hated to ask, but she didn't know what else to do.

"He's coming in your room at night? Hell! Honey, I'm so sorry."

"Sssss," she made a small noise of pain when he put alcohol on the raw places. "Where did you get that stuff? It burns!"

"Sorry, if it stings. I bought it at the drug store with some of the money I filched. We have too many 'accidents' as it is, we don't need an infection, to boot." He longed to protect her. But, could she sleep with him? Damn! Would it be a sin? He liked girls; and he liked Nada, a lot. But, she was only thirteen and he was sixteen – old enough to know better. This little angel was innocent.

Nada understood. Beau hadn't said anything when she had asked to stay with him. That meant he would rather she didn't. She wouldn't ask again. After all, she was nobody. She was Nada. That was her name. The word Nada meant nothing, nobody. Her father had given her that name, put it on her birth certificate, and ground it into her head everyday – *'you are nobody'*. *'Nobody will ever want you.*

You are nothing.' Years of abuse and humiliation taught her to expect nothing. So, when she asked for something, Nada would only ask once and would show no emotion when she was told 'no'. "That's okay. I appreciate you doing this for me."

"All right, I'm finished; you can put your shirt back on." He turned away while she pulled it back over her head. When she was dressed again, he faced her. Nada's dark hair hung in gentle waves and her amber eyes were huge in a face which reflected too much sadness for one so young.

"Thank you, Beau." She noticed his face was bruised, and she couldn't help but reach out to touch it. "Do you need me to doctor you anywhere?"

"No, I'm all right." He put the lid on the disinfectant and hung up the cloth in the bathroom. When he came back, she was leaving. "Where are you going?"

"Back to my room." She looked confused. "Why?"

"Stay with me." He held out his hand. "I'll take care of you." When she smiled, his heart contracted. It was wrong, the way he felt about her. She was too young. And so damn fragile.

"Really? I need to go get my pajamas." She was about to go when he stopped her.

"Stay, you're already here. We don't want to attract too much attention. They've already done room check for the night. You can sleep in one of my t-shirts. How's that?" Beau pulled back the covers on the narrow bed and considered that they would have to sleep close. He just hoped he could hold her during the night and not get a boner. That would be the last thing she needed. He wouldn't hurt her for the world, but he was a guy and she was a very beautiful girl. Somehow, he didn't think she realized how lovely she was. Opening a drawer in the dresser, he took out a clean shirt for her to wear. "You go change and I'll get in the bed. I'm through in the

7

bathroom."

"Okay." Nada scurried to the bathroom and did her business, rubbing her teeth with a bit of toothpaste on her finger. She was about to sleep with a boy! Oh, not really – she knew that. He wasn't interested in her that way. But this was still the most special night of her life – she was going to be close to him. It was a small bed; he might even hold her. Looking in the small mirror, she studied her own face. She was nothing special, obviously. Her boobs hadn't budded much beyond an A cup and the rest of her body was a little too curvy by popular standards. Tonight was a gift; Nada knew that, a precious gift.

"Are you okay in there?" Beau tapped on the door. It's almost time for lights out; we don't want to give anyone a reason to come in."

After only a few more minutes, she shut off the bathroom light, and walked out into the bedroom. It was dark. "Are you sure you want me?" she began hesitantly. "I mean are you sure you want me to stay in here with you?" Her voice was a whisper.

"Come here, Nada. I want you with me." And he did. Beau knew this place would be unbearable without her. She divided her food with him. Pell had a cruel streak, and he withheld food from some of the bigger boys to try and keep them in line. But his Nada would slip extra rolls in her napkin and put them back for him. Anything she could sneak from the kitchen, she hoarded back to supplement his short rations. And that wasn't all, a couple of times when Pell had been about to thrash him for not meeting his quota, Nada would knock something over – spill something – do anything she could to get the focus off of him and onto her. Pell made her pay for that kindness, harshly. Beau threw the bedcovers back. "Walk straight ahead; it's just a couple of steps." When he felt the mattress give under her slight weight, he felt a thrill. "That's my girl."

'His girl'. He'd never know how much she longed to be his girl. The nights had been cool and the thought of curling up next to him while she slept was intoxicating. "Where are you?" She knew he would be able to hear the excitement in her voice. "This is sort of like a sleep over, or a slumber party. Isn't it?" As she slipped beneath the covers, her legs came into contact with his. They were strong, muscled and hair-roughened and his maleness made her go soft inside.

"Lie down on my arm and let me hold you." He held his breath as she nestled her small body down against his. Her head rested on his arm and she fit herself to him, automatically throwing an arm around his waist and a leg over his lower regions. Hell! There was no way his body would be immune to her nearness. She let out a deep, restful, relieved sigh as if the weight of the world had been lifted from her shoulders.

"I like this," she whispered. "Nothing in the world can bother me here."

"No, you're safe with me," he kissed her forehead. He couldn't resist.

Rivulets of fire raced over Nada. She didn't exactly understand why her body felt so electrified, but she did know there was no other place she'd rather be than with this boy. "Beau, what's going to happen to us? Are we ever going to be able to get away? Living on the street is safer than being here." As she talked, she stroked his arm – up and down - over and over again, enjoying the feel of hard muscle beneath her fingers.

"Soon, I'm going to try and get away, go get some help." A plan was forming in his mind, he had been thinking about it for some time. But knowing how scared Nada was, he realized time might be running out for them. He had no idea that Pell had been going into her room at night. "Until then, I want you to be careful. Do you hear me?" He pulled her tight against him. "I don't know what I'd do if anything happened to you. You belong to me. I'll do whatever it takes to protect you." Against all better judgment, he lowered his head to kiss her on the lips. In the dark, he sought her mouth with his own. It was a sweet, gentle kiss – mostly innocent – a clinging of the lips, a mixing of their breaths, an exchange of promises, hopes and dreams. "You are mine, Nada. Don't ever forget my words. You are mine."

His words thrilled her heart almost as much as his kiss. She had never been claimed by anyone, before. Surely, there was no better feeling in the world. "I trust you, Beau-ray. I trust you."

He had held her close throughout the night – it was the first and last time she had been truly happy.

Chapter One

Philadelphia, PA – LibertyOne Plaza – Socorro – Present Day

"What in the name of God, are we going to do now, Chief?" The younger member of the Philadelphia bomb squad was white as a sheet. "There's no way in hell we can use the robot to get to this one."

Chief Murphy looked up at the tall high rise that was destined to transform the Philadelphia skyline. "I think that was the idea, Tim." He was more worried than he let on to his crew. If the explosive device on the tenth floor main truss were to detonate, the whole structure would come down and he hated to think about what the blast would do to the apartment buildings surrounding Liberty One Plaza. "That's why ATF is bringing in Socorro."

"What has Socorro got that we don't, Sir?"

"Socorro has Harley Montoya. If anyone can get in there and diffuse this monster, Harley can." Shouts from uniformed cops let the Chief know that Socorro was approaching. A path was cleared and a black H1 Hummer came rolling up beside them and slowed to a standstill. Several ATF agents approached the vehicle ready to provide whatever assistance necessary. The driver's side door opened and someone hopped out.

"Is that him, Chief? He's not very tall." Tim craned his neck to see the man who had been called in to save the day.

"That's because Harley Montoya is a woman, son" A very beautiful woman, he could have added, but that wouldn't have been professional. "She is a former Navy Special Forces captain, a very talented one. Some say she's psychic and that gives her an edge, others say she has a

11

magic touch. Either way, she has diffused bombs that no one else would even attempt. Harley left the Navy two years ago, only she knows why. But our government keeps her on the payroll and when she's needed – she comes. In the world of Explosive Ordinance Disposal, she is one of the undisputed authorities."

"Wow," Tim Renfro watched the petite dark-haired woman slip on the 80-pound protective suit. He knew it was outfitted with internal cooling, amplified hearing and embedded radio communications that would allow her to talk to the control area while she tried to disarm the massive bomb. "I can't believe a woman that looks like her has the know-how to go in there and do what all of these man can't."

Murphy chuckled, "Watch her." He had seen Harley in action before and a cooler head he had never encountered. "You can bet she's already been briefed and while she drove in, she was rehearsing a plan of action in her mind. They say she has one of those analytical minds that allows her to visualize every step before she places herself in the hot seat. When Harley goes in, and she goes in alone, she will know exactly what to do."

"I hope you're right." Renfro stepped aside as the men in blue forced all unnecessary personnel behind a hastily erected protective barrier. "I'd hate to pin all of my hopes on that pint-size pixie, unless I was hoping for a good time," he muttered under his breath as the scream of sirens heralded the arrival of ambulances. EMT's and the fire department had been called in, just in case everything fell apart.

* * *

Harley took the long walk. That's how she always thought of it, no matter if it were a mile, two hundred yards or twenty feet. It was a long walk. She faced death with no one beside her, no partner, no team, no one to back her up or take her place. What she focused on was saving the situation, she knew if she failed there was more at stake than the loss of her life, there were the lives of others.

At least she had no hostages to fortune. If the worst happened, Harley left no one behind that would mourn her passing. The fact that she was a solitary gave her strength to face the unthinkable. She could look her mortality in the face and know she was expendable. She had no husband, no children, no parents. No one who would wake up the next day after her death and be devastated to know she was gone, and that's the way she wanted it. She had no desire to bear the burden of someone else's happiness.

The very name of her company Socorro said it all. A Socorro was a type of mourning dove and the dove was a symbol of peace. Harley felt that the work she did, ridding the world of dangerous explosive devices, was her gift of peace. And since the Socorro dove was known as the solitary dove, never spotted in a flock. Always alone, it just fit her. The very word Socorro meant to offer help, so she identified with it. She was Socorro.

The construction elevator was small and rattled like a two-bit radio. All sounds were muffled in the suit and the ice vest cooling unit made her feel as if she were sitting naked in a deep freeze. Her arms ached from carrying the portable x-ray machine and her bag of tools, in addition to having to move around in the heavy suit. That was the only drawback she had ever had. Her size. But what she lacked in size, she made up for in determination and grit. With a jerk and a loud creak, the temporary construction elevator ground to a halt. She stepped out on the deserted platform, about 108 feet off the ground. Harley disliked heights with a passion. She picked her way across the girders and tried not to look down.

The bomb came into view. Good Lord! They had to be

dealing with a seriously psychotic individual. Somebody wanted to do this city, and her friend's family, some major damage. On the way today, she had been informed who owned this building. It was quite a coincidence that she was close to the Gaines Family. Not that she would work any harder to disarm this bomb than any other that crossed her path. She put the same amount of effort into each one, everything she had.

The device had to have been brought up in sections. As she drew nearer, she determined that the explosives themselves were housed in three grocer boxes. From the report she received, the boxes were full of semtex, a deadly plastic explosive. There was enough power here to do untold damage. The blast wave alone would shatter glass for several city blocks.

Falling to her knees next to the bomb, she set up her x-ray equipment to analyze where the fuses were and how she could neutralize the threat with the least amount of invasive scrutiny. Looking through the LED screen, she saw a tangle of wires between the layers of semtex. This made no sense. Bomb makers today used remote controls and microchips that could be dealt with through trepanation, a boring of a hole in the side of the bomb where the triggers could be liquefied with an acid bath. No, this would have to be done the old-fashioned way. She would have to snip wires and pray she picked the right ones.

With delicate moves, she began lifting out bricks of semtex to get to inner workings. How tempting it was to just try and empty the boxes of the plastic explosive, but she knew time was of the essence. There was no countdown display, and that made her need to be methodical, maddening. Now, there were probably only seconds left. She would have to act, and act fast.

Quickly, she removed the last layer, exposing the

colored plastic wires. For a moment, she was stunned. This looked familiar, she knew this pattern. Impossible. He was dead, she had seen him die. Was this some kind of cruel trick? Closing her eyes for just a moment, she used her secret weapon. Rubbing her fingers over the cluster of wires, she used a combination of knowledge and insight, took her wire cutters and held her breath. Snip. Breathe. Moving the blue wire out of the way, she snipped the green one. Breathe. She wore no gloves; they would just get in the way. Using one fingernail, she lifted the yellow wire. Yellow or black, yellow or black. It could be either. Making her mind a blank, she waited for the answer. Yellow. Snip. Breathe. No explosion. Every muscle in her body relaxed. She would live another day.

* * *

Deep in the South - Atchafalaya Basin – Louisiana

Beau LeBlanc steered his pickup down the levee road toward the Guidry homestead. He would have liked to be out in his airboat plowing through the water lilies, fishing for catfish. Instead, he and Indiana had been called to wrangle a big bull gator who had been plaguing the fisherman trying to make a living along Bayou Chene. These Cajuns had known too many problems, recently. The BP oil spill, the Mississippi River flooding and now a rogue alligator who was getting too aggressive around their homes. The locals had named him Godzilla; he had begun his reign of terror by tearing up their traps and snapping their trotlines and continued it by crawling up in their yards and eating their dogs and cats. Most of them were afraid to let their children out to play. So Beau had been summoned to move the old monster to a safe place before he became a man-eater and would have to be destroyed.

As luck would have it, Godzilla had got himself into a predicament before traps could be set for him. He had been in the process of crawling between irrigation ditches at the Guidry place, when old man Guidry had walked upon him. The old gator had tried to get away from the human and instead of heading for one of the manmade waterways; he slid underneath the connecting pipe right into an enclosed deep water well. The watery trap was likely to become his grave unless Beau could get him out. It was a wonder the homeowner hadn't shot the old reptile. But he hadn't, and for that Beau was grateful. He had a soft heart for things no one else cared about. Beau ran SAFEPLACE, a Sanctuary for endangered and threatened animals. Godzilla wouldn't end up there; he was still able to make it on his own. They would relocate him somewhere deeper in the swamp, away from man.

"That's the Guidry house." Indiana pointed over at the dog-trot style, Louisiana swamp house. A tall thin man stood out front waiting, two hound dogs flanked him on either side. Beau pulled in and climbed out, breathing in the atmosphere like life giving oxygen. The swamp was a spiritual place for Cajuns. He could close his eyes and smell his home, the bayou was where he belonged. The familiar aroma was so many things melded together into a gumbo of sights, sounds and experiences. The hot sun, dark green water, crawfish, mud, cypress trees, and humidity all carried on a thick damp breeze.

The cellphone on his hip buzzed. Glancing at the number, he turned to Indy. "It's the store. I wonder what's up? We left them working on converting those stock Uzi's to competition grade." Punching the talk button, he answered. "LeBlanc, here."

"How much longer are you gonna be, boss?" As Beau listened to his employee, he poked Indiana, pointing out at the water. Out in the bayou, they could see the tell-tale eyes and a little bit of a snout showing above the water. An alligator.

"Not too much longer, we've gotta pull Godzilla out of a hole and then Indy will move him deeper into the Atchafalaya. I'll come on back as soon as he heads out. What's going on?"

Rick Gentry was excited. When he got excited, he stuttered a little bit like now. "You, you, you will never believe what's coming into our shop this afternoon. A woman called and she, she, she has a Ma Deuce she wants us to look at."

That got Beau's attention. "A Ma Deuce? Damn! I'll be there. If she arrives before I do, don't let her leave, or at least hold on to the gun."

Firepower Munitions – Breaux Bridge Louisiana

Harley rang the doorbell at Firepower Munitions and waited to be admitted. She found the locked door to be slightly odd, but she had been told by those in the know, that this establishment was the place to come to get a gun accurized. Her birthday present to herself had been a Remington 5R .308. She wanted the .308 converted into a souped-up sniper rifle. It might not be politically correct, but there was nothing more exciting than being able to hit a target 800 meters away. To each their own, she supposed. Firing a powerful weapon was the way she dealt with stress and the pressure of living her life alone. But the custom job wasn't the main reason for her visit to Firepower; she had come to rid herself of a bad memory.

"Hey, come in." While she had been deep in thought, the door had opened and a pretty girl with coal-black hair stood there inviting her inside. "Ms. Montoya, it's good to meet you. My name is Dandi LeBlanc. Beau is my cousin."

The owner's name was Beau. That fact had struck a sad note in her heart. She would never forget her Beau as long as she lived. "Thank you, Dandi." She stepped into the gun shop. "It's good to meet you, too."

The front room of the shop wasn't very big. The glass

display counter held a few pistols and knives, but Firearms Munitions wasn't a normal gun store. In fact, customers were required to make an appointment. The services they offered were unique and Harley respected the knowledge and the connections they were purported to have. A military contractor she knew had commissioned them to design specific mounts with a swivel arm for a Mag 58 to be used on a helicopter. So, her request was certainly within their scope of work. "Do I know you?" Dandi spoke right behind her. "You look really familiar."

"I'm nobody special," Harley was quick to assure her. There was no reason Miss LeBlanc would be familiar with her face or her work, either in the Navy or in Socorro.

She had been forced to go by Nada in the service, because that was her legal name. But she longed to be somebody – anybody else – other than who she was. So one night, Nada had been reading a motorcycle magazine one of the guys had left lying around and the name Harley just hit her – it seemed right. So, Nada became Harley Montoya. She took her father's name, even if he didn't want her to have it. It seemed, to her, to be the least he could do.

"Are you sure?" Dandi looked at her, pointedly. "Oh well, it will come to me."

Harley hoped not. She wanted to live here in St. Martin's Parish and no one ever learn about her unusual line of work. It was just better that way. Noises and voices from the back told her where the action was taking place. Harley was tempted to ask to look around, but didn't really have time. There was no way she could miss the appointment she had scheduled this afternoon, the tests were required for her insurance coverage. Following Dandi to the counter, she laid the gun case holding the .308 in front of her, but the Ma Deuce was still in the back of the Hummer, for that she would need to borrow some muscle.

"Beau's in the back, I'll call him. Did you bring the .50 caliber with you?"

Harley was amused. The younger girl was clearly a gun aficionado; she spoke the lingo as easily as some people talked about the weather. "It's in my Hummer.

"You drive a Hummer?" Dandi's eyes widened and her excitement doubled. "H2? H3?"

"Actually, it's a H1."

"Wow, I think the Hummer is one sexy machine." With a wistful look on her face, Dandi took out an order book. "Now, what did you bring beside the machine gun?"

"A 308," she unzipped the case. "I want to know what your cousin thinks about the new reaper conversion I've heard about."

"I know he's done one, there are a lot of different options to choose from. Let me get him for you." Dandi held up a finger to pause their conversation and punched an intercom button. "Beau, the Ma Deuce is here." Harley smiled; it was easy to tell what excited Dandi. The Ma Deuce!

* * *

"I'll be right there," he released the speaker button to the intercom and picked his cell back up, where Indiana was waiting. "Did you have any trouble finding somebody to help you unload Godzilla?" It had taken them a half hour to get a noose over the big bull's head and another ten minutes to get him loaded in the back of the truck. Beau couldn't resist weighing and measuring the big gator and he had been an impressive thirteen feet and a thousand twenty-five pounds.

"No, I ran into the Welch brothers and they were glad to help. You know they're the best trappers in South Louisiana. Did the Ma Deuce show up?"

"It's out front, waiting on me. Did Godzilla give you any trouble? I should have gone along to help you."

"No trouble, will you quit worrying about every little thing?" Indiana groused about Beau's tendency to worry about everyone he cared about. "Just get out there and check out that gun. Then call me when you can. I'll be waiting."

"Why aren't you coming in?" Beau tightened the last screw on a replacement stock for a Ruger 10/22. "Or do I want to know?" Indy was his right hand man, but he pulled double duty and set his own hours.

"I have a date."

"Whooeee, really?" Beau couldn't help the little tone of amusement that crept into his voice. "With Nita?" He knew his friend was sweet on an elementary school teacher who lived over near Lafayette.

"Yes, with Nita. Now, quit worrying about my business and take care of your own. It's not every day something comes into the shop like what you've got waiting for you. I suggest you get out there and appreciate what's fallen in your lap."

* * *

Mon Dieu! Beau stood frozen at the entrance to the lobby, stunned at exactly what had fallen into his lap. If Indiana only knew! This sweetheart was much better than a gun, no matter what the caliber.

There was no way in the world he could take his eyes off of her. She was absolutely delectable. The Ma Deuce was forgotten, he'd check it out later, much later. He'd much rather talk to this hot little honey. Lord Have Mercy! She had her back to him, but what he could see caused his cock to swell. Tight little blue jeans cupped a behind so round and sweet, he wanted to go to his knees and genuflect. Her hair, swear to God, hung to the top of that little rump and all he could think about was lying beneath her, letting that curtain of dark silk enclose them in their own private paradise. Damn! And he hadn't even seen her face yet.

She was making a point and he was entranced at the way she moved her hand and cocked her hip. It really didn't matter why she had come, he would give her anything she wanted. Hell! What if she was married? Surely God wouldn't be that cruel.

"There you are." Dandi motioned him over and when she did, sweet-doll turned around and Beau audibly growled. Okay, he surrendered. It was over. This was the future Mrs. Beau LeBlanc. His eyes almost crossed, he couldn't decide whether to stare at her perfectly adorable face or the two handfuls of tit-heaven that seemed to be begging for his touch. "What's wrong with you?" Dandi asked. Thank God, his cousin couldn't recognize that he was completely lust-struck. "Come meet Harley Montoya. She has a couple of questions for you."

Her heart almost stopped beating. It was impossible – absolutely impossible. Harley couldn't believe it. Every psychic nerve in her body tingled – even before she made a move to turn around. Never, ever had she expected to see Beau again. All breath fled her body. It was Beau, and he was drop-dead gorgeous. Taking one-step toward him, she prepared herself to greet the person who meant the most to her in this world. Did he recognize her? Her mouth had gone dry. Meeting his gaze, Harley searched his beautiful blue-black eyes for any hint he knew who she was.

He didn't.

He was smiling, but there didn't seem to be any surprise in his expression. He grinned and there it was, that little half dimple she had dreamed about so often. Her Beau. God! She wanted to sink to her knees and thank heaven. He was alive and within touching distance. She had to drive her fingernails into her palms to keep from reaching for him. Harley didn't know what to do; she was so tempted to just launch herself into his arms. But, she resisted. Not only would it shock him but her ingrained fear of intimacy made her skittish. There was no need to embarrass both of them. The only thing she allowed herself to do was extend one trembling hand in greeting.

"Hello, cher," Instead of shaking it, Beau surprised her when he brought it to his lips and kissed it. "What a pleasure it is to meet you. I'm Beau LeBlanc."

No, he didn't know her. At all. Harley didn't know whether to be relieved or disappointed. "I'm Harley. It's nice to - uh - see you, Beau." The name slipped off her tongue like a prayer. She had known the owner of Firepower Munitions was named Beau, but Beaureguarde and its derivative were common in South Louisiana. Plus, she had never known her Beau's last name, and he certainly had not known hers. Details like that hadn't been important. They had been more concerned with just staying alive. Still, she drank in his face with her eyes, her whole body shaking from the shock. "I've heard wonderful things about your weapons business."

"Thank you, I'm proud of it," he was staring at her face so hard, she just knew any moment he would realize who she was. But he didn't. "Do you live near here?"

"Yes, I just moved from Southeast Texas, before that I lived near San Diego." Why was she being so specific? There was no need for her to share so much, unless she intended to remind him of days gone by. Would he want to know? Harley wondered if Beau would even remember the thirteen year old scrap of humanity named 'nothing' that had clung to him like he was a life preserver.

"Well, welcome to the Atchafalaya Basin. I'm sure you'll love it here. As a home-grown boy, I sure would be glad to show you around. Would you like that? "

He looked so expectant she had to smile. His voice had the same sexy Cajun cadence she remembered from their youth. Sixteen years might have gone by, but she would have recognized him anywhere. His hair was the same. Longish, slightly curly and black as sin. High cheekbones, a chiseled face and a smile that would make any woman in the world sigh with longing. It was all just as she remembered, except mature and perfect. The last time she had seen him, he had been climbing out the window to safety. She had stayed behind to provide a distraction for Pell while he escaped. Harley had never seen Beau again, until this moment. She had often wondered how he had fared. Hopefully, better than she had. Pell had beaten her six ways to Sunday for aiding in the loss of his star pickpocket. And that wasn't all he had done. But, she pushed the painful thought from her mind. No use dwelling on that nightmare. Beau had gotten away, and she had escaped. Pell's final attack on her had given Harley enough courage to take the risk and get out of that hellish place. After all, with Beau gone, there had been no reason to stay.

Wait! What had he said? He was asking her out? Harley was so distracted by the wonder of finding him again that it was difficult to process simple English. She was about to try and answer him, but Dandi cleared her throat, reminding them both she was there. "Harley wants to talk to you about a conversion job." It was obvious she was growing bored with their by-play.

Beau's mind was fogged by arousal. Conversion job? He wasn't familiar with that term; all he could think of was blow jobs, hand jobs. You know, critical jobs. "Did you bring your weapon with you?" He didn't need for her to answer that; he could tell she was fully armed and dangerous. And he was cocked and primed and on a short fuse. Hell, he was beyond aroused!

"Yes, I did." Harley tore her eyes from his and unzipped the gun case, removing the Remington rifle for his inspection. "I'd like to see about getting a reaper conversion and having it accurized, if that's possible."

23

Beau held his breath while he asked the next question. "Is this a surprise gift for your boyfriend?" There was no way this baby-doll could handle a sniper rifle. Everything within him hoped her answer was no.

Boyfriend? Harley paused before answering. "No, there's no boyfriend. This is a birthday gift. Do you think you can do it?" She didn't explain that the gun was a gift to herself.

Boyfriend? That was almost funny. If he only knew her crazy history. To start off with, for three years she had lived as a boy after leaving Brownwood. After escaping, Harley had run off into the night, hiding underneath one of the bridge overpasses near the river. A homeless man had loaned her a knife and she had sawed off all of her long, dark hair. After what had happened with Pell, if she could have stripped herself of her femininity, she would have. She handed the .308 to Beau, anxious to get the focus back on the gun and off of her.

No boyfriend. He couldn't help but smirk. Okay, so the coast was clear. She sure as hell fascinated him. All he could think about was what her kiss was going to taste like and how it would feel to run his hands all over her incredible body. Taking the gun from her, Beau admitted that Harley handled the firearm pretty well, for a girl. Beau was intrigued. He had seen women shoot big guns before, but the thought of this woman handling a rifle was turning him on to no end. God, he'd love to feel her hands on his weapon. "Well, sweetheart, it would be my pleasure to do this for you."

"Okay, good." Harley felt so torn. What should she do? But, he deserved the truth, didn't he? "Beau, there's something that I need to. . . ."

"Here's the brochures," Dandi breezed back in and gave them to Harley. "Have you brought in the Ma Deuce, yet?"

That got his attention. "You're the owner of the .50 caliber?" Damn! He hadn't even thought about the machine gun. She was just so beautiful everything else had slipped his mind.

"It's in my vehicle."

"She drives a Hummer." Dandi shared the information like she was whispering the most delicious gossip.

"Dehelyousaye?" There was more to this woman than met the eye, and he couldn't wait to peel back every layer...of clothing. Feeling his cock jerk in his jeans, Beau found himself smiling again. "Shall we bring it in? And what do you want to do with it?" Fighting to regain a little decorum, Beau couldn't believe he was acting like a sex-starved teenager and liking it.

"Sure," Harley felt like she had gotten a reprieve. It would give her a few more minutes to get her thoughts together for her confession. "I inherited the machine gun. I hope you can help me find a buyer for it."

"Damn! I'd sure love to have it." Beau ran a hand through his thick hair, ruffling it.

Harley was entranced by his hands. They were strong, wide and capable. The veins stood out prominently on the top and she found herself wanting to trace them with her tongue. Land sakes! What was wrong with her? Beau was talking; she tried to focus on what he was saying.

"Depending on the condition, those things are going for fifty to fifty-five thousand dollars."

'This was perfect,' Harley thought. "It's in mint condition. Of course, I encourage you to check it out." She could get rid of the gun and do something nice for Beau. "If it passes your inspection – how does ten thousand sound?"

"Ten thousand?" Beau was flabbergasted. "Why? If it's all you say it is, I could find you a buyer in a couple of days who would be glad to pay you full price." Was she that hard up for money? He had no desire to cheat her.

"No, I'm not interested in making a big profit. I just want to get rid of it. So, if you're interested, it's yours."

"Hell yeah, I'm interested." This was turning out to be his lucky day, in more ways than one. "I'm interested in the gun, but I'm more interested in you." Beau grinned. He was happy. There was no two ways about it. And he wasn't shy, so he just decided to lay all of his cards on the table. "You are the most incredible looking woman I've ever laid eyes on." Behind him, Dandi choked. Crap! He had forgotten about his cousin being in the room. And his little bombshell, Harley? She blushed! Good Lord in Heaven, the little darling blushed!

Digging the keys out of her jeans pocket, Harley held them out to him. "You've just bought yourself a .50 caliber machine gun. It's in the back of my truck. Let's go get it." She decided not to comment on Beau's admission that he found her attractive. It would be better if she just ignored it. Her body seemed to have other ideas, however. Harley felt her nipples puffing up and her pussy began to swell and an unfamiliar ache started deep within her sex. God, she was turned on! A myriad of emotions flooded through her. This type of reaction to a man was unheard of for her. But this was no ordinary man, this was Beau. "Come on."

She led him outside and Beau had a good time trailing her. Fuck! He couldn't decide if she looked better coming or going. If he had ever seen a hotter woman, he couldn't remember it. She walked with confidence, yet sensuality defined every step she took. The sway of her hips mesmerized him and he vowed he would have his hands on that ass before the week was out. Now that he had found this tempting morsel, he wasn't going to let up until he was pumping between her thighs. Damn! He shifted his package around in his jeans, grateful that she was a couple of steps ahead of him, unaware of his aroused state.

"Here we are."

Beau looked up. He had been so captivated by Harley; he hadn't noticed he was in the presence of another beauty. "Wow." Now, this was a ride! "You drive this?" He loved powerful machinery and the Hummer sitting in his parking lot was the ultimate machine. This wasn't just an H1. This was a custom, military-outfitted Humvee. The real deal. It even had the helicopter hook so it could be picked up and moved through the air to another destination.

"Yeah, I manage to keep it between the ditches." His skepticism about her choice of a vehicle was something she had heard before, way too many times. Standing back, she watched him open the double doors to the large storage compartment. "Actually, I've owned this truck for a couple of years."

What in the world was all of this? Beau stood at the rear of the Humvee in amazement. "Baby, what kind of work do you do?" He had never seen so much technical looking hardware in one place. The Ma Deuce was there, within easy reaching distance but it was surrounded by other equally intriguing items. Electronic gadgets and tools were neatly arranged, and he had no idea what they were for. His fingers itched to pull them out and inspect them more closely. "This stuff looks like Radio Shack on steroids!"

Harley laughed. Beau was having a typical male reaction to her chosen mode of transportation. And as far as the explosive ordinance gear, she knew how to be evasive. "I'm a government contractor."

"That tells me a helluva lot." Beau realized she didn't care to elaborate and that was all right for now. "Man, that's a pretty lady." He pulled the machine gun closer to him. "Where did you get this?"

Well, there was no secret there. "I inherited it from my father." And that was why she didn't want it. He hadn't

27

cared anything about her when he was alive and she couldn't muster up any sympathy for him now that he was dead. In the Navy, Harley had always been surrounded by men. In her line of work, a female was the exception not the norm. But there had only been a handful of men in her life she had trusted implicitly: Captain Thibodeaux, Admiral Gaines and Beau. She had never trusted her father; Manuel Montoya had rejected her from the moment he had laid eyes on her. Being born with a caul over her face had been a sign of the devil to her superstitious parents. Manuel had made it clear to her, in every way possible, that he wanted nothing to do with her. That was the reason he had named her 'nothing' - Nada. The only reason she had ended up with the gun and a few other items was because she was his only living relative at the time of his death.

"I can't wait to try it out." Beau picked it up. It weighed about a hundred and fifty pounds, but he carried it easily. "All we need to do is get all the transfer papers filled out and I'll write you a check."

Harley hurried ahead of him and opened the door. Dandi was there anxiously waiting to admire Beau's newest acquisition. Clearly, she was as taken with it as he was. He carried it into his office, a large adjoining room that was crowded with stacks and piles of books and papers; there was barely room to walk. Organized chaos. She was fascinated to see this side of Beau. There was so much she didn't know about him and she was hungry to know it all.

While they were inspecting the Ma Deuce, Harley watched him. He was so good-looking. There hadn't been anyone in her memory with a body better than his, and she had worked with the best - Navy Seals, Black Ops. Beau's shoulders were so wide; she would love to stand close to him on tiptoe and see how far her arms would go around him. Despite her problems, she could still appreciate male beauty. So she stole a few glances at him. When she heard a throat clear, she realized Dandi was watching her. Hastily, she tried to at least pretend to study the papers in her hand. How unprofessional could she get? "I think this will do for the .308. I like the way it looks." Glancing at the clock on the wall, she saw it was time for her to leave for the doctor's office. Lord, she dreaded this visit. "Look, I've got to go. Why don't I come back later in the week and we can get things settled with both transactions?"

"Wait," Beau stood up, there was no way he was letting her leave without a little more information, like when she was going to go out with him. "Where do you live?" He hadn't recognized the street name when he reviewed the firearm transfer papers. "I could drop off your check tonight and get your signature on the bill of sale and we could iron out the reaper conversion details. I need to get some measurements and make sure we get the stock the right length." He started to ask the identity of the lucky man she was giving the gun to but one thing at a time.

Beau wanted to come to her house? Harley didn't know if this visit was such a good idea. The more she thought about it, the more she was questioning the wisdom of spending a lot of time with him. To her surprise, she was feeling urges she thought were long dead, and with her history that couldn't be good. Still, he was looking at her with such heat; all she wanted to do was draw closer. Like a moth to a flame. "That sounds okay. I just moved into Willowbend." She was about to tell him where it was located, but his knowing chuckle stopped her. "What?"

"So, you're the one who moved into the old Sonnier place. I wondered about that. You do know it's haunted, don't you?"

"Well, I do now." Her tone was chastising. She couldn't help but smile back at him. "I could have done without that particular piece of knowledge, thank you.

Now, I'll jump at every creak and groan the old house makes." She might be brave when faced with a live bomb, but ghosts and snakes were another matter entirely. Stepping backwards, Harley tripped over a pile of gun manuals. If Beau hadn't reached out to grab her, she would have fallen.

"I've got you," Beau caught her and hugged her close, glad for the opportunity to get his hands on her. He swayed a little bit, just enjoying how she felt in his arms. God, nothing had ever felt so right. The only thing that could be better would be to have his cock buried balls deep inside her sweet body. Now that was a dream worth having. "Ah, love I'll protect you from the boogeyman. Just wait until you hear the loup garou howl deep in the night as he slinks through the swamp hunting his prey." He was teasing her now, and loving every minute of it. Thank God, Dandi had showed enough manners to leave them alone. It was time to make his move.

Harley's whole body went on alert. She hadn't been this close to a man, not willingly, in a long time. An overwhelming urge to pull away assaulted her. But she didn't want to make a scene. Calling upon every inner strength she had, Harley pretended to be normal. "Stop that," she playfully punched him on the shoulder. "You'll have me too scared to sleep there alone at night."

Before he could talk himself out of it, Beau did what he had wanted to do since the moment he saw her. He kissed her. Oh, not on the lips, like he longed to do but tenderly on each eyelid and at the corner of her captivating mouth. "That's the idea, love. That's the idea."

Chapter Two

Yuck! Harley hated going to the doctor, especially to the gynecologist. Even though she owned Socorro, she had to abide by the insurance carrier's rules. Lying on this cold hard table, Harley thought she would rather be anywhere but here. But, at least Dr. Young met her main requirement, she was female. The room smelled of antiseptic and it was painted a pleasant shade of pastel yellow. Overhead, the fluorescent lights buzzed monotonously. When the door suddenly opened, Harley almost jumped out of her skin. Damn! What was wrong with her? Harley had faced enemy combatants; dangerous situations and today she had been more of a wuss than she could ever remember being. First, she had thoroughly chickened out around Beau. Looking back, she realized she should have been straight with him from the very start. What difference did it make? They were childhood friends – well, not even that. Their paths had crossed thirteen years ago; she would be lucky if he even remembered her. He was a grown man now, that period of his life was probably nothing more than an unpleasant memory.

And he had kissed her. She couldn't forget that. She would never forget that, or her response. Beau had probably kissed hundreds of girls, but she bet that was the first time one had reacted like a frightened deer. In her mind's eye, she relived the embarrassing moment. He had been holding her and for a second, it had been glorious. She had wanted to feel his lips on hers. The kiss they shared at Brownwood had always been the one memory in her life she could cherish. Now, she had ruined that memory. Because this time, Harley had pulled away. Closing her eyes, she tried to forget the confused look on Beau's face.

31

"Well, hello." The door opened and a woman came in. The tag on her white coat identified her as the physician. Dr. Young came to her left side and slid a stool up so she could talk. She had a pleasant smile. They were probably about the same age. "I see from your chart that you are here for the full workup. Pap smear, mammogram, and a general check-up." The other woman was so calm and friendly that she put Harley at ease.

"Yes, I put off going to the doctor until the last minute, I'm afraid."

"Why is that?" She moved to the end of the table. "Put your feet in the stirrups and let's see what we've got here."

Could there be more unpleasant words than 'put your feet in the stirrups'? Harley followed the doctor's directions and opened herself up. She felt so vulnerable. Even though the gynecologist was a woman, she couldn't be still. At the first touch of her gloved hand – Harley jerked. "Are my hands cold?"

"No," Harley answered in a small voice. "I just don't like this, I'm sorry."

Dr. Young made a sympathetic noise. "Some women are a bit nervous about having another woman touch them intimately. Remember, I'm your doctor. I only want what's best for you." Harley steeled herself as the doctor opened her wider and inserted the mirrored probe into her vagina. "Do you need to get your birth control pills refilled?"

Harley had been biting her lip so hard, she was sure she had brought blood. "I'm not on birth control pills."

"Why not? I see in your folder that your cycle is not always regular and that you suffer from severe cramps. Birth control pills are the best answer for those problems. Besides, a woman that is sexually active needs the protection – unless you are anxious to get pregnant." Harley felt the doctor insert a swab, getting a sample for the pap smear.

"I'm not sexually active." Foot! She hadn't intended for this to turn into confession time.

The doctor said nothing for a few moments. Then, she scooted her stool back. "Sit up, Nada."

The name startled Harley. She didn't think of herself by that name very often. But obviously the doctor would use her legal name. "If you think I need birth control pills, I'll take them." That should stem any awkward discussions. But it didn't. The doctor was too astute, by far.

"Yes, I think you should be on the pill. I'll write you a prescription. When was the last time you had sex? And I'm asking this because you are obviously nervous. You are so tense that I'm afraid you might break. Is there something you need to tell me? I'm a good listener, you know."

Harley took her feet out of the hated stirrups and sat up, tucking the paper gown around her thighs and crossing her ankles. She felt exposed and vulnerable. How could a person who faced death on a regular basis be so cowardly? "My sex life has been a disaster. Being intimate with a man just doesn't work for me. I've been raped twice and the consensual encounters I attempted were complete failures."

The silence in the room was overwhelming. Harley hung her head in shame.

"Hey," the doctor spoke in a gentle, but firm tone. "Look at me." When Harley complied, she saw only sympathy and understanding. "Have you been to counseling?"

"No, I was too ashamed." She knew how stupid that sounded. Harley wasn't dumb. Her IQ was exceptional; she was a college graduate and a decorated war hero. Still, when it came to sex, she was handicapped.

"Nada, I don't really know your circumstances, but there is no need for a woman as beautiful as you to throw her intimate life away just because of a tragedy. Don't give the idiots who abused you that much power." Dr. Young laid her instruments and her chart aside. "Would you go to a sex therapist if I arranged it?"

"What?" Harley was totally shocked. "She had been expecting the doctor to suggest a psychiatrist, maybe. But not a sex therapist. "I don't think so."

Dr. Young stood. "Let me get a nurse in here and get your mammogram and then meet me in my office and we'll discuss this further." After she left the room, another woman came in and Harley followed her instructions and moved over to the torture device that would squeeze her breasts and tell her what she already knew, she was cancer free.

Harley was psychic to a degree, sometimes she just knew things. She didn't read people's thoughts, thank goodness. But she picked up impressions from objects. This gift came in handy in bomb disposal. Sometimes she would know the feelings of the bomber. At times she had been able to give her superiors insight into their motive. Her gift had kept her alive more than once. But it had also been a burden. Harley's ability had stolen her family. They just couldn't handle her 'knowing' things. And when she was small, she hadn't learned how to hide that knowledge. She had blurted things out and her father had hated her for it. That was why she had left her home and Beaumont when she turned thirteen and taken to the streets. Ending up in New Orleans and finally in Brownwood, where she had met Beau.

After enduring the mammogram, Harley dressed and was led down the hall to where Dr. Young sat at a desk, typing on a laptop. "So, what are we going to do with you?"

If the doctor hadn't been so sincere, Harley would have been offended. She didn't want anything 'done' to her. She was satisfied with her life. Wasn't she? Looking back at the day and the incredible sexual feelings Beau had awakened in her, and her miserable reaction to him, she wondered if it was time to face her demons. "I don't know. What are my options?" Memories of Jed Martin came to mind. Harley had tried with him, she had really tried. They had met at a BBQ at Mariner's Park celebrating Asian-Pacific Heritage month. He had been very sweet and had talked her into joining him at a picnic table and later for a walk. One thing had led to another and Harley had agreed to go out on a date with him. He wasn't a big man, so his closeness didn't resurrect the shameful flashbacks like what had happened with Beau today. Jed had been non-threatening and she had thought that just maybe he would be the one to coax her back into the world of sex.

After a couple of dates, he had made a move to take the next step. It had all started out well enough, but she'd been hesitant and he had been shy. When he'd asked her what the problem was she had made the mistake of telling him the truth. Never as long as she lived, would she forget the look of disgust that had come over his blandly handsome face. He had backed up from her like she had the plague and said, "I don't think I can be with a woman who's been raped." His reaction had been a shock to her, but she had hoped he would be an exception, not the rule.

A few months later she had developed a relationship with another man. Sonny Garrison had been a breath of fresh air. He had hailed from Houston, so they had a lot of things to talk about. Both were Astros fans and had swam in the warm waters of the Gulf of Mexico. They had shared memories of the State Fair and the Big Thicket Natural Preserve, but when he had coaxed her into an embrace, everything had fallen apart. She had resisted, he had asked questions and she had blurted out the ugly facts. His words and reaction had been so close to Jed's it made her think they were reading from a script. That was when Harley realized that what had happened to her had affected much more than her own body. It would affect how any other man would ever feel about her.

Dr. Young looked at her with sympathy. "Are you happy? Do you want more out of life? Do you want to know what it's like to know the love of a good man?"

"Well, when you put it that way..." Harley wanted so bad to laugh at herself, but the whole situation was just too sad. Meeting Beau today just seemed to cap it all off. The way he made her feel before the panic attack just highlighted how empty her existence had become and how she was just watching life pass her by. If it wasn't for her work at Socorro, she wouldn't have a purpose at all.

"Look, let me make you an appointment with someone I trust – implicitly. Dr. Wagner can help you. I know he can. And get those pills filled – today."

* * *

Harley stared at the appointment card like it was a poisonous snake. She didn't know if she had the courage to go to a sex therapist and bare her soul. Thank goodness she had a month to think about it. Pulling on a pair of blue jeans, she grabbed a yellow sweater off a rack and skimmed it over her head. She had followed the doctor's orders and gotten the prescription filled. And as soon as she had gotten home, she had swallowed a once-a-month birth control pill and tried to relax in the shower. Going to the gynecologist always made her feel funny. The jelly they used to ease the insertion of the probe always made her feel like she had been violated, again.

As she hung up her clothes and straightened the bathroom, a noise from across the hall caught her attention. It sounded like a door creaking and swear to God, she heard the sound of a child's little voice waft on the air. Every hair rose on the back of her neck. Great! Now she was hearing ghosts.

Moving slowly, Harley left her room and eased across the hall. Maybe the sounds had come from outside. Sure, that was it, it had to be. Beau had told her a tale and she had fallen for it. Hook, line and sinker. Still, she was going to check and make sure. Just before she opened the door to the guest room, she heard another noise; it sounded like people talking in her kitchen. All right, this was just too much. Going back to slip on her sandals, she scooted downstairs. Her heart was racing a mile a minute. She had never really believed in ghosts, but she had spent enough time in New Orleans to realize there were more strange things in this world than she had ever imagined. Peeking into the kitchen, she was relieved to see nothing out of place.

It wouldn't take but a moment for her to look around the whole first floor and she wouldn't rest until she knew there were no intruders lurking around the next corner ready to jump out at her. As she headed through the entry hall on the way to the dining room, a lilting little laugh seemed to come from directly behind her. The very next moment, the front door bell chimed and Harley panicked, threw open the door, saw Beau, and launched herself right into his arms.

"Hey, precious!" Beau couldn't imagine a better welcome. This was way better than yesterday. All day, he had worried about the way she had reacted to his kiss. If she didn't enjoy his touch, it just might kill him. Then, he realized she was trembling. "What in the world?" She wrapped her arms so tight around him; he had trouble taking a breath. Beau didn't mind that a bit. "Harley, is something wrong?" He cradled her close; aware of every luscious inch of her body nestled close to his.

"I heard noises. I think it was the ghost." Her voice was shaking and Beau wanted to smile. He had never been grateful to a ghost before, but he definitely owed the specters of Willowbend.

"I'm here. It's okay, love. I'll protect you." Lord, what a perfect armful. He could feel her tits pushing against his chest as she tried to crawl into his skin. Kissing her temple, he marveled at how right it felt.

How wonderful to be held! Harley clung to him a second longer, trying to calm down. Gradually, she began to feel foolish. Some brave Special Ops soldier she was; falling apart and going all girly over a ghost! And then, there it was, the niggle of unease. Beau was so precious, but he was a large male and being in his arms brought back painful memories. Gee, she was pitiful! Pushing back from him, she managed to put a few inches between them. "Sorry, I feel so stupid."

He let her distance herself for a little bit, the night was young. At least she had turned to him when she felt afraid. Beau was old-fashioned. He was the protector. There was one thing he believed more than any other. It was a man's place to protect his woman, to shield her from whatever threat she might face. If everything went the way he hoped, he'd get her back in his arms before the evening was over or he wasn't the ragin' Cajun he thought he was. "You stay right here and I'll go check everything out and make sure you don't have an intruder." She stood there by him looking like a China doll, a wary trust in her eyes. Right then, he vowed in his heart that he would never, ever let her down. "God, you're beautiful." Stealing a kiss from her worried little forehead, he looked into eyes the color of amber jewels. Where had he seen eyes that shade before? "Don't fret, lamb. I'll take care of things." It made him feel great to be able to take care of her. She had knocked him for a loop and all he could think about was getting to know her and seeing if the incredible connection he felt with her was real.

"Okay, I trust you." Harley knew she should be the one

to check out her home, she was perfectly capable. But Lord, it was nice to have someone want to take care of her. Their gazes held for just a moment and she was struck anew by his sheer size and masculinity. Even though she was emotionally damaged – she wasn't blind. Beau was built. He was strong and sure of himself; yet kind and so considerate. And sexy, incredibly sexy.

I trust you. I trust you. Harley's words rang in Beau's ears. Searching her face, he looked for his own ghost. Was he imagining things? What he saw was a drop-dead gorgeous woman who had more sensual appeal than should be legal. More importantly, she had just leapt into his arms like she belonged there. Still, those words 'I trust you' haunted him. Despite the provocative prospect of spending time with Harley, Beau still remembered Nada. It had been sixteen long years, but not a day went by that he didn't think of her. She had saved his life, asking nothing in return. His heart still broke every time he thought of the night he had led the police back to Brownwood to save her and the others, only to find that Pell had killed her in anger because she had been foolish enough to help him escape. That was the last words he had heard Nada say, 'I trust you. I trust you, Beau-ray'.

"I'll be right back." Fighting off the ancient memory, he decided to enjoy the blessings of the present. Entering the big double doors of Willowbend, he found that Harley had been busy. It wasn't like she was trying to turn back time, but she had tried to stay true to the spirit of the place. That thought made him smile. He hadn't really been joking about the place being haunted, he had heard it was. And the person who told him, Savannah Doucet, would know. Savannah was their local ghost hunter. She haunted more cemeteries and battlefields than the dead did. According to Miss Doucet, this beautiful old home was still inhabited by the mulatto mistress of Joshua Conway and their two mixed race children. Tales of visitations by Lillian, the mistress, were commonplace. Most would see her or hear her in the kitchen and the little girl and the little boy were most often heard – their little voices carrying on the wind, laughing and playing in the twilight.

Beau walked into the living room. Harley had done a good job with the house. He was just a good ole' boy, but her sense of style appealed to him. The colors were warm and inviting – blues and earth tones with touches of burgundy. He would feel right at home, here. She had brought the richness of Louisiana and the mystery of the bayou into every aspect. Audubon prints were on the walls and wooden carvings of wildlife sat on the table. It was amazing.

Making his way through the plantation house, Beau looked for clues as to what defined Harley. Everything was comfortable, not overly feminine, but tasteful and well put together. When he came to her bedroom, he stared at the big bed covered in pillows and imagined being there with her, loving on that incredible body and making her cry out with passion. Mon Dieu! He couldn't wait to see her naked, those breasts were going to be spectacular. Beau's cock grew hard and thick just thinking about cupping them and sucking on them. He loved a woman's breasts and he couldn't wait to get his hands on Harley's. Out of the corner of his eye, he saw a figure go by. Thinking it was Harley, he made a grab for her and his hand closed around nothing. "Well, shit!" he laughed. Continuing on with his inspection, he had to conclude that there was no one in the house but them. No one alive, at any rate.

When he went back downstairs, he found Harley standing in the front hall at the base of the stairs. She began to apologize. "Look, I'm sorry. I was foolish. My imagination just got the best of me. I can't believe I attacked you at the door, like I did." He walked right up to her, making her realize what a height advantage he had. She stood five-four and he was easily a foot taller without those shit-kicker boots he wore.

Beau couldn't keep his hands off of her if he tried. Taking her stubborn little chin in his hand, he tilted her face up to his. She visibly trembled and he noticed it was all she could do to stand still. What was up? This was one mystery he definitely intended to solve. "It was my fault. If I hadn't filled your head with scary stories, you would have just ignored the unusual noises. And don't you know that I want you in my arms? The greeting you gave me at the door was the fulfillment of a fantasy, love. Not something you need to apologize for."

"I don't think I could have ignored the laughter of a little child. It sounded too real." He was standing so close and her whole body was reacting to him in conflicting ways. Harley was mystified; she hadn't realized she could still feel this way. Not only was she a bit nervous, she was beginning to feel sexually excited. And it wasn't just that he was a virile, exciting, handsome man. No, it was because he was Beau. Her Beau-ray. "I'm just thankful it was you outside my door. I could have thrown myself into the arms of the UPS guy."

"I'm glad it was me, too. I don't want anybody else holding you tight. I'm claiming that job for my own." He smiled, watching her cheeks grow warm, again. God, she was a delight! Beau debated whether or not to tell her the legends or what he had seen upstairs. He decided against it, for now. "I just don't want you to be scared."

"I'm okay, now."

He couldn't resist, he placed the back of his hand on her face, her cheek was so soft. Jesus, he wanted to kiss her. "Look, let me take you out to eat, and we'll talk about everything over supper. I have your check and some papers on the conversion I want you to take a look at. And there's no charge for the conversion." Her big doe eyes pulled at his heartstrings. "But to be honest, I just want to spend the evening with you. I couldn't stay away, cher. Will you do me the honor of keeping company with me tonight?" He waited, expectantly, studying her face.

And then she surprised them both. She rose up on tiptoe, put her arms around his neck and kissed him on the side of the face. It was a quick embrace, but it was a start. "I would love to have dinner with you. But, you're in business and I will pay for the conversion."

Beau didn't know what to do. He started to put his arms around her but let them fall and then, he gave in to his desires. "No more talk of money." He clasped her to him so tight that he was afraid he might break her. "God, baby! You do know how to turn a man inside out."

Harley struggled with herself and forced her body to remain still. She could feel the ridge of his cock, hard against her stomach. For a moment, she wanted to rub herself against it. Embarrassed by her own desire, and a fear that the panicky feelings would start, she pulled back. Again. "Sorry, I got carried away." What was she thinking? The realization that a physical relationship with Beau might be a possibility stunned her. He wanted her, or he thought he did. There was no attempt on his part to hide his interest. But what would Beau have to say when he found out her secrets? And she had so many. . . . .

"Don't you dare apologize to me. Having you in my arms is absolute heaven." Watching her cast her gaze to the ground, he wondered at her innocence. She gave out an almost virginal vibe. But, surely not. She was fully-grown, filled out, and a fuck-fantasy if he ever saw one! But she was also a lady and he would never, ever dare forget that. This sweet doll was a class act, and he was going to make sure he did everything just right. "I want to be alone with you more than I want to eat, but I'm determined to show you a good time. So, let's go out while I still have the strength to resist you." Putting a hand in the small of her back, he showed her to his truck and helped her inside. For the first time, he wished for bench seats so he could have her sit right next to him. "Have you ever been to Mulate's?"

"No, but I've heard about it. They are supposed to have some of the best Cajun food around." Breathing deeply, Harley inhaled his scent. He smelled so clean, like salt spray and crisp autumn air. They pulled out of her drive and headed toward the small downtown area of the sleepy south Louisiana town. "Where do you live, Beau?" She couldn't resist asking about him. Now that she had found him, she was hungry to know every detail she could learn.

She was interested in him! Yes! "Most of the year; I live on a houseboat. There's nothing in the world like it. I can't wait to take you out on it. Also, I have a house a few miles from yours, deeper in the swamp at my game preserve. You'll love it. It sits on stilts and there is this meandering staircase and deck that I've built that goes from the decks off my living room and bedroom and winds down around trees and over swampy places and ends up right on the bayou. There's a dock there that you can sit on and fish. If you'll come over one night, I'll grill steaks and we can eat down there." He had to touch her hair. It seemed imperative. Yes, it was as soft as he imagined it would be. Stroking the silky strands from her face, he tucked a little bit behind one pink shell of an ear. This time she didn't tremble. Good. "Would you like that?"

She hesitated, not because she didn't think she would have a good time, but she knew there was so much they needed to discuss before they could embark on a real friendship and thinking about anything else was more than she could process right now. "Why don't we wait until after dinner tonight and see if you still want to see me again?" She said it lightheartedly, but meant every word.

"Do you remember that innocent kiss from yesterday?" He drove into the parking lot of the inauspicious restaurant and slowed to a stop. Not waiting for an answer, he asked another question. "I didn't get to keep you in my arms for very long. But the amount of time I had you there was heaven." Their eyes were locked, she watched him as closely as a frightened deer. He could tell she was listening intently. "Do you remember how it felt to be in my arms a few minutes ago, when you ran to me for protection?" The expression on her face wasn't hard to read. It was longing, pure and simple. "I do, sugar. And I'll be honest with you. I've never felt this way about a woman before. I want you, Harley Montoya. I want you every way that a man can want a woman."

She felt hypnotized. No one had ever spoken to her this way before. The closest had been the night she had lain in Beau's arms when she had been thirteen and he had told her she belonged to him. Lord, she owed him so much. She owed him the truth about who she was. Right now, she had no intention of telling him about the rapes; she had learned her lesson on sharing that detail from her past. Later she might feel differently, but right now she didn't want that ugliness to mar their reunion. God, she didn't know what to do, but she could be honest about one thing. "I'm glad I'm with you. There's nowhere else I'd rather be."

"Well, hallelujah" Was all he could say.

On the way to the restaurant, she tried to get all of this sorted out in her mind. God, she wanted to share herself with him, to acknowledge their connection and their past. But would that be wise? So much water had run under the bridge and the last thing she wanted to do was for him to bear blame for what happened to her. He had escaped and she had provided the distraction. It was a risk she had been willing to take. After the midnight visits to her room, Pell's reaction shouldn't have come as a surprise. Harley could still feel his cruel hands as he'd forced her into the back room where he had made her pay dearly for his loss. Harley, or rather Nada - separating the past from the present helped her cope - had been cruelly raped. But that single act of violence had given her the courage to run away from Brownwood. So while Pell had removed the bloody rubber and jerked the soiled sheet from his bed, she had fled.

The only regret she had was losing Beau that day. How often she had thought of him and prayed he was doing well. Harley would have given anything if she could have left with him, but she had understood it was impossible. He hadn't offered to take her and she hadn't realized he was going until just moments before he escaped. She had been able to help him, and for that she was grateful. As he had turned to go, she had mouthed the words 'Run, I'll slow him down'. If only they could have found one another later, but she had never known Beau's last name or where to find him, until today when she had walked into his shop and stood face to face with her past.

A crowd was gathered in the parking lot, so Beau found a place and helped her out of his truck, escorting her to the door with a possessive arm on her shoulder. When they walked through the modest entrance of the restaurant, the rhythmic music of Cajun zydeco met her ears. It was all she could do to keep her bottom still; the peppy, driving beat made her want to dance. As they made their way through the entry hall, Beau showed her all of the photos and signatures of famous people who had performed at the club. Muddy Waters, Huey Lewis and even Paul Simon. "I can't wait to get you in my arms on the dance floor" he whispered in her ear.

Dancing with Beau. Just the thought of it sent a shiver through her body. The only times she had ever indulged was in a crowd setting, to fast music. She had never been held in a man's arms while they swayed to the music. Could she do it? Did she want to try? "I'm not very good at dancing. My lifestyle hasn't given me much of a chance to indulge." There, that was as good an explanation as any.

"Well, that's just sad, mon cher." He took her by the hand. "We'll have to remedy that." When they walked into the large room, Harley was hit by several things at once. The smells of fried seafood, the sound of a French Cajun wailing about a lost love, and the raucous laughter and conversation of an excited, happy clientele. A waitress asked Beau where he'd rather sit, near the band or in a more secluded area at the back. He pointed to a darkened section lit by hurricane lamps where couples sat enjoying one another's company.

It only took a few moments for the waitress to seat them, get their menus and take drink orders. Soon, they were alone. "It all looks good," Harley mused. "What would you suggest?"

"I'm going for the crawfish platter. If that's too much food, you might try the etouffee. It's a savory dish that consists of crawfish cooked in a roux and flavored with the holy trinity. The holy trinity is. . . ."

"The holy trinity is celery, onion and bell pepper. I cooked at a restaurant in New Orleans when I was younger." Younger – that was an understatement. She had started out washing dishes at some of the bars on Bourbon Street. Gradually, she had hung around until some of the managers let her help out in the kitchen. Nada had been a quick study and it wasn't long before she was preparing poboys, muffalettas, jambalayas and beignets. That was when Captain Thibodeaux had offered her a job on the tugboat. Of course the Captain had assumed she was a boy, since that was the guise she had lived under for almost a year. Nada had hated to trick him, but she had needed the job and being a boy was the safest way of existing she could think of.

"You'll have to cook for me sometimes. I bet I'd love anything you did for me."

Again, his expression told her he wasn't referring to food. Harley bit her lower lip and prayed she wasn't making a mistake. "Okay, it's a date." Those were brave words, for her.

Damn, the way she looked at him, licking her lower lip with that little pink tongue. If they hadn't been in a public place, Beau would have swept her up in his arms and ravished her. The waitress interrupted his fantasy time, so he ordered quickly just to get rid of her. "We'll take an order of crawfish etouffee and a crawfish platter and a pitcher of beer." He looked to Harley for affirmation, which she gave. But the waitress wasn't in any mood to leave.

"Hey, aren't you the guy who goes around catching alligators?" She leaned in real close, and stooped over so Beau couldn't help but see down her blouse.

Harley was a bit amused, but she was also a tad jealous. Beau, however, handled the woman with polite dismissal. "Yes, I own the game preserve. I appreciate you taking our order so promptly; my date and I are looking forward to the wonderful food."

When he covered Harley's hand with his own, the waitress sighed and winked at him. "Got it. Too bad. Your food will be right out."

"Sorry about that." Her hand was so soft; he took advantage of the chance to trace sensual patterns on her silky skin. He heard her gasp. She tried to slip her hand away, but he held on to it and after one more small tug, she relented. Neither of them acknowledged the tiny war of wills. "So, tell me about the lucky guy who's getting the sniper rifle for his birthday." Beau hoped he was hiding the jealousy factor, keeping it casual was hard. God, he was hard. Damn! Beau wasn't sex-starved, but he was particular and since meeting Harley, he knew no other woman was going to satisfy him. He wanted Harley. Period.

Honesty, she would practice it as much as possible. "The gun is for me."

"What?" He couldn't keep the amazement off of his face or out of his voice. "Well, that surprises the hell out of me; you are just so damn dainty. I don't think you can handle a rifle that big, baby."

Oh, boy. She had a lot of explaining to do. "I can shoot," she admitted, carefully.

"Really? I'd like to see that," he admitted. "One day soon, we'll do some target practice." Any excuse. He had it bad. He'd take any excuse to spend time with her. He didn't care if she could hit the broad side of a barn. He'd love to play with her. Anyhow, anyway he could.

"We'll make a date out of it. Okay?"

"What will you do if I outshoot you?" she teased. 'Was she flirting?' Harley asked herself. Surely, not. She was so out of practice, it was pathetic.

Oh, this was going to be fun. "If you outshoot me," he pretended to ponder the question; "I'll let you have your wicked way with me." When her mouth opened and her eyes got big! He cracked up. "God, I'm going to enjoy you. You are absolutely precious."

While she was trying to figure out if he was serious, he stood up, "Now, make me happy, baby. Dance with me."

He held his hand out and she placed hers in it. The gesture felt momentous, it was as if she were agreeing to more than just a dance. At that moment, she knew she was going to tell him everything. Eventually, when the time was right.

The band was playing a French song, one from the 60's, Ma Belle Ami. It wasn't fast, but one that gave her the chance to enjoy the novelty of being held close. He was holding her lightly and they were surrounded by people. So far, so good. Harley hummed with the music, it was a beautiful tune. And when it came to the part where the song said, 'my beautiful friend, I'm in love with you', a lump came into her throat. This was Beau, her Beau, and he didn't even know. "Beau, I need to tell you something."

"I'm listening, baby." He rested his chin on the top of her head. How long had it been since he enjoyed being with a woman so much? The song was almost over, and the final thought it left you with was hope. Whoever the woman in the song had walked away from, for whatever reason, was history. And the man who would take his place was ready, willing and able to do so. Beau didn't know who Harley had been with before; it didn't really matter, because the man after him was here. He buried his face in her hair and breathed her in, "God, you smell good – like brown sugar and cinnamon. I could just eat you up." The music died down and he didn't want to let her go.

But the crowd wasn't in the same romantic bubble that Beau lived in. Someone called out the name of a song and the band ripped into a fast number that woke the whole room up. Beau spun her out and pulled her back so fast it made her head swim. "Beau!" she gasped as she made a grab for him, trying to regain her balance.

"I've got you. Don't worry. I won't let you fall."

"Okay, I trust you, Beau-ray." Harley said the words automatically. She hadn't meant to use the term of endearment that Nada has coined so many years ago, but it had slipped out.

In his mind, the sounds of the music died away, the noise of the crowd dissipated – it was as if they were alone. Beau froze in his tracks and stared at her. Now, he was the one that looked like he was seeing a ghost. "Nada?" On all sides, couples danced around them. They stood in the midst of happy people like an island in a fast moving stream. Harley stared at him like she was afraid he was going to strike her, then she tore away and ran from the restaurant as fast as she could.

"Nada? Harley?" Shit, he didn't know what to call her. He was flabbergasted. Beau didn't know what to think. The only thing he knew was that he had to go after her. "We'll be right back," he hollered at the waitress, as he ran to the door. Out in the parking lot, he glanced around. There just wasn't that many places she could go. "Harley?"

She leaned against his truck, trying to catch her breath. It had been stupid to run. For Beau to be shocked was perfectly normal. He was probably put out at her because she hadn't revealed herself to him right away. Instead, she had pretended they were strangers. And in a way, they were. Sixteen years was a long time to be apart. They had both changed, in many ways, she most of all. But the one thing she didn't want to be was a coward. "I'm over here," she called to him. Harley stood there, her arms wrapped tight around herself – head lowered, waiting to see what his reaction would be. "I guess you'll want to take me home." She didn't have long to wait.

Beau walked up to her, stood right in front of her - close. "Damn, right, I want to take you home. Look at me." She did, and what she saw made her heart jump in her chest. She meant something to him. How long had it been since she knew that to be true of anyone – the answer was easy – sixteen years. At that instant she lost her fear. Beau would never hurt her. Now, all she had to do was convince her body of that fact. Taking her by the shoulders, he pulled her in his arms. "I thought you were dead." Cradling her to him, she could feel his heart pounding. "My God, I can't believe I've found you."

Standing on tiptoe, Harley buried her face in his neck. "This was what I was about to confess. And I wanted to tell you, before. So much. When you walked into your shop and I saw you for the first time, I almost died. It was so hard to pretend I didn't recognize you."

"I can't believe you're alive!" My God, he couldn't get close enough to her. Beau picked her up and swung her around. "Why did you pretend? Why didn't you just tell me?" His voice was deep and husky with emotion.

She clung to him. "I don't know. It had been so long, I didn't know how you'd react." She knew that sounded lame. "I was afraid, I guess."

"Afraid? My God!" He pulled her up even tighter. "Do you realize how much I longed for you? I have longed for you a million times. I came back for you, you know. But Pell told me he murdered you. And, Goddammit! I believed him." Lord, there was so much he wanted, no needed, to know. "How about if I go back in and get our food to go? I need to be alone with you. I want you to tell me everything." Unlocking the door to his truck, he picked her up and set her on the seat. "You sit here and I will be right back." He kissed her quick and hard "and don't you move." He took a step or two, and then looked back as if to make sure she was still there.

Harley put her fingers to her lips. He had kissed her on the mouth. She could still feel his heat. "My stars and garters" she whispered. If she wasn't careful she was going to fall head over heels in love with her Beau. As she sat there and waited, Harley rehearsed what she was going to say. A short nervous laugh escaped her lips. He seemed as thrilled to be with her as she was with him. "Lord, please let this work out," she prayed. She wasn't exactly sure what she meant by that but she knew she didn't want either one of them to be hurt.

"Thanks," he paid the cashier and left a generous tip for the waitress. His heart was thumping like a jackhammer in his chest. *Nada was sitting in his truck.* And she was beautiful and safe and he knew he was grinning like an idiot, but this was the best gift he could ever dream of getting. "Thank you, God." He breathed a prayer as he carried the two Styrofoam containers filled with fragrant crawfish. Oh, he had been attracted to Harley big time. But Beau was awed at the difference it made in his heart to know that she was Nada. Before he had been lust-struck, anxious to know everything he could about sexy Harley Montoya. Now he still felt that same hunger, but it was sweetened by the knowledge that he had prior claim to this woman, they were bound by ties that could not be easily broken.

He peered through the darkness and let out a breath he hadn't realized he had been holding. She was still there. Balancing the food in one hand, he opened the back door of his double cab truck and sat the containers on the floorboard. "I'm back, baby." He couldn't stop looking at her. "Are you okay?" he asked as he climbed into the truck beside her.

"Sure," she smiled back at him. "There's just so much I want to say to you. So many questions I want to ask and I'm not sure where to start."

"Start anywhere. At the beginning if you need to. I've got as much catching up to do as you." He turned the key, put the truck in gear and pulled out on the highway. "We didn't get to talk that day. It all happened so fast. I saw an opportunity and I took it and you covered for me, didn't you?" There was no doubt in his mind that she had, and he was almost afraid to ask what happened next.

"Yes," she answered quietly. "You came back to Brownwood?" Even in the excitement of their discovery, she hadn't missed that startlingly wonderful information. He had returned for her!

Had she doubted he would? That thought made him pause. Even though they had talked about escaping Pell's clutches, there had been no definite plan. That night, circumstances had just worked for him. Pell had been busy with a new guy that was causing problems and both of his cronies, Ron and Lonnie, had been picking up a load of drugs that Pell was about to coerce them into pushing. That was one of the reasons he had felt the urgency to act when he did. Once drugs were involved, the danger factor would increase tenfold. So when he got the chance, he took it. Beau had just assumed she would understand that he would move heaven and earth to return to her, with help. "Of course, I came back. I came back for you. Don't tell me you thought I was just going to abandon you there?" He was driving carefully, but glancing over at her at every opportunity. All he cared about was looking at her, being with her, understanding what had separated them so long ago.

For the moment, she savored what he said, the momentous fact that he had come back for her. That was almost too much to take. It hurt to think about what might have been. "When Pell discovered you were gone, he was furious. He was about to take out after you, and that terrified me. I wanted to give you as much time as possible to get away." Harley could feel him looking at her, but at the moment, she couldn't bring herself to meet his gaze. "So, I went into his room and broke his jazz records."

She didn't have to say anything more. Beau felt his heart contract. Those old 45's had been Pell's prized possession. "What did he do to you?" He could just imagine the beating she received for him.

"Just more of the same, really, he beat me." Harley refused to tell him about the rape. Maybe someday. Maybe not. Once again, Jed and Sonny's repulsed faces came to mind. And the thought of seeing that same look on Beau's countenance was the worst thing she could think of.

Beau could tell she was holding something back. He

didn't know what that could be, but he could tell the memory haunted her. "So, what happened? When I got back you were gone. I tore into him, demanding to know where you were." The police had pulled him off the sleazebag. After Beau had testified, the detectives had felt Pell was probably responsible for several unsolved murders. All they would need would be to compare his DNA to samples they had extracted from the victim's fingernails. So knowing he was going to be charged with multiple murders, Pell had chosen to torture Beau. "He told me he had knocked you in the head and threw your body off the river bridge. I died a little that night, Nada."

She couldn't resist, Harley covered his hand on the steering wheel, offering him comfort. "I'm sorry. Not too long after you left, I got a chance to escape. He was – uh – preoccupied and I slipped out the kitchen door. It was a fluke chance, really. Everyone was out on the take and Cook had gone to refill Pell's liquor cabinet. We were all alone." She swallowed hard, remembering that she had ran with torn clothing and virginal blood running down her thigh. But at least she had gotten away.

"There's so much I want to know." He might be pushing things, but he had no choice. There was no way he was letting her out of his sight, not for a while and hopefully, not tonight. "Can I take you to my houseboat, Nada? For some reason I just need to get you on my home turf. It's a man-thing. Okay?"

Beau knew how to pull her heartstrings. "That sounds wonderful, Beau. I would love to spend some time with you."

As soon as she agreed, he made the turn to head to where his boat was docked. He wasn't about to give her time to rethink her decision. "You won't be sorry." As he waited at a stoplight, he leaned over toward her, looking into her eyes. "God, I'm happy. But, it's funny I'm just not sure what to call you."

"Call me, Harley. I haven't been Nada for a long time."

"Harley, it is." He knew what he wanted to call her. Mine.

Chapter Three

"Beau, did you know there is an alligator walking up the gangplank?" Harley couldn't help herself. She backed up against the wall as the huge reptile lumbered onto the boat. She wasn't armed and didn't know if she could shoot the monster if she had the opportunity. He didn't look hungry, he looked sort of happy. Still, she wasn't going to stand still and get eaten. "Beau!" she called. "Please come get me!"

"Awwww, come here, baby." A door she hadn't noticed opened up behind her and a strong arm pulled her close to the safest place she had ever known. Harley turned in his arms and nestled close, finding his closeness much more preferable than facing the alligator.

"That's my gator, Harley. His name is Amos Moses and he doesn't have a tooth in his head." Beau planted kisses all over the top of her hair. "I didn't mean for him to scare you. He doesn't usually come aboard this time of day."

Harley turned her head slightly, peeking around. "He doesn't have any teeth. Why?"

"I'm not real sure, I found him half-starved when he was about three foot long. Somebody had pulled all of his teeth, probably thought they would keep him as a pet. He would have died, if I hadn't taken him in. He's lived on ground meat for almost ten years."

Harley turned in his arms and smiled as the big gator ambled to the back of the boat to a place where he could bask in the sun. "So, he comes and goes as he pleases?" Gradually her heartbeat returned to normal. She became aware that he still held her tight, and she was holding on to his arm like it was her soul's anchor.

"Yea, he keeps the burglars scared off." Beau closed his eyes and celebrated the miracle of having Nada, Harley, in his life again. "Come on in, I want to talk. I need to know everything you've been doing since I lost you."

Harley let him draw her into the cabin. "This is beautiful. I've never been on a houseboat before." She was amazed at how nice it was. There was a large leather sectional sofa, a wood-burning fireplace and a fully equipped kitchen.

"I'll show you the rest of the place in a bit," yea, he hoped to show her his stateroom up close and personal. "Here, love; I fixed you some hot chocolate. I remember how you loved hot chocolate." Beau picked up a cup from the bar and handed it to her and as their fingers touched, the memories flashed between them. A chilly day in the French Quarter of New Orleans when Beau bought Nada a cup of warm cocoa to stave off the winter chill.

"Thank you, I can't believe you remembered." They sank into the welcoming cushions of the couch and sat close, facing one another. Harley sat with one leg tucked underneath her. Her body was tingling, literally tingling. She tried to attribute it to nerves, but she knew that wasn't it. Harley was sexually excited. Being this close to Beau and seeing the hunger in his eyes was turning her on. And God, he was aroused. She tried not to look at the bulge in his jeans, but it was really too big to miss.

"It's all right, baby." Beau saw where she was looking and he saw her hand tremble. "I can't help how you make me feel, and I can't hide it either. You know that old saying, it's a plain as the nose on your face? Well, I have a big nose and big other parts, too." He laughed as she ducked her head. God, was she as innocent as she appeared? The thought that she might be untouched excited him no end.

"Sorry, I shouldn't have stared."

"Look all you want, treasure. It already belongs to

you." He took a sip of the fragrant chocolate. "Drink your cocoa, doll. We've got a lot of catching up to do." He debated how to start the conversation. Perhaps it was better to start with a safer topic. "Do you need a right or left hand stock?"

She looked relieved, "Right hand and a cheek piece, if you don't mind. And I would love for you to put some nightforce optics on it."

"You're turning me on, you do realize that don't you?" Beau laughed. "How do you know about nightforce optics?"

"I told you I could shoot."

When she smiled, his heart skipped a beat. "Can I hold you?"

The question was so unexpected and he spoke so softly and evenly that she thought at first she had misheard him. But when he held out his arms, she realized that he wanted her to sit in his lap. The very thought made her head spin. "You want me . . . . ."

"Damn right, I want you. Come here. I want to be as close to you as possible."

If it had been anyone but Beau she wouldn't have considered it in a million years but, she did consider it. She even made a move, until something deep inside of her put the brakes on it. Nothing in her body would cooperate. "I can't, I'm sorry."

He took the cocoa from her unsteady hand and placed both cups on the side table. "No problem, cher. Is it me, do I make you nervous? That scares the shit out of me, you know."

"It's not you. I know you. Don't think that."

"You have no reason to be apprehensive, I would never hurt you. You know that, don't you?" Beau searched her face, but he could read nothing in it. It was very carefully blank. What in the world could be wrong?

"I know that. It's just too soon. Okay?"

All right, he'd abide by her wishes, mostly. "Can I touch your face? Would that be okay?"

"Oh, my goodness," she whispered, not sure of what was happening. He waited until she gave her permission. "Sure, I don't mind." It was hard to be still. She didn't know whether to jump in his arms or flee.

Slowly he raised one big hand and with the most gentle of touches ran his thumb over her cheek, then cupped one side of her face. "Now, let me look at you. Yea, there they are, amber eyes. That same sweet little mouth I kissed so long ago. Well, of course, you're my Nada. Why didn't I see it before?"

Beau's voice was so tender, Harley almost cried. "It's not so bad when you say it."

"When I say what?" Kiss. He wanted to kiss her so bad. It was hard to think when she was so close.

"Nada."

"Why would that be bad? Isn't that your name?" Something was bothering her, so he stoked the fire in his blood and gave her his complete attention. "What do you mean?"

"Don't you know? It means I'm nothing."

"Nothing?" What did she mean? He was missing something.

"When I was born, I had a caul over my face. Do you know what that is?"

Why did she look ashamed? "Sure, that's when the baby has a bit of membrane over its face, and people used to believe that child was born with second sight." Beau watched her press her eyes together and bite her lip. "I don't understand – that's a good thing. Old-timers around here would say you were blessed." He played with the loose material, soothing the front of her shirt, just anxious to touch her anywhere he could. She covered his hands with her own, stilling the movement of his fingers.

"Hardly. My father thought the veil over my face meant that I was spiritually cursed, that's why he named me 'nothing'."

Damn! "Nothing? That's what the word nada means? And it wasn't an accident, he told you that?" Beau wanted to hit something.

"Over and over again, everyday he told me how worthless I was. That's why I ran away from home when I was thirteen." That was how she ended up in Brownwood.

"Oh, sweetheart," he leaned over and kissed her forehead before she could stop him. She didn't move away, thank God. "I am so sorry. His loss is my gain. Now that I've found you again, I'm never letting you go. I'll admit it. Before, I was entranced with you." His voice was husky and he ran a hand up and down her arm, as if he were trying to soothe away every cruel word that had been said to her. "I fell fuckin' head over heels for you when I only knew you as sexy Harley. And now I find out that you are the one precious thing in my life I thought I had lost. Do you understand what this means to me? Baby, I'm holding on to you with both hands. I may never let you out of my sight again."

His words were like another language, one so foreign that she only recognized a few phrases. But the gentle look in his eyes made her feel safe. Every taunt her father had thrown at her was being made powerless. And before she could protest, he leaned in and captured her lips for a quick kiss and the world stopped turning on its axis. Heat. Peace. Hunger. Emotions that Harley thought she had no claim to, burst forth into her heart. His lips were coaxing and warm and she had to grab the material of his shirt to keep from clinging to his broad, broad shoulders.

"Mmmmmm," he groaned into her mouth. He couldn't help it; his hands wouldn't stay where he put them to save his life. They found their way to her back, coaxing her up against him so there was no doubt in her mind that he was fully engaged, mind as well as body. "Cher, cher my God, you are like the sweetest honey. I could get so addicted to you." He had to have more. Hungrily, his lips slid down her neck, nuzzling her throat, scraping his teeth on her skin and sucking enough to leave a tiny mark. He couldn't remember ever being so instantly voracious for a woman.

With a little whimper of surprise and surrender, Harley tentatively brought her arms around his neck. It was like coming home.

Hallelujah! Beau hugged her. "That's my girl." She was gorgeous, she was sexy as hell, a mixture of softness and strength that literally made him ache with longing. "You're far from nothing. You are a treasure, a precious jewel. You are my all in all." All the time he was talking, he was rubbing his lips and nose on the side of her face, inhaling her scent, marking her as sure as one the ghost cats of the swamp marked its territory. Black panthers were real. Even though their existence was denied by the authorities, Beau had seen them with his own eyes. When they wanted to claim something as their own, they rubbed their scent on it by passing their mouth across the object, leaving a brand of possession, the same way he was marking Harley.

Her body hungered while her mind whirled at the myriad of wondrous things she was feeling. So this was what she had been missing, this amazing need to belong to someone. But. . . but. . what if? God, what if she couldn't? What if he couldn't? She put her hands up between them, pushing back making a space between them. "Stop, Beau."

"Too fast?" She nodded her head, slightly. "I understand, baby. We're not strangers, but it has been years." He had no intention of rushing her. She was just too precious.

"There's so much you don't know," she whispered.

"You can tell me anything," he nudged her face with his, his lips grazing her skin.

"I want to. Beau..." Lord, she didn't know what she was about to say, when her beeper sounded and made her bounce in his embrace like a Mexican jumping bean. Immediately his arms tightened around her.

"I got cha' precious," he kissed her neck. "Whoever is calling you, tell them you are otherwise occupied. With me."

Harley looked down. Shit! "As much as I would like to stay, I have to take care of this. Duty calls." Casting aside her doubts, she laid her head on his shoulder and hugged him tight. "This has been wonderful. I can't tell you what it means to find you again. Thank you, for everything."

She started to get up, but he stopped her. "Hey, wait a minute. Are you sure you have to go?" He wasn't ready for their evening to be over. Not by a long shot. Would he ever tire of looking at her face? High cheekbones, a sweetly curved jaw, and a pair of lips capable of transporting him to paradise. Each feature was pleasing to the eye, but combined they were lethal to his self-control. "Do you have any idea how beautiful you are?"

"I'm not," she protested as she placed her hands on his biceps, half-heartedly keeping him at a distance. "Thank you for saying so, though. I wish I didn't have to go. It's my job. There's an emergency."

He let her get up, reluctantly. "Okay, I'll take you home."

"Thank you, I appreciate it." As she gathered her things, her mind was already racing ahead wondering where she would have to go and what she would have to face. "I'm sorry to rush off like this."

"It's okay, honey." She seemed worried. And that worried him. "Do you want to talk about it?"

They hurried down the gangplank and onto the dock. Harley was aware of her surroundings. The cypress knees and the Spanish moss; it was all so beautiful she wished she could stay and not face whatever new horror some maniac had devised to blow people up. "It's a long story and I will tell you about it, I promise." He opened the door for her and hurried around, realizing she was anxious.

She was texting on her phone when he got behind the wheel, so he started up and gunned it – not wanting to disturb her focus. When she finished, he pressed again. "When will you be back?" Damn, he felt possessive! "I told you I didn't want to let you out of my sight."

A thrill shot through Harley. No one had ever worried about her before, and he had no idea where she was going or what her job entailed. "I'm never gone long. I'll be back tomorrow; it will all be over by then."

"Tomorrow, what time?" Beau got amused at himself.

"Just stop by the Hummer, I keep a change of clothes in there and I need to get on the road." As he pulled next to her vehicle, she gave him one last long look before she got out. "I can't say for sure what time I'll be back, but I will call you." Reaching for the door handle, she was brought up short by a strong, but gentle hand around her neck.

"Promise?" He held her gaze for a long, intense moment.

"I promise." Without asking permission, he leaned over and kissed her once more. A chaste kiss full of longing.

"Give me your phone." She handed it over and he put his number in, and gave it back. "I'll be waiting." With that, she got out, leaving him sitting there, watching her go. Harley knew everything had changed, because this time when she left part of her heart stayed behind.

This was hitting too close to home. The bomb in Philadelphia had been placed in a building owned by her mentor's family. At first she had been convinced it was a coincidence, but once she got this text – she knew it was personal. An anonymous tip had been received at the sheriff's department in Port Arthur, Texas. A bomb had been placed in the Transco Logistics Terminal – where her mother had worked for thirty-eight years. Again, the device had been placed above ground level where a robotic device could not reach, this time on the side of a huge storage tank. The nightmare scenario was compounded by the contents and location of the tank. Not only did it hold 300,000 gallons of gasoline, but it was just one of fifty such tanks that sat very near oil refineries with similar setups. If you flew over the area, the sheer number of white tanks filled with gas and oil would look like fields of mushrooms. Each was a potential bomb in itself, and if one blew up there would be a chain reaction of explosions that would take out half the city. A more horrific accident, she couldn't imagine. .

What compounded the problem was the fact that the Transco Logistics Terminal had twenty-one pipelines pumping oil into the facility, as well as trains, barges and tankers sitting nearby waiting to be unloaded. A detonating bomb here would be worse than the Texas City Disaster of 1947 which was still on the books as the worst industrial accident in U. S. history. It had begun with a small fire on board a ship filled with ammonium nitrate, but ended up causing multiple explosions on other ships, oil storage tanks, and oil refineries. Five hundred homes, the seaport, 1100 vehicles, and 300 freight cars had been destroyed. The death toll reported at a little over five hundred was thought to be woefully underestimated due to foreign seamen, immigrant laborers and their families and an unknown number of travelers being in the vicinity. As she drove into Port Arthur on Highway 69, she prayed she could stop this. If not, it was going to make the Texas City disaster look like a Sunday picnic.

The road was blocked and she had to weave her way in between barriers and fire trucks. Didn't they realize if this thing went off, all of these vehicles would be blown sky-high? Pulling through the gate, a uniformed security guard met her, "Ms. Montoya, we're relieved you're here." He pointed toward the group of men standing near a small office complex. "If you'll head that way, they'll show you our little problem." His words were brave, but she could see the pulse point on his neck throbbing with nerves. With a curt nod, she rolled her window back up and eased the Hummer on toward the throng of tense men. She could tell they were tense by their stance. All ram-rod straight, shoulders back like they were preparing for battle. Only, they wouldn't be on the front line. That would be her. This time she had called Waco to join her. He wouldn't go to the bomb itself. She wouldn't let him, but he could help her get everything ready to go and be nearby to coordinate things if it all went horribly wrong. Part of her wanted to assume this bomb would be like the last, but until she looked at it, she wouldn't know that for certain. Saying that time was of the essence was so cliché, but in this case it was the greatest of truths.

Even in the enclosed vehicle, she could hear shouting. And there were several trailers filled with expensive looking equipment being moved out of the way. She didn't want to laugh, but the idea they were worried about computers and analyzers was typical. If the number of white vans loaded down with people heading out the gate was any indication, at least some of the employees were being transported out of the area. Taking a deep breath to steady her nerves, Harley parked and exited the hummer. It was such a peaceful night, the sky was blanketed with stars, the moon was full and there was a hint of chill fostering the hope that fall was on its way. This part of Texas was flat, humid and close enough to the Gulf that a tinge of the sea was in the air. The world looked entirely too normal for the possibility to exist that this whole area could soon become hell on earth. And if it did, she wouldn't survive and that wasn't acceptable. For the first time in a long time, Harley had an overwhelming desire to see tomorrow. Finding Beau had changed all of that. Reuniting with her childhood friend was wonderful, but the way he made her feel…that was everything.

"Socorro is here!" she heard one of the deputy's shout. Hearing herself identified by that term brought a wry laugh to her lips. It was their way of dehumanizing her. If they could label the fragile looking woman with a synonym the brawny he-men could retain their swagger. Unfortunately, she was surrounded by people who had no business here. This was a one-man job, or in this case, a one-woman job. SWAT team members, EMT's, police…good gracious, there were even a few highway patrol officers. Why in the world hadn't the Golden Triangle bomb squad taken more precautions? These folks weren't going to be any help. And they certainly didn't need to be this close to ground zero if the worst happened.

Hell! There was no time to go hunt whoever was in charge. They would just have to find her. After all, they knew she had arrived. Harley went to the back of her Hummer, opened the doors and began pulling out her protective gear. A lot of good it would do, but it was protocol.

"Hey boss," a gruff East Texas accent met her ears, a welcome sound. Harley looked over her shoulder at the handsome man who would do anything she asked him to. Waco Rainwater was anxious to learn everything she could teach him, and Harley would eventually turn over more responsibility but it was hard. She had this underlying belief that these were her battles, not his. "Here, give me that." He picked up the heavy suit and held it for her while she climbed into it. "When are you going to let me handle one of these jobs?" There was a smile on his face, but she could tell he wasn't kidding.

"Soon," she smiled at him weakly. "I feel funny about this one, let me handle it and I promise that next time I'll let you go up with me. This one is different than the others we've faced. In fact, I want you to help me get the stuff to the tank and then I am ordering you to leave. Drive away, at least a mile. If it explodes, the shock wave will rip the other tanks open and this whole area will be one huge fireball and I don't want you anywhere near here." She could tell Waco didn't like what she had to say. And he let her know it.

"Harley," he spoke her name, softly. There was a ton of emotion in his tone. "How do you think you make me feel?" Waco was all man. He had the devil of a time stepping back and letting a small woman take risks while he stood in the clear.

"I know what I'm doing," she tried to speak in a confident tone. He didn't respond, but finished fastening the seals on the side of her suit. Picking up the helmet, she looked up at him. He was tall, as tall as Beau. "My radar will keep me safe, it always has. Trust me, Waco. Next time, I promise we go in together. Please?" She could have pulled rank. She wasn't only his boss, he was Navy too and had served under her in Iraq.

"I would take care of you, if you would let me." His eyes spoke volumes to her. Harley was a bit shocked, she knew he cared for her but this seemed to be more.

"My sweet friend," she said in a rush, but Waco was important, "I appreciate your concern, but I will be fine. Pray for me, you can do that." She would have to deal with this and she hoped his feelings would not get in the way of their working relationship. At one time, maybe…no, she didn't have sexual feelings for Waco, not like she did for Beau. Beau! God! Beau just the thought of him made her heart race. "Let's go."

A mask dropped over his face and they prepared to do what needed to be done. "Yes, ma'am. But, we will talk about this."

His retort surprised her, but it shouldn't have. Waco Rainwater was a determined, strong man but he wasn't the man she had dreamed of for sixteen years. He gathered up two suitcases full of instruments and followed his superior officer. As they walked toward the tank, a harrowed looking, older man wearing a hardhat started toward her. He carried a clipboard and Harley wondered what he was tracking. A devastation quotient? She could read the fear on his face; at least the gentleman understood the possibilities. "Ms. Montoya? Thank God, you're here! I have never seen anything like this in all of my born days. Who in the world would do something like this?"

"We don't know, Sir. That's not really our job. There will be investigations from the CIA, the FBI and Homeland Security, you can be sure of that." Waco spoke up, and Harley didn't mind a bit. She had to focus. A huge part of her success was mental.

"Let's focus on keeping this a failed threat," Harley stepped ahead of them, already concentrating on the task at hand. The closer she got to the bomb location, the more she realized how dire this scenario actually was. Two men were standing at the base of the massive tank, and it dwarfed them. Great, this monstrosity was something else high for her to climb. Why couldn't these crazy psychos put an explosive device on ground level? A whisper of uneasiness snaked down her spine. She knew why. Whoever was behind this didn't want the bomb diffused by remote means, they wanted her to do it. She couldn't deny the obvious. This was hitting too close to home. Pushing that thought out of her head, she tried to concentrate. It didn't matter. She had to deal with this either way. "I'm going up," she spoke evenly to Waco. "I'll call you when I'm through." Taking out the tools she thought she would need, she attached them to her suit and began to climb the ladder.

Refusing to look down, Harley hoped that Waco would do as she asked. Ordered. God, she should have begged for him to leave. Rung by rung, she made her way upward. Over her head, the platform was adhered to the side of the tank like a window washer's scaffold clinging precariously to the side of a skyscraper. "Please God, let me be able to take care of this." She didn't often pray. Harley wasn't convinced an appeal to a higher being did any good, but now was the time for a step of faith. Pulling herself up on the shaky structure, Harley gasped at what she found. Compared to the work of art in Philadelphia, this was crude, but deadly. She didn't have to look very closely she just knew. Pure C-4 was packed tightly in soft-side suitcases and hung from the side of the tank. Her hand shook as she reached for the zipper on the first one. She had to look to find out how it was wired and what the trigger would be. Hell! This was far more volatile than she had thought. Liquid nitroglycerin in fragile vials was woven among the blocks, so there was no possibility of removing the cases and relocating them. They would detonate in her hand. Wires connected the cases, but only the cases; she knew they were on a timer, not a fuse. But where was the timer? That was the question.

Harley just stopped and stood still for a moment, she didn't have time to search for the timer, she needed to know where it was. Now. "Please she prayed, don't fail me now." There were seven cases, the large kind that people rolled behind them as they hurried to catch a plane. This was a huge amount of explosives and the tanks themselves were highly incendiary. For the first time, she doubted. What if she couldn't do this? Panic coated her soul and seemed to stifle the connection she always had with whatever power gave her a glimpse into the unknown. "No, no, no," she gently laid her hands on the first suitcase and sought a trance-like state. Evening out her breathing, she let her mind go blank and waited. Three, three, three, the number flashed red in her mind, blinking like a neon sign. So, she opened her eyes and stared at the third bag. It must be here. She tugged on the zipper and the case swayed and she gasped, waiting on a flash of white-hot heat. Nothing. Good God! She needed to retire.

3:43 3:42 3:41 "Merciful Lord," she whispered. There wasn't much time. Hastily, she examined the maze of wires. "Sadistic bastard." Before, there had been colored wires which was the norm. Bombers used colored wires for their own safety, so they could be sure of what they were doing and not blow themselves up. Not this time. All of the wiring was black; just a mass of tangled strands, specifically designed to confuse and frustrate. There appeared to be no rhyme or reason and Harley knew most of them were fake. They were just placed in the design to make it harder for her to know what to do. Someone was playing a game with her, she could feel their hatred emanating off the plastic he had touched and arranged for her sole amusement. 2:49 2:48 2:47. All she could think about was Fox Crocker. It smelled like him. That Old Spice smell that he wore to ad nauseum. But she had watched him go overboard as he was evading arrest for her rape. 2:40 2:39 2:38. Taking a pair of clippers from her belt, she held them in front of her like a dousing rod. This was impossible! There was no way she could figure this out in…2:15 2:14 2:13.

Harley knelt in front of the device, as if she were praying to it, asking for mercy. Staring at the wires, she saw Beau's face. Tears welled in her eyes and she wished with everything in her that she was safe in his arms and far away from this unbelievable situation. 1:47 1:46 1:45 Damn! She wanted to live! Calling forth every molecule of belief and faith she had, Harley stared at the mass and willed the riddle to make itself known. Brushing her fingers over the wires, she tried to reason it out, what she would do if she had been the one to make this monstrosity. One wire caught her eyes, it was looped low and seemed to have no use; then it coiled up and the end was soldered into the back of the small control panel. 57 56 55 54 "Please, God!" she begged. "I want to go home to Beau." For the first time there was someone waiting for her, and she didn't want him hearing about her death on the news along with the slaughter of countless others. Picking up her hand she poised it, waiting for some kind of confirmation or hint that she wasn't making a mistake. It made sense. It was what she would do - - - and then - - - it happened. The wire began to glow, just the least little bit. At first, Harley thought it was too late, the bomb was detonating. But then, she realized this was her sign. Taking a deep breath she steadied her hand; 44, 43, 42, 41 and snipped. The light on the LED screen died and Harley almost fainted with relief.

* * *

"Where the hell is she?" Beau talked to himself as he walked from one end of the workshop to the other. He was trying to ignore them, but he was aware his employees followed his movements. Step by step.

"What's wrong with him?" Rick asked. "He's pacing like a caged tiger."

"What the hell could she be doing?" He knew he was attracting attention, but he just didn't give a damn. He had called her home number several times, and damn! He could have shot himself for not getting her cell number. She had his, but he hadn't been smart enough to get hers. Idiot!

Dandi entered the workshop behind him, her face betrayed the fact that she was enjoying the spectacle he made as much as the men did. Well, tough. He didn't care; he was worried sick. It had been twenty-four hours and still no word from her.

"Who is this 'she' of whom you speak? If it's your cousin, 'she' is right behind you."

Beau could tell that Indy was trying to be funny, but he wasn't in the mood. "No, I'm not talking about Dandi." He didn't elaborate and his expression let the men know their questions wouldn't be welcome.

"If you've got time, come over here and look at your Ma Deuce. I've cleaned her up and she's a real beauty." Indiana polished the barrel and lovingly ran his hand down its length like he was caressing the long sleek leg of a woman.

"That's not the beauty he's worried about," Dandi smirked. "It's Harley Montoya. The woman who sold him that dream gun. I think he wants to see if his weapon will fit in her holster."

Dandi's attempt at locker room humor brought a groan from the men. Beau thought about lecturing her on lady-like conduct, but he had more important things to worry about than her crude comments. "Look, it's more than that; I used to know her a long time ago. We were both at Brownwood in New Orleans. She saved my life."

"What?" Rick Gentry stepped closer to Beau. "I know about Brownwood. Remember my family lived in New Orleans; my father was one of the cops that brought Pell down. Was she one of the kids that Dad rescued?"

"No," Beau began to explain, but Dandi walked up close and put her arms around him, effectively shutting him up.

"Beau, who is Harley? I heard you cursing earlier, you used the name Nada."

"I thought Nada was dead." Indiana sounded confused.

Beau looked at his best friend. Indiana knew his history better than anyone. They had confessed their sins and drug out their tarnished memories as they fished the bayou on many a dark night. "I did too, until yesterday." The whole room went quite, everyone waiting to see what he would say or do. Beau felt their concern. Finally, he broke the silence. "All right everyone back to work. We've got deadlines." He dry washed his face with the palm of his hand. "Where are we on that Reaper conversion?"

As the men went back to work, Dandi went to the front to file some invoices. The small TV was on a news program and for a few moments, she didn't pay it much attention. But then she heard the word 'bomb' and glanced over to see where the incident had occurred. The news announcer was pale and shaken. "We avoided a near catastrophe yesterday, ladies and gentleman. If it hadn't been for Socorro, the landscape of Southeast Texas might look very different". Dandi was shocked as the familiar face showed up on the screen. "Oh, my God. Beau is going to have a Cajun fit. So, that's why Harley looked so familiar."

* * *

Goodness, she was tired! Willowbend hadn't been her home for very long, but she was definitely glad to get back to it. It had taken her longer than usual due to the briefings she gave homeland security and the FBI about her take on the bomb and the bomber. She might be making a mistake, but Harley had decided to keep her suspicions about Fox Crocker to herself for now. Accusing a dead man never went over very well.

Shedding her clothes as she walked, Harley paused and listened to the house. She hadn't been back in it since hearing the voices and laughter. Nothing. It was as still as death. Oh, not a good analogy. She laughed at her own

73

jumpiness. Heading into the bedroom, she tossed her discarded clothes on the end of the bed and noticed the answering machine light blinking. A tiny leap in her chest betrayed her excitement. Could it be Beau? Checking the read-out, she grinned. There were three messages; she smiled and hit Play.

Message One – Harley, this is Beau. I hoped you would be back by now. I'm worried. Give me a call. You have my number.

Message Two – Harley, this is Beau. Again. I hope nothing's wrong. Call me as soon as you get this message.

Message Three – Nada, damn it all! Where are you? To hell with it, I'm coming over there. His concern warmed her heart and she pulled out her cell phone and went to contacts, touching his name he had entered. He picked up on the first ring. "Harley?"

"I'm home." She said the words softly, as if she were sharing a precious secret.

"I know. I see the Hummer. I'm at your front door."

"I'll be right there." Realizing she was standing there completely nude, she hung up, squealed, and ran to the closet for a robe. Slipping it on, she padded downstairs clad only in the thinnest cotton wrap. No underwear, no shoes. God, she was becoming brazen. Flinging open the door, she didn't have time to say a word. Beau grabbed her up and held her tight.

"God, I missed you." His breathing was ragged. "I was so worried. Where were you? Are you okay?"

"Yes, I'm fine. I can't believe you came over." She hugged him hard, "I'm so glad to see you."

"Stand still and let me look at you," she obeyed his rumbling command. "My God, baby, you're a luscious little morsel. You don't have enough material on to make a good size table napkin." At first she thought he might be displeased, but his next words dispelled that notion. "I

74

can't wait to make love to you."

Okay. Time to slow things down, at least until she could be sure she wouldn't embarrass either one of them. "I guess I should get dressed." She said the words and he heard them, but neither one of them turned loose of the other for a few more long moments.

"Okay, I'll let you cover all that sugar up. For now. I came to take you on a little jaunt, if you'll go with me. I want to take you to my game preserve, I'd like for you to meet my girls and boys." Beau stepped back and Harley could swear she saw a tremor shake through his body, but it might have been her imagination.

"There's nothing I would like better," she told him sincerely. They were standing close and he was so big and broad; she wanted nothing more than to melt back into the haven of his arms. But until she wrestled her demons, it wouldn't be fair.

An almost harsh laugh escaped his lips, "Cher, there's something I would like better, for sure." He looked her up and down. A scalding, slow rake of his gaze that let her know he was aware that she was woman, and that she was aroused And so was he. "But, we will take it slow for a bit longer. I want to do this right." He picked up a strand of her hair and caressed it between his fingertips. "Go put on some tomboy clothes and I will introduce you to more of my world."

"Okay," she turned and hurried away while she still could, leaving him standing just inside her doorway. Rushing up the stairs, she untied her robe while she ran. Happiness made her want to throw her arms in the air and twirl in a circle like a small child, but she contained herself. Taking time to hang up her robe, she chose a pair of jeans and a top, grabbed some underwear and headed to take a shower. She didn't lock the door, knowing that Beau was too much of a gentleman to barge in on her uninvited.

75

The bathroom had been completely renovated in blues, greens and earth tones – the color of the sand, sea and surf. Turning on the water, she couldn't help but think about sharing a bath or shower with Beau. That was one thing she fantasized about – steamy visions of a man running his hands over her body as the water sluiced over them. Now that man had a face, a body, and a name.

Climbing beneath the spray, Harley decided not to wet her hair; she didn't want to take time to dry it. Instead, she soaped her loofah and ran it over her arms and breasts, cleaning away the horrid memories of yesterday. After the recap interviews with the authorities, she had spent some time with Waco. He was so important to her. It had been hard, but she had come to terms with him. More responsibility was what he was asking for and she wanted to give it to him. If only she could figure out this latest rash of bombs and if they were just wild coincidences or if someone, somewhere was trying to send her a message. As far as her and Waco's personal relationship, she made it clear that he was family to her. But after she found herself mentioning Beau every other breath, she figured he had gotten the message. And so had she, because it hadn't been an act, he had figured naturally in her thoughts, and conversation about him had just flowed. Before she knew it, she had told Waco about Brownwood and Beau and their finding one another again. And before she was through, he had covered her hand with his and told her he hoped it all worked out between them. Now, she had to convince herself. But before anything could happen between them, she had a helluva lot of thinking to do.

God, the water felt good. As she ran the sponge down her thighs and between her legs, she felt a longing, a yearning. This wasn't normal for her, she didn't masturbate. But now, with every swipe of the sponge, the hunger grew. Bracing one hand on the marble tile, she began to rub and caress her slit. Moving the sponge up and down, teasing her clit. God, it felt good! A little moan of need slipped out, "Oh, yeah!" She moved the loofah feverishly, riding it as her hips pumped in time to her excited pants. "Please, please, love me, oh it feels good. Oh Beau, I want you so much." As her orgasm hit her, she cried out the name of the man who from fantasy alone, had made her cum harder than she ever had before.

Chapter Four

"Jesus Christ!" Beau leaned his head against the door and listened to Harley cry out his name in ecstasy. It took every molecule of strength he had to keep this door closed between them. It wasn't locked, he had tested it and he had had no intention of interrupting her while she was temptingly naked and wet. . . . damn. "Be strong, Leblanc." He wanted to do this courtship right. It was just too important. So, he had come upstairs to tell her there was a man at the door who said he was here to give her an estimate on a new roof. "Lord Have Mercy." Had his cock ever been so hard? Pre-Cum was leaking from his dick and all he could do was rub it and promise he would give it relief as soon as possible. "Later, buddy, promise."

Adjusting his engorged package, he went back downstairs to tell the man he'd just have to reschedule. Beau took the roofer's card and his good-natured ribbing about the obvious erection he was sporting. "Good luck, man. I don't blame you for putting this off. There are just some things in life more important." He hadn't known the fella, but apparently the contractor had been in Firepower a time or two, because he had called Beau by name. He hoped Harley didn't mind that he had changed her plans.

"I'm ready." The soft-spoken words sent chills down his spine. Turning, he found her standing right behind him, cute as a button and hot as hell. "Was someone at the door?"

"Yea," he handed her the card. "He said he would call and reschedule since we had plans and all." The blush on her cheeks intrigued him. It wasn't make-up – it was residual passion, because he saw a matching hue on her upper chest and it was all he could do to keep from testing

78

to see if that sexy flush would burn his fingers. "I hope that was all right."

"Of course, I had forgotten all about the appointment. I'm glad you were here to take care of it. I probably wouldn't have heard him knocking over the water running in the shower." She smiled so sweetly at him that he almost sank to his knees.

"No problem, cher." He had to struggle to keep from commenting on what he had heard from her in the shower, but he had no desire to embarrass her. "Shall we go?" He offered her his arm and she took it, and he just felt like he had won hit the biggest Powerball lottery, ever. Talk about a fuckin' high! He was so over the top for this woman, he might never come down.

They made their way out to his truck, and he calmed his over anxious libido by taking note of the things she had done in her yard. "You've done a good job re-establishing some traditional Southern plants. I like it." There was magnolias, crepe myrtles, Louisiana Iris. A myriad of flowers and bushes that spoke of decades of history and the passing of life and love through the hour glass of time.

"This is the first real home I've owned." She stood still while he opened the truck door for her and before she could protest, he picked her up and held her close; stealing a quick kiss before depositing her in the seat. "Oh, I like that," she whispered and kissed him back for good measure. "I enjoy being with you."

A simple statement, but one that made his blood pressure escalate to dangerous levels. "There is no where else on earth I'd rather be than with you." Lowering his head, he nuzzled her cheek, inhaling the essence of his Nada. "Push me away, or we'll never get anywhere." Playfully, she did as he asked and he shut her securely in, and went around to join her. "Are you ready to tell me where you went yesterday?" When she hesitated, he gave her a reprieve. "Okay. We'll wait on that. Instead, tell me what you did after you left Brownwood."

For just a moment, she paused. But Harley knew he wouldn't judge, so she pivoted in the seat a bit so she could look at his face. Once again, she was struck by how devastatingly handsome he was. The chambray shirt he wore was light blue and the sleeves were rolled up, giving her an opportunity to see how strong his forearms were; the veins prominent, the muscles large and defined. She knew how good it felt to have those arms around her, how safe and secure. And she wasn't used to relying on someone else for her well-being. Remembering the weeks and months after Brownwood was hard. "I ran and ran, hiding anywhere I could. All I could think about was Pell finding me; I had no idea he had been arrested. During the night, I came upon a homeless family and they let me hang around with them."

"Damn!" Beau maneuvered the truck off of her property and onto the river road. "Anything could have happened to you. I should have realized that bastard was lying. Pell was a sadistic son-of-a-bitch and telling me you were dead was his last ditch effort to torture me." He slammed his hand on the steering wheel. "Honey, I'm so sorry. If I hadn't been so young and stupid, I would have had enough sense to come looking for you."

The scenery they were passing was captivating. Glimpses of the bayou could be seen peeking through the trees. Leaves with all the colors of the rainbow heralded that the year was waning down. But none of it held her interest, only the man before her was important. "Stop," she placed a hand on his arm. "There was no way for you to know. Nothing else bad happened in New Orleans after I left Brownwood. Not really. The Watson's, the homeless family, they were kind and warned me about the dangers of being on my own, not that I didn't already know, but it was nice to have somebody care. At first I thought they had two boys, but as it turned out, the children were girls. That shocked me. The Mom explained that they were dressed that way on purpose, with their hair cut short and wearing boy's shoes. Perils of the street seemed mild compared to what I'd been through, but if I could make myself invisible, I wanted to do that. So I borrowed a knife and they helped me cut my hair right then. Even though they didn't have much, they shared what they could and when I walked away from them, I was a boy."

"There is no way in hell you were a convincing male, sweetheart. You are decidedly the most feminine female I have ever seen." Harley studied his face, looking for signs of disgust. There were none. What she saw was anger for her. Remorse. A longing to turn back time. A muscle in his strong jaw jumped, betraying the unleashed tension he was holding in. "I want to know everything, but I will be honest with you. The thought of you alone on the streets, thinking that I wouldn't care enough to come back for you, that tears me up, Nada." The old name slipped out, evidence of his turmoil. He slowed down as they approached a denser portion of the swamp. A small dirt road led off to the right marked by a sign that said, 'Reptile Preserve'. "We should have talked it out, made plans. I just had no idea that you would run away before I came back to rescue you."

Gravel and rock on the road crunched under the tires. A bigger sign with an alligator in bright green with his tale curled over his back announced they had arrived. As he slowed to a stop, Harley knew she had to explain enough to make him realize what had happened was neither of their faults. "We were kids, Beau. I was thirteen and you were sixteen. Pell was a professional criminal and the worst kind of bully. After you left, he turned on me and I knew that I had to get out when the opportunity arose." When he turned off the engine, she unfastened her seat belt and shifted until she was kneeling, facing him. Harley wanted to look in his eyes; his beautiful eyes and reassure him. "When you escaped, I was so relieved. If you had stayed there, one of two things would have happened. He would have pulled you so deep in the mire of his criminal activities that you would have been lost, or he would have ended up killing you. Never, not once, did I regret you had gotten away. My running off, my escape, was not because I didn't have faith in you. Somehow I just knew, I was convinced I had to get out of there. Pell would have killed me."

"Christ!" Beau shifted his seat all the way back with his left hand and clasped her around the waist with his right. "Come here, baby. And this time let me hold you, please. I just want to hold you. Nothing else." She let him move her to his lap where she lay between him and the steering wheel, her head on his shoulder and his arm anchoring her in place. "Tell me what happened next."

Cradled in his arms, her palm on his chest, she could feel his heart beating. The hard muscles of his torso felt like the safest resting place in the world. This close, she could see the growth of his beard, the five o'clock shadow that always showed up ahead of time. God, Beau was all man. Unbidden, she cupped his jaw, reveling in the rasp of his beard against her skin. "Have you ever heard of PoBoys?" At his nod, she continued, her hand still stroking his face. He leaned into her caress like a big, contented cat. "It was several days later, after I had left the Watson's and realized I was out of options. Hunger drove me to knock on the back door of a restaurant and offer to wash dishes or mop floors in exchange for something to eat." At his harsh sigh, she placed one finger over his mouth to quell his regret. "It was my lucky day. Raquel Dumaine opened her door and her heart to me. She fed me, let me work that day and the next and soon I was not only cleaning, but cooking too. Lucky for me, she put a cot in the backroom and I lived right on the premises. Raquel figured out I was a girl, pretty quick. But she went along with my wish to disguise myself. In fact, she would perpetuate the idea by talking to me and about me in front of others and she always referred to me as 'her little lad'. The regulars bought my act, for the most part. Although once or twice I would feel interested stares. Of course, there are plenty of men who lust after young boys, so that could have been an explanation."

Beau kissed the palm of her hand. "How long did you work there?" Shouts from outside the vehicle made Beau glance up, but he waved a hand at whoever was making the racket and turned his attention back to her. "Were you happy?"

How did she answer that? Happiness was never her goal; survival had been Harley's motivation. "I wasn't unhappy. Working at PoBoys's taught me a lot. And I met my next employer – a man who gave me a chance and was better to me than anyone in my life, but you."

A slight grimace came on Beau's face. "You're making me jealous, babe. Who was this man?"

Harley couldn't help but chuckle as she thought about her savior. No human being had ever looked more like Santa Claus than Captain Jerald Thibodeaux. And he had managed to bring peace and good will into her life as well. "There was one man; a rotund gentleman who came in quite frequently and he always ordered a Denver omelet and I made sure it was hot, and just the way he liked it with extra cheese and peppers. One day, he offered me a job. I spent two years cooking for him and his crew on The Crescent Moon. A big tug boat that moved barges up and down the Mississippi River."

Beau looked amazed. "I can't believe you. You worked on a tugboat? And you were still passing yourself off as a boy?" Harley was finding it hard to be still, he was rubbing her leg from knee to the apex of her thighs and the smooth, sensual strokes were setting her on fire. Before she realized, she lifted her hips, offering herself to him and the gesture did not go unnoticed. With an audible growl, Beau captured her lips. "If I don't get inside of you soon, I'm going to go stark-raving-fuckin' mad." He ground the words against her mouth and sucked on her bottom lip, "I heard you in the shower. Those sweet, little moans you were making, you said my name, come on baby, say it again."

He had heard her? She felt the blush rise. "I got to get up," What could she say? "I – uh – I uh . . ." as she was struggling for words, a tap on the window caused her to leap in his arms.

"I got you, baby." Beau scowled at Indiana. Rolling down the window, he fussed. "Your timing is lousy, buddy."

"The gharials are about to mate. You wanna watch?" His expression was one of true wonder. There had been no intent to interrupt.

"They're not the only ones who were trying to mate," Beau muttered under his breath and Harley got tickled. Beau felt her giggle and smiled and hugged her, kissing her on her forehead. "We'll finish this conversation later, sugar. I want to know when you're going to let me love you. Okay?"

She gave a brief, hesitant nod before he turned his attention to Indiana. "We'll be right there. Just give us a minute. Okay?" Slowly, comprehension dawned on Indy's face and his mouth opened in a slight, apologetic 'O' and he backed away. "Are you okay? You're still trembling." He stroked down the soft skin of her arm.

"Yes," she chewed on her bottom lip. "I was just embarrassed to find out you heard me in the shower." The thought of making love with Beau had been on her mind a lot lately, but discussing it with him was scary. "What's a gharial?"

"Trying to change the subject?" He laughed and held her close with one hand while he brushed a strand of hair out of her face. "Don't be embarrassed. It nearly killed me, but I loved every moment of it."

"Yes, I am," she answered solemnly. "I don't want to be the cause of you not joining your friend."

Lowering his voice, he pushed his groin against her soft hip. "The reason we're delaying a second or two is to give my cock a chance to return to normal size."

Pink bloomed on her cheeks and Beau was amazed. "Nada, my love, how can you seem so innocent? It's as if you are untouched." Before his eyes, everything changed. Harley stiffened and moved out of his arms, straightening her clothes. "What did I say?"

"Nothing," But, he could tell she was upset. Shit!

Did she think he wanted her to be completely inexperienced? He knew better. She was almost thirty years old. "Baby, I didn't mean that I expected you to be a virgin?" Hell, open mouth, insert foot.

"Well, I'm not...a virgin, that is. Far from it." She looked embarrassed, uncomfortable – and he felt like a heel.

"I didn't mean. . . ." he began trying to make amends without knowing what to be sorry for. She opened the passenger side door then walked a piece off from the truck and stood, her arms crossed around her waist, holding herself tightly. Hell! He slammed the door and went to her. "Baby, what did I say?"

She lifted her tear-streaked face and he wanted to hit someone, but he was the one who made her cry. Wiping the tears from her face, she gave him a faint smile. "I'll tell you later, I promise. Just don't press me now. Let's go see your animals." Holding out her hand, she waited for him to take it. All he wanted to do was grab her up and haul her off to his man-cave, but he forced himself to take it slow. Something was up; he didn't know what yet, but he was determined to set it right if it was in his power to do so.

"All right, sugar." He took her hand, squeezing it lightly and led her down the path to where the crocs and alligators were kept. "Before we got distracted, you were telling me about your days on the mighty Mississippi. Were you able to maintain your male persona all that time?"

"Yea," she laughed wryly, "Until my breasts began to develop. I was a late bloomer, but when I blossomed, it was hard to hide them." Almost self-consciously, she folded one arm over her breasts as if remembering. "When Captain Thibodeaux discovered the truth, he was very kind."

"Over here, Boss." Indy motioned for them to come to a special holding pen.

"Wait till you see this pair. They are incredible. I call them Cyrano and Roxanne and soon you'll see why." He led her up to a sturdy mesh fence and there they saw two huge crocodiles. "These beauties are very special. They are on the critically endangered list, and I am giving them a safe and secure place to breed." Harley seemed to be fascinated.

"I have seen pictures, but never been this close to one. They're huge."

Beau loved to talk about his boys and girls. "The Gharial crocodile is one of the largest crocodile species in the world. Look at that elongated and narrow snout which becomes thinner with age. Cyrano has a bulbous growth on the tip of his snout, known as a 'ghara'. Only the males have that distinctive bulge and the Gharial are the only reptile where you can tell the difference in the sexes by just looking at their faces." He pulled Harley close and laid his chin on her hair. "And they are big, reaching a length of twenty three feet." She shuddered in his arms, so he laid it on thick. "And look at those jaws, they're razor sharp." As he said the last two words, he squeezed her quick and hard. Making her jump.

"You!" she immediately gasped and grabbed his arms, partially amused and partially annoyed. "Don't try and scare me. I'm not afraid"

"There they go." Indy pointed as the two monsters slid into the deep holding pool.

Beau could tell that his friend and employee was intrigued by his affection for Harley. He gave his buddy a smile and a tilt of his head to indicate that he wanted him to keep his distance. He wanted some time alone with his woman. So, Indy dropped back, following at a respectable distance. "Watch this, crocodile sex takes place underwater. Cyrano will approach her and touch her softly, blowing bubbles underneath her and rubbing his jaw against her." Just like he said, the big male courted the female. "If Roxanne accepts him, he will gently push her under the water. It's not a fast process, he'll take his time with her; make her happy." Much to his delight, Harley was rubbing his arm like she was absorbing strength from him. Strength that was hers for the taking. "And it won't be a one-time thing," he whispered in her ear. He was speaking for himself and for Cyrano. "He will take her numerous times to ensure that he plants his seed and the eggs are fertilized." A mighty splash in the water pronounced that the deed was well underway. "Come on, they deserve some privacy."

They walked on down the shady path, surrounded on both sides by high protective fencing. Up ahead a smaller brown alligator watched them as he paced the fence. His eyes never leaving them. "What is he doing?"

"That's Castro and he is wishing you would get close enough so he can take a bite."

"What kind of crocodile is he? He's beautiful."

"That's a Cuban crocodile and their habitat is disappearing as fast as the home of the Indian Gharials." At that moment, Indy came up by them and tossed a dead chicken over the fence and the croc literally sprung up in the air and caught the treat.

Harley clapped her hands in delight and the two men laughed. "He's so agile."

"Carmen!" At Beau's call, another Cuban rose up out of the water and started a slow march to the fence. "These are my favorite," Beau explained. "No other species of croc or gator even comes close to the intelligence of these creatures. It'd be like comparing a dolphin to a gold fish. Watch this, Indy give our girl some supper." Indy tossed another chicken over the fence and Carmen caught it in her powerful jaws. "Water!" Obediently both big reptiles turned and made their way back to the dark green waters of their safe haven.

"Boss, we got fire-ants in the Cuban's pen. We're gonna have to move them down in your slough for a few days soon to clean this up."

"Do what you need to, just make damn sure that the fencing, underwater and above ground, is secure. We don't want to lose these babies, plus we don't want them eating any locals. That wouldn't be good publicity."

"You are providing these animals with a second chance." Harley looked at Beau in wonder.

"How many others do you have?"

"Only three more right now - the Dwarf Crocodile, Morelet's Crocodile or the Mexican Crocodile, and the Orinoco which is from South America. It's my hope to get these endangered animals started in places where they'll be safe. Programs are in place to attempt to retain enough of their natural habitat to ensure that they don't disappear."

Harley put an arm around Beau. "People like you are the true heroes in this world."

"Thanks, love." Her words meant more to him than a Congressional Medal would have. He was about to show her the rest of his pets when his beeper went off. He unfastened it and read the message. "I've got to head to Beaumont. There's a gator in a residential area, taking a dip in somebody's pool. I'm sorry, honey, but that's part of the work we do here. Any time an alligator is found in a place where he isn't welcome, we go in and catch him and move him to some place safe."

"Can I go with you?"

Beau was pleasantly surprised. "You want to help me catch the gator?" She was so delicate and feminine; he couldn't believe she would choose to spend an afternoon watching him wrangle a reptile.

"Unless you'd rather I didn't." She looked a bit unsure of herself.

"Hell, no," he was emphatic. "By my side is where you belong. Don't worry, I'll keep you safe." Beau couldn't remember ever being so happy. "Come on, we'll take the other truck," he pointed to a black double cab dually. "It's equipped with all of our reptile control tools."

"Do you do this often?" Harley asked after they had climbed in, excitement sparking through her veins. Even though her life was fraught with danger, this day with this man felt like a great adventure,

"Two or three times a month," he ably maneuvered the vehicle from the swamp road onto the blacktop that would lead to I10 west.

Beaumont was just a few miles west of Port Arthur where she had dismantled the bomb at the Transco Facility just the day before. "Where do you take the alligators that you relocate?"

"Mostly, I take them deep into the Atchafalaya, the largest swamp in the United States It's amazing that people are so familiar with the Everglades, but don't even realize

89

the Atchafalaya even exists."

"I knew about it. We've never talked about our early years very much, but I grew up in Beaumont. Funny, though – I don't remember hearing about alligators invading homes the way you say they do nowadays."

"That's because all of the new housing additions they've been building are on lands that used to be rice paddies." He slipped his hand under her hair and began to massage her neck. She totally relaxed into his touch, letting him make her feel good. "Progress has encroached upon the natural habitat of the gators and they are just moving in the same place their kind has moved for thousands of years. Only this time man is trying to share that space with them. So they go out into their yards, and there they are. They look in their pools, and they have a guest. One woman even came home and found a good size young female had come through the doggie door after her cat."

She had leaned back into his hand, letting him rub her neck, and every once in a while a little contented sound escaped her lips. He kept talking. His cock solidified, but his heart was happy. When he told the story of the home invasion, she reacted to that, "What about the cat? Did the alligator eat it?"

Beau laughed, "No, the cat just jumped up on the kitchen cabinet and they had a staring contest. The cat won."

"Good. Where did you grow up, Beau?" Knowing he ended up in Brownwood, there was no doubt he had endured some type of tragedy. When he moved his hand from her neck, she thought her question had offended him. It didn't, he took her hand in his and held it tight, as if drawing strength from their union.

"My early days were spent in a little town called Church Point, Louisiana. My Mom and Dad were good people." He smiled at her, and Harley felt a warmth start to grow around her heart. If she wasn't careful, she would have an urge to start picking out china patterns. It might be her wishful imagination, but she was beginning to see forever in his eyes. "All my memories were good ones until I was five, when Hurricane Juan destroyed my world." For a moment, he stared out the window. They were going through Lake Charles and he seemed fascinated by the refineries and smoke stacks on the horizon.

"You don't have to tell me, if you don't want to." Some people valued their privacy; she surely had no room to talk.

"I want to tell you everything," he spoke simply, giving her hand a squeeze. "I'm a big believer that everything happens for a reason. It's true that I've had some hard times, but all the events in my life wove themselves into the path that led me to you, cher. How can I regret that?"

Lord in heaven, he was getting serious quickly. A shiver of unease passed over her. There was no guarantee she could ever be what he wanted or needed. And neither one of them deserved to be hurt. They had known enough of that to last a lifetime. What he was about to say was still unclear, but it wouldn't be pretty. She knew that. And the funny thing was, she agreed with him. "I don't regret the path that led me to you, either. Just knowing that you are alive and well and happy is worth more than you know." 'Yea, I'm pushing him away with both hands', she inwardly laughed at her own contradictory behavior. They were in big trouble.

"My Dad worked on an oil rig out in the Gulf. So he would be offshore for three weeks, then home for three weeks. Lordy, when he was home - laissez les bon temps rouler - the good times rolled. Pop loved to party. My memories are hazy, but what I have are bright ones. Mama, she loved my daddy and I can still remember how tender

91

he was with her. Like I want to be with you, cher." He rubbed the pad of his thumb over her knuckles. "All that changed when Juan blew in. He wasn't a Katrina or a Carmen or Camille," he named huge deadly storms, "but he was big enough to devastate my world. It tore up a lotta shit. Two hundred cattle drowned in Terrebonne Paris and Grand Isle was underwater. Offshore, it got a helluva lot worse. An old wooden lighthouse was destroyed over on Timbalier Bay. Dad's oil rig collapsed, then smashed into another rig. Some of the crew was rescued, he was one of them. But the ship that picked them up sank during the rescue mission. Twelve people died in Juan, and my Pop was one of them." Harley picked up his hand and kissed it, then held it as tight as she could to her breast. He didn't react, seemingly lost in his story. "When my Mom heard the news, she panicked. There was no way she was going to believe he was dead 'til she saw his body. I can remember her dragging me out of bed, justa screaming. It was still pouring down rain when she dropped me off at her brother's house. I never saw her again. She died in a head-on collision halfway to the boat docks. The only consolation I had was that they were together. But, I was alone."

"God, I'm sorry Beau-ray. Your pain makes my childhood seem like a trip to Walt Disney World. Were you not happy at your uncle's? Was he not good to you?" She knew there had to be some reason he ended up on the streets of New Orleans.

"He was a single man with a job; there was no way he could keep me. So I was passed around like some stray puppy that no one had time for. It was a wonder the state didn't step in and put me in a foster home. It was a good thing that Mama had a big family, because I never stayed anywhere very long. No one was really mean or cruel to me, they just didn't care. The best place I stayed was at my

Great Aunt Lejune's. She was good to me, and Lord she could cook. But, she passed away about four months after I'd moved in with her. I mourned her almost as much as I did my mama and daddy." As he reminisced, they passed through the monotonous landscape of far western Louisiana and crossed the border into Texas. All the while she caressed his hand, trying to absorb his remembered pain. "When I was fourteen, I'd had enough of being the human hot potato. One night at my Cousin Prejean's trailer house, I just opened the bedroom window and crawled out. It was a hot June night, and I can still hear the sounds of the crickets and the bullfrogs. I walked nine miles to the interstate and hitch-hike to New Orleans."

"I wonder why The Big Easy is so attractive to runaways?" Harley mused. "For me, it seemed a place of vast possibilities. Mystery is so much a part of its natural fabric and I had been so condemned for my psychic abilities. It just seemed to me that if I could get to New Orleans I'd be . . . normal."

"How psychic are you?"

The question wasn't asked with any motive or hidden tone other than mere curiosity. She could read that much, plainly enough. "By most standards, my ability is weak. I get impressions from objects. Rarely can I read anyone's thoughts, and even if I did, I would doubt what I was picking up. What freaked my parents out was that I always knew where they'd been, who they'd seen during the day and what they had been doing. Since my father was trying to hide a gambling problem from my mother and my mother was trying to hide a drinking problem from my father, my propensity for spouting off what I picked up from their clothes or their possessions just made them hate each other and fear me. So, I saw no reason to stay. They didn't love me and I could do without the daily beatings; that's for sure." The next thing she knew, Beau was pulling off the road, turning down a driveway that led to a mechanic's shop. He didn't go all the way, just far enough off the road to be safe.

Unbuckling his seat belt, he leaned over her and unbuckled hers, as well. She had no idea what was going on. "Those days are behind us, mon ange." She knew enough French to know he had just called her 'his angel'. "I need to hold you, just a bit. My arms feel so empty without you."

Gathering her in his arms, he tucked her close and rocked her, as if to erase every cruel word and stinging blow she had endured. God, he was sweet. Men were supposed to be hard and stoic, unyielding and harsh. Not Beau. He was big and macho, but his heart was the biggest thing about him. At that thought, she smiled to herself. He might possess other large parts as well, that would be interesting to find out. Lord, how far she had come in so short of a time! To ponder the size of a man's cock had never crossed her mind before today. "I needed for you to hold me. Thank you." And that was the truth. She wasn't feeling any anxiety from his closeness, only happiness. Now, anything beyond a hug was still up in the air. A blast from an air horn broke their reverie. "Perhaps, we should get back on the road."

"You're right. Give me some sugar, to tide me over." This time he waited for her to do the kissing. She delayed for a microsecond, and then pressed her lips to his cheek, his chin and the corner of his mouth.

Damn! And he was supposed to go alligator hunting? He'd much rather hunt a bed and stay there for a week with this treasure. She rubbed her lips over his, much like he had when he was marking her like the noir panthere, the black panther. That was fine. He wanted to bear her mark. "Tongue, cher't bebe."

His Cajun terms of endearment were causing her to

quiver with happiness. Cher wasn't pronounced like the singer, it was soft – sha. And when he called her his dear baby, she melted. He opened his mouth and she slid him just a bit of tongue and he groaned his appreciation. Sipping from her lips like they were the finest wine, Beau stole the small remainder of her heart that she was holding in reserve.

Another blast from a passing eighteen-wheeler brought them back to reality. "Let's go before I ravish you here, my treasure." Feeling a little dazed and a lot horny, she eased back to her side of the truck and managed to exhale a ragged breath. "I feel the same way, Nada. Soon, you will be in my bed. I won't survive if you don't." His words hung between them, giving her something serious to think about.

Pulling back into traffic, they headed toward Beaumont. A few miles down the road, when they had themselves under control, he became curious. "Touch my truck seat or whatever, and tell me what I've been up to lately."

Was this a test? She dreaded doing anything that would upset their tender camaraderie. But the look he gave her was full of gentle curiosity and tender concern. So she put a hand on the dashboard and the other on his steering wheel and concentrated; calling forth whatever residual energy lay in the common materials which would give her a glimpse into the recent past. As if watching a 3D movie, she saw a large alligator throw open its jaws and lunge at her. She jumped. About as quick as it had come, the monster morphed into a cartoon figure of Japanese movie fame "Godzilla," she said aloud. The mythical creature was attempting to climb from a well. Interesting.

"Damn!" Beau exclaimed, "You saw Godzilla?"

She opened her eyes to see if he was laughing at her. He wasn't. What she had seen made no sense, but it was all she had. "Actually, I saw a large alligator. It was aggressive, that's why I jumped. But then it changed and became the movie monster fighting to get out of a deep hole."

"Shit, baby! You nailed it!" He was shocked. There was no way she could have known. He hadn't told Dandi and she'd never met Indiana. "Right before I met you, my buddy and I rescued a big gator from a well. His name was Godzilla."

"Good, I'm glad I haven't lost my touch." Yea, since her gift kept her alive, she wanted to keep her psychic antennae clear and free from static. The voice of his navigation system told him where to turn and they maneuvered through a cookie-cutter housing addition filled with median priced homes, sitting too close together with not enough landscaping for Harley's tastes. She much preferred older, more traditional homes with big yards and a tangible history, like Willowbend. "Look at that crowd gathered, that must be the place." She pointed to a house at the end of the cul-de-sac where multiple vehicles were haphazardly parked. Neighbors were gawking about and peeking over the fence like they were sneaking a glimpse at a peepshow.

Beau pulled in and got out, gathering his equipment that included very little; nets, ropes, tape and two sticks with hooks and a noose. "Do you want to stay in the truck till I get back?"

"Heck, no." She was out and around where he was before he could say Andrew By-God Jackson.

"Hell, baby. You just stick close to me so I can keep you safe."

His request sounded reasonable to her. Once they pushed through the crowd and made it to the backyard....it all happened fast. Harley was amazed to see the large reptile was jammed into a corner, hissing and doing its best to back through a wooden fence. "It's scared," she stated the obvious.

"Yeah," Beau addressed the useless audience. "Everybody stay back. When they feel threatened is when they're the most dangerous. Keep your distance and I'll have it under control as quick as I can." He took the stick noose and moved it close to the animals head. The big gator lunged forward about two feet. "Watch it, baby. Where are you?" he was thinking of her first.

"Here to help you, just tell me what to do."

"Nah, cher. This big bruiser means business." He managed to get close enough; quickly to push the loop over its head, but the gator began whipping its head side-to-side, desperately trying to dislodge the rope. "I need two hands." He glanced around to see which man would step forward to help. None did.

"I can do it, Beau. I have nerves of steel," she sounded like she was joking, but actually she wasn't.

"Sweet doll, I don't know." She touched his elbow, showing her support. "Hold this, carefully, and I'll put another one on and try to get behind it." He handed her the stick and immediately the huge animal reared, but Harley spread her feet, tightened her body and held tight.

Beau was right there. If the gator came for Harley, he would have to go through Beau; but still, he wasted no time throwing another rope around its neck and pulling tight. "On land, these things are ten times more dangerous than water. They can move thirty-five miles an hour." As Beau moved to its side, the gator tried to turn, but Harley went the opposite direction and kept him from flipping around on Beau. "Good girl, baby-doll."

With quick agile moves, Beau subdued the creature by sheer force. He got on top of it and with brute strength forced its head to the ground. Only the tail was whipping now. "Can you tape his jaws for me, brave-girl?" he asked

Harley with a smile.

"Yes, sir," she took the tape from the ground and knelt down in front of the alligator. "He smells pretty bad."

"Yea. That's fear. He's thrown his musk." He pressed down on the head and snout while she wrapped the heavy-duty tape around and around. "Make sure you leave his nose holes open so he can breathe."

"Okay," she did what he asked, quickly and efficiently. The gator seemed to calm and Beau, with Harley's help, flipped him over and tied his front and back legs together. "Now he's all trussed up like a Christmas turkey."

She sounded so proud, but she wasn't nearly as proud as he was. "You handled yourself like a pro. After Amos and the ghosts, I expected you to be leery of all this."

Harley was glad she hadn't embarrassed herself. "Amos took me by surprise and I am nervous of ghosts and snakes, but not much else."

After the reptile was secure, the bystanders came close and Beau got a couple of them to help him load the gator in the back of his truck. Leading her out, he put his arm around her. "I loved that you shared that with me, my brave girl," he kissed her on the head.

"I think it's time I told you what I do for a living," she spoke slowly and evenly.

"I got the feeling I'm not going to like this," he muttered.

As he helped her in the truck and buckled the seatbelt, she took the bull by the horns. "We need to talk about what happened to us both, after Brownwood. Come over tonight, and we'll have confession time." As he climbed in his side of the truck he faced her, looking anxious. She sought to reassure him; after all, she was the one with the secrets. "Don't look like that, we don't have to let the past matter." God, she hoped that was true. When – no, if – she ever told him about the rapes – were he to reject her, she would die.

"You're right," he agreed. "I've found you again and that's all that matters."

Chapter Five

At her insistence, he took her home. "I have a lot to do," she insisted with a smile as he peppered her face with kisses. "A neighbor lady is coming today; I've hired her to help me with the housework. Plus, I want to cook for you and get beautiful for you and cast a few spells so I can catch your eye," she was teasing, but he stopped her words with a hot kiss.

"Honey, you've got the last two items on your list all buttoned up. There's no way you can get more beautiful and I'm already enchanted. You have me under your spell as sure as if Marie Leveau herself was working her mojo on me."

When he mentioned the voodoo queen, Harley giggled. "You don't look hoodooed, Beau-ray, you look sexy."

She was picking at him, but he went serious. "Do you know what you do to me when you call me Beau-ray? God, that's got to be the sweetest sound in the world," he picked her up and hugged her tight. "I'll be back, cher, at six-thirty, and the devil himself couldn't keep me away."

* * *

With a duster and a can of lemon furniture polish, Harley made her way through the living room. Like most women, she didn't want to be judged for her lack of housekeeping skills, not even with the housekeeper. Noting the irony, she hoped her house was clean enough to pass the white glove test of her neighbor. It had been a busy couple of hours since Beau had left. She had made the roux for her gumbo, baked six dozen chocolate chip cookies and washed her hair. Whew! She was already tired! Now, all she needed was for her new help to come and get everything spic and span. Right on cue, the doorbell rang and she hurried to let them in. She knew it was a 'them' because Mrs. Prescott had asked if it would be okay to bring her son along. Laura Prescott was about Harley's age. She was very attractive and so was her son. Unable to resist, Harley knelt down to get eye to eye with the precious little boy. "Well, hello. I'm so glad you came with your Mama. You're going to brighten up my house quicker than Christmas lights." He was precious with big brown eyes and freckles all across the bridge of his nose.

"Howdy, lady," he stuck out his hand like a big man and she shook it, solemnly. "My name's Morris. I brought me a whole bag of goodies to play with."

"I can see that. Morris is a fine name. I'm so pleased to meet you, I'd like for you and your mom to call me Harley."

"That's a deal, Harley."

"This young man isn't shy. Is he?" Both of the women laughed and Harley got up and stepped back to admit them. "I'm so glad you're here. Totally unlike me, I've invited someone to dinner. So while you make yourself at home, I'm going to be in the kitchen."

"Call me Laura, please. This is a beautiful home. I have to tell you, I've looked forward to exploring this old place for years."

Harley walked her through the house, showing her where all the cleaning supplies and the vacuum cleaner were kept.

"Where can Morris play? I don't want him to be in the way."

"Believe me; I'll enjoy having him around. There is one room he might like." She led them into a large room she had set up as a sitting room. It was open, cheery and had a TV. "Will this do?"

"Sure thing, lady," Morris made himself at home. Squatting down on the floor, he dumped out his bag of treasures and went to work racing a car around and around on the braided rug.

"Good, I'll be in the kitchen if you need me."

The time passed swiftly. Harley loved to cook and gumbo was one of her special dishes. She made hers with chicken, sausage and shrimp and lots of spices. The recipe had come from one of the premier New Orleans chefs. He had his own restaurant in the French Quarter, but once a week he would patronize the restaurant where she worked and he always ordered the same thing - a muffalata. He had been as wide as he was tall, but Harley grew to love him and as a reward for the extra attention she gave him, he passed on his world-class recipe for gumbo.

Stirring the big pot of soup, Harley imagined cooking this for her own family someday. Talking to Morris had tugged at her heartstrings. Never before had she seriously missed being a mother, but she was feeling the urge today. Forcing her mind elsewhere, she put that impossible hope aside. Right now, she had a dangerous job and no assurance she could even have sex with a man. Not even Beau.

Out of nowhere, the phone rang and she nearly jumped out of her skin. Dashing to it, she reminded herself that it wouldn't be for Socorro. Calls for her unique services only came through the red cell phone in her pocket. "Hello? This is Harley Montoya speaking."

"Ms. Montoya, it's good to speak with you. My name is Dane Wagner with the Touch Institute. I received a referral from Dr. Young. She asked me to call you and confirm your appointment."

Uncomfortable niggles of doubt inched their way up her spine. Just the thought of opening up to a stranger about her sexual shortcomings terrified her. "Thank you for calling, Dr. Dane."

A friendly laugh from her caller made Harley smile, "Please, call me Dane. Dr. Dane makes me sound like the star of a poorly written sitcom."

"Okay, Dane. And you can call me Harley." She let out a shaky sigh. "I'm considering coming to see you. Frankly, this is a huge step for me and I'm not sure I'm ready to take it."

"Of course, Harley. I'm here to help you, not force you into anything. Dr. Young only told me a bit about you, I prefer to find out the details from my patient."

"You seem very kind. She told me the date, but could you confirm it please? Just in case, I don't chicken out." She took a pen and a pad to write down the information.

He confirmed what she had been told. "I tell you what; I'll pencil you in and hold it for you. No pressure. You think about it, and give me a call in two weeks, either way. And if you decide you need to come in earlier, just let me know. I can always work you in."

"How generous of you, Dane, thank you." She hung up the phone and went back to stir the gumbo. Could she open up to a stranger? And would it help her if she did?

"Lady! Lady!" Morris came tearing through the house, skidded into the kitchen and wrapped his arms around her knees. "Me and that little girl up there, we sure would like some cookies!"

Harley laughed as she steadied herself. "Cookies? I have cookies. Do you think your mom would mind?"

"I don't think so," he smiled a toothless grin at her. Apparently, the tooth fairy had been by to visit. "That little girl, she said for me to come ask you. She said you made chocolate chip cookies this morning."

Wait! What? "You have a good nose. Those cookies are sealed up in plastic containers." And then she realized what he had said. "What little girl?" Goosebumps swept up her arms as she waited for his answer.

"That little girl with yeller hair that's sitting on the light thingy in your room, she told me all about you."

"What light thingy?" What little girl?

"You know the thing high up that has lights on it. Come see," he pulled. "And brang the cookies." She grabbed the canister and let herself be pulled along.

"Are you talking about the chandelier?" Surely not. How would a child get in the chandelier? Her mind was whirling...unless. . . . Nah!

"Yep, I think so. Come see, she said you heard her laughing yesterday. She thinks you're funny."

By the time they made it to the sitting room, every hair was standing up on the back of Harley's neck. "There she is!" he pointed up at the ceiling. Harley looked in the direction Morris was pointing, but she saw nothing, only the light fixture.

"What's going on?" Laura Prescott asked; broom in hand. "Morris what are you yelling about?"

"If I'm not mistaken," Harley spoke in a hushed tone, over the little boy's head. "I think Morris saw a ghost."

Laura Prescott's reaction wasn't exactly what Harley had been expecting. Instead of snatching up her child and pooh-poohing her way down the stairs, Laura went to her car after a camera and when she returned, she began to take picture after picture. "You need to get Savannah over here. She might be able to pick up some EVP's."

"EV – what's?"

"Electronic Voice Phenomenon, the voices of the dead caught on a digital recorder. Savannah does that all the time. She caught one over in the old cemetery at Lafayette that will blow your mind."

"It's pretty much already blown," she murmured.

"Oh, this is incredible." Laura talked as she snapped. "I didn't ask you if I could do this...take pictures, I mean? Is it okay?"

"Sure," Harley had no real problem with it. It just made her nervous, but she did live in an old plantation house . . . and they purportedly came with former inhabitants intact. It reminded her of the old joke about the woman who had a house full of potted plants. One day the husband came home and found her atop a chair with her hair standing straight up, and the caption read "I told you so, dear. When you live in a jungle, you have to expect snakes." At the thought, she shivered. Harley was no fonder of snakes than she was of ghosts. "What happened at the Lafayette cemetery?" Did she really want to know?

Laura was into the story; she practically salivated as she told it. "Savannah was investigating in the oldest part of the cemetery where some Civil War soldiers were buried. They came upon the grave of a man named William Joseph Sheets. It said he died at Antietam. We had all known of that battle and had visited there and the battlefield of Gettysburg several times. Savannah asked him about the war and – I swear to God – I was there and while we didn't hear it with our naked ears . . ." Harley got tickled about the naked ears part. "When we played the tape back there was a very clear and distinctive voice could be heard - that wasn't one of us. The question she had asked was simple, but the answer he gave was chilling. She asked who he fought with and a southern voice clearly replied, 'with the Louisiana 14th Infantry, Sharpsburg, ma'am.' At first, that didn't make sense to us. Later, we checked the historical records and his name was listed as having fought and died with the 14th Infantry at Sharpsburg, Maryland. Also known as the battle of Antietam."

A tug on Harley's skirt made her jump, "Lady, I sure would like some of them cookies."

Ah, a voice of reason. Harley sank down and opened the container and placed two cookies in a chubby waiting hand. "Here, you go." Harley had fought enough battles in her life. This time her philosophy was 'if you can't beat them, join them'. "How many cookies will your little friend have?"

* * *

He had time to grab a shower, if he hurried. The smell of gator musk was not known to be an aphrodisiac, so he turned the water on as hot as he could stand it, stripped and stepped beneath the spray. Holding his head up and letting the water hit him in the face, he began to fantasize. It wasn't his hands rubbing soap over his body. It was Nada. God, she was gorgeous. He couldn't help but wonder what her nipples looked like, what they tasted like. Would they be coral colored or cocoa brown? What would her pussy look like? When he got the chance, he was going to spread her out on his bed and make a meal. He could just imagine laying her on his bed and covering her, like the big panthers of the swamp over their prey. He would suck on her neck, scrape his teeth on that sensitive cord, and lick his way down to her nipples. God, he loved to suck tit. Like most men, he loved everything about a woman's breasts, but thinking about Harley's lushness. . . shit, he wanted to suckle at her like he was starving for her milk. As he lived it out in his mind, his hand was pumping his cock. God, he was engorged…full, thick, throbbing with the need to fuck.

Leaning back against the shower wall, he spread his legs and fisted himself. Precum was leaking, his balls were tight and his hips bucked sympathetically. They were aching to be pushing against the cushion of her ass. God, he wanted her. He wanted her in every way imaginable. His cock in her mouth, his mouth on her pussy, buried hilt deep from the rear, her impaled and on top, and yes, his favorite; he wanted to hold her down, dominate, fill her pussy so full of cock that she'd wrap herself around him like a vine and beg for more. Shit! Hot streams of cum splashed across the dark green marble. It looked like somebody was trying to be artistically inclined with cake glaze. Helplessly, his hips still pumped and he rubbed his aching cock until every last drop was dispensed. Lord, he needed to fuck. He needed to fuck Harley and he didn't know how much longer he could wait.

* * *

He was right on time, in fact he was five minutes early. She had been standing at the dining table looking at two of the photos that Laura Prescott had printed for her. The woman was prepared. She had not only had a digital camera, but a portable photo printer as well. And one of the images was haunting; there was no other word for it. It showed a swirl of mist, about the same height as Morris. Intriguing, very intriguing.

A tap on the kitchen door made her heart jump, for several reasons. As soon as she opened it, she was captured in a hug. "Man, it smells good in here. I'm starving. for you." She barely got to focus on his face before he began eating at her lips. This time a wave of longing hit Harley, so hard. Gone was the fear, she needed more.

Beau held her face in both of his hands, smooching and teasing. She joined in the game, darting her tongue out to draw him in. A whimper of longing disappeared into his mouth, and he answered it with a groan. Pushing her back against the door, his big body pressed against her, holding her immobile and she panicked. "Stop, stop" she pushed against him. "Wait, Beau. I need a minute." Harley wasn't screaming, she was speaking fairly softly, but her heart was pounding, not from excitement but from an unreasonable feeling of being trapped. Flashes of Pell and Fox Crocker holding her down overwhelmed her mind's eye.

"What's wrong? You're trembling!" Instead of backing up and letting her go, he cradled her to him and she fought the urge to bolt. This was Beau. This was Beau. Then it seemed to hit him. He separated them a fraction and looked down at her, stunned. "Are you afraid of me? My God, don't you know I'd cut off my arm before I'd ever hurt you?"

His heartfelt disbelief only made her feel worse. "No, I'm not afraid of you, per se. Sometimes I just can't make my body understand." With that confession, she tore away and ran from the kitchen to the living room. She didn't get very far, because he caught up with her. "Easy, precious. Just stop. You are safer with me than you are anywhere in the world. Now, explain to me what you meant before I go crazy." He tried to lead her in the living room.

"I don't want to sit down. I'm too tense."

"No problem, we'll stand." He gentled her by rubbing her arms, her shoulders. "Just relax. In my arms is where you belong. I never should have let you out of them to start with." She didn't move toward him, so he moved toward her, just barely touching. Just enough so she could feel the heat of his presence. "Now, we talk. There's something going on with you and I want to know what it is."

"I don't know how to say it."

Taking her chin, he waited until she met his gaze. "Somebody hurt you. Who was it?"

Shame immediately filled her chest. Harley found it nearly impossible to form the words.

"Nada," he whispered. "Don't you trust me?"

Something broke free in her heart, "Yes, I do. And I'm not afraid of you, really I'm not. It's just that when you held me so that I couldn't move, it reminded me of . . ." Closing her eyes, she didn't want to see his reaction, not yet. She might be making the biggest mistake of her life. Twice she had been rejected. Would this be the third time? "Pell raped me the night you left."

"What?" Beau's whole body stiffened, and then he

walked away from her. Exactly as she figured he would.

Pure black rage boiled up inside of Beau. It was his fault, "Dammit," he hit the doorjamb with his fist, bringing blood. "Why didn't you tell me before? Didn't you think I'd want to know?"

His voice was hoarse with emotion. This was worse than she thought. "You don't have to explain," she offered, trying to at least save their friendship. "I understand why you would feel the way you do. It's very common."

"What way?" Raking his hand through his hair, he stared at her almost blankly.

"Disgusted with me," she stated simply as if she believed what she spoke was the gospel truth. She stood stiff, her fingernails digging into her palms. The play of his muscles under his tight black t-shirt reminded her of his strength. Yet, she had no fear of him. The only way he could ever hurt her was by walking away.

"What?" He looked so angry and hurt. Yes, he looked hurt. "God, no, baby. O God, no. I'm not disgusted with you! How could I ever be disgusted with you? I'm disgusted with me and the stupid fuckin' circumstances that put you in danger in the first place!" He was yelling, but it wasn't at her, she realized. He was yelling for her. "I should have been there for you!" In two steps he was there, about to sweep her up in his arms. "Can I hold you?" He waited; his arms outstretched until she walked into them. Clasping her close, he repeated brokenly. "I came back for you. I came back for you. I was just too late. I'm so sorry, so goddamn sorry."

Beau clasped her tight and buried his face into her neck. She couldn't help herself; she cupped the back of his head and held him close. "It wasn't your fault." A distinct dampness amazed her. He was crying for her? A sense of awe and wonder dawned in her heart. Perhaps this time it could be different. "Sometimes bad things happen and they're nobody's fault." Biting her lip, she knew she had to tell him the rest. God, please don't let this new information hurt him, she prayed. "Beau," she touched his face, tenderly. "Look at me." He did and what she saw in his face made her fall totally and completely in love. "Let's sit down, its time I told you my story and it's complicated."

"Did he hurt you?" Picking her up, he carried her to the couch and laid her down and he knelt at her side.

She looked up at him, not wanting to answer. "Why am I lying here flat of my back while you're sitting up?"

"So, I can do this." He wrapped an arm over her middle and began to kiss a path from her neck to her lips.

"Oh, that's important, then." If she didn't have to tell him such a tragic bit of information, she would have laughed. "I was a virgin, of course. But no, he didn't hurt me. Not really, I guess. I mean it hurt, a lot, and it made me sick, but I was able to run away. While he was cleaning himself up, I escaped."

"I am so sorry, Nada. If I had only known you were still alive, I wouldn't have rested till I found you." He laid his head on her tummy.

Okay, here goes, "I am a total failure at sex. I've been told that I'm frigid because I can't respond to a man's touch."

She was about to explain further, when he raised his head and glared at her. "I beg to differ, pumpkin. I would say you've enjoyed my touch and kisses these past few days." Even though his voice was gruff, there was a look of total vulnerability in his eyes. "And there is no way in hell that you're frigid, you respond to me like a fuckin' dream."

"It's different with you, I can't deny that. Or at least, it has been so far." She held up her head and kissed him. "You make me forget the bad stuff." No time like the present. "You see, Beau. I'm nervous about being touched because I wasn't raped just once…it was twice. The second time was in the Navy. We served on the same EOD team, and he hated me."

"What the fuck?" Beau sat back on his heels, stunned. "Twice? My God, Harley!" He got up and paced back and forth, this time she didn't fear him leaving. What she feared was…Lord, she didn't know what to feel. Obviously, he was in the same hell she was.

Unable to be still, she went to him. Holding out her hands imploringly, she spoke softly "I know it's a lot to deal with. Can't you see? I'm broken and dirty and totally ignorant of how it should be between a man and a woman."

"Stop! Stop!" He grabbed her hands. They were cold as ice. "You don't know what the hell you're talking about."

Harley continued speaking, as if he had said nothing. "I'm trying to fix it; I've even made an appointment with a therapist."

"Hush, hush," Beau pulled her in his arms. His heart was breaking. "Nada, listen to me." Over and over again he kissed the side of her face and her hair. "You are not broken and you are damn sure not dirty." She trembled in his arms. "Close your eyes, lay your head on my shoulder and feel, baby. Know that it's me holding you. It's Beau-ray. I cherish you. There is nothing in this world I wouldn't do for you. Come on, let's sit down. I need to hold you."

"The gumbo, I need to turn it down and check on the rice."

Beau chuckled, glad to hear her talk about everyday things. Mon Dieu! He had a lot of work to do. Healing work. It horrified him to know what she had been through. Raped twice? It was unthinkable. "I think we can handle that." Picking her up like a bride he started to the kitchen.

"I could walk, you know." With hesitant small touches, she rubbed her fingers over his shirt, caressing the hard planes of his chest. He was still here. He hadn't run away, not yet. Of course, making love with her might be a different story.

"Nope," he moved through the rooms, narrowly avoiding collisions with furniture and making her laugh. "I have a new mission in life. To show you how perfect we are going to be together. It's going to be a pleasure to teach you how responsive you can be to me."

As she stirred the gumbo and turned the burner down, it was from the safety and security of his arms. She marveled at his attitude. It was nothing like she had expected. "I can't reach the rice."

"Hold on," he shifted her position, pretending to nearly drop her and she squealed in delight. "God, your laughter is a beautiful sound. I didn't get to hear it too often in Brownwood. We didn't have a lot to laugh about, did we?"

"No, we didn't."

Being a coon-ass, he knew his rice. "We got twenty minutes before its gumbo time. Let's go." He carried her back to the couch easily, as if she were a child. Sitting down in a corner of the overstuffed sofa, he placed a big soft pillow in his lap and then arranged her on top of it, just in case. This was no time to let her know how much she affected him. "Okay, I want to know more." With a light touch, he pushed a strand of hair from her face. "First and God, please be honest with me. We've kissed and you responded to me, but sometimes you back off and push me away. I thought it was because we were moving too fast. What do you feel when I touch you?"

Harley let out a sigh and looked him right in the eye. "Beau, most of the time when you touch me, I melt. It's, at the same time, the most exciting and the scariest thing in the world. I want your touch. I dream about you making love to me."

112

"Thank God."

She ran a hand up his chest to cup the back of his neck. "Like I told you before, I can work all of this out in my head. It's just that sometimes my body remembers the feeling of being trapped and the pain and that's what it expects. Because it has . . . never known . . . anything different," her voice trailed off into nothing.

For a few long seconds, Beau didn't comment. Could he be hearing her correctly? "You're twenty-nine years old, Nada. Are you telling me that no man has ever given you pleasure?"

Answering him could have been much worse, but his fingers were tracing patterns on her cheek and she could see a warm light of compassion in his eyes. "Yes, it's pitiful, I know. After Pell, I lived as a boy for three years, until the Captain, well one of his men, discovered I was a girl and ratted me out to the Captain. They were good to me though, and Captain Thibodeaux helped me get into the Navy. There, I pretty much kept to myself until I found my niche."

Beau laid his head back on the couch. "Sacre bleu! You are blowing my mind, sugar. I guess I thought you were frozen in amber, unchanged from when I knew you. You are full of surprises! There's no way a little bitty sweet thing like you were in the Navy." As he said that he ran his hand up her arm as if he were checking for muscles.

"I told you I could shoot."

"And that thought alone is enough to get me hard," he tapped her on the end of the nose. "Now help me understand…you ran away from Pell and what happened next? I remember you saying you ran into that family under the bridge and you worked in a restaurant. What happened in between? Did you live on the streets?"

Tightening his arm, he cradled her close, making it easier for her to open up about the hard times. "The first few nights were difficult. As you know, there's a lot of gang activity and the pimps have look-outs all over, ready to scoop up girls that are on the streets and put them into the business. But since I had hacked all my hair off, I managed to evade them. One thing I knew for sure, I wanted to avoid the system. Getting picked up and sent into another shelter or halfway house was my biggest fear. I know they aren't all like Brownwood, but I couldn't risk it." It was almost hypnotic, she rubbed her thumb on his shirt and he rubbed his lips on her hair

"And nobody picked up on your femininity? That's so hard for me to comprehend, because that night you slept in my arms and we kissed, you were a little doll. Oh baby, you had to know I wanted you. I got so hard that night and you were just a slip of a girl. I felt like the world's biggest pervert because I got aroused."

"Really? I didn't realize it; you were a perfect gentleman to me." She smiled and laid her face against his chest. "I was so thrilled to be in your bed. When you kissed me that night, it was the single best moment of my life . . . until I kissed you again."

Shit! Already he was erect and needing to be buried inside of her. Having her lying on him like this was ultimate torture, but he loved it. To think she was, for all intents and purposes innocent, just blew his mind. "Honey, I can give you a lifetime of moments like that."

She began playing with his belt buckle. If it had been any other girl, he would think she was up for a blow-job, but this was his Nada, his innocent Nada.

"You don't have to say that, I know guys aren't usually interested in a girl like me."

Picking her up with one strong arm, he pulled the pillow out that she had been sitting on. He scooted her down his thighs, closer to his knees. She didn't know what was going on. "Give me your hand." He held his out. She placed hers in it. "Now, I'm not being aggressive, I wouldn't scare you for anything but, I just want to show you how turned off I am about being close to you." Gently, he placed her palm over the bulge in his pants.

"Oh, my goodness. Thank you, I think." He was aroused, hugely aroused. Harley let her hand rest there, just for a second more, then moved it. He pulled her up and over his erection and the feeling of it under her hips was consolation, in a way.

"So polite. You're very welcome." Taking her chin in his hand, he tenderly kissed her lips. "Now, who was this second man who hurt you? Can you tell me about him?"

"Yea, I will tell you. Fox and I were singled out. We were both good at our jobs. Sometimes, I would best him at something, he didn't like that. When I got selected for Special Forces. . ."

"I need a drink."

Harley wiggled to get up. "Did you want coffee, tea or . . ." Whoosh!

She didn't get very far, he held her fast. "If the next word out of your mouth is 'Me' that'll be my choice."

"Uh – me, maybe?"

"Good. Now, explain. Special Forces? You mean like the Navy Seals?"

"No," she laughed. "They don't let women in the Seals."

"Well, thank God for small favors. What were you? Intelligence?"

"No, bomb squad. I diffuse bombs for a living."

There was an explosion, but it wasn't a bomb, it was one pissed off Coon-ass.

Honestly, Harley wouldn't have tolerated that kind of tirade from anyone else. He didn't dump her on the floor. No, he picked her up and set her gently aside. Rising to his feet, he proceed to stomp back and forth across the living room speaking Cajun French so fast and furious that she only caught every third or fourth word and those weren't nice words, either.

"C'est des conneries!" Harley calmly followed his movements as he waved his hands around and looked to the Lord in heaven for consolation. "Chiant ca me fait chier!" After a few moments, he went to the wall and leaned on it, breathing hard. "Merde!" Finally, he turned to look at her.

"Did you just have a Cajun fit?" she asked him calmly. There was one miraculous fact that emerged from his heated display. He didn't turn any of that anger toward her, and she wasn't afraid of him, not one little bit.

"Yes, I did." He stood hands on hips and looked stoic and damned magnificent. Wide shoulders, bulging biceps...he was all man. And when he picked up his T-shirt to wipe the perspiration from his face, she almost fainted. Abs! Lots of abs were just waiting for her fingers and lips. Right then, Harley promised herself that someday she would trace every one of those ridges with her tongue. "Can you throw a Hispanic one like that?" he asked with a hint of a smile.

"I don't know, I could try," she offered grinning at him. For the first time, she had the distinct feeling things might be okay.

"Let's go get something to eat, I'm starving. I need sustenance before I spank your cute ass for putting your sweet life in jeopardy." Harley had been walking toward the kitchen and that remark brought her up short. She turned around, in place, to look at him. "Yea, you heard me, Nada."

"You could try," she teased him. "In the last two years, I've become quite proficient in Krav Maga."

"Oh you have? You know Israeli martial arts, quite impressive." He lifted an eyebrow and looked her up and down, real slow. "I go one on one with big gators, baby. I would be game to take you on, anytime. Just the thought - damn - that turns me on. I'd love to wrestle with you."

"Let's eat first, we'll wrestle, later." She grabbed him by the hand and led him to the table where she served him the steaming Louisiana stew, rice, French bread and homemade cookies. "I had company today," then she told him about Laura Prescott and her son, Morris and the possible ghost of the little girl who wanted her cookies.

"Why don't you invite Savannah over," he suggested. "Even if you aren't interested in her ectoplasmic expertise, she's a very nice woman. I imagine she would love to get to know you, she's had a hard time."

Pouring them both a glass of iced tea, she listened with interest. A hard time? She knew about those types of circumstances. "What do you mean?"

Beau laid down his spoon and met her gaze, "Savannah was engaged to be married to a good man. He served in Afghanistan, but he didn't come home. She took it hard...she's still taking it hard," that was all he said about that.

Harley had nothing to add either, except a vow. "I will invite her over," she had known too many good men who didn't make it home. "It will be a pleasure." They ate in silence for a few moments.

"You're a damn good cook, baby."

"Thank you, I enjoy cooking. For me, it's one of life's pleasures."

"See, I knew we were a perfect match. You love to cook and I sure love to eat. Let's see. You can cook, shoot, hold down a job," he waved his spoon around, "you're turning this house into the showplace it used to be. Am I missing something?" he grinned at her.

"No, I don't think so." He was embarrassing her.

Leaning back in his chair, he penned her with a stare.

"Let me see if I've got a handle on this. Here you are, my precious Nada." Beau placed his hand over hers, dwarfing it. "You are alive and you're my dream woman. Honey, I can't say it any plainer than that. When you told me about being raped - not once, but twice, I've got to be honest, it broke my heart. I want to kill the bastards that did this to you. My new mission in life is to show you that a man can love a woman. Tenderly, passionately, and not hurt them. I can heal you, baby. I want to give you pleasure more than I want to live to see the sun rise tomorrow."

"Are you sure?" This was so important. Beau meant more to her than all the rest of the world combined. If he rejected her, she didn't know if she could go on.

"You're damn right, I'm sure. Harley, you've knocked me for a loop. My cock has been strutted with lust from the moment I saw you in my shop. You're my miracle; the one missing piece of my heart that I thought was lost to me forever. But I have to be honest. I'm damn glad you're out of the Navy."

Harley felt dismay wash over her. "I still do work for the government, Beau. I'm a contractor, an Explosive Ordinance Specialist. Socorro is called out when a device is found that the bomb squads can't handle or don't want to handle."

She waited for the explosion, like before. But, it didn't happen. Instead he swallowed, stood up, kissed her on the forehead. "I need a few minutes. I'm gonna take a walk." And left.

Harley sat perfectly still. Well, damn.

Beau headed out from the main house down to the Bayou. The slow moving waters and the sounds of the bayou soothed his soul. Shit! He had just walked off and left her sitting there. What did that say about him? But he had to think.

Reasoning it out, he remembered their first meeting.

The Hummer, the MaDeuce, the sniper rifle. It all was beginning to make sense. She had used a name, what was it? Socorro. He racked his brain and knew he had heard the name before. Yes, he had and it was all in connection with a rash of bomb threats all over the U.S. Cold chills ran over his body. To think that angel put her life on the line for others over and over again, nearly killed him. Hell, he didn't know if he could handle it or not. Every protective instinct in his soul reared up and protested. But, he was damn sure gonna try. She needed him and he needed her, it was as simple as that. Was he going to pressure her to quit and remove herself from danger? Hell Yeah!

For a few minutes more, he stood on Bayou Chene and watched an alligator glide by. Just a few days ago, his life was full of guns and gators, fairly simple - for him. Now, he was on the verge of having it all, if he handled it just right. Taking a deep breath, he made a decision. Nada was worth it, no matter what he had to do. Nada was worth it all.

The first order of business would be loving on her as much and as often as she'd let him.

Harley watched him out the window. At first, she had assumed he had left. She wouldn't have blamed him. Her reality was not ideal by any stretch of the imagination. Not only was she damaged goods, she played with fire – literally. But when she glanced out the window, there he was, standing so still down by the water. He was a formidable figure of a man, a born warrior. Yet at the same time, he was gentle and caring. He was her Beau.

When he turned and started back, she hoped he wouldn't leave. If he wanted her, she was going to try and be what he needed. She held her breath as he approached. Would he turn to the driveway or come in the house? Her question was answered as he headed her way. She met him at the door. "I'm sorry, Beau." This time she didn't wait for him to pull her close, she threw herself at him and he caught her. Deftly.

"You have no reason to apologize. For sixteen years, you've been living your life without me or any other man telling you what to do. And you've done a damn fine job of it. I remember Socorro now. Honey you are the big leagues. You are considered to be THE expert in safe bomb disposal. When you're talking weapons, you're talking my language. I know something about this stuff and I respect you to no end. Still, that doesn't mean my heart won't be in my throat every time you get called out. Have you ever considered changing careers?" Walking deeper into the kitchen with her, he sat her up on the counter, and settled himself between her legs.

"No, not really. I'm good at what I do, and I'm needed. Most of the time I have an advantage. That psychic ability I told you about has never failed me yet." When it looked like her answer didn't satisfy him, she tried again. Reaching deep down in the hidden recesses of her dreams, she said, "I've never had a reason to consider quitting before. Being alone worked to my advantage, I had no hostages to fortune. I have no family, no one who would mourn if I," she paused and looked away and whispered, "If I didn't come home." Lifting her face to him, she acknowledged how they felt. "Until now. Until you."

"Would you think about getting out of it, for me?" He asked gently.

"I'll consider the options." She wouldn't say 'yes', not yet. The last two incidents were troubling. Fox Crocker was dead, but something or someone was playing with her. Maybe. And until she figured that out, she couldn't promise Beau, or anyone else, anything.

"That's all I can ask. Well, no…I do have another question. I think you've already answered it, but I want to be clear, just for the record."

"Okay," she didn't know what he was getting at.

"Are you ready to take the next step and let me love on you?"

He studied her face, his eyes roving over her features. She had his full and complete attention. This was new territory for Harley. A razor-sharp shaft of dread sliced through her. What if she failed? What if she panicked? What if she disgusted him? She knew there was no physical evidence of the rapes remaining on her body, but the others - Jed and Sonny - had told her men didn't like to be with a woman after she had been violated. And they had been very attracted to her before they knew. Before they got too close. But Beau was here, and this was her chance at happiness or at least to know the pleasure that the rest of the world took for granted. "I'm willing to try."

"Good," he kissed her cheek. "Cause, I don't know what I'd have done if you'd said no." Now, when's your appointment with that therapist fella?"

"In a month, but he said he could work me in if I called."

"Call him and get your appointment moved up and tell him you're bringing me with you."

Chapter Six

"You want to go with me to the therapist?" Her voice got a little louder with each word. She didn't dare say sex therapist, that was just too hard to think about. Part of her wanted to run screaming from the room. And part of her wanted to beg him to carry her to bed. The impulses were so different all she could do was sit still. "Okay. You do realize that scares me to death, don't you?"

He gave her a big smile, smooched her right on the lips and put a hand on either side of her hips. "You scared? Impossible. Not of me. All I want to do is love you. Don't you know that?" Yes, she did. Throwing her arms around his neck, she hugged him hard.

Her nipples were so swollen and hard! Oh, she knew it would be like this, only it was better. God, his body was so beautiful. Rubbing her tits on his chest, she let her body drag over his, loving every luxurious sensation. "Am I pleasing you?" she asked feverishly.

"God, yes." He took her by the waist and pulled her farther up. "I need to kiss your breasts."

"Please, I've dreamed of that." She held herself up by the arms and watched as he closed his eyes and took her nipple in his mouth. "Oh, oh, oh, that feels good. I can feel the tugs between my legs." She loved to watch him nurse at her breasts. He cupped her tit and feasted. She squirmed a little and he drug them both backwards until he was sitting leaning against the headboard and she straddling one of his muscular legs. And boy, did it hit the spot.

Letting go of her nipple, he pushed her breasts together and licked her cleavage. "Ride my leg, Nada. While I suck." She was hesitant, but oh, she needed the stimulation. So, as he pulled at her nipple she rocked against the hard muscles of his thigh.

"Oh, Beau…my God, this feels so good." Feverishly she humped his leg, each hard suck of his mouth sending zings of pleasure right to her clitoris. Clasping him by the head, she let herself go. No fear. No shame. No holding back. An orgasm hit her so hard, she screamed. "Beau!"

And woke herself up.

Trembling, she laid there, her lower body jerking with pure pleasure. Throwing her arm across her eyes, she moaned. It had all been a dream. A good dream. If only she could be brave enough to it come true.

* * *

"Hand me that scraper tool," Beau held out his hand.

"Here you go," Indiana tossed it to him and Beau almost missed it.

"Ass." With deft movements, Beau cleaned the carbon from the gas regulator of the M249 Squad Automatic Weapon – every Marine sniper's gun of choice.

"What kind of modifications do you plan to make on that SAW?"

"Well, I have several ideas. It's too heavy, for one thing. Mainly because the SAW is built like a box. This receiver assembly has more nooks and crannies for brass, carbon, and dirt to build up in than necessary. My thinking is that is needs be a little smoother and sleeker. If we smooth out these corners, it'll be lighter and easier to clean."

"What about the blank firing adapter?" Indiana leaned closer. "It never seems to fit right."

"I agree," Beau studied the end of the weapon. "Why don't we create a longer screw assembly, one that can be modified easily to fit the M16."

"That oughta work. You know what? We got a report of a nesting female gator on the Cypress Bend golf course up around Many."

"Really?" Beau started to ask Indiana to take care of it, but thought it might be a fun place to take Harley after the tension of seeing the therapist. She had gotten her appointment moved up and he figured she would enjoy a trip after it was all over. "They've got a pretty nice clubhouse and hotel up there, don't they?"

Indiana grinned, "Yea, they do. It's scenic, romantic and secluded. Are you planning on taking your woman up there?"

"Maybe," Beau wasn't ready to talk about his relationship, yet. Not until he was sure he had one. "Do we still have our membership at that shooting range up at Natchitoches?"

"Yea, we do. Gonna show off your skills to the little lady?"

Indy thought he was in the know, but Beau had news for him. News, he was surprisingly proud to share. "Actually, Harley has some skills of her own. I bet you'd never guess she's former Navy Special Ops. My little girl is one of the premier bomb squad techs in the nation."

"Dehellusaye!?!" Indiana was suitably impressed. "Shit! How does that mesh with your macho, old-fashioned, protective instincts?"

Beau grimaced and looked sheepish. "I'm working on it. Look, I'm meeting Harley in half an hour and if she agrees, I'll head up to Cypress Bend and take care of that mama gator and then we'll make a weekend out of it. You can reach me on my cell, but we'll probably stay there or up on Caddo Lake."

"Sure thing, boss. Don't do anything I wouldn't do." They had always shared good-natured ribbing about their love lives, but this time Beau didn't bite. What he had with Harley was too fragile and too precious to kid about.

* * *

"I'm nervous," Harley admitted as she walked through the door Beau held for her. "I looked up this type of therapy on the internet and found out more than I wanted to know."

"Good morning," a grandmotherly receptionist clasped her hands together and greeted them like they were arriving at a family reunion. "We've been waiting on you. After you called this morning, I told Dane 'I think I'll make some sugar cookies.' They're his favorite. And I've made a pot of pumpkin spiced coffee." She patted Beau on the shoulder. "My name is Joyce, and I'm so glad you came with Ms. Montoya. Did you say your name was LeBlanc? I have some LeBlanc's on my mother's side. I wonder if we're related." She was talking so fast that Beau and Harley didn't even try and interject a word. They just let her lead them back to the Dr's office and the connecting waiting room. "You sit here Mr. LeBlanc and Dane will come out and get you when it's time for you to join them."

"Thank you," was all Harley managed to get out before Dr. Dane Wagner joined them. She managed not to react, but he was one of the best looking men she had ever come across. Not as good-looking as Beau, of course. But having them both in the same room was intimidating.

"Harley, Beau, it's good to meet you." He shook hands with both of them. "Harley, if you'll come with me, we'll call for Beau in a few minutes."

Beau sat down, reluctantly. He didn't like Harley going off with that pretty-boy. He didn't like it at all. But he wanted her to get better, so he'd put up with it. "I'll be waiting." As they walked off, Beau tried to give the man that 'she's mine' glare and the doctor picked up on it because he gave him a knowing, somewhat cocky, grin.

Taking her seat, Harley folded her hands in her lap and bit the inside of her lip, nervously.

Dr. Dane leaned back in his chair and tried to reassure her. "There's nothing to be apprehensive about. We're just going to talk. Dr. Young only told me the vaguest details, why don't you explain to me about the rapes and how they've affected you." She started to speak, but he lifted up his hand. "I only have one question that I need you to answer, before we start. And that's very simple. Do you want to get better? Do you want to be able to have a normal sexual relationship with a man?"

"Yes, if that's . . . possible. I mean, if he wants to have one with me," Harley found herself stammering and stuttering. Clearing her throat, she tried to explain. "I don't want to disappoint Beau. I'm afraid of making him feel rejected, if I get uncomfortable." There was more to it than that, but she wasn't ready to share the rejections she had experienced, not even with the doctor. Closing her eyes, she shut out the image of Dane Wager. He was a compelling man. Surely, he understood what she meant.

"I understand that Beau is interested in a relationship with you." When she nodded, he leaned forward, speaking to her intently. "Any man worth his salt; is going to understand how you feel. Putting you first and helping you get past your fear will be his main concern. I'll talk to him and explain all of this. You don't worry about him being disappointed or feeling rejected. That's just a crock of shit; if you'll excuse my French."

His comment made Harley laugh. His French wasn't nearly as explicit and earthy as Beau's had been. Sobering, she went on to explain why she felt as she did. "Beau and I have a history. He was my hero long ago when we were together in a runaway shelter in New Orleans. Due to a misunderstanding we were separated, but I never forgot him and our reunion has been totally unexpected and the fulfillment of a dream. If I were to ever love and trust anyone, it would be this man. And the thought of hurting him or making him think that I place him in the same category as my rapist horrifies me. But the flashbacks happen, I can't help it. We've only kissed so far, he hasn't pushed me, but I have felt the stirrings of panic. It's unreasonable, I know."

"No, Harley. It's not unreasonable. What you are experiencing is totally normal. Flashbacks and anxiety attacks are to be expected."

"So, what do you suggest?"

"After you answer some questions for me and I explain some things to you, I'm going to call your friend in and discuss a proposed treatment with him. Does that meet with your approval?"

Harley wanted to curl up and hide. Just the thought of these two men discussing her problem filled her stomach with butterflies. The only thing that kept her from fleeing the scene was her intense desire to get past this. It was true. She wanted to get better. Harley wanted to have sex with Beau. She wanted to be like any other woman. "Yes, I agree with your plan."

"All right, then. Let's begin. Tell me about your early life and what led up to the first rape."

* * *

An hour and half later, Beau saw the door open and Harley came out. Her eyes immediately sought his and he could tell she had been crying. Damn! He went to her; "Are you all right?" he looked at the pretty doctor who motioned for him to enter his office. Beau held up a hand, "I'll be right there."

"Are you sure you want to do this?" she asked him. "You don't have to."

"Yes, I do. It's as important to me as it is to you." He took her by the shoulders and kissed her on the forehead. "I printed out some information from the Internet this morning. It's over there where I was sitting. While I talk to the Doc, you go check it out. And if you like what you see, we'll go pack you an overnight bag and head north."

Harley's heart quickened, "A trip? Together?" He was so considerate. She knew he was doing this to get her mind off of things, and make time for them to be together. "Thank you. I can't wait to see what you've planned."

"You sit tight. I'll be right back." Tucking her hair behind one ear, he looked deep into her eyes. "And don't worry. I'm going to take good care of you."

* * *

"Sit down, Mr. LeBlanc. I'm glad you came."

"I want to help Harley."

"I know you do, and I'm going to do everything I can to make that happen. Harley tells me that you knew one another as children in a home in New Orleans."

"Yeah, she was raped there because she helped me escape."

The doctor wrote something down, Beau strained to see what it was. "So, I have to ask, Mr. LeBlanc. Could your interest in Harley now stem from gratitude and guilt?"

Beau snorted. "Are you kidding me? Are you blind? Did you get a good look at that woman?"

Dane Wagner grinned, "Good answer."

"I have a connection with Harley, don't get me wrong. This isn't just sexual attraction; I have tender feelings for her. Having said that, I also intend to have her in my bed. Permanently."

"Understood."

"So, tell me what to do to help her."

"I'm about to. But first, I want you to remember that I'm looking out for Harley's well-being – just like I'm supposed to. She is a very special, beautiful woman." The doctor met his stare look for look, and if Beau wasn't mistaken, the good doctor would like the chance to step into Beau's shoes with Harley, if he made even one misstep.

"I appreciate your help. She doesn't realize it yet, but Harley belongs to me. I want to take responsibility for her. Her happiness is my happiness, and if her insurance doesn't cover this, I'll gladly pay." Joining the doctor at the coffee pot, Beau poured himself a cup of what he generally termed sissy coffee. "Plus, I want you to know that if there's any sexual interaction to be done like touching or anything like that, I will be the one to do it. I'll follow your guidelines, I'll take your suggestion, but I don't want you to even think about her naked." Beau stood toe-to-toe with the other man and staked his claim. "I don't know how you operate here, but I've done a little investigating about sex therapists on the Internet. I respect what you do, but I will be filling the role of her sex partner, exclusively."

To Beau's surprise, the other man didn't argue. Rather, he smiled and clasped him on the shoulder. "She and I have discussed that very thing and we were just waiting on your agreement. Shall we get started with the details?"

"The sooner the better." They both sat back down and Beau started to take notes, but the Dr. handed him a small pamphlet. He gave him some verbal instructions as well.

"One of the main side effects of sexual assault is flashbacks. These vivid memories often occur during sexual contact. The flashbacks can be feelings, images, or thoughts and for a brief period the victim relives her trauma. This can be confusing, making the woman feel guilty for having any sexual desire at all. If they happen during sex, you may have to stop or just hold her till the discomfort and panic subsides. Over time, the occurrence of flashbacks can lessen. I think because Harley has been a rape victim twice, her symptoms are more complicated. You may find that just letting the flashback happen and talking her through them will make it lose its importance. The only thing I can tell you at this point is that Harley understands what is happening to her. She wants to get better and she wants you to be a part of that. In all actuality, she is a very brave and strong woman."

"I agree." One other topic he had researched online had been Harley's company. What he had found had made him proud and scared the shit out of him, simultaneously. "She faces danger and death regularly, better than most men. It baffles me how she can compartmentalize this tragic area of life and still function so well in all the rest." They sat in silence for a moment. Beau leaned forward, his arms resting on his knees. "If she agrees, I'm taking her away this weekend to someplace romantic. What I want to know is how to start. I want to make her comfortable, yet make it clear that I want her more than anything. Doc, I want her to feel cherished, aroused and safe."

"My suggestion is to take it slow. Make sure she realizes that she can tell you anything. Once you understand how she feels about something, do your best to show her that you support her decisions. She may interrupt you at some point during the lovemaking, and if she asks you to stop. Do it. Stop any contact immediately until her fear and discomfort subsides. If it were me, I'd start with sensual touching. A lot of touching. And not just you touching her. Allow her to learn your body and associate it with protection and strength. When you're touching her, don't concentrate just on the breasts and genitalia, touch all of her. Show her that there isn't a part of her that you don't find beautiful and desirable." As the doctor spoke, Beau's mind was spinning. Making plans and dreaming up ways he could please Harley. "You might take a bath together and take turns washing each other. Cuddling under the covers would be good and massages would work well. Add the little extras that make a woman feel special like her favorite music or candles. Baby her, Mr. LeBlanc. Pet her, pamper her and show her that there is no place in the world you'd rather be than at her side."

"I think I can handle that," Beau said dryly. "Anything else? I'm a mite anxious to get this show on the road."

"Just take it slow. Show her how good you can make her feel and how much you love to be touched by her. Put her needs before your own. I've told Harley that I want to see her again very soon. Have her call me the day after you get back. Call me, day or night if you have any questions or concerns." Dane handed Beau his card and they stood up and shook hands. "Good luck; and you're a damn lucky man, LeBlanc."

"I realize that and I'm counting my blessings every day."

* * *

As they drove north on I-49 through Alexandria, Harley was both excited and skittish. She had packed carefully, knowing that Beau intended for them to be intimate to some degree. As she gathered her lingerie and sleepwear, she had wished for a trip to Victoria's Secret, but there wasn't time. Just the thought of what they were going to do had her trembling, both from anticipation and trepidation. It was what she wanted though; she needed to find out if her life could be more than solitude and work. "So, we're going to Cypress Bend first?"

Beau adjusted the radio; he was more interested in what she had to say than he was in the top forty countdown. "I thought we'd stay at the resort tonight. It won't take me long to relocate that gator. The local wildlife officers are going to transport her to another spot on Toledo Bend, so all I have to do is catch her and restrain her, and honey, I can do that in my sleep. You'll love Cypress Bend. Do you like to play golf?"

"Yes," she said, and she did enjoy playing. But that wasn't the game she was interested in at the moment. "I understand they have a beautiful course."

"They do, it has a real tropical feel...lots of water. But honey, I have something much more enjoyable to share with you than golf." Beau let his eyes rove slowly down her body. In a very non-threatening fashion, he wanted to start turning up the heat. "Is that gonna be okay with you?"

"Yes," her answer was almost a whisper. Harley was happy that he agreed with her. Seduction wasn't her strong suit.

"But don't worry; we're going to do other things, too," he assured her, hearing the slight edge of nerves in her voice. "That's why I brought some guns. I wanna have a friendly little competition with you. Really, I can't wait to see you in action. The idea of you shooting a rifle makes me hard." As soon as he said it, he regretted the reference, but it didn't seem to faze her and she took her hand in his and squeezed it.

"That will be fun. And I've always wanted to explore Natchitoches. Steel Magnolia's was always one of my favorite films. It was shot there, right?"

"Yea, and there are several interesting plantations nearby, but you live in one of those, so that might not thrill you too much."

Wanting tonight to be special, she spoke what was on her heart. "You thrill me, Beau. Just the idea that we might find pleasure together is beyond my wildest dreams."

"Damn, you have to say that on the Interstate; and me with no place to pull off and ravish you." He winked at her. "I promise you this, Nada. Tonight will be a night you'll never forget or I'm not the Ragin Cajun of the Atchafalaya Basin."

"Good Lord," she laughed at his rhyme.

When they arrived at Cypress Bend, Harley was

reminded of how big Toledo Bend Reservoir actually was. It was huge. On the way up, she had read a pamphlet declaring that the lake was sixty-five miles in length, with 1200 miles of shore-line. What she loved about it was the surrounding pine forests. It was peaceful; there was a natural harmony with the woods and the water. Best of all there was a mystery to it. An almost primitive feel in the bayous and coves that formed the shoreline. She had never had the time to become a birdwatcher, but she was still fascinated by the number of species that called the lake home: pelicans, cranes, bald eagles, egrets and several species of ducks.

For privacy's sake, Beau opted for one of the golf suites. This wasn't their honeymoon, but if his baby wanted to be vocal in her pleasure, he didn't want anyone overhearing her. Just thinking about caressing her to orgasm, if she was ready, had him as hard as a steel beam. "Let's get you settled and then I'm gonna make short work of that alligator wrangling job."

"Can I help you?"

"Sure, you're my best partner." But, he fully intended to keep her safe.

Making their way to the pro shop to meet the golf course superintendent, Harley couldn't resist asking, "I see people are still playing golf. Don't they know there is an alligator lurking about or are they not told?"

"That's a good question, lady bug," he chuckled. "Courses that are on the water like this, in the reptile's natural habitat, are expected to have some incidents of alligator sightings. Usually the golfers and the gators can coexist in peace, but this one is a nesting mama and she's become more aggressive and territorial. What they're doing to ensure the safety is – and I'm not lying – someone is babysitting that female. I understand that they've got grounds keepers sitting in a portable tree-stand making sure she doesn't charge some unsuspecting golfer or their family. Instead of hollering 'fore', they're yelling 'gator'. Of course, this is Louisiana; people expect and even enjoy the possibility of catching a glimpse of one of our swamp creatures. We just don't want anything to happen here like what happened down in South Carolina. One golfer lost his hand reaching into the water after a ball. The poor old guy was seventy years old and it grabbed him and pulled him in and tore his arm off in the struggle."

"You be careful, Beau," she chided him. "I don't want you losing any valuable body parts."

"Don't worry, cher. I won't be dangling my dick in the water."

"Stop teasing me," she fussed as he held the door open to the pro shop. They met with the superintendent and he notified Parks and Wildlife officials that Beau had arrived. While they waited, Beau got them both a cold drink and they passed the time watching the golfers tee-off at the first hole. When everyone was ready, they told Beau where to pull his truck to get as close to the area as possible. He and Harley made their way around the scenic course and she enjoyed seeing the water lilies and other blooming plants. "There they are," she pointed. "Look, that guy just jumped three feet in the air."

Beau parked and yelled at the guy. "Stay back, before you lose a leg!" He took out his gear and handed Harley one of the hooks. "When I get down there, let me get up close and personal and you don't step up until I tell you. Okay, doll?"

"Okay." She thought how different it would be if they were approaching a bomb. She would be the one with the skills, doing her best to protect him. Approaching the female alligator, Harley was amazed to see that this one was considerably larger than the one in the housing addition in Beaumont had been. "What will we do about her eggs?"

"Don't worry, the Parks guys will gather them up and move them together and even help her set up another nest. They'll take care of her."

Beau worked fast and even though there were others there to help, he let her tape the mouth shut. When she finished, she held her hands up in triumph – "two wraps and a hooey!" She smiled; mimicking the move she had seen rodeo calf ropers do when they had tied off the calves legs in record time.

Beau ate her up with his eyes. Even though onlookers surrounded them, he couldn't resist. "You're precious, did you know that? I'm so damn glad you walked back into my life."

* * *

"If it's okay with you, we'll eat on the balcony," Beau offered. Shit, he was nervous. Now, wasn't that a fine how-do-you-do. "I ordered grilled shrimp, rice pilaf and cheesecake. Sound good?"

"Oh yes," she sighed. "And look at the sunset over the water." She put her arms around his neck, "Thank you so much for bringing me. You've made me so happy."

Beau got a little choked up, he cleared his throat. "Oh doll, I intend to make you a lot happier than this." He knew this was important; this night was huge. It all depended on him being gentle enough and supportive enough to lead her through the maze of anxieties her fears had constructed as a barrier to accepting physical love.

He held her chair out for her. "Thanks," she put her napkin in her lap and they began to eat.

"Tell me about Socorro," he prompted. If they were going to be together, he needed to understand. It was his hope that she would change her focus with the company, maybe become an adviser or a consultant. Let someone else

135

take the risks, but he couldn't push. Not yet. He knew how he would feel if someone tried to tell him to stop doing what he did best. Not every woman would approve of his dealings with weapons or the risks he took with the reptiles he wrangled.

Harley took another bite and chewed slowly, considering where to start. "When I decided to test for Special Forces, I was considering trying out to be a diver or a member of the Special Warfare Combatant Craft Crewman. They work as support staff for the SEAL missions, including intelligence. But when I began the aptitude testing, my superior officers said that I was more suited to the EOD unit. I had a knack for it. It wasn't something I shared, but my psychic ability gave me an edge. I just knew how to safely diffuse the bombs; it was like I could connect with the mind of the maker of the bomb. Not only could I determine the fastest and safest way to detonate or disarm them, sometimes I could pick up insights concerning motivation. That doesn't happen often, but so far my gift hasn't failed me and I have had some really, really close calls."

Beau didn't like to think about really, really close calls. "Why did you decide to leave the Navy and strike out on your own?"

"Fox Crocker," she stated simply. "He made my life a living hell. I tried to handle it on my own, but it just kept getting worse. There were times he would set booby traps for me and undercut my projects. Anything he could do to make me look bad, he tried. The competition was fierce between us, and because I was female, it was a blow to his masculinity when I would score higher or complete a task faster. When it came down to who would be squadron leader, I won. That pushed him over the edge and he began to physically threaten me. At first he came on to me, but I wasn't attracted to Crocker, nor did I want to be attracted to him."

"What would he do to you?" Beau couldn't help but want to know. He felt his chest tighten with anger at the idea of the bastard bullying her around.

"Ships have a lot of small spaces and nooks. He would corner me in those places and hold me down. Sometimes he would kiss me, but he wasn't really interested in sex with me. I fought him off, and I even went so far as pressing charges on him. But my immediate superior officer didn't approve of sexual harassment accusations. He told me to toughen up and act like a Special Ops officer. So, I tried. But Fox got worse; he was trying to ruin my career. If it hadn't been for Admiral Gaines, he would have succeeded. The Admiral reprimanded him and pulled him off the team. Fox got his revenge, though. He caught me alone in the head and attacked me in the shower stall. This time I fought back, and I did some damage, but he was stronger. Another person walked in on us, and he was apprehended and taken into custody. When they were about to take him off ship by helicopter, he broke away and jumped overboard. His body wasn't recovered."

Beau had listened carefully, wishing he hadn't brought the topic up. Now, she was sad and tense and he was furious. These were not emotions conducive to good sex. "Good enough for him, I say."

"Fox was good at what he did. Really, in some ways, he was better than me. Here lately, it seems like I'm seeing his handiwork. We had to study all types of explosives and understand them completely – so in order to diffuse a bomb, you have to know how it's built. I have seen Fox's work. He took short cuts, I know the knots he used, and I swear to God – the last two bombs I disarmed could have been built by him and they were left in places that meant something to me." By this time, it was as if she was talking to herself. But Beau was right there hearing every word.

137

"Do you think the asshole is still alive and trying to get to you?"

"Believe me, the thought crossed my mind. But, I saw him jump overboard! And we were out at sea! His chances of survival were slim to none."

"Have you mentioned this to anyone?"

"No," she tore her roll in half, skipping the tempting butter. "I don't want to sound paranoid. The FBI has questioned me twice about possible suspects and I did say that the work was similar to Crocker's and they might need to check for possible associates of his."

"Who calls you? I mean, when the government needs your help, who contacts you?"

"Usually, Homeland Security, but Socorro responds to any request made by a state or city. Last year, I averaged two incidents a month. Most of these were overseas, dealing with American interests. Waco has been asking to take on more responsibility and I've promised him that he could." She enjoyed the pleased, hopeful look that came over Beau's face.

"One more question and then we move on to more pleasurable topic," he gave her a hot wicked grin. "With all of the expertise in the world, it amazes me that they utilize a company like yours so often. Don't they have robots designed to lessen the need for human contact to render one of these bombs harmless?"

Folding her napkin and placing it beside her place, Harley avoided his eyes. "Yes, there are some fantastic bomb disposal robots in service. Unfortunately, some bombs are deliberately placed where a robot cannot go. I'm small and my success rate is one hundred percent, or I wouldn't be sitting here. So when the job is difficult or unusually dangerous, Socorro is called."

He wished he hadn't asked. Ignorance is bliss. "Hell, baby. I may never sleep again."

Wanting to see him smile, she squeezed his knee. "I'm not interested in sleeping. Not just yet."

Beau made a sound deep in his chest that sounded just like a growl. "I can't wait to touch you. I am going to make you so damn happy." Or he was going to die trying. Earlier, he had made arrangements for the concierge to add some special touches to the room while they dined al fresco. Housekeeping was also going to access the balcony from the outside stairs to clear away their dishes. "Come on inside, I have some surprises for you." He stood and helped her with her chair, brushing her hair back off her shoulder. "You have the most beautiful soft skin. Soon, I'm going to kiss every inch of you that you'll permit." Wrapping his arms around her shoulders, he pulled her back against his chest.

Shivers ran over her body. Good shivers. Harley could feel his breath move on her neck and when his lips grazed her skin; she leaned back into him, encouraging more contact.

Instantly, his cock started to rise. Angling his hips back, he avoided contact, not wanting to spook her. "God, what you do to me!" He kissed her again and led her to the double French doors. "Yeah, I think we've had company."

"Oh, my," she looked around in amazement. "This is beautiful. I can't believe you went to so much trouble!" Candles were everywhere and their light danced all over the room. The king size bed was turned down invitingly and looked lush with pillows. As she stepped closer, she saw the sheets were sprinkled with deep red rose petals and a bottle of champagne was chilling on the nightstand. Low strains of Spanish music were playing. He had totally set the stage.

"It wasn't any trouble, not for you."

"Oh, look. They even lit the fireplace," she exclaimed. "I love to watch a fire."

Beau shrugged off his black jacket. "It's not exactly fireplace weather, but the thermostat has been turned down. I think it will feel nice, especially if we lose a few of our clothes." She watched him, mesmerized, as he removed his boots and socks. "Don't look so apprehensive, baby. Nothing is going to happen that you aren't literally begging me for. The shirt and pants will stay on until you pull them off of me. How's that?"

"Uh, yea, that will be fine." Concentrating enough to speak while contemplating the possibility of seeing him naked; was difficult. Damn, he was fine. She slipped off her own shoes and pulled her dress over her head, leaving her in a sheer top and slip.

"Leave the rest, precious. I want you to be completely at ease with me."

"Okay," she stepped forward toward the thick rug. Beau knelt down and offered his hand. He looked like a handsome prince from a long ago fairy tale. "I'm not innocent of sexual knowledge, Beau. My life has been lived in the company of men. So, it won't shock me if you become sexually aroused." If he didn't, she'd know it was her fault.

"Baby, I've been aroused since the moment I saw you in my shop, that heart-shaped little rear caught my eye. Your hair was dancing on the top of your hips, and when you turned around, the only thing sweeter than your luscious breasts was your gorgeous face." Not even the dim light could disguise the flush that rose from her upper chest and swept up as high as her cheeks. The camisole and slip she wore did nothing to hide the lushness of her beautiful body. "You look like an angel." He helped her sit down on the rug. "Let's face one another, Indian-style. I want to hold hands with my best girl."

"Hold hands?" The warmth from the fire felt good, even against her heated skin. "Okay, I guess."

"Don't despair, lady-fair, I'm working up to something. Us Southern boys, we move slow; like a panther in the swamp. But when we get near our luscious little swamp hen, we pounce!" As he grabbed at her, every muscle in her body sprang into action. But instead of fleeing, she launched herself right into his arms. "Damn!" How stupid could he get? But her reaction, Lord God, her reaction . . . "That's right, baby. Just right. You run to me, never away from me. I'll be your sanctuary. In my arms is where you belong." Cupping the back of her head, he wondered how far he had set them back. Him and his stupid games! Lord, she was crying! He could feel her whole body quaking, and then she giggled. She was laughing! Thank God.

"You are so bad," she nipped him on his chest and his heart flipped over. If things were different, he would push her back, rip her panties off and bury himself balls deep. But he couldn't, he had promised. He had to go slow. At least she was comfortable enough to tease him; that was a start.

"I pride myself in my badness, baby," he murmured. "But tonight, all you will see is my good side." Setting her back a bit, he reached for her hand. "Do you remember when we would walk in the French Quarter? You were still in that stage where friends held hands. As we moved through the crowd, I'd feel your little hand grasping for mine. You never said anything; you just took what you wanted." Cradling her small hand in his, he began to rub the center of her palm with the pad of his thumb. "I want you to be like that again with me. Take what you want. That's my fondest dream, to have you so sure of me that you'll take charge and show me how to please you." Leaning over he nuzzled her cheek, "'Cause that's what will please me. Pleasing you."

Ripples of awareness coursed through Harley's body.

She wasn't afraid, she was on alert, not knowing what to expect. It wasn't fight or flight syndrome, it was the same sensation one would get if they were standing near a live wire. There was a sense of caged power close at hand. Beau…he was caged power. And he was holding all of that back, just for her. "I want to learn to please you," she confessed.

"Just being near you pleases me," he looked at their linked hands. Her skin tone was golden and his was sun-darkened, making them very near the same color. They belonged together. He had no doubt of that at all. Now, it was up to him to prove it to her. "Me touching you is a language without words. I want you to place your whole body in my care, just as your hand rests in mine. Feel how our heart rates are pacing themselves together." He put his thumb against her pulse point, and she did the same and they let an awareness flow over them. Two hearts, indeed, could beat as one. "I want you to let me push the worry and fear right out of your mind. My touch is a gift to you, a gift I long for you to accept."

"You're making my body sing," she let the truth flow from her lips. "I'm not afraid of you, Beau. I'm only afraid of failing you."

Raising her hand to his lips, he let his teeth scrape the center of her palm, then he soothed it with his kiss. "There is no possibility of your failing me. Tonight, there are no expectations. We are just enjoying one another, that's all. And baby, I enjoy being with you; every moment, in every way." Taking her hand in both of his, he began massaging it; the space between the thumb and her first finger became a playground. "You are so soft. I dream of your hands on my body. Mon Dieu! You should have seen me in the shower, yesterday. I pleasured myself imagining how your hands would stroke me, cher." As he talked, he soothed. With one hand, he intertwined their fingers, rubbing her palm with his thumb. And with the other, he took one finger and rubbed a path of heat from just under her chin down the slope of her neck. He let it slide almost to the swell of her breast. Almost.

"You are being so sweet to me."

Her breathing was getting shallower and faster. She was excited. Good. "Easiest thing I've ever done. Let's see how sweet you taste," lifting her hand to his lips, he began to kiss it softly; taking little licks in the sensitive area between her fingers.

"I like that," she whispered. Their heads were so close, she couldn't resist, and she rubbed her lips over his cheek. And when he took her forefinger in his mouth and began to suck, she whimpered. She knew he wanted her, he wanted her hands and mouth on his body, and she longed for the courage to make that happen. Knowing she had to start somewhere, she endeavored to give it a try. "Do you know what I want?"

He stopped, waiting, "What, baby?" If she wanted something, he was the man for the job.

"I want to look at you, all of you."

Look? But not touch? Could he survive this? Damn, he'd sure try. "All right." His hands went to the buttons of his shirt.

"Let me."

Beau held his breath while she undid his shirt. Her hands were shaking. She pushed it from his shoulders and he helped the rest of the way. "Everything?" He didn't want to assume too much.

"I want to see you. Do you mind? I'm not ready to go all the way, but I . . ." she let her hands drop.

Standing up, Beau shed his clothes with economical movements. "Harley, honey. You've said that you can trust me and I am going to show you how much. I want you to touch me, if you want too. Familiarize yourself with my

143

body and know that it's yours to command. I will never hurt you." When he was naked, he returned to the floor next to her. The firelight played over the planes and angles of his body. He was beautiful. "Where do you want me?"

"Lie down, I guess." He did. Reclining back on the rug, Beau offered himself up to her. The only precaution he took was covering his privates with a towel that the maid had left at his request by the fireplace. Harley scooted closer. "There's so much of you, I'm not sure where to start."

"Make yourself at home. All that you see belongs to you."

Her mind went back to Brownwood and how she felt to be close to him. And now, he was placing himself at her mercy. She would not let him down. Moving to his head, Harley knelt down. "You have the kindest face," she allowed herself to caress him. She touched his forehead, cupped his cheek, and leaned over to kiss his lips. It was a chaste meeting of their mouths, almost sacred. Next, she ran her fingers through his hair. "Your hair is longer now."

"Too long, I need a haircut."

"No," she spoke quickly. "I love it. It fits you. Wild, untamed, and sexy."

"I feel like Sampson. You have me at your mercy, Delilah," he teased. She smiled and that was a reward in itself.

"Angel face," she murmured. "I used to look at you across the table at Brownwood and imagine that the archangels looked like you." Her fingers traced lightly over his face. "High cheekbones, straight nose," she moved closer for another kiss. "And those dimples, they don't come out to play very often. Strong jaw, perfectly kissable lips," Harley stole another kiss.

"Do you realize what a miracle it is that we have found one another again?"

Now, she was using both hands. Harley stroked his neck and his wide, wide shoulders. The flesh beneath her fingers was firm, the muscles defined. "Yes, I was drawn to the area. I don't know why. Maybe, my psychic abilities played a part. It was never a conscious thought. It never occurred to me that I would find you here. Truly, I had no hope that I would ever see you again. After all, we shared so little of our lives beyond the day-to-day weary routine of surviving."

Her hands were magical. She massaged his chest, kneading his pecs, smiling a secret little smile when his nipples hardened under her fingertips. When a hoarse groan escaped, she glanced up at him to make sure she was still welcome. "Don't you dare stop. I love your hands on me." To put her back at ease, he picked up on their previous conversation. "I always thought I had more time to share with you, I guess. Our former lives seem so faraway. Looking back, I realize I should have found out every detail about you that I could. I was your protector and I let you down."

"Shhhh," Harley didn't want to think about Pell right now. Touching Beau's body was making her excited and that thrilled her. "Your biceps are so big; I can't reach around them with both hands." Beau flexed for her and she giggled. "I think I would like for you to be my protector now. You're built like Conan the Barbarian."

"Taking care of you is Job Number One, baby."

She explored his forearms; so firmly muscled and thick. Sturdy wrists and the most beautiful manly hands she had ever seen. Picking up his left hand, she held it to her cheek. "I love your hands. They are broad and capable. And the veins on top are so sexy."

When she traced them with her tongue, he had to close his eyes and force himself to be still. There was one part of him that wasn't behaving. His cock had a mind of its own.

The towel was beginning to rise like a magician's trick. "Don't pay no attention to my dick, baby. He can't help it."

"I know." She moved down his body, skipping the part that seemed to want her most. She just wasn't ready for that yet. "I guess you've been with many beautiful women, haven't you?" His feet didn't escape her notice, or his calves or knees. Harley left no part of him feeling neglected. Except one.

"I'm thirty-two, Harley. No one would ever mistake me for a monk."

His thigh muscles fascinated her. She rubbed her palms from his knee to his groin and back. "No, I suppose not." Her eyes were drawn to where his manhood was sheltered. She gasped. There was no mistaking his size, even under the cover of modesty. A hungry sensation began deep inside her pussy. Harley was horny.

"Are you sure you want to . . ." she paused. Now what was she trying to ask? The sight of his arousal was all she could see or think about. "Uh – are you sure you want to waste your time with me? Look at you. You're every woman's dream. And I can't – I can't even. . ."

He was up and she was in his arms before she could say another word. "You mean more to me than anybody, Nada. We can work through this. All I'm asking for is a chance."

"I feel the same way, Beau." She pressed her face into his throat. "I just don't want to take advantage of you or frustrate you." Both of them became aware of what lay between them, and it wasn't a misunderstanding. The light was dim, but the towel had fallen away. And like a magnet, her eyes were drawn to the evidence of his desire for her. Hesitantly, she lifted her hand and then drew it back.

"It's okay, baby. Touch me. That part of me only wants to please you, make you feel good."

"I know that. My mind can sort it out, it's just my body

doesn't always obey." Seeing that she was feeling uncomfortable, he stood and led her to the couch and they sat down. Beau drew her close, tucking her under his arm and she rested her head on his shoulder. He waited. His cock was standing straight up, stiff, hard as a board. It was all up to her.

"Give me your mouth," he whispered. She didn't make him wait long. She touched. They both gasped in the midst of the kiss, sharing their breath as they shared the ecstasy of discovery. Beau didn't let it be awkward; he cupped her face and drank from her lips while she rubbed his cock. With tentative strokes, she learned his shape and texture, the wonder of it throbbing in her hand. "Having your hand on me is heaven." He smooched at her lips and let her play with his cock. It wasn't even close to being an expert hand-job, but it didn't need to be. It was his Nada touching him and that made all the difference. Against his chest, he felt her nipple harden and Beau knew she was aroused.

"Ummm, Beau…you feel so good. I love touching you." And that was all it took, her admission added to her innocent caress caused him to come in her hand.

Hot, wet pulses drew her attention. She pulled back to look at the wonder of it. Streams of creamy colored sperm shot out onto his stomach and dripped down her hand. Harley held him until he was through. Then she rubbed her thumb over the tip, and he jerked a bit. "It's sensitive."

Harley pulled back. "Let me get a washrag."

She was escaping. He didn't know if it was because she was embarrassed or if she regretted it or if she was just scared. He let her go. When she returned, she handed it to him, and he cleaned himself up. "Thanks. Now, I want to hold you. God, I love to touch you. That was incredible. Being with you anyway I can, is a dream come true."

Harley met his gaze, longing in her eyes. "Compared to what you're used to, that was probably pitiful. And while

I loved every second of that, I'm afraid to go further."

"You gave me more pleasure than I can even begin to explain to you." He took her chin in his hand and kissed her full on the mouth. "This is more than I anticipated for our first time. We're going to take this slow. It's too important to me. To us. Okay?"

Entwining her arms around his neck, she almost sobbed with relief. "Okay. I can't believe you're being this understanding. Are you real?"

"Pinch me and see."

Harley couldn't help but laugh through her tears. How did she ever get so lucky? She just prayed her luck held out.

* * *

Beau took his cell phone and stepped out on the balcony. Harley was taking a shower. And while he would love to have joined her, he wanted to be sure not to mess up his progress. Taking a chance that he could get hold of Dane Wagner, he placed a call. It seemed odd to confer with another man on his sex life, but here goes.

"Dr. Wagner's answering service. May I help you?"

"Yes, ma'am. This is Beau LeBlanc and I'd like a word with Dr. Wagner, if he's available."

"Certainly, Mr. LeBlanc. He left word that your calls should be put through." In a few seconds, Dane was on the line.

"Beau? How is the trip going?"

"Good, so far. We have made some headway. Like you suggested, I got her to touch me and well, I . . ."

"She brought you to orgasm?"

Clinical devil, Beau thought. He wondered what kind of a sex life the sex therapist had. "It didn't take much. I'm putty in her hand." Then he laughed. "That didn't sound right."

"I got your drift. Good." They shared a man moment.

"I'm glad. How did she react to your climax? Did she become aroused?"

It bugged the shit out of Beau to talk about Harley with another man. "Yea, I recognized a few signs of arousal." Be damned, if he would tell the Doc her nipples got as hard as little rocks.

"Sounds like you're on the right track. Just take it slow. I can't emphasize that enough. Take it slow." Beau could almost swear he could hear the good doctor grinning. "And keep me posted."

Beau grumbled as he folded his phone. "You won't know any more than I have to tell you, you bastard. Beau LeBlanc does not like to share."

Harley slipped out of the bathroom. How did one go about seducing a sexy man like Beau? She, who had no experience, weighed her options. The first thing that came to mind was sexy clothes, but she had on the sexiest thing she possessed. The only other thing she could think of was going up to Beau and touching him, showing him what she wanted, but since she didn't know what that was, that idea didn't hold water either. Maybe she could just talk to him. Yeah, that sounded good.

When Beau stepped back into the room and pulled the French doors shut, he saw a vision waiting on him. She wore a short midnight blue nightgown. It was demure by most standards, but on her little goddess body, it was perfection. "How beautiful you are." He stood still, waiting to see what she would do. The bed was right there. It was a massive king size filled with soft pillows and the color of the spread was a suggestive deep burgundy. The color of passion.

"Thank you." He had pulled on a pair of lounge pants. No shirt. No shoes or socks. He looked good enough to eat. But as she stood there, she felt her courage dissipate like air being let slowly out of a balloon. Perhaps, she'd better not push it. It had been a banner day for major steps forward in the intimacy department and asking for more was just being greedy. "I want to sleep in your arms tonight. Just sleep. Would that be okay?"

"That's just fine." One miracle a day was enough for him. "To have you in my arms, at any time, in any way you'll allow is heaven."

She was back in his bed, after sixteen years, she was back in his bed. If she closed her eyes, it was almost as if no time had passed. Beau held her as if she were of great value. It made her want to cry. He was so warm and she felt so safe. How different life could have been if they had never been separated. Just like the last time, she half laid on his big body. Her head was on his shoulder and she was cradled in his arms. The events of the last few hours were overwhelming; she had no idea that a man could be so gentle. Tender feelings of love and hope unfurled in Harley's heart and, unbidden, tears began to flow.

Beau was exploring uncharted territory for him. Here he lay, wanting to make love to this woman more than anything, and knowing it wasn't going to happen. Not yet, anyway. And he was still happier than he could ever remember being. They had made progress, undoubtedly. So, when her body began to shake with tight little sobs, he reacted. "Baby? What is it, darling?" Tilting her face up to his, he traced the pattern of tears on her face. Light from the bathroom gave the room a soft glow. "Why are you crying?"

He had such a dear face. She cupped his cheek and tried to be honest. "I can't believe you are being so understanding and tender about all of this. Why are you doing that?"

"Why? Simple. I'm in this for the long haul, Nada. The reward for my patience and care is you. Don't you understand that? You are the prize. You are the unexpected gift that has taken my heart by storm. To me, your value is far above rubies. You are my heart."

Beau's sincere outpouring of love enveloped Harley in peace and happiness. She pressed her lips to his chest and kissed him. There was just so much of him to love, she smiled through her tears. Especially that part...she could feel his massive erection nestled between them. Feeling unusually bold, she slid a hand to her goal, and whispered. "Can we? Do you want to?"

His cock jumped with the realization that she was offering to take it further. How much further he didn't know. He had been lucky enough to feel her hands on his body once tonight; there was no use being greedy. The doctor's words kept ringing in his ears. Take it slow. Beau planned on keeping that promise, even if it killed him. "There is nothing,nothing in the world I want more." He cupped the back of her head and kissed her cheek. "But tonight we weave the dreams and tomorrow...tomorrow we make them come true."

"Okay," Harley pulled her hand away from him so fast; it was as if burned her. Maybe, he didn't want her hands on his body. She tried to reason with herself. And that was difficult as she lay in Beau's arms. Trust in him warred with her own self-doubts.

Beau felt her tense up. "Stop. Right now, I know what you're thinking." He bumped his erection against her. "He wants you and I want you, but this is too important. I want you to sleep in my arms tonight with the absolute assurance that I adore you. I would never hurt you and I want to play house with you more than anything in the world."

"Play house?"

"Yes, I want to be with you, often. Eventually, I want it to be more. That is, if you think you could put up looking at my ugly mug all the time."

"You're beyond handsome, and you know it."

Although she still had some doubt – a lack of sexual self-confidence was too deeply ingrained, but she decided to believe him. Harley nestled down into his arms and sighed, letting all the tension and worry evaporate from her mind and body. And when she dropped off to sleep, her dreams were sweeter than they had ever been.

* * *

"I can't believe you brought my sniper rifle!" The surprised joy on Harley's face was worth the extra thousand dollars Beau had forked over to gain them exclusive time at the shooting range. Special targets had been erected and other necessary precautions had been taken to ensure safety.

"My aim is to please, mam," he admired how she looked in tight jeans and a lacy top. His Nada was all woman; and if she could shoot she was a wet-dream. Memories of last night kept flitting through his mind. The taste of her kiss, the way his body felt when she touched him, and the pure hell he had endured keeping his cock out of her pussy.

"Mr. LeBlanc, we've got you set up for 500, 800 and 1000 yard shooting. Hopefully, there's everything you'll need, if not, I'll be up at the front office. You two have a good time." Beau had almost forgotten the range manager was standing right by him. He looked down at his package and saw that he hadn't embarrassed himself…yet. Hiding his grin, he wanted to laugh at himself. He had never been hard for so long, nor done without sex for this length of time. There was one thing for sure, he was going to have to get himself in check so he could give her all the pleasure she deserved.

"Thanks, Malcolm, I think I can figure everything out." With a wave of the hand, the man was gone, leaving them blessedly alone. "Are you ready to try it out? The reaper conversion worked like a dream on this gun. It shoots damn well."

She held out her hands for the rifle and it was all he could do not to offer to carry it for her, but she looked confident. "I see you have sand bags all set up for the shooting rest. That's good. I shoot better from a prone position. Did you bring a spotting scope?"

Beau snorted. "I do this sort of thing for a living, sugar britches."

"Of course you do, I'm sorry." He could see that it was a strain for her to carry it, but she carried it well. Not one complaint. "What are we going to do first?"

He steered her out to the range and helped her get set up to take the first shot. "Let's do the 500, start off with something easy." There were two shooting rests and two targets side-by-side waiting for them to test their mettle. Beau joined her on the ground, his own 380 in his hand. "You can go first, treasure. And I'll watch."

"Let's both go at the same time. Best out of five," she gave him a cocky little grin. They put on their noise muffling headsets; the fancy kind that allowed them to hear and speak to one another and still be protected. "Ready?"

"You betcha, baby," he gave her a slow wink. "But if we're going to do something at the same time, I think I'd rather cum."

He said it so matter-of-factly that Harley almost missed it. Since he had stopped her from touching him last night, she had been afraid he might have changed his mind about wanting her. A tiny smile played around her lips - - apparently not. "I'm think I'm ready, Beau. I can't wait for you to make me cum." After dropping that bomb, she announced. "Ready? Aim! Fire!"

Fire? What? He couldn't get past the incredible news that she was ready for him to give her an orgasm. Damn! "Ready?" She was ready? Hell, he wasn't. He missed the first two shots; he knew he had because he wasn't even aiming. "You did that on purpose!" To his delight, she broke into a fit of giggles.

"No, I just thought it, so I said it. Sorry. How did we do?"

"Who cares? You're ready to let me touch you." She was happy, which made him happy. Yes, he would own her orgasms before the sun went down. Looking through the scope, he exclaimed. "Damn, baby. You're good." He wasn't really surprised, but she had been right on the money. One bull's eye and four within the smallest circle. He had two wild ones and three within the inner circle. They were a good match, just like he knew they would be.

As they moved on to the farther targets the results didn't change. Beau was completely enchanted. His Nada was more than capable. She was a top shot and sexy as hell. After they had satisfied their friendly competition, Beau drove her into Natchitoches and they walked the banks of the Cane River and visited where the movie Steel Magnolias was filmed. He had seen it all before, but having her at his side made it a rare and wonderful experience, especially when she would rise up on tiptoe and kiss his cheek. They walked into an old-fashioned mercantile that had everything in it from paintings by local artists to the kitchen sink. Literally.

"I'm so happy, Beau. Thanks for bringing me. And I had a good time at the shooting range."

Putting his arm around her, he pulled her close so another couple could pass them on the narrow aisle. "You are a true marksman. What other kinds of things did you have to do to qualify for Special Ops?" Actually, he wasn't sure he wanted to know. But she belonged to him and he needed to know.

She turned in his arms and nestled close, laying her head on his chest. "I dive, I jump out of airplanes, I can run a mile and a half in ten minutes and do forty-two pushups in ninety seconds; or I used to be able to - now I'm getting fat." About that time, she goosed him and he fixed her wagon. He just picked her up and kissed her full on the mouth.

"You're perfect, that's what you are." He knew she had told him all of that and then did something to take his mind off of it. And it worked, sorta. He still didn't like to think of her diving or jumping out of airplanes or dismantling explosive devices. Harley was too precious, she was his Nada and he didn't know if he could survive if he lost her again. "Have you seen enough or are you ready to go back to the hotel. We'll eat at the restaurant, they have excellent snapper and then we'll head north to Uncertain, Texas."

"Sounds good to me." Holding hands, they walked back to his truck and he picked her up, placing her carefully in the seat and fastening the seatbelt. Taking her hand, he raised it to his lips and kissed her. She found it hard to breathe as he leaned in and whispered next to her face. "I know you're capable of taking care of yourself. You are strong and sharp and talented beyond belief, but I crave to be the one you run to, the one you turn to when you need to be held. I want to be the man that makes all your dreams come true."

Harley melted. Resting her cheek next to his; she slipped an arm around his neck. "You've always been that man. I just didn't know where you were or how to find you."

* * *

"Two for lunch, please." Beau talked to the hostess and as she was checking her book, his cell phone rang. When he saw Dane Wagner's name, he stepped outside to take the call. "Hey, Doc. I'm glad you called."

155

"How's my patient?"

Beau appreciated that Wagner called him instead of Harley. He wanted to help her through this; it was his highest priority. "Pretty good, we just got back from the shooting range and a sightseeing trip."

"Great. The reason I called was to reinforce the point that you'll have to gauge her response to you, and act accordingly. Be affectionate, but let her make the first moves. And it doesn't have to be much of a move. If you get any indication that she is open to more sensual play, then go for it. Harley has extreme insecurity issues, so any advance she makes toward you might be so slight you would miss it in any other woman."

"Oh, hell," Beau could have kicked himself.

"Talk to me. What's going on? How is she reacting to you?"

"Last night, she reached out to me. I had a hard-on and she touched me and offered . . ."

"Excellent, she's feeling more confident."

"I told her no," Beau spat out the words. "You told me to take it slow."

Dr. Wagner threw out a few choice phrases. "Going slow is critical, but her self-confidence is even more so. How is she reacting now? Has she withdrawn? Does she seem happy?"

"Slow down, Doc. You're making me nervous." Had he screwed up? "She's been laughing and talking. She's even been teasing me about having sex with her." He remembered the comment she made at the shooting range.

Dane let out a long breath. "I hope so. Look, this isn't your fault. It's mine. For all intents and purposes, Harley is her own woman. I had no idea that she would feel free enough to make a move like that so soon. She must really trust you, LeBlanc."

God, he hoped so. And to think he had pushed her

back. Reliving the moment made him feel like a first class heel. "So, what do I do? Should I try and reenact what happened last night? Set the stage or let Harley make her first move for the second time?" He knew he wasn't hiding his frustration very well.

"Give her a little space, but don't you dare give her a reason to doubt herself. Look at this from her point of view. Harley is feminine, affectionate and beautiful, yet all she has ever known from men is violence. If she reaches out to you, she is giving you a priceless gift. Don't make her regret it, or you'll have to deal with me."

Beau didn't even argue with the doctor. If he fucked this up with Harley, he'd kick his own ass.

* * *

Cypress Bend's hotel was a beautiful place. As Beau saw to their lunch reservations, Harley walked around the lobby and admired the décor. So much glass and the view of the golf course was spectacular. She moved around the lobby and saw that there were large statues of rabbits, everywhere. This made her smile. She petted one, rubbing a hand over his ears and down his back. "You like that big ole' bunny?" Beau asked as he nudged up against her. She loved the feel of their bodies touching.

"Yes, I love rabbits. I have two ceramic ones next to my fireplace back at Willowbend. Is our table ready?"

"Sure, come on." He offered his arm and led her into the dining room. "Let's sit by the window." Since it was a weekday, the place wasn't packed. After the waitress took their order, Beau decided to find out more about Socorro. "Tell me about the last time Socorro was called out?"

There were a lot of things she would rather have discussed with Beau, but these issues would have to be addressed sometimes, it might as well be now. "My last job was at one of the oil refinery storage facilities in Port

157

Arthur, and before that it was at a high-rise construction site in Philadelphia."

Beau watched a change come over her face. She set aside her vulnerable, soft nature and became capable and analytical. Perhaps this was necessary for her to be able to function in such a high-pressure environment. "I heard Dandi talking about it, but I didn't catch the report. If I had known it was about you, I would have watched it."

Harley folded and refolded her napkin. "The newscasters tend to be dramatic. Although both episodes could have been horrific and deadly, especially the one in Port Arthur, we were able to defuse them and halt the danger. The potential for widespread carnage was much higher at the refinery. The bomber used extremely volatile explosives yet, it seems more like a game he's playing rather than a cause he's warring against. Frankly, I don't think he's trying to manipulate the price of oil or make some grand statement about our overseas policy or the environment."

Beau buttered a piece of bread and broke off a chunk, offering it to her. Harley accepted it, licking his fingers in the process. Sitting here with him, discussing this, was absolutely precious to her. Oh, she had talked to Waco and government officials, even her mentor, but never with someone who valued her so completely.

"What does your gut tell you?"

She was having a hard time concentrating. Beau was magnetic, she was hungry to be closer to him and at least four women were openly gaping at him. Jealousy and possessiveness streaked through her – it was a brand new feeling. And she liked it. "My gut tells me that Fox Crocker isn't dead. I have no proof other than what I can see with my own eyes. The placement of the wiring and the explosives is almost identical to schematics that he drew-up when we were in training and learning about the possibilities we could face. Plus, the locales that he chose were meaningful to me. The way the bombs were placed would ensure that human intervention was necessary. I think the bombs were set to lure me, to involve me, specifically." A stern, almost desperate look came over Beau's face. Harley knew instantly, that he was upset. She hadn't meant to do that.

"I want you out of danger, whatever it takes." He was about to say more, but their waitress arrived with their food.

He had said this before, so she knew it would be something they would have to work out, eventually. That is, if they were to have a future together. A future. Thoughts such as that were alien to her. But she could see it, vaguely. Sharing a home, a life, maybe even a child. "I'm working on it." That wasn't quite true, yet, but she could make it true if the ghost of Fox Crocker would disappear. Beau looked like he wanted to lecture her, but he didn't. Instead, he told her more about the day he had planned for them. She was listening, truly. But, he was just so damn sexy.

"We'll finish up here and go up and pack. Check out time is in half an hour. We're only a couple of hours away from Caddo Lake and I've rented us a cabin right on the water. You'll love it. Caddo Lake is the largest natural lake in the South and used to be home to river boat ports." Harley wasn't seated across from him, rather she was to his left and when he placed a hand on her knee and let it glide northward, every molecule of her body sizzled. "I'm going to take you on a moonlight boat ride. Can we neck?"

Lunch was over, as far as Harley was concerned. "I'd like that. Yes." Just the thought of kissing him made her heart pound and her breathing go shallow. "I can't wait to kiss you, again. Waiting till tonight seems like waiting for an eternity to pass."

The sparkle of heat in her eyes told Beau this was an opportunity too sweet to pass up. "Hell, yeah," Beau threw down his napkin and motioned for the waitress, meeting her halfway. Not waiting for the check, he handed her a fifty and came back for Harley. "Damn, baby. Let's get out of here. I need to get you alone."

As they walked, he rubbed her back up and down. God, he couldn't keep his hands off of her. She was quiet, God he hoped she didn't change her mind. "What are you thinking, Sunshine?" The walk from the hotel to the golf suites seemed to take forever. His cock was growing by leaps and bounds.

"I'm thinking how happy I am and how lucky I am to be with you." And how stupid I'm going to feel if you push me away, again. Of course, she didn't say that part out loud. But wow, she was brave. That was pretty plain speaking for her.

The reaction she got was unexpected. Beau groaned. "You have me, baby. I'm playing for keeps. As far as what didn't happen last night, I've counted myself a fool a thousand times already." He gently backed her up against their door. "Believe me, I'll never make that mistake again. I was just trying to be considerate and be a gentleman. What I should have done was get down and kiss your feet and tell you what a lucky son-of-a-bitch I am."

About that time, somebody walked past and Beau pulled back, quickly letting them in. As he opened the door, it was apparent the maid had been there. All the candles and petals were gone and the room was spiffed up and clean. The bed was remade and looked inviting and images of sleeping next to him made a shiver pass over her body.

"So, what can I do for you, precious?" He pushed her hair back over her shoulder. "I'll do anything and everything you'll allow."

Inhaling once, deeply; she pushed aside her anxiety

and went after what she wanted. If she didn't take risks, she would never gain the prize. Beau. "I want to sit in your lap like you asked me to at Willowbend. I've been dreaming of what I missed."

He was easily led. "Oh honey, I can definitely do that." Moving to the couch, he sat down and pulled her close. Before she knew it, he had taken her by the waist and set her astraddle his legs, facing him.

"Are you sure I won't mash you?" She could feel his manhood beneath her. "I could sit a little farther back," she suddenly felt very awkward.

"Don't you move," instead he drew her closer. Yeah, that was better. Harley might be protesting a little, but her nipples had a mind of their own. They were poking out hard and anxious like they were begging to be noticed. He noticed. Before he could stop himself, he was pressing his dick into her softness, lifting his hips, pumping against her, letting her know that he was helplessly, hopelessly at her mercy.

"You feel good to me." Harley was relieved that she was thrilled at his nearness. After the rape and the rejections, her sexuality had gone dormant. But she was more relieved that he found her attractive enough to respond. Lifting her face, she fitted her lips to his. And they kissed. Beau had given her that treasured first kiss so long ago and now she was getting to kiss him again. There was no way he knew how momentous it was, how huge. Tenderly, he caressed her mouth, licking a fiery path all along the seam of her lips. "Let me taste you." With an almost imperceptible gasp of surrender, she opened to him and felt Beau's full and complete passion for the first time. His tongue teased her, pleased her, and made her chase it with her own. "Oh yea, aren't you precious."

She wanted more. He pulled back to let them catch a breath and she followed, seeking his lips blindly. Breathing was secondary. "Please, more," she demanded.

Beau chuckled. "Yes, ma'am, I aim to please." Hell, how lucky could a man get? And when she framed his face and began kissing him, hungrily, his cock rose up even firmer and gave her his version of a standing ovation. "Damn, baby." The kiss was so much more than she had ever dreamed. Reverent, tender and powerful. Harley was amazed that her desire was to get closer to him instead of pulling back. Sensations swept over her body, a longing and an edgy excitement that demanded fulfillment. God, she wanted to move. If she could just get a little closer . . . her hips moved of their own accord, rubbing her clit against the seam of her blue jeans. She wanted him to touch her there so badly she could die.

When she moved that tiny bit, Beau pulled back. "Are you okay?"

"I tingle all over," she confessed.

"Good answer," he murmured as he covered her mouth with smothering kisses, feasting at her lips over and over; one deep, delicious open-mouthed kiss after another. Beau couldn't help but see the irony. He was thirty-two fuckin' years old and here he was making out on the couch. It had been literally years since he had done this. Usually it was a kiss or two and he was bedroom bound. Even though he couldn't wait to be with Harley, he wouldn't have missed this for the world.

Harley didn't even think. One of his hands slid around to cup her butt and she acted instinctively, pushing against him, her soft center nestled right over his crotch.

"God, I want you." His breathing was ragged as he drug his mouth from hers, kissing a path down her neck and nipping her once, right where her neck joined her shoulder. "Do you know how much I want you?"

"I don't know about that," she whispered. "But what I do know is that I've never felt this way before. I feel electric." It was far from an unpleasant feeling. She was completely aroused and it was all she could do to keep from rocking her private parts against his hardness.

"I need to see you, just a glimpse," he looked deep into her eyes for permission. And with big hands made clumsy by excitement, he undid the top two buttons of her shirt. Beau could see the rapid beating of her heart; the little soft spot at her pulse point was fluttering like a butterfly in a jar. "Cher, you are so damn beautiful." He could only see the top swells of her breasts, but they were full and round. Then with a groan, he buried his face in the valley of her cleavage and kissed first one side and then the other.

"Touch me, please." Her cry of excited desperation made his heart pound. Raising his hands, he was about to undo her shirt, when she stopped him. "No, here," she drug his hand where she wanted it to go. Damn! Realization dawned on him as she placed his hand over the mound of her pussy and lifted against it. "Please?"

"You don't have to beg, baby. I'll do it gladly. Mmmmm, God, yes." He cupped her vulva and began to work it with his fingers, massaging her through the rough fabric of her jeans. Desperately she arched into him and spread her legs wider, anxious for more of his Cajun magic.

"Does that feel good?" Beau's eyes were smoldering.

"Better - than – I – ever – dreamed," she stammered, as she closed her eyes in ecstasy and moved against his hand, faster and faster.

Her little grunts and groans were driving Beau over the edge. "You look hot as hell, Harley. I want to fuck you till you can't stand up."

Harley marveled that she enjoyed his sex-talk. So far, everything was different with Beau. And when he said, "Cum for me, Nada," and applied even more exquisite pressure to her clit, she spiraled out of control. Harley grasped his shoulders like she had dreamed and curled into him, riding his hand while writhing in the throes of an intense orgasm. "Beau! God, Beau!" Harley kissed him feverishly on his neck, his jaw, and his lips, letting him know how grateful she was. "I can't believe we did that. You inspire me."

"I like to inspire you," Beau continued to rub Harley between her legs, loving the little jerking movements her body made as she enjoyed the aftershocks.

Hiding her face against his chest, he felt her whole body tense up, as if what she had to say was hard to confess. "That's not something I've done very often."

"Let a man make you cum?" As soon as he got the words out of his mouth, he knew how wrong it was. She pulled back from him and God, she looked ashamed. Like it was her fault the whole fuckin' male race were morons.

"No, not a man. Me. I haven't made myself cum too many times. Sex rarely crossed my mind. Touching myself in the shower the other day was the first time in a very, very long time. Thank you for making me feel this way." She kissed him on the cheek. If she had more courage, she would have touched him again, but once burned, twice shy.

"Oh, Harley, honey. You are so welcome." He kissed her forehead, his cock was in such a bind that he had to adjust his package to keep from passing out. Beau was just about to say to hell with check-out time and ask for an encore, when his cell phone started playing 'Desperado.' Joseph McCoy. "Now, this is somebody I want you to meet. Hold on, sugar." She would have gotten off his lap, but he kept her anchored down. "Talk to me, Tex."

"Beau, hell! It's good to hear your voice, man. How are you?"

"Better than I've been in a long time." He picked up Harley's hand and kissed it. "Did you get those contracts I sent you on the sponsors for the rodeo?"

"I sure did. But that's not why I called. I wanted to

make sure you're coming to Aron and Libby's wedding. My fiancé and I would like a chance to take you out to dinner."

"Fiancé? Who's the lucky girl?" He knew who he hoped it was. If Daredevil McCoy had let sweet Cady Renaud slip through his fingers, he was going to personally whip his ass.

"My angel Cady has agreed to marry me and when we tie the knot, I want you to stand up with me."

"Damn, that's wonderful. Cady Renaud is a catch. You are one damn lucky man. When's the big day?" As he talked marriage with his best friend, he thought about how wonderful it would be to watch Harley walk down the aisle to him.

"Soon, Cady's pregnant. But we haven't set an official date yet. She's talking things over with her family. Believe me, you'll be one of the first to know. By the time you get here for the wedding, I'll know something."

"Pregnant?" Beau laughed out loud with joy. "That's the best news I've heard in a while. I want to be godfather. And don't you forget it."

"Your name is always first on the list. So, you'll be here?"

"You know I wouldn't miss it. Those McCoy shindigs are worth the drive half way across Texas. Can I bring a date?" 'Will you go with me?' he mouthed to Harley and she nodded.

"Of course." Joseph sounded intrigued. "It's unusual for Rogue LeBlanc to be traveling in tandem with somebody. Usually you are a love em' and leave em' kind of guy." Beau started to say something, but Joseph beat him to it. "I know. it's the pot calling the kettle black. Those days are behind me, I've been caught, hog-tied. trussed up and I wouldn't go back to my playboy ways for anything. Cady has made me happy, really happy. I worship the ground she walks on."

The sincerity in his friend's voice moved Beau. "When you find the right woman, buddy she changes everything. I know. Mine is sitting in my lap, right now, looking at me with the biggest, sweetest brown eyes you've ever seen." Harley blushed and he stole a kiss.

"Tell her hello for me. What's her name? Have you ever mentioned her to me?"

"Yeah, I have. My Nada has come back in my life. You remember me telling you about the girl who stole my heart so long ago?"

"Yeah, I do remember. How could I forget?" Joseph was silent for a moment. "There's a story there, and I want to hear it." Beau knew Joseph must have remembered that Nada was presumed dead. "You must be in heaven right now. I'm happy for you."

"We're both blessed. Tell Aron and Libby that my girl and I wouldn't miss their big day for anything. I thought it was going to be a double wedding? What happened to Jacob and Jessie? Don't tell me he let her get away? She seemed to be just what he needed."

"They're already married. It's a long story; I'll fill you in when you get here. Take care of yourself…all right? Don't go letting one of them alligators get the best of you."

"Don't you worry, McCoy." Beau looked deep in Harley's eyes. "I have a reason to live now, and I plan on enjoying every day the Lord grants me."

Chapter Seven

Uncertain, Texas had a population of only one hundred and fifty people. Beau had fallen in love with it when he had come to help an old friend of his set up a gator park and petting zoo. "Our cabin is just around the bend." He glanced over at the beautiful woman who held his heart in her hand. "I've rented the steamboat to take you on a tour of the lake. The largest cypress forest in the world is here and I have heard tales that Big Foot has been spotted in these woods."

"Stop it!" She playfully pinched his knee, but she held on to his leg instead of letting go. "What is it with you? First ghosts and the loup garou and now Big Foot. You enjoy scaring me, don't you?"

The woman had a killer smile and when she gave it to him; he couldn't help but smile back. "No, I enjoy your hands on me." He covered her smaller hand with his own. "You gravitate to me when you're unnerved and that I love."

Harley looked at him with all seriousness in her eyes, "I can't imagine a time when I wouldn't turn to you for comfort. Throughout my life, in my darkest moments, I always ran to you in my heart."

Beau swallowed hard, the pain of their separation a familiar ache. "We're together now and that's all that matters." He guided the truck into the driveway, the dark greenish blue waters of Caddo Lake in the background. "Okay, we're here. Let's go in and rest a bit and then we'll go exploring."

Harley knew what she wanted to explore. Him. As he got their luggage out of the back, she looked around. The area around Caddo Lake and Jefferson, Texas had always

167

been an area she wanted to visit. Uncertain surprised her, however. It was small, and sleepy but full of more primitive, earthy vibrations than anyplace she had ever been. Perhaps it was the residual energy left over from the Caddo Indians or the riverboat era, but whatever it was gave her a sense of days long gone by. The plants and the trees grew densely and everything was a deep green and damp looking. Truly, it wouldn't have been too much of a shock to see a big prehistoric dinosaur come stalking out of the underbrush. Harley decided she liked it here.

The cabin was small, but cozy and when she touched the bed, a hazy vision of the last couple who had stayed here swept into her mind and she saw the man taking the woman, pumping between her thighs as she clutched his shoulders, her legs wrapped around his waist, her cries of ecstasy bouncing off the walls. That was what she wanted; she wanted to feel passion and pleasure. Beau's hands on her shoulders made her jump.

"Sorry, doll. I didn't mean to scare you."

With renewed courage, her heart pounding she turned in his arms. "Would you like to play with me?"

Her tempting suggestion instantly had his cock doing push-ups. "More than you could ever imagine." He did manage to keep from pumping his fist and saying – Yes! "How about if I give you a massage?" A massage seemed like a good idea, he could get his hands on her and still maintain some semblance of control…maybe.

Not waiting for her to move, he went to her and closed the curtains in the bedroom on the way. He wanted to be able to see and appreciate her, but he sure didn't want to share her beauty with anyone else. "Can we take off that top? Like a child, she raised her arms over her head and let him lift the camisole. No bra, Lord have mercy, Jesus. He was still for a moment, just appreciating the view. "You've got the prettiest titties in the world." Holding the piece of cotton in his hand, he couldn't help but stare. "You're perfect, Harley. Damn!" High, round, full globes of firm female flesh were decorated with big nipples; mouth size nipples. "Oh doll, you make me want to lay you down and suck on you all night long."

"I've never . . ." she tried to tell him that she had never known a man's lips on her flesh. She pushed the two violent encounters from her mind; this was nothing like them, this was Beau.

"Lay down, baby; let's get those jeans and panties off. Is that okay?" he wanted to be so careful with her. She was like spun glass; fragile and oh, so beautiful. When she settled back on the bed, he couldn't believe the picture she made. No playboy centerfold could ever be sexier than she was. Every breath she took made those tits move just right. Her waist was small, and those hips flared out, just so, making him want to trace their heart shaped perfection as he buried his face between her legs. And when she lifted her hips so he could remove the remainder of her filmy underwear, the gesture caused him to groan. It was so trusting, so giving. His heart began to race like an untried schoolboy. Slowly, he pulled down the small bikini panties that were so shear he could see straight to paradise. Paradise was better up close. "Lord, you're pretty, girl." The only touch he would allow himself was one finger right down the little runway that appeared to be designed strictly for his pleasure. Her whole body jerked at the touch, "Easy, baby. We're taking it slow."

"What should I do?" she asked with a slight tremor in her voice.

Oh, the things he would like for her to do... 'Patience, LeBlanc'. She was the important one. "Lay there and look pretty and enjoy yourself." Carefully, he moved so he could reach her feet. The reason he was moving carefully was so he wouldn't damage the goods. His cock was so heavy, and pulsing with such force that his jeans were binding him like a strait jacket. "What a dainty little foot," he picked it up and caressed the instep. "Are you ticklish?"

"No," she answered rather hoarsely. "I can't believe you're doing this, you can see right up my business."

"Yes, and you've got the sexiest, sweetest business I've ever seen." He held her foot, rubbing the arch, knowing that this small foot carried her down paths of danger where few men chose to tread. "Speaking of your pussy, did you know that I see glistening dew, baby?" The evidence of her excitement was a total relief; he had been so afraid she wouldn't respond to him.

"I'm wet you mean?" She wasn't surprised, she felt odd, a good odd. "I feel sorta melty and empty."

Raising her foot to his lips, he kissed her toes, ran his hand down to her knee and slowly let it glide back up. "Oh, empty is good, that means you want me to fill you up."

"Possibly, possibly," Harley was having a hard time thinking. "I love what you're doing, but I sure would love to kiss your lips."

This time he didn't move quite as carefully, he was in a hurry. She wanted to kiss him and he wasn't going to make her wait one second longer than necessary. Lying down beside her he got close, but didn't let their bodies touch. Not yet. He intended to let her come to him, if he lived that long. She turned her body to face him. "Side by side is good," she whispered. "It's the being held down with my face pressed into the mattress that was so bad. I couldn't breathe."

"I know, baby." Damn! Comments like that made him want to kill somebody.

"Would you take off your clothes so I can feel your skin against mine?"

"I was just waiting for you to ask," he shed them in record time and rejoined her on the bed, making sure he got in the exact position he had abandoned. Oh, yeah! That was it. Her nipples were grazing his chest, this was a major breakthrough. She was making deliberate contact with his body. "We'll touch one another however makes you most comfortable." Her eyes were deep wells of golden amber, and he just wanted to stare at her forever. "After we were parted Nada, I dreamed of you so often. I would wake up in a cold sweat, thinking you were crying out for me."

Her breath hitched in her throat, "I did cry out for you in my sleep, sometimes." With that admission, she eased forward and fit her mouth to his, just barely touching. "Kiss me, please?"

"God, yes." He hadn't been privileged to kiss her near enough. She inched closer to him, keeping their mouths melding, tongues mating. Breaking for air, he had to know, "How you doing, baby? Any anxiety?"

"No," she admitted softly. "But maybe it's because I know we're taking it slow. You won't do anything that I don't want, will you?"

"Never." Tipping his head toward her a scant inch, he touched his forehead to hers. "Making you feel happy and loved is what I want." Like Eskimos' he rubbed noses with her. "Where does my baby want to be touched?"

Reaching between them, she groped for his hand and moved it to her breast. "Please? I want you, here"

Fuck, yes! "Oh, cher, oh baby, you've got me." Easing her on her back, he sat up next to her. "Put your hands over your head. God, just look at you." He framed the quivering tender globes and caressed them from the outside, then around, making a complete circle. "Perfect, you are absolutely perfect." He had expected her nipples to be some shade of brown; instead they were a dark coral, a beautiful contrast to her golden skin. Over and over again he repeated the circle, massaging the flesh, plumping them, lifting them. Yet, he didn't touch the nipples. He wanted her to ask. Hell, he wanted her to beg.

Harley wouldn't shut her eyes, even though what Beau was doing made her want to revel in the joy he was bestowing. No, she wanted to remember every second, exactly who was touching her. If she could ingrain that reality in her mind and heart, maybe everything would be different. "Your hands are making magic on my skin," she murmured. "Could you – please?" Arching her back, she offered him everything.

Not plain enough, he needed a specific request. He didn't dare make a mistake. "What do you want, doll? I'll give you anything, but you have to ask. I can't risk misreading you, this is too important."

"It's hard to ask," her voice sounded almost near to tears. "I'm afraid you'll tell me 'no'."

Beau stopped his sensual assault, "Try me," he challenged her. "I can promise you it would be next to impossible for me to deny you anything. Honey, if you asked me for the world, somehow I'd get it."

"I need…I wish…please touch and kiss my nipples?" The look on her face was so hesitant, so unsure. How could she doubt her attraction so much?

"My pleasure, precious. My pleasure." Going down on one elbow next to her, he lay down beside her. "Can I come back down here with you?" She pressed her hand to his chest. "Give me some sugar, bele."

Bele, she recognized the Cajun word for beautiful and in that moment, she felt beautiful.

He bent closer, and she could feel his breath on her cheek. Harley's heart was pounding when he finally settled his mouth on hers and nudged her lips open with his tongue. Oh, he tasted so good. Gone were the bad memories. Fox and Pell didn't exist. When he dipped his tongue in her mouth, she began to kiss him passionately, pushing her body against him, their tongues mating. Taking heart, he made a bold move. As if approaching the gates of paradise, he swept one hand from knee to thigh, stroking – barely grazing over her mound.

"Hmmmmm," she gave him her approval. "Nipples, Beau," she reminded him and he chuckled.

"No way I've forgotten. I'm just stoking the fire."

Brushing the underside of her breast, he made his move, running his fingertips over one nipple. When it hardened instantly, Beau knew she was aroused. And when she arched her back he thanked heavens that her trust in him could overcome her fear. "Feels so good," Harley pressed herself against his hand. So he gave her what he thought she needed. He began to tease the nipple, working it between his thumb and first finger, rubbing it tenderly and then giving it a gentle pinch.

A haze of pleasure fogged her mind. She was responding to Beau. Her pussy muscles were closing on nothing and she had never felt so empty in her life. For the first time, she craved a man's touch. Pushing her body closer, she moaned softly as she felt him find her other breast and begin to squeeze the nipple with a milking motion. "Oh Lord, Beau, I never knew it could be like this."

"Me either," he whispered as his mouth moved down her body. Kissing her neck, he let his lips graze over her collarbone and the top of her breast. For just a second he hesitated… "Can I?"

"If you don't, I might faint."

Beau was surprised to find he was shaking. God, he wanted her so much. Just having her in his arms was paradise. What he wouldn't give to bury himself in her heat, but right now he had to think of her. She was in his arms and that was all that mattered, the rest would come. Glancing up at her face, he made sure she was still with him before his tongue darted out and lapped at the flesh right next to her areola several times. When she moved her body toward him, just a little bit, a tiny push, he covered her nipple with his mouth, latching on to it with his lips. Shit, this was good, having his mouth on her was the hottest thing he had ever done. Beau felt like a horny teenager. And her reaction was so total, so complete, he was entranced. Harley probably didn't realize the hungry little sounds she was making or the fact that she had wrapped her leg over his hip and was pushing her pussy right into his groin. For a moment, he just buried his head in her cleavage and relished the moment.

"Don't stop," she groaned and he had to laugh.

"Yes, ma'am." Renewing his commitment to suckling her tit, he opened his mouth wide, like he was enveloping an ice cream cone. Using the flat of his tongue, he worked the nipple as he pulled on the entire areola. Against his tongue, her nipple hardened further and he scraped it with his teeth, gently. Molding her tit, shaping and kneading it, he worshiped his Nada.

"Beau-ray, I feel desperate," she whispered as she pumped her hips into him. Knowing what she needed he kept nursing and slid a hand down her body. All he had to do was dip his fingers into her pussy once. It was a simple graze to her clit and she shattered in his arms. As he cupped her vulva, her whole body began to convulse. Bo raised his head and captured her mouth, wanting to share this moment in every way that he could. She whimpered and mewled and kissed all the while, her body jerked and convulsed against him. Beau found her response to him irresistible. His whole body rejoiced in her orgasm, so much that he joined her in the party. Without a single touch - it was a first for him, but Beaureguarde LeBlanc jetted his cum all over Harley's belly and thighs. Hell! "Damn," he whispered, regret clear in his tone.

Harley fizzled and sparkled. She clung to Beau's shoulders and realized what it was like to leave one's body in rapture. Nothing was penetrating her euphoria till he whispered the one word of remorse. Disgust literally dripped from the single syllable. Pushing back from him, she tried to move. "I'm sorry." The sudden awareness of his disapproval appalled her. "I couldn't help it, I didn't mean to. . . " It was happening again with Beau. "Excuse me, please. I need to leave." Again, she tried to extricate herself, but she didn't get very far.

For a moment, Beau didn't understand what was going on. He had cum so hard his head had almost exploded. Thinking clearly wasn't easy, but when he understood. He latched on to her like a vise. "Not on your life, Nada."

"It's okay, Beau, I just need to get up."

His body was blocking the light. Reading her expression might be difficult, but the quaver in her voice was unmistakable. She thought he regretted what had happened. Hell, no. "Don't you feel it? I came all over you, baby. I messed us both up good. That's what I was carrying on about." He settled his lower body on hers. He'd have to clean them both up, but that was okay. Teaching her this lesson was far more important. "Now we'll just get stuck together," he rubbed his face against hers and whispered. "I loved how you came, that was the hottest thing I've ever done. You just exploded and all I did was suck on your beautiful tits and finger your pussy for just barely a second. It makes me happy how you respond to me so completely."

She studied his face, needing to be sure. "When you touched me, it didn't remind you of...the rapes?" All she could think of was strength. With one move, Beau rose over her. He held himself up like he was doing push-ups on top of her.

"Hell, no. What kind of a question is that?" Harley bit her lip; she looked like she was about to cry. "Are you afraid of me?" he asked, hoarsely.

"No, that's not it." Her voice trembled. With an

175

economy of movement, Beau pushed himself to his feet and gathered her up in his arms. "Where are we going?" she wrapped her arms around his neck.

"To the bathroom to get cleaned up, I'm going to wash away all your cares and woes. And get my mess off the both of us. Now smile." He pitched her up in the air, making her giggle a little.

Really, this was extraordinary. Her Beau was carrying her to the bathroom. When he stood her down and began to ready the shower, all she could think about was the last time they had been like this. When he had cleaned her up after Pell had beat her. As he adjusted the temperature and gathered up a towel, she couldn't help but look at him. He was truly magnificent. His body was broad and strong and if any man in the world could be described as ripped, it was him. Beau was muscle bound, not the pretty-boy muscles of a gym junkie, but the real deal, life-lived on the edge, wrestling alligators type of strength. Unbidden, her eyes gravitated to his manhood. It had only been minutes ago that he had had an orgasm, yet he was already big and hard. Wow.

"If you keep looking at me like that, it's gonna happen again. You'll have my cock erupting as regular as clockwork, just like that Old Faithful geyser."

Averting her eyes, she blushed. "Sorry."

"Ah, cher. Don't be sorry," he took her hand and pulled her under the spray. The warmth of the water was soothing, but she couldn't relax. After all, she was naked in the shower with a handsome virile man. Actually she didn't know what to do with her hands, so she put them behind her. What she wanted to do was run them over his body. He had a light furring of hair on his chest and when it became damp from the spray, she had an incredible urge to lick the droplets from his skin. She waited. tense with excitement, to see what he would do. Her body was reacting to his nearness. Harley could feel her nipples harden. Being here with him like this was almost more than she could comprehend. Instead of using a washcloth, he squeezed soap in his hands and rubbed them together. They gazed at one another. He smiled. A heart-stopping smile. That dimple that she loved so well was right there in front of her and she couldn't resist standing on tiptoe and kissing it. "Are you trying to kill me, girl?" Gently but surely, he pushed her back against the shower wall and kissed her with pent-up passion. As he ate at her mouth, he soaped her body, he hands moving feverishly over her flesh.

Harley wanted in on the act. She didn't have any soap, but she began touching his body. "This is so unreal," she mused as he bit at the side of her neck. Beau didn't just kiss; he put his whole body into it. And Harley was turned on, she felt like she was truly alive for the first time in her life. As he sucked at her lips, he took her nipples and began massaging them until she couldn't be still.

"Want more?" he asked harshly.

"Yes," she moaned. All thought fled, there was only sensation. Harley was stunned when he went to his knees at her feet.

"Here, let me," he picked up one of her legs and put it over his shoulder and steadied her until she got the other one in place My God! While she leaned back against the wall, he had his head buried in her pussy. And what he was doing to her! Nothing in her life had ever prepared her for what she was feeling. His mouth was very talented. Beau licked her vagina from stem to stern, delving his tongue deep into her channel and chewing on her nether lips until Harley was mindless with pleasure.

"God Beau, I don't think I will survive this," she panted. Beau smiled around her clit. She tasted like pure happiness to him. Lord, he was lovin' on his baby. Could it get any better than this? Oh yeah! His cock reminded him, it could get better. She was holding his head in her hands and rubbing his scalp, tangling her fingers in his hair. Steady, LeBlanc – don't embarrass yourself twice in one day.

"Oh baby, don't stop, don't stop, don't ever stop! I'm cumming again," she wailed and pushed forward so hard into his face that he had to brace himself. Sweet Jesus! Harley exploded and when she did, she spurted her cream all over his face. Supreme satisfaction flooded Beau. It was going to be all right. Everything would be all right.

* * *

They were having their first argument. "I cannot believe you did that! Have you lost your mind?" She stood with her hands on her hips, her breasts heaving and her eyes flashing pure Hispanic fire. "What if that was something important? I do run a business, you know."

Beau stood his ground, and Lord he covered the ground he stood on. He didn't look mad. Actually, he looked tolerant and a tad amused. "Little darling, you asked me to answer your phone. So, I did. I didn't even get a chance to say hello before this male voice came on the line and called you 'Harley Baby'. It damn sure didn't sound like business to me. So, I hung up on him."

"That was Waco. He works for me. Sometimes, he calls me stuff like that." It was rare, but since their conversation after the Port Arthur incident, he had taken to speaking to her with terms of endearment.

"You are my baby, no one else's. Amarillo's lucky that I didn't do more than hang up on him."

"Waco's his name, not Amarillo." Her mad was dissipating and quickly turning into something else entirely.

"I knew it wasn't Socorro business, you said that only comes through on your red cell phone."

She had to smile. "You listened to me."

"I hear every word you say."

"Waco knows about you. I told him the score the day I went to Port Arthur."

Now, he didn't even try to hide his grin. "I'll call him back and apologize, if you'll tell me what the score is."

They stood outside the door of the cabin, having returned from shopping and eating supper in Jefferson, Texas. Chicken and dumplings at The Bakery Restaurant and two new pair of shoes from a downtown boutique had made both of them happy. On the way back, she had been hanging over the back seat, digging in the shoe bag, when her phone rang. Little did she know that he couldn't be trusted to take a simple message. "You know the score," she blushed. "I'm not interested in another man, only you. But if you act like that every time somebody says something to me, we're going to have trouble."

Beau was tickled pink. She was actually tapping one of her little feet and if he wasn't mistaken, her nipples were hard. Time to test the waters. "What kind of trouble are we going to have?"

A tiny laugh escaped, "Big trouble."

"Are you as turned on as I am?"

"Maybe more."

He managed to get the door open after unsuccessfully poking the card in three times. "Having trouble poking it in the hole, Beau?" she teased him with a snort.

"Watch it, Sassy-pants," he grumbled. "You've got my dick all excited and I've lost my eye-hand coordination. No blood in my brain." He stepped aside to let her in and slapped her playfully on the butt as she went past. She walked across the room and put her purchases on the couch. "Are we gonna have make up . . ." he was about to say 'sex' when she started slinking across toward him with a wiggle in her walk that almost brought him to his knees. Lord

Have Mercy!

"We've got on way too many clothes, Beau-ray." She unbuttoned her shirt and threw it off, revealing a little black stretch tube-top that didn't do squat to cover her ample breasts. Her beautiful caramel colored skin looked like the sweetest candy to him and he wanted to consume her. Literally, consume her. His gaze ventured down, down and he thought leather and studs had never looked so good. She wore a black belt, almost biker looking that held up her fashionably well-worn blue jeans. "I was getting a little warm. Now, for you." She sauntered, yes sauntered to him with a saucy little swing in her hips. "May I help you off with your shirt?"

Shit! "Help yourself, doll-face," he probably should ask her if she was sure about all of this but dammit, he didn't want her to stop. Slowly, she unbuttoned his shirt. The look she was giving him was pure eroticism. That pink tongue kept dancing on her lips and her fingers were shaking. Sliding it off his shoulders, he stood stock still, waiting to see what her next move would be. Ye gods! She placed both palms on his chest and rubbed.

"Ay Dios Mio," she murmured reverently. "You are one beautiful man."

Easing him backwards against the wall, Harley came on to him. She began to kiss and lick his chest, tickling his nipples with her tongue, tracing his ripped muscles, licking a path downward as she sank to her knees. There she palmed his rampaging erection as she nipped and lapped at his flat, rippled abs.

Beau didn't know what to do, except enjoy. He cupped the side of her face with one hand and held his own hair off his face so he could clearly see every moved she made. Was she about to do what he had been dreaming of? "God, don't tease me hot-stuff, be merciful."

Harley didn't let up, she wasn't teasing. "Let me,

please?" Planting open mouth kisses all over his stomach and chest, she began to unbuckle his belt.

Easing down his zipper, she looked up to find him staring at her intently. "Make yourself at home. My cock is your cock."

"Good to know," she clasped his pants on either side of his crotch and tugged them down. "You are well endowed, Mr. LeBlanc. And very, very hard."

"Baby, I've been walking around with my Harley-bone on for over a week. It's petrified by now."

"What?" she couldn't help but laugh. "I was in the Navy and never heard that phrase before." This was Beau, she could play with him. She could trust him, because she knew he would never, ever hurt her. And right now, he was standing in front of her, hotter than Michelangelo's David ever thought about being. Peeling down his shorts, she jumped a little bit as his cock jutted toward her.

"It's okay, baby. He's in love with you, that's all." Harley could feel a rush of wetness in her panties when he said those words. No one had said words of love to her…ever. Wanting him to know how touched she was, she nuzzled her face against his thigh before moving over to rub her cheek against the hot, smooth shaft. She heard Beau catch his breath as if waiting, so she didn't make him wait long. Taking the tip of his cock between her lips, she licked around the head. "Damn!"

Harley pulled back, "Was that a good damn or a bad damn?"

"Good," he whispered through clenched teeth. "I want you to do that - again - repeatedly." Granting his request, Harley began to suck on the head. And Beau wasn't quiet. He talked to her in low, dulcet tones, but she couldn't understand a word he said. He was speaking French, or the Acadian equivalent. And it was music to her ears. She considered stopping and begging him to take her, to push her back and take her. Fuck her on the floor. At that instant, it seemed like she wanted the full weight of his body pressing her down. But, she couldn't ask. She was afraid that her old enemy, panic would make itself known and she didn't want to spoil the magic of this moment.

"Merci beaucoup, bebe. Mon Dieu, amore, tres bien!" That much she understood. He liked what she was doing. Very much. Wrapping her hand around the base of his rod, she began to stroke slowly. Lord, she hoped she remembered what to do. After all, she had watched porn a little bit. Never one to indulge in fantasies, she had very little to go on other than pure instinct and a desire to please. And Lord in heaven, did she want to please him. Harley took her time, relishing his reaction as he pumped his hips gently filling her mouth over and over. Pulling back to take a much needed breath, she heard him hiss as if he was afraid she was quitting.

"I'm coming back, I just want to explore." There was a lot of territory to cover, and she didn't want to miss an inch. Once more, she slid her tongue around the head before licking a path down his shaft. "Am I making you feel good?" In answer, he grunted and pulsed in her hand. "I'll take that as a yes." Harley was surprised, she loved this and it made her feel so fulfilled. For the first time she was giving pleasure to a man. Her man. Licking the veins that ran up his cock, she noticed that she could feel his heart beating beneath her tongue. Her heart swelled and her pussy throbbed. This was incredible, something she would never, ever forget.

"I need more, baby. Suck it, please?" Drawing a bit closer, Harley sought to give him what he needed. With a final swirl of her tongue around the large purple head, she finally slipped her lips over and down. "Fuck!" he exclaimed as she took him deeper. When the tip touched the back of her throat, Harley had to fight the gag reflex, but she did. Concentration had helped her through a lot less pleasurable tasks than this.

"So good, baby. You are so good." This might be her first time, but Beau wouldn't have changed one thing. As she worked on him so sweetly, he tangled his fingers in her hair and made sure she knew he was loving everything she did for him. A feeling of urgency was building in his balls and he needed to move, just a little bit. "I can't be still, Harley."

Gladly, she let him take control and loved it. He moved his cock in and out of her mouth, while she licked and sucked all along his considerable length. To her amazement, Harley discovered she was a giver. All she could think of was gifting him with as much pleasure as possible. Almost instinctively, she began to pump his cock as he slid in an out of her mouth.

"Oh, yes. Baby, I'm gonna love you all night long," he promised. Fire swept through his veins, creating a primal rhythm. Beau wanted to fuck. He felt himself grow longer and thicker. Days of starving for her touch had made him voracious. "Touch me, sweetheart."

Touch him? Well, she did have two hands. Keeping a hold of his cock, she zeroed in on the area that drew her like a moth to a flame. His balls. Tentatively, she took them in her palm. Oh, they felt nice. So hard and smooth, so male. Caressing them, she almost forgot to keep up the rest of the process. Pumping, sucking, fondling, and feeling. Harley was so aroused, she was almost…beyond…thinking.

"Baby, I'm gonna have to cum, soon. This is so damn good; I can't hold it back much longer." He expected her to pull away, but she didn't. She moved closer, increasing the motion of her hands and mouth. upping the intensity. "Fuck, he said. "Lord, you know just what to do. Baby, if you don't move, I'm gonna cum in your mouth."

Shaking her head 'no', she took him deeper. Sliding her mouth up and down his cock, she bobbed her head in time with the pounding of his heart. Helplessly, his body began to buck. Shit! "Hell, yes," he groaned. "Nothing…nothing is as good as this."

Harley was on the verge of cumming herself. A trickle of passion was gliding down her thighs and her sex felt swollen and needy. There was nothing in the world she wanted more than Beau. She wanted to rub on something, she wanted to grab his hand and put it between her legs. Or beg him to kiss her there, again…or fuck her there.

"Yes!" he groaned. "Fuck, baby! Don't stop! Just like that. Suck me hard!" His words made her nipples hard and Harley wanted to be filled, she wanted to be stretched. She wanted his cum to shoot deep inside of her. The heat of her thoughts only made what she was doing better. Putting every ounce of passion she had in her loving of Beau, he jerked and bellowed, filling her mouth with his seed. She wasn't turned off by it, but swallowing it was difficult. It was just so new. But she did and the taste wasn't unpleasant. It was Beau. "Cher, cher…I am blown away," he sighed above her.

Harley knew the feeling. She didn't want to let him go. Rising up on her knees, she hugged him tight, pressing her face against him. "I love you, Beau-ray." She couldn't have held back that declaration if her life had depended on it.

Leaning back against the wall, he cradled her head in his hands, letting his heart pound and the aftershocks of passion spark through his body. "God, I love you, too. That was the sweetest gift you just gave me. Thank you."

"I like gifts, too," she nipped him right by his belly button. "You can take me on that boat ride now, how's that?"

Drawing her to her feet, he kissed her softly – reverently. "A small price to pay for rapture, baby. Just wait till tonight; you're gonna think it's Christmas. I can't wait to give you a great big gift. Me."

* * *

There are certain things in life that you should see before you die and Caddo Lake by water was one of them. Harley felt transported back in time. Truly, it was one of the most beautiful and peaceful places she'd ever had the fortune to visit. The picturesque haven was the kind of place you see in tourist pamphlets but aren't really sure they actually exist. Beautiful swamps, tall cypress tress dripping with Spanish moss and an almost magical atmosphere. And the fact that they filmed part of her favorite show, True Blood, in the area, sure didn't hurt.

The Graceful Ghost was a steam-driven paddleboat that ran on burning wood in the boiler, which ran steam pistons to drive a single rear-mounted paddle. There was no one on the boat but the two of them and the Captain, and he was holed up in the front and they had the whole deck to themselves. "Is the water deep?" she asked, shivering a bit.

Beau held her cradled to him, loving the feel of her warmth and her nearness. "No, it's only about eight to ten feet, unless you go down one of the bayous, and there it gets as deep as twenty-seven feet." A white heron flew over them, almost like a phantom passing in the night. He loved that she leaned back into him, seeking more of his protection.

"I love it out here," she turned to give him a kiss. "Thanks for bringing me, and I'm sorry I got miffed at you earlier, I have nothing to hide from you. Waco is just my friend."

"You are welcome. And it's all right, if your getting miffed leads to that kind of erotic romp, I have no complaints." He wrapped his arms around her, tighter, pulling her closer. "I have something to ask you."

"What?"

"Do you want to have another session with the therapist before we make love, or are you ready to place yourself in my care?"

She said something, and he had to bend his head closer to hear, but it was worth it. "We will make love, I believe that. But, I would like a bit more time. Isn't there anything else we could do? I've loved everything we've done so far. Can we play some more tonight?"

"We can play as much as you want to." Beau was tempted to have the boat turn around or swim for shore. But some things were worth waiting for.

* * *

"Are you going to jack-off or just lay there and ache?" They had returned to the cabin, but something was wrong. Harley had waited for Beau to make a move, but he hadn't. Her imagination was beginning to run away with her. Doubts and uncertainties tended to flare up in her mind like leftover coals at a campfire site. If left to smolder, they could become a raging forest fire of insecurity.

At her risqué words, he pushed her back, flipped on the bedside lamp and stared at her. Honestly, he wanted her so bad he ached. That's why he hadn't made a move after they returned from the boat ride. His control was just hanging by a thread, and he didn't want to scare her. So, he had decided to do nothing. Just sleep.

But lying beside her in this bed, feeling her warmth, smelling her scent, feeling her edging nearer to him, was almost unbearable. And then the little doll surprised the hell out of him. Again. "What did you say?"

For a moment she thought he was angry. Until he laughed.

"I can't believe those words came out of your mouth."

A little bit of devilment came to mind. "Why not? I was in the Navy, after all. One cannot be in the Navy and not see and hear anything and everything about sex. Just because I managed to avoid it for myself, mostly, does not mean I was oblivious. I even caught a couple of men masturbating in the head." Rising up on one elbow, she let her eyes rove over the sheer male magnificence before her. Unable to resist, she reached out and laid a palm on his chest and rubbed a circle, drawing a groan from Beau like water from a well. "Could I watch you?"

"Shit!" Beau let the curse word slip. "You do realize you're making it almost impossible to keep my good intentions intact." Even as he protested, he was uncovering the Washington monument.

"Oh, Lord," Harley breathed. "You look ready to burst." She leaned just a bit closer and fit her palm around it and slid her hand slowly to the crest. Beau visibly shuddered. She removed her hand and watched him with hungry eyes.

"Jesus, give me strength!" he prayed. "Harley, baby soon, I'm going to do everything to you that either one of us can dream up." Taking her pillow, he slung it down toward the foot. "Lay down there and watch me watching you." She followed his direction and reversed her place on the bed, lying facing him. Almost in a 69 type position.

From where she was sitting she had the most interesting view. Peering closer, she studied his strong legs, his massive thighs and best of all, she could see his balls. "God, you're hung, Beau."

"Would you stop?" he growled, choking back a laugh. Really, he couldn't have stopped if he wanted, to. His cock was engorged, his balls were tight and he wanted to rut like a horny stag.

Like a magnet, his hand connected with his hungry cock. "You look like a damn siren laying down there baby." Slowly, he began to pump his aching dick. Yet, he never took his eyes off of her. And when she licked her lips and groaned a little moan, he felt like his blood was on fire. "Look at your pretty titties. Do you know how much I loved sucking them?"

"You did?" Could she do this? Did she dare? Hell, yeah- she was brave. She diffused bombs for a living! "It felt good to me, too. My nipples are hard right now, can you tell?" She rolled over on her side, so she could see him fisting his cock.

Fuck! Beau's hips bucked in time to his heartbeat. "Your nipples are like hard candy – the sweetest I've ever sucked." She was a temptress! If she ever got her footing in bed, Harley would be a damn hellcat! "God Harley, I'm gonna love making love with you." He was about to close his eyes and relish the moment when he saw her hands move. Shit!

Harley was excited, seeing Beau masturbate was making her so needy. Harley wanted. She wanted to be touched, so she touched. Cupping her own breasts she began to weigh them, lift them, knead them. "God, this is good." And her nipples…oh, they needed to be touched and pinched and pulled and rubbed. "Hmmmmm, I love how this feels." The very air was charged with excitement. Being here with Beau like this was intoxicating. He was pumping his cock. Hard. Harder than she would have ever dreamed a man would tug at himself. And she could feel the rhythmic jerks and pulls right between her legs. Their eyes devoured one another. Harley could feel moisture between her legs and she felt swollen and desperate. "I need. . . . ." she whimpered. Turning loose of one breast, she zeroed in on the part of her that was screaming for release.

"Holy Mother of God!" Beau breathed as he watched Harley touch herself. With one hand she massaged her tit and with the other she began to feverishly rub her pussy. "Easy baby, that's my pussy you're petting down there. Stroke it sweet, rub it gently." Damn, this was the hottest thing he'd ever seen. There was no way he could be still. Not a snowball's chance in hell. Going to his knees, he rose up in the bed – still working his cock. "God, just look at you. You are damn perfection. That is the sweetest pussy I've ever seen. "If I don't get my hands on you soon I'll go crazy." Lying down beside of her, he pushed her hand out of the way and replaced it with his. "Okay, baby?"

"Anything, just please make me cum," she begged. So, Beau did. He lusciously rubbed her vulva, sucked on her breasts and humped his cock on the side of her hip till he spilled out every drop he had. "Beau, oh baby!" she cried out as all the colors in the universe showered down on her.

He could not get enough of her. As his body moved against her, almost involuntarily, he kissed and smooched her arm and neck and upper chest. "You belong to me, Nada. Nobody else. We are going to have it all, baby. I'm going to give you a happy ever after... just wait and see."

* * *

It wasn't hard for Beau to pretend he didn't see the man. It was obvious the shitass thought he was staying out of sight. Wrong. He was used to spotting alligators in high grass, there was no way he missed the idiot in the camouflage jumpsuit smoking one of those thin cigars and chunking the butt off into the grass. Good thing it wasn't dry or the place would go up like a tinderbox. Beau started to go give the man a piece of his mind – but it wasn't worth it. All he could figure out was that he had intended to steal his truck or something in it. Tough. Not today. Today, he had more important fish to fry. Spending time with Harley was his top priority. When he pulled up at the front of their cabin she was out waiting for him. Lord, he was going to have to beat men off with a stick.

He would have gotten out to open the door for her, but she didn't wait. "I love it here. Can you believe that I saw a bald eagle fly over? I've never seen one that close before."

"We'll see lots of birds and other creatures down by the bayou." She looked happy and that was worth more than a million dollars to him. "When we get back home, I'll take you out into the Atchafalaya on my houseboat. You and Amos can sunbathe naked. Is it a date?"

"I wouldn't miss it!"

As they drove away, he pointed out a blue heron that took flight right over their vehicle. But all the while he was keeping an eye out for the man who had been watching their cabin so closely. Jerk. "I'll take you down to Avery Island. Have you ever been down there?"

"No, but I'd love to go. That's where they make the famous pepper sauce, isn't it?"

"Yes, but the real attraction on the island is the jungle gardens. You'd love it there. We could stroll through the grounds and hold hands." He captured her hand and kissed it.

"Beau, I'm hungry."

He almost bit his tongue.

She knew what he was thinking, because she smiled.

"Could you stop at a convenience store and let me get some cheese crackers?"

"Oh, you're hungry for food! You had me going there for a minute," he laughed. "Around you, I have sex on the brain." Turning onto the main highway, he pointed up ahead. "I can do better than cheese crackers. We're going to The Lodge to eat. I think you'll like it."

They rode in companionable silence until they came to a rustic building on the banks of Big Cypress Bayou. "They have the best catfish in the world," Beau announced as he parked under the shade of a big spreading oak.

As the waitress seated them, Beau pulled her chair closer to his. "I need you close," he announced unashamedly.

She patted his shoulder, as if telling him she was in perfect agreement. Harley was fascinated by the view of the bayou. "I love to look at the water; it doesn't really matter to me if it's the ocean, a river or a lake. I stare at it hoping to see a creature emerge, I guess."

"You know they did film *The Legend of Boggy Creek* here, and like I told you earlier, there are many tales of sightings of a Big Foot type creature in this very area." He leaned forward, "Maybe we'll see something like that when we go for a walk later tonight." Much to his surprise, she didn't flinch this time; she leaned forward and stole a kiss, thereby stealing what was left of his heart.

"As long as you are with me, holding me tight, I don't care what we see. I know you'll protect me. My faith and trust in you is absolute." After what they'd shared earlier, she had no qualms about giving him everything else. "When we go home, could I spend the night with you on your houseboat sometime?"

"Absolutely." He was just about to pin down a time so she wouldn't back out, when the waitress came to take their order. Harley chose the catfish and as Beau decided on his sides, Harley studied the crowd. She loved to people watch. A family with two young children sat to their right, the baby had a mop of curly black hair and not a tooth in his head and she felt an uncharacteristic yearning for one of her own. The little boy let out a squeal and threw his napkin in the air. She watched as a passing man bent over to retrieve it and as he raised up, he grinned at her. Harley froze. She was looking at the face of a dead man. Surely her eyes were playing tricks. Instantly, she grabbed for Beau's hand. Calmly, the man who so closely resembled

Fox Crocker walked out of the restaurant. Harley got up to follow him. She had to be sure. Throwing down her napkin, she took off.

"What the hell?" Beau was right behind her. "Harley? What's wrong?"

She had sprinted across the hard wood floors and through the heavy double door. But by the time she had made it out on the porch; he was nowhere in sight. Glancing around, she didn't see him. Her heart was hammering in her chest. Unwilling to give up, she took off into the parking lot, weaving her way through the cars and pickups. She even stooped and looked under vehicles. What would she do if she found him? Well, her planning didn't go quite that far. A hand touched her shoulder and immediately Harley went into defense mode. She was just about to use her elbow and her weight to throw her attacker when he said one word.

"Baby."

Harley went limp. "Beau."

"What are you doing? What's wrong?"

"Just a minute, I've got to keep looking." She pulled from his hold and headed around the restaurant to the water's edge. A boat motor in the distance answered her question for her. If it was Fox, he was long gone. She heard Beau's footfalls behind her. "He must have gone around the back. I lost him, he got away."

"Stop, Harley." He grasped her arms, turning her to face him. "What's going on? Who are you chasing after?"

"I don't know," she pushed her hair off her forehead. Beau could see she was upset. "It looked like Fox Crocker, the man who raped me."

He put an arm around her and pulled her to his side, putting himself between the waterfront and her. "Where did you see him?"

"In the restaurant, he was standing by the table closest

to the door." She shuddered in his arms, and he kissed the top of her head. "Do you think I'm imagining things?"

"What was he wearing?" Beau had an uneasy feeling.

"Camouflage coveralls, you know – those one piece jumpsuits."

Damn. It was the same man. "Let's go in and eat, sweetheart. We'll talk about it and see what we can come up with." He didn't like it; he didn't like it at all. They returned to their table and Beau held out her chair. "Did the man make eye contact with you?"

Harley took a long sip of tea, trying to settle her nerves. What was wrong with her? She was turning into a girl! "Oh yeah…he sneered at me. It took me a second or two to process who it was, or who I think it was."

"Eat, then we're getting out of here. We'll come back another time. I'm not risking taking you out in the open with some nut following you around. We're going back to my stomping ground, so I can protect you."

"You can't stay with me all the time, you have things to do," Harley protested.

"Watch me." Beau was dead serious. "I have no trouble setting priorities in my life and you are #1, nothing else even comes close."

Harley fell silent. She had never known such concern for her well-being before.

"Look at me, Nada." She did. "I love you. You realize that, don't you?"

"I'm beginning to." Feelings of joy warred with a sense of dread. She was responsible for Beau's happiness. He was her hostage to fortune, and that scared her to death.

Chapter Eight

"You can take care of the office for a few days, Dandi. Just have Indiana bring me those specifications so I can take a look at them. Yes, the ones for the Ferret Scout vehicle. I'm working on a plan to add some riot control equipment. The New Orleans Police Department has contacted me about converting a fleet of them for their SWAT team."

Her rug would never be the same; Beau was pacing a hole in it. He would walk to the window and look out and then march to the door and look through the glass. Harley had plans to take some precautions also. She had looked up a number for a security company; they were coming out in several days to give her an estimate on an alarm system.

"Sounds good, and tell Rick that I want to see him, too." Beau snorted at something Dandi said. "Yes, I'm staying with Harley and if I have to leave for some reason, I want Rick to be available to take care of her till I can get back."

Harley glared at him and he smiled the sweetest, sexiest smile, it made her knees go weak. How could she get mad at him? It was impossible. As he was taking care of business, she retrieved Dr. Wagner's number and gave him a call. Her original appointment was scheduled for tomorrow, so the likelihood of getting in to see him today was small. But she was anxious to make love to Beau – so she was prepared to beg.

"Good morning? Dr. Wagner's office. How may I help you?" The receptionist syrupy drawl made Harley smile.

"This is Harley Montoya and I would like to see if I could move my appointment up to today. I was scheduled to come in tomorrow."

"Hold on a moment, please." After a few moments, the receptionist returned and Harley was told to be there in an hour.

Looking out the kitchen window, she was surprised to see a movement in the bushes down beside the bayou. Her property was fenced and no one should have been on the place except her and Beau. She stood on tiptoe and looked again. This time she saw no one. Maybe her imagination was working overtime. Or perhaps it was just an animal.

"Did you get ahold of the doc?" Beau came up behind her and enclosed her in a bear hug.

"Yeah, I get to go in an hour." Should she tell Beau what she saw?

"I'll drive you. There's a man I need to meet in Lafayette, he has a cannon he wants to sell me. It won't take but a minute; I could catch him before our appointment if we leave now."

So, she wouldn't tell him. Not now anyway. "Okay," she knew better than to argue about them going together. He had made it pretty clear that he didn't want her to be alone. "But I don't want you to talk to Dr. Wagner this time. I want to do it by myself. Okay?"

"Why?" Beau nudged her around, so they were facing one another. He looked confused.

"Just let me handle it this time, you know all of this is embarrassing to me. And now that we've done intimate things, the idea of the two of you talking about me makes me extremely uncomfortable." Maybe, she wasn't being reasonable, but it was how she felt.

Beau took a deep breath, knowing what he had to say wouldn't go over very well. "I guess I should tell you that the Doc and I have talked on the phone a few times. I'd rather you hear that news from me, rather than him."

Humiliation flashed over Harley, making her redden with unease. "You've been talking to the doctor about what we're doing in bed?" She placed her hands over her cheeks, trying to imagine what their conversations had been like. "Did he tell you what to do? Has any of this been real at all? Did you tell him I masturbated in front of you? Or that I begged you . . ." she couldn't go on.

He took her by the shoulders, not roughly, but he had a good grip on her. "You know better than that, Nada! I gave him the barest of explanations. He's a doctor. A sex therapist, helping us is his job." When she lowered her head, unable to look at him, he cupped her cheek rubbing a thumb across the dampness under one eye. "You know I would give my life for you. For you to be healed and able to accept me in your bed is my greatest desire. Embarrassing you or laughing at you is the farthest thing from my mind. The only reason I spoke to him at all was so I wouldn't make any stupid mistakes. I didn't want to rush you or do anything that would harm you. We were just trying to make sure that I did what was right for you."

"And what is right for me?" Through tears, she looked into his eyes. This was Beau, she had to remember that. He would never hurt her. Would he?

"What is right is that you feel safe and loved. Have I done that so far?"

"Yes you have," she couldn't lie about that.

"So why don't you want me to speak with the doctor this time?"

"It's difficult for me to explain." Harley needed to voice her doubts and fears to the doctor and she didn't want what she had to say to get back to Beau, in any way, shape or form.

"Very well," he conceded. Beau didn't like it, but he wasn't going to push her.

* * *

"So tell me…how was your trip?" Dane was leaning

back in his chair, with his feet on his desk looking entirely too relaxed and smug to suit Harley.

"I presume you already know. I understand you have been talking about me with Beau."

He wasn't fazed by her accusative tone. "That's right; Beau was determined to not make a mistake with you. He talked to me so I could advise him, that's all. There was no details or male locker room talk. I can assure you of that."

"I'm still not sure how I feel about that."

The doctor pressed on. "So what have you been doing? How do you feel about your progress so far?"

Harley blushed. This was going to be impossible. "I think we've made some headway. We've slept in the same bed and kissed and touched." That was enough detail. Wasn't it?

"Have you had intercourse yet? Full vaginal penetration?"

Ye gods! Apparently not. She covered her face. "No, not yet."

"So you tell me, in your own words. Are you satisfied with where you are or do you want to go farther?"

"Like I said, we have kissed and touched . . ." she stopped.

"Is that all?"

The man was sadistic. Harley gritted her teeth and answered. "Well, the kissing and touching did lead to lower kissing and touching." For heaven's sake! She was a grown woman. Why was this so hard?

"So you participated in oral sex? Cunnilingus or fellatio?"

"Yes, both," she croaked.

"Do you want to make love with him?" Dane's voice softened.

"Yes, but I'm afraid," Harley could only whisper the sentence.

Dane came around his desk to sit on the edge of it, right in front of her. "I don't think you have anything to fear. If you have already been intimate to that extent, full penetration should be achievable. Explain your reservations to me. Are you afraid of the pain?"

Taking a deep breath, Harley pressed on. "Maybe, a little bit. Penetration, full penetration, I'm afraid it will remind me of the rapes."

"Beau knows to be gentle with you. He wants to help you more than anything. So are you afraid of the panic attacks? Not being able to go through with it to climax?"

God, the man was clinical. "No, I'm afraid he will leave."

For the first time, Dr. Wagner looked confused. "Leave? What are you talking about?"

"At first, I didn't realize how men felt about, you know…how turned off they are about touching someone who's been raped. And once I understood that, I knew not to expect . . ."

An understanding came into to the doctor's eyes. He was always amazed at how rape could warp reality for people. Frankly, this was one of the most amazing looking women he had ever laid eyes on. She was totally hot, and didn't have clue one that every man she met found her absolutely stunning. Rape was a hideous crime, but what it had done to this woman's self-confidence was barbaric. "Harley, what you are feeling is normal. Many women feel changed after a rape. Somehow, you get the idea that is strips you of your sex appeal and your worth…" She didn't let him finish.

"I tried to date a few times, but it didn't work out. A couple of men flatly stated that they couldn't stand the thought of touching me, much less having sex with me."

"Some men do feel that way, and they need therapy as much as the victim does. However, their feelings of rejection are no more correct than your feelings of insecurity."

Tears were beginning to come into her eyes. Dane's explanation was heartening, but it wasn't his opinion that mattered. "So, can you guarantee that Beau won't act like that? Can you give me assurance that one day Beau won't realize he's making love to a tainted woman?"

"No, I can't. But, if I were a betting man, I'd put every dime I had on Beau LeBlanc. That man cares more about you than he does himself. If you are attracted to him, if you want to be a woman with him, my recommendation is that you go home and enjoy one another. You deserve to know the joys that intimacy can bring into your life and I see no reason that can't happen between you and Beau."

* * *

He had waited for her. It had been an eternity. When she had emerged from the doctor's office, she had been subdued. Beau felt it wise not to push. But, he couldn't help but ask. "Are you okay, baby?"

"Yes, I'm fine. Can we go home now?" They made the trip in relative silence. The only breaks came when he told her about the cannon and the work he was doing on the Ferret. Since leaving Uncertain, he was uncertain. What if she decided that she couldn't be intimate with him? Her mood was hard to read. It had been a long day. What with the turmoil and the long drive, he hadn't even unloaded their luggage from the trip. Now, all he wanted to do was get her in bed and in his arms. If anything else happened, he'd be ecstatic, but having her close was essential to his existence. They were pulling into the driveway, when he had an idea. "Why don't we run back into town and get a pizza and just come back home and crash. It's been an emotional time, what with that idiot Crocker and your visit to the…"

Her unexpected statement stopped his thought in midsentence. "I want to try and make love to you."

Beau was out of the truck and getting luggage faster than a wink. He had them on the porch and through the door...looked around and realized he had left behind the most important ingredient. Harley. "Hell!" She was almost out of the truck when he reached her. He went back after her, opened the door and kissed her. "You've got me so turned on. I don't know whether I'm coming or going." Picking her up, he pushed the truck door closed with his hip and carried her into Willowbend.

She tried to calm down, but her heart was fluttering like a hummingbird's wings. She couldn't help it; she was excited, yet apprehensive. This was such a big step for her, and she prayed she didn't do something to screw it up. "I don't want to disappoint you," she mumbled as she rested her head on his shoulder.

Beau climbed the stairs and set her down to open the bedroom door. "Okay, before we go in, let's get one thing straight." He framed her face and looked deep into her eyes. She felt small and fragile next to his wide, hard body. "There is no way under heaven you could ever disappoint me. This isn't a performance, and it's not a game. This is me and you getting a second chance at forever."

"I'm nervous," she confessed as they stepped into her bedroom. No matter what happened, she would never forget how Beau looked standing in her private space. Never had she expected to share her life or body with a man.

"If it helps, I am too." The bed was big. Good. He needed room to work. Sitting her down, he began to undress. She began to pull at her clothes, too, but he stopped her. "No, let me do that. I want to touch you while I peel away the layers. I've dreamed of doing that. I want to fulfill that dream." Her hands stilled and she just watched him as he disrobed.

Gone were the images of Pell and Crocker. Standing before her was male perfection. Big biceps, powerful shoulders, sculpted pecs and defined abs that proved the term six-pack to be woefully inadequate. His upper body was a powerful wedge that drew her eyes downward to the evidence that he really and truly desired her. "I'm on the pill, please don't wear a condom. I want to feel you and know it's you." She didn't say so, but the other two had worn rubbers and that was one of the sensations that had stuck with her. The uncomfortable drag of alien plastic over her dry tissues. Oh, she had been grateful they had worn a condom; it had been the one thing that had kept her sane. There had been a barrier, a thin one between their perversion and her body. Plus a baby or an unwanted venereal disease would only have compounded her nightmare.

As he pulled the last of his clothes off and tossed them aside, he took his cock in hand and ran his palm up and down the length of it. "Baby, I have never not worn a rubber with a woman."

"Oh, okay," she replied and looked away quickly. His adamancy was unmistakable. "I don't blame you, after all I've been . . ."

"Until you. I want nothing between me and you...ever." Placing one knee on the thick comforter, he pushed her shirt off her shoulders. "I love you in this camisole – it's sexy as hell. Hold up your arms."

"Thanks," she said as the tight garment skimmed over her head muffling her words. "It unhooks in the back, you know."

Beau chuckled, his dimples flashing. "Yeah, but this way is more fun and quick . . . damn! No bra." He pushed her back and straddled her. "Tell me...stop me. Let me know anytime or anyway, if I make you nervous. I know

I'm big, and I want you so much. Harley, I'm an alpha male and right now, every instinct in my body is screaming out to possess you. Do you want me?"

"Yes," no doubt about that. She lifted her hips as he worked her pants down and off.

"I've never wanted anybody before, only you."

He stopped and just looked at her, raking his eyes from top to bottom, then closed his eyes as if in prayer. "You've got a body that will make a man drop to his knees, Nada."

Harley could see he was visibly shaking.

"I will be gentle, I promise. But I want this to be good for you, and I'm scared to death, baby. I don't want to do anything you aren't ready for me to do."

He waited and she held out her hand. "Love me, that's all I ask."

"Done."

This would be her first time…the first time that counted. Her body wanted to respond, but an icy uneasiness was tingling down her spine. Harley bit her lip, determined to be the kind of woman Beau would enjoy having sex with. She didn't know what to expect, but when he laid down and pulled her on top of him, her back to his front, that wasn't it. Kissing her neck, he wrapped his arms around her waist and held her tight. "You feel good in my arms." At that simple declaration, she let out the breath she held, letting her whole body relax on his. Here, she was completely and utterly safe.

"I do?"

Her husky voice did wild things to his libido. "Lord, yes. You do." He took a handful of her hair and tipped her head back. "Kiss me." Helping her turn over on top of him, he fit their mouths together. Slanting his lips over hers, he kissed her hard. She shivered and he wondered if it were from arousal or nerves. A wild core of lust pushed him to bury his cock deep in her lush heat. In his fantasies, he had fucked her over and over until she was so full of his cum it would run down her thighs when they were through. It was a primal instinct. Beau wanted to place his brand on her so any man would know who she belonged to. Soon, he promised himself.

First, he had to prepare her, both physically and mentally. Harley's breasts pressed into his chest and the feel of her nipples hard against his flesh brought his cock to straining, hungry life. 'Patience, LeBlanc, patience', he cautioned himself. Seduction, a tender seduction; that was his plan. Her beautiful face was right in front of him, and he catalogued every feature. Ah, those lips. "I could kiss you for hours. Did you know that?"

"I like the sound of that."

She said the right words, but he could still hear a little trepidation in her voice. Determined to get past her inhibitions, Beau tickled her lips with his tongue. Gently he stroked their plump fullness with just the tip, teasing the corners of her mouth until she let out a little moan. Heartened by her response, he repeated the move at the other corner just because he loved the way she lifted herself up to him. Gratefully, he eased his tongue into the sweet heat of her mouth. They had kissed before. Hot passionate kisses, but this was different. They both knew where this was headed…all the way, baby…all the way. For a microsecond she did not respond, gradually she moved her tongue against his. He felt her body shift upward, her hands coming up to cling to his shoulders. 'Oh yeah, that's it baby. Let yourself go.' He would have spoken out loud, but he was just so busy with important things like kissing on his woman. Tilting his head, he moved a bit, giving them both a better angle. Hungrily, he deepened the kiss, cupping his hands under her ass and pulling her body tighter to his. To his amazement, she pushed back against him, making him groan as her thigh made contact with his aching dick. Hell, he longed to revel in her, luxuriate in her softness, immerse himself in her very being. "How?" he had to ask. "How do you want me? Missionary? From behind? You on top?"

Harley thought before she answered. "Not from behind, please. That's the only one that really scares me. And on top...I don't really know how." She sounded embarrassed.

"That's okay, baby. We've got all the time in the world to find out what we like together. For now, we'll just feel our way...how about that?" There was such a hungry yearning in her eyes.

"I'm sorry. I wish I was more experienced for you. I wish I wasn't broken." She smoothed his hair back from his face. The gesture was so sincere and gentle it made his heart ache.

"You hush, Harley. You are not broken. You are perfect. I don't want a woman with experience. Hell, I want you. Haven't I made myself clear?" Slowly, he eased out from under her, moving and adjusting their bodies until she was on bottom and he was on top. "Look at my cock, Harley. Look how hungry I am for you." Bearing his weight on his forearms, he fitted his cock into the cleft of her thighs. Now, she could feel his need. Precum leaked out onto her skin and Harley gasped. "Do you want me to continue?"

"Please," Harley wasn't about to back down now. She wanted this more than anything in the world.

Beau gently pushed against her thigh with his cock. It was turgid and throbbing, anxious to gain entrance to her pussy. "He wants you so much. You are so hot, sugar." Mon Dieu! He wanted to do this right. Despite the sexual assaults, she was so innocent and unaware of just how sexy and tempting she was. The contradiction was driving him crazy. He had to fight for control. At the same time, he wanted to take her hard. Fuck her raw till she couldn't walk and he also wanted to whisk her away to some safe place and protect her from everything. Even himself.

"I'm ready, Beau."

"Almost, there are parts of you that I haven't paid proper homage to yet, but I'm getting there." Easing down her body, he pushed her tits together and rubbed his face on their lushness. "God, I love your breasts. I'm going to spend a lifetime sucking these beauties." He smooched one nipple and licked and lapped at it like a hungry tomcat.

"Suck, Beau," she urged.

He didn't argue, but settled in for a feast. With swirls of his tongue he massaged one nipple, while he tweaked the other one between his fingers. Her little mewls of pleasure turned him on almost as much as the mouthful of woman flesh he was sucking on. When her hips started undulating, he knew she was almost to the point he needed her to be. Coming up for air, he praised her. "You have me totally at your mercy, Nada. I don't know whether to put you on a pedestal and worship you or tie you to my bed for eternity."

"Love me, that's all I ask."

"I already do, angel baby. I already do. Open your legs." She did, splaying herself open for him. As if drawn by her heat, the broad head of his cock slid in her slit and found it blessedly slick with cream. Beau groaned in relief. Holding himself up, he pumped his hips, letting his cock bathe in her juices. She raised her head, seeking his lips, so he kissed her again. Their tongues tangled as the flames rose higher between them. Unable to control it, he nudged her clit with rhythmic short jabs. His cock was courting her, riding her slit, begging for attention. She gave it to him. When she lifted her hips and spread her legs wider, he knew she was ready. So was he; beyond ready. "I'm aching for you."

"Let me feel," she slipped her hand between them and closed her fingers around the thick shaft. "I love the way you're made."

Beau froze as she played with him. He held himself up on his arms, muscles straining, letting her get comfortable with his size and shape. "I can't hold out much longer." Settling down on his side, he dipped his fingers into her pussy. "God, you are so ready for me. Honey, your little cunt is so wet and slippery."

"Take me, Beau."

Holy God, Beau had never been more ready for anything in his life. Raising up, he was thankful they were making love while it was still light. The room was bathed in the afternoon sun as it filtered through the curtain. Harley lay there like a centerfold, her hair spread out on the pillow, her beautiful tits quivering with passion and her legs spread wide open. She was the picture of feminine surrender, yet he knew she was braver than most men. The loveliest of contradictions. Taking his cock in hand, he fit it to the small, near virginal opening and pushed in.

Ye gods! Harley had never felt anything like it. This was nothing like she had expected. Since meeting Beau again, she had fantasized what it would be like. What she would feel…the exact sensations she would experience. Oh, it was good…mostly. Her flesh throbbed and she could feel her vagina stretching and burning as her body struggled to accept his claiming. Mainly it was good because it was Beau making love to her and it felt good to him too, that much she could tell. Their eyes locked and he groaned as he worked his way inside of her. He was so big and he was on top of her and he was holding her down. A tightness in her chest made in hard for Harley to breathe. 'O Lord, not now, not now, please not now' she couldn't do this to Beau.

Beau felt her whole body tighten up. God, it felt good.

She was pleasing him, perfectly. How did she know to do that? "Nada, nada…you are gonna make me lose control." Then, he looked at her face. Her eyes were glazed over and he realized she wasn't trying to make him feel good, her body was trying to expel him. She wasn't fighting him, thank God, but she wasn't enjoying it, either. Immediately, he enfolded himself down over her and stopped thrusting. "Breathe, baby, for me. It's Beau, look at me. It's Beau." Rubbing his thumb against her cheek, he peppered tiny kisses over her face. "I wouldn't hurt you for the world. You belong to me. No one will ever hurt you again. I won't let them. Trust me. You're my baby." The doctor had said to hold her close and work through things and by God that was what he was going to do. "It's just me Harley. It's Beau-ray."

Beau-ray. Slowly, the panic attack subsided. Beau was stroking her face and neck and saying tender, gentle phrases of love. Harley realized he was accepting her burdens and her fears as his own. She felt the weight of the world shift from her shoulders to his. Harley was not alone, anymore. The pain was gone and she was desperate to feel anything else. "I'm sorry."

"Don't you dare be sorry." Beau felt her body begin to relax. Shit, he should have pulled out – but he refused to give up the ground he had gained. His erection was not diminished, and he was still inside of her, but just barely. "I'm gonna make you feel so good. Is that okay?"

"Please." With shaking hands, she began to caress his beloved face and shoulders. "I see you, Beau. I know it's you." She canted her hips giving him permission to continue their lovemaking.

He kissed her neck as he slowly began to move, rocking his cock into her. "Feel us together, Harley. It's just me inside of you. Just relax and let me in a little more, sugar."

The tingling began to spread and pleasure overpowered pain and panic. She let herself be aware of what was happening. Beau was lovingly moving against her, his lips never leaving some part of her skin. She opened her legs wider to make it easier for him. But he wasn't pushing deeper, he was just letting his cock massage the rim of her channel.

"Oh, you are so precious, baby. So sweet. Your little pussy is so warm and tender."

Beau was loving on her. Petting her with words and touch. Harley felt her temperature begin to rise. Desire mounted within her and soon, she began to need more. Exultation filled her heart. "It feels good now." And it did. Her body and mind were working together and it seemed like she was on the verge of something momentous. Every molecule of her body was priming itself for a great discovery. "I'm wet, aren't I? Still?"

"Oh yeah," Beau breathed. She was welcoming him. He could feel her pussy flesh growing softer and more open. His Nada was relaxing for him and now he could show her how wonderful sex could actually be.

Harley was fascinated. Mesmerized. Above her, in all of his male glory, was a man that meant the world to her. And he was beautiful, sexy, kind, and he was worshiping her body. There was really no other word for it. With every gentle thrust of his hips, he was pushing inside of her a fraction more. And her body was accommodating him, and wanting more. It came as a great surprise, but she wanted to be possessed and pleasured by Beau.

"Let's try this from a different angle. I want to use my hands." He rose up and sat back on his heels, and she was afraid he was going to separate from her so she clamped down and tried to push up to take more of him in. "Steady, angel. I'm not going anywhere." He arranged her thighs over his, and this new position had her pussy right there in front of him. "Now, I can play."

Holding her in place with one hand on her upper thigh, he proceeded to pump into her until his large cock had stretched her and made itself at home. But there was a bonus, he took his fingers and began rubbing her clit over and over again. Swirls of ecstasy began to spiral in her vagina and radiate out and up making her nipples feel like they were connected to her clit by invisible wires. "Beau, my God!" she exclaimed.

Little whimpers of need came from her lips and this satisfied Beau almost as much as an orgasm could have.

Need. Want. God, she felt the urge to mate. "More!" she begged, a frenzied urge to move overcame her. She covered his hand with her own, pushing it down on her flesh, showing him that she wanted him to give her more…of everything. The other hand covered her own breast and she cupped it and squeezed it and above her Beau watched with hooded eyes.

"Oh, Harley…you are so damn hot. And tight…my God, girl. Your pussy was created for my cock. I need you so much, baby." She was his. He had no doubt about that, and he would tell her so, just as soon as he could think.

"I need you, too!" she almost shouted. Her body wanted to be filled like this again and again. Her heart needed filling too, and her life. Beau was the answer to all of her needs. For years she had been empty, just existing. Now, she knew what was missing. Him. Harley needed Beau to complete her life.

"You got me, baby."

He hiked her a little closer, and bent over and took both nipples between his thumbs and forefingers and rubbed. What a simple word - rubbed. There was nothing simple about the way he was making her feel. She was getting so close to orgasm that if she didn't make it there, the world might end. "Fuck me hard, Beau," she pleaded.

Beau laughed in celebration. "You want more, my baby? Let me get serious about this." Holding on to her he scooted back until he could stand up and then he lifted her bottom and pushed deeper until he was buried to the hilt. "You're going to need to hold on to something."

He was right. Harley held on to the bedspread as Beau hammered into her. Hard, fast, relentlessly. His grunts and growls of pleasure turned her inside out. It was all she could do to keep from panting. Pleasure was whipping through her and she couldn't be still. Her body jerked and she arched her back, pushing down on his cock and squeezing him for all she was worth. An orgasm tore through her that ripped her soul from the tethers of reality and slung her out into a vast sea of erotic delight. "Beau!" That was the only word that seemed to matter.

He never wanted this to end. Harley was coming apart before his eyes and the sight of her in the throes of ecstasy was unbelievable. It was too much. The pleasure was too much. He couldn't have held back if his life depended on it. Surging into her, he let himself go and his cum boiled out of him and filled her up, just like his dream. He shot his seed deep inside of her and it mixed with the essence of her arousal. The alpha part of him wanted to make a baby, right now. Anything that would tie this woman to him forever. He didn't want to spend another day apart from her. Pulsating aftershocks kept their pleasure going and Beau kept pushing his cock into her heat, loving the way her body kept grasping him as if she wanted to keep him inside of her for as long as possible.

Amazing. Harley opened her eyes and saw that Beau was gazing at her intently. "Thank you, I loved that. You have changed my life," she whispered.

"Oh baby, this is just the beginning," he pulled out and stretched next to her, pulling her close. "I'm gonna love being married to you."

* * *

Married. No, she hadn't missed that reference at all. She hadn't responded, but she hid it away in her heart to savor it over and over again. All night, she had held on to Beau and fantasized about being married to him.

As she stood in front of the bathroom mirror, Harley felt a little silly. She couldn't quit smiling. She...Harley Montoya...no, even better...Nada 'nothing' Montoya had had sex with a man...AND SHE HAD LIKED IT!! She had had an orgasm. An orgasm!!

"Harley, I'm waiting for Indy. He's on his way with some specs; I'll be down here if you need me." How wonderful it was to have him in her home. Harley was happier than she had ever been.

"Okay," she called. "I'm almost ready." She would have been dressed ten minutes ago if she could calm down and quit dancing around and hugging herself. Her whole world seemed like a brighter place. Fastening a small gold locket around her neck, she checked her make-up one more time. All she could think about was how much she loved Beau and how good it had felt to express that love. Exiting the bathroom, she took another look at the bed where her miracle had happened. With a squeal, she launched herself in the air and landed with a bounce right in the middle of the mattress. "You, Nada Montoya, are one lucky senorita!"

She lay there with arms and legs extended, just being happy and still. Screech! Harley almost levitated off the bed. There was no sound in the house like it; she had heard it a hundred times since she had been here. The vanity bench in front of her makeup mirror had just been scooted back. Only this time, she wasn't sitting in it. Scrambling off the bed, she hurried through the connecting door, completely unarmed. Taking the traditional Krav Maga fighting stance, she stood ready to engage . . . nothing. There was nothing there. Her heart was beating ninety to nothing. Every instinct she possessed had told her that Fox Crocker had been standing in here just waiting for her.

Breathlessly, she stared down at the bench. The bathroom floor was ceramic tile and every time she got up from putting on her make-up, she pushed that bench backwards and it always made the same dragging noise. Nothing else sounded like it. She stood there not really knowing what to do. Could she have imagined it? No, she didn't think so.

A creepy eerie feeling came over her. If it wasn't Fox, it could have been a ghost. Crap, she hadn't thought about that. Glancing in the mirror, she was grateful to see that nothing was hovering behind her. With a slight shiver, she whirled around to leave…and SCREECH! It moved again. For a moment, Harley just bounced in place. She didn't know whether to stay and investigate or turn and run. Turning and running won out. Big time.

She didn't fly, but she came close. "Gotcha!" Beau huffed as he literally caught her at the foot of the stairs. "Did you see a ghost?" he couldn't resist teasing her. Actually, he was grateful every time she gave him opportunity to hold her. He cuddled her close, "Aw, baby-love, your heart is hammering out of your chest. What happened?"

"I didn't see a ghost, but I heard one," she managed to croak out. "I'm glad you'll be sleeping with me tonight."

He rubbed her back, doing his best to calm her breathing. "Me, too." Then, he chuckled; he just couldn't hold it back. "I'm glad to be sleeping with you too, but for a whole different reason I bet."

"Don't laugh at me," she nipped him on the shoulder. "I'm looking forward to having sex with you, again – more than you can imagine. I loved it. But I'll also be glad to snuggle up against you in the dark."

He kissed her, full on the mouth. "I loved making love to you, too. Now, what happened, exactly?" They walked toward the kitchen.

She explained to him about the vanity bench and what a distinct noise it made and that it had happened twice, once when she had been standing right over it. Beau listened intently. "That's interesting. Let me get some tape and we'll put it under the legs and see if it moves again. Do you have some duct tape?"

"Yes, I do." A heavenly aroma surprised her. "What smells so good?"

"I hope you don't mind, I knew you were tired, so I had the meat market deliver some boudain, stuffed pork loin and dirty rice. All we have to do is keep it warm and make some tea and we'll be set." He opened the drawer she indicated and removed the tape.

"Mind? This is wonderful. I know its last minute, but do you mind if we call Savannah and ask if she'd join us for lunch? That is, if she doesn't have any plans?" She longed to get to the bottom of all the supernatural happenings. Harley thought that if she could just understand what was going on she might not be so jumpy.

"I think that's a great idea, cher. If she's free, Savannah would appreciate the invitation. Let's go put the tape under the legs of the bench and we'll see if it moves again. You wouldn't have a video camera that we could set up to capture evidence, do you?"

He sounded experienced in this sort of thing. "Have you done this before? Ghost hunted, I mean?"

"Nah," Beau walked behind her as she headed back upstairs. "I've watched some TV shows and heard Savannah discuss it. But, my evidence gathering is more in the realm of game cameras: I like to hunt." In a few minutes they had the camera set up and the legs of the vanity bench situated on top of four pieces of tape so they could document if it moved on its own, again.

"This is sort of fun, isn't it?" She knelt by him and watched his big hands at work. "Being with you is very pleasurable." Out of the blue, she leaned over and kissed his cheek.

A velvety mouth that close to his was too tempting to resist. Meeting her lips, he took a tender bite from them. She crept closer and he indulged himself, tracing her mouth with his tongue and feasting on the honeyed sweetness of her kiss.

Her heart beat fast, but she managed to breathe. Beau licked her cheek and nibbled on her chin, then gently sucked on her lower lip, sweeping his tongue inside. Desire swirled through her body, as he mapped her mouth and coaxed her tongue to play with his. Damn, he needed to stop. "Later, my Dove, I'm going to love you within an inch of your life." He drew Harley to her feet. Cupping the back of her neck, he massaged the tension away. "Tell me the truth. Does my touch bring you only pleasure or do you still have twinges of unease?" By the way she relaxed into his care; he thought he knew the answer.

"I only feel trust and great desire," she answered truthfully.

"Damn, I just did myself in. Now, I'm gonna walk around the rest of a day with a hard-on." Nada would probably never understand how much pleasure it gave a male for his woman to accept his protection.

Despite the tenderness, Harley laughed. "Anticipation will make it better." Pulling from him, she raced downstairs and after he got over the shock at her playful behavior, he followed. "Do you know Savannah's number?" He did one better; he found her in his contacts and placed the call.

A very pleasant, soft voice answered. "Hello, this is

Savannah."

"Hi, Savannah, this is Harley Montoya, I live at Willowbend. I'm friends," she pinned Beau with a stare and a smile, "with Beau LeBlanc and he was telling me all about you."

"Hey, how nice it is to speak with you. Laura told me a little about you. I've always been fascinated by Willowbend and its history."

"Actually, that's why I called. There have been a couple of incidents that I can't explain. It's last minute, I know. . . ." Harley hesitated, but Beau rubbed her back, encouraging her to continue. "Would you be interested in having lunch with us? Beau had some fantastic food delivered. It won't be fancy; but we would love to have you."

"What time?"

"Great! Eleven-thirty?"

"Sounds good."

"We'll see you then."

"I hate to ask, but could I bring my dog? Two reasons...she won't leave my side and she's pretty sensitive to the supernatural."

"Of course, bring the dog. I love animals."

When they had rung off, Beau spoke up. "She's bringing Patrick's dog?" he spoke as he set the table without being asked. Good man.

"Savannah's bringing a dog, yes. She didn't say anything about Patrick." Harley thought a minute as she handed him the napkins and silverware. "I guess Patrick was the soldier fiancé she lost?"

"That's right. I didn't know him well, but Savannah thought he hung the moon. When he was home on leave, they were inseparable."

"How sad," Harley couldn't help think how she would feel if something happened to Beau or how Beau would

215

feel if something happened to her. A cold chill ran up her back and she shivered.

"What's wrong?"

He didn't miss anything. "Nothing," she smiled. "Someone just walked over my grave. That's all."

"Don't say that," Beau protested. "I don't want to think about your grave. I plan on dying before you, and don't you forget it."

He tried to make a joke of it, but she could tell he was uneasy about everything. And to tell the truth, she was too. It wasn't the ghosts of Willowbend that bothered her; it was not knowing when or if the madman would strike next. Forcing those thoughts from her mind, Harley watched the big man as he tried to fold a napkin properly. And he didn't do a half-bad job. "Are we playing house, now?"

Harley's teasing question earned her a heart-stopping grin. "No, that comes later…in bed." She couldn't wait.'

* * *

At eleven-thirty on the nose, the doorbell rang and Harley ran to answer it. "Get the rolls out of the oven for me please."

"Got 'em snookems."

Snookems? Harley giggled like a schoolgirl. This 'playing house' stuff was fun. Who was she kidding? Being with Beau was incredible. When she opened the door, Harley was surprised. With a name like Savannah, Harley was expecting a Southern Belle. Lots of blonde hair and big blue eyes, maybe with an umbrella and a mint julep. Instead, it was almost like looking in a mirror. Savannah wasn't of Hispanic descent, but the resemblance was uncanny. "Well, hello there."

Savannah blinked and laughed. "Have I seen you somewhere, before?"

"Every time I look in the mirror." Their eyes were

different Harley observed. where hers were brown, Savannah's were almost black, maybe navy blue. Her skin was not quite as dark, but their features were very similar. "I didn't realize I had a sister."

"Well, you do now. It's wonderful to meet you." Savannah shook Harley's hand warmly.

Hearing footsteps behind her, Harley realized Beau had joined them. Turning to him, she put her hands on her hips. "Why didn't you tell me that Savannah and I look alike." They both turned to gaze at him, expectantly.

He looked at first one girl, then the other. Deep in concentration, he wrinkled up his brow and narrowed his eyes. Harley thought he looked so cute, that sexy long hair, all of those hunky muscles. She couldn't believe he actually belonged to her. "I don't see it," he spoke just like a typical guy.

A canine whimper drew their attention. "What a beautiful dog." A black lab stood just as close to Savannah's leg as possible.

"Ciara wants to come in," Savannah translated.

"Come in, Ciara," Harley stepped back and let them enter. "I'd ask you to sit down and have a drink but Beau says he is starving to death, so let's get to the good stuff first." They sat down around the table and filled their plates with Cajun delicacies. "How about Ciara?" Harley started to get up and get another plate.

"No," Savannah stopped her. "That's not necessary. Patrick has her impeccably trained. She eats at a certain time of day out of a certain bowl." As she talked about Ciara, the young woman placed a hand on the dog's head that rested in her lap.

"She certainly seems devoted to you," Beau commented. He had always loved dogs.

"Only recently. And I'm not sure what changed. She has been living with me since Patrick and I became engaged." Savannah smiled sadly. "This may sound strange, but she has always been polite to me, but distant. It's been three years . . ." she stopped and waited a moment as if to compose herself. "It's been three years since I lost him, and she has allowed me to care for her, but this affectionate behavior is brand new. Ciara has never stopped looking for him. I've carried her to his grave, but she refuses to give up."

Harley could read between the lines. In her own way, Savannah wasn't giving up either. "I'm so sorry for your loss," she covered the young woman's hand, offering sympathy. "I'm former Navy and I grieve for each soldier who never comes home."

"Patrick was a Marine sniper."

Harley continued her own brand of comfort, "I'm sure he was a wonderful man. There is no greater gift a soldier can give than to die for one's country, but the loved ones left behind are required to sacrifice equally. They just don't have the solace of death."

Seeing the women were very near tears, Beau tried to lighten the mood. Harley's talk of death made him uneasy. "Savannah, I understand you were on an episode of one of those ghost hunting television shows. Was it fun?"

A smile brightened her face. "It was fascinating. Most folks think these shows are all staged, but the PROOF team makes a sincere effort to find and substantiate claims of supernatural activity." While they talked, they ate, enjoying one another's company. Harley drank a lot of tea, the boudain was good but very spicy. "What were you investigating? Anything local?" She thought about her own experiences and couldn't wait to hear Savannah's.

"Yes, it was local, the Broussard house on the north side of town. At one time it was a slave auction house. At present, it's a private residence and the family had the whole gamut of experiences, from full body apparitions to disembodied voices to furniture being moved." At the last revelation, Harley looked at Beau. Savannah picked up on the exchange. "What? Do you think something moved here at Willowbend?"

"The vanity bench in my bathroom all but walked across the room to me." Harley's eyes were big; the memory was still very fresh in her mind.

"Seriously?" Savannah was all ears. "Because I've seen a chair do that, one leg at a time. That was one thing that completely unnerved me. Ever since then I've been nervous of chairs."

"No, it wasn't quite that predatory, but it was bad enough. It was as if someone pushed it toward me."

Beau got amused when Harley shivered and shuddered. "You should have seen her, Savannah. She came flying down the stairs as if the devil himself were after her."

Giving him a warning look, she pinched his knee, playfully. "If I knew what they wanted, I might not be so scared. Seeing someone who looked like Fox Crocker didn't help either."

"Perhaps, I can be of assistance . . . ." Savannah began to speak when there was a loud crash from upstairs. "Is that our cue?"

Beau ran first, closely followed by the two women and the dog. What they found made Harley's blood run cold. The vanity bench had not only moved, it had been been picked up and tossed against the shower wall.

* * *

"Okay, now this is what we're going to do," Savannah explained as she laid out the equipment. "We're going to do a walk-through of the house, snap photos and ask questions. You carry the digital recorder and talk to them like you would anyone else. From my experience, ghosts are just people. Dead people, but just people.

As Harley familiarized herself with the recorder, she wondered... "What does all of this mean? Could the ghosts want something from me? Do I offend them because I live in their home?"

Savannah stopped what she was doing to look at her. "Perhaps we'll get an answer to your questions. Many times, I think they just crave attention. Not many people are aware that spirits inhabit the same world we do. I don't pretend to understand it, but when someone like me comes along who is actively seeking them, they take advantage of the attention. Who knows? Maybe they are lonely." As Harley watched her, she dashed a tear from her eye. "I'm sorry. The reason I do this is to find answers. I've heard voices, but never the one I long to hear. Many nights I have sat by his grave and pleaded for him to come to me; to say just one word in his beloved voice, but nothing."

"Patrick, you mean?" They were sitting in Willowbend's formal receiving room. Beau's assistant, Indiana, had arrived and he had eyed Savannah with appreciation. She had been courteous, but oblivious. Not even reacting to his interest at all.

"Yes, I wasn't ready to let him go. He was my world. I loved him more than life."

"Why do you think he doesn't come through? Doesn't contact you?" Harley scooted closer and put a comforting arm around Savannah.

"I don't know," she whispered. "Maybe he's being kind. He has to know that, until lately, if he were to have talked to me, I would have been very tempted to join him." Savannah placed a protective hand over her abdomen. The gesture wasn't lost on Harley, but she didn't feel comfortable asking personal questions. Not yet, anyway.

"Nada!" Both women jumped. The voice had come from upstairs and it hadn't been Beau's. It was a woman's voice and the insistent, mournful tone made Harley's blood run cold. To add to the eeriness, Ciara lifted her head and wailed a mournful howl.

"Who or what's Nada?"

"That's me...long story."

"Well, I think you're being paged. Let's go." Savannah stood and began purposely walking to the stairs, the lab right on her heels. She was already taking pictures. "I'll go up first and we'll start in your room. Directions?"

"First door on your right." Harley swallowed hard. She could do this.

Savannah led her into the bedroom. "Okay, begin." As her new friend moved slowly around the room taking photos, Harley talked. At first, she felt silly, but she pressed on. "Hello, my name is Harley Montoya. I'm also called Nada. Thank you for letting me live here with you. What's your name?" She paused, just as Savannah had instructed. If you were going to ask questions, Savannah had explained, you had to give them a chance to answer. "Is there a little girl here who likes cookies?" At that, Savannah smiled at her. She even opened up the closet and took pictures inside of it. Harley walked toward the bathroom where the stool still lay on its side. "Are you angry because I am here? Do you have a message for me?"

The women moved from room to room, methodically taking pictures and asking questions. At one point, Beau stood at the door and watched them, a look of concern on his face. When they had finished to Savannah's satisfaction, they returned to the kitchen to find that Beau had cleaned everything and put the food away. "Thank you, baby." Harley was touched at his thoughtfulness. She didn't hesitate but went right up to him and kissed him on the cheek.

"Did you girls have any luck?" Beau certainly had. He had notified the county sheriff and put him on alert that

221

there might be trouble in the area. Now, he was assured that a patrol would be made through the area every hour or so. Because what he had found at the side of the house, right under Harley's bedroom window had made his blood run cold.

"We're about to see," Savannah sat down and pulled her laptop out of her bag. "Scoot over, Ciara," she gently pushed the dog aside. "I don't know what's gotten into her. You'd think she loved me or something."

"Maybe, she does," Beau observed. "She certainly acts like it to me."

"I hope so, but I'm skeptical," Savannah muttered. She clicked the memory card in place and started pulling up photos. Pushing the computer toward Beau, she instructed. "Look through these for anything weird." Hauling out another laptop, she took the digital recorder from Harley and hooked it to the second computer via a USB cable. "Now, let's see if we can hear anything."

They sat quietly – Beau looking through photos – and all listening as Harley asked question after question. Finally, they had a response – and it was one that put Beau in high gear. The question Harley asked was, "Do you have a message from me? Is there something you want me to know?" A woman's faraway, yet distinct voice answered. "My name is Lillian and you are in grave danger. If you stay here you will die."

Chapter Nine

"I don't think that was a threat, Beau." Harley insisted as she filled a suitcase. He hadn't given her time to argue. As soon as he had helped Savannah pack up and got her safely ensconced in her vehicle, he had come back and informed her they were moving to his houseboat.

"I don't care if it was a threat or a warning; you're not staying another night in this house until we know for sure what's going on." He hadn't told her about what he found outside and he wasn't going to until he knew more. All he could think about was getting her somewhere safe.

"Do you think she could have been referring to Crocker? How would she know? Is information like that just floating around in the netherworld?"

"Sugar, I don't know, but I'm damn sure not taking a chance." As soon as she finished zipping, he grabbed it up and waited for her to go ahead of him. "We'll go to the houseboat and head out into the Atchafalaya. There are places to anchor there that few white men have ever seen." The swamp was his turf; he knew it like the back of his hand.

"Wait, I've got to get my cell phones." She had been in such a hurry that she almost forgot them. Hurrying to the kitchen, she retrieved them. Checking the red Socorro phone, she was relieved that there were no messages. God, she couldn't believe how careless she had been.

"I've locked everything up, let's go."

Harley didn't really understand Beau's urgency, but when she touched his arm as he held the door for her, she knew. A vision of him looking down at the tale-tell sign of a trespasser jarred her equilibrium. "He's been here hasn't he?" Stopping, she looked up into Beau's worried face.

223

"That's why we're leaving...it wasn't just the ghost was it?"

"Can't hide anything from you," he attempted to quip. "I'll have to remember that."

"Sorry," Harley was reminded of her parent's displeasure. "I won't do it again."

Her change in demeanor did not escape his attention. "Harley, there is nothing that I will ever do or think or say that is off-limits to you." He was in a hurry, but this was important. Cupping the back of her neck, he stopped her forward momentum. "Do you understand? You are my priority."

Relief filled her heart.

* * *

"Do you mind if Amos comes with us?" Beau stood at the gangplank and watched the old gator lumber toward the boat. "He's hungry."

"Not at all," Harley was ready to embrace Beau's pet. "Why doesn't he live at the game preserve with your other alligators?" She thought it was a reasonable question. They stood there while Amos lumbered aboard and made his way to the back where Beau had left him his morning meal.

"I enjoy him, for one thing. It reminds me of those old Miami Vice reruns when Don Johnson had his gator named Elvis on his boat. Secondly, he does deter those who would vandalize my boat. Amos is a pretty good watchdog."

Harley settled in a chair inside the cabin and felt excitement roll over her as they pulled from their moorings and set off. "It's beautiful here, truly haunting." She loved everything about the swamp.

As they made their way down the bayou toward the Atchafalaya, Beau pointed out creatures along the bank and in the water. "Look at that snapping turtle baby, if he latches onto you, he won't let go till it thunders."

"Really?" she looked skeptical. "He's huge. And mean looking." She stood up to get a better look at the large turtle basking on a half submerged fallen tree.

"He probably weighs a hundred and seventy five pounds and his bite could take off a finger. Thunder wouldn't have anything to do with it, but they are known for being ill-tempered." Beau fanned at a mosquito buzzing around his face. "We need to spray for these smaller varmints. They're much more likely to bite." Rounding a bend, the waters of Bayou Chene opened up into a wider swath of water. "Look over there, a big gator."

Harley followed to where he was pointing then gasped as the beast lunged sideways and snapped up another creature in its jaws. "What was that?"

"He caught him a nutria rat." Beau edged the boat closer so he could get a better look.

"When I saw my first nutria, I thought it was a beaver," Harley confessed as she stood to watch the semi-gruesome sight.

"The nutria isn't native to our part of the world. Actually, it's from Argentina. It was introduced in the 1930's by the rich naturalist, E. A. McIlhenny, to his home on Avery Island. He intended to start a fur trade. A storm blew in and the swamp beavers escaped and now there are twenty million of them destroying the coastal wetlands. They eat the roots of plants and this escalates erosion. Their only claim to good fortune is that they have helped in the comeback of the alligator population. And to be fair, their fur has become a viable trade item with France." Harley listened as he talked. She was so proud of Beau. He was a true environmentalist.

"I was going to ask if we could go swimming, but I don't know if it would be safe. Would it?" She had brought her swimsuit, just in case.

"No, cher. I'm not risking your precious hide in these

225

waters." Beau brushed a lock of hair out of her eyes. "If you want to swim, I'll take you to the Hilton or to the beach."

"Can we fish?"

Her eyes were big with excitement and he chuckled. "Yes, I brought some cane poles and bobbers. Are you gonna bait your own hook?"

"Yes," she said a bit hesitantly. "But, if you'll do it for me – I'll make it worth your while." A sly, slight little smile let him know what she really meant. "I could cook for you, satisfy any hunger…you might have."

Beau stared at her a moment and then laughed out loud. "You little vixen! It won't be ten minutes till we get to the cove and then I'm going to satisfy my hunger, but it won't be for food."

His dick reacted, instantly. As Harley had packed, he had called Dane Wagner and informed him that his services were no longer needed. He was feeling a bit cocky, thinking he could hang out his shingle as a sex therapist. But when Harley stood and leaned over the counter to get a soda, the sight of her gorgeous ass reminded him that he had all the business he could handle, right here. Watching his Nada sparkle and shine in the throes of ecstasy was all he was interested in.

"I can't wait," she turned and shocked him. Stepping close, she took a small chip of ice, traced his lips, then stood on tiptoe to lick the drops away. "I want you, so much."

"Hell, baby." Beau decided they were in as good a spot as any, to anchor. Maneuvering out of the boating lane, he came to a stop, safely shut down the engine and reached for her. Smoothly, she slipped from his grasp. With a little wiggle to her walk, she stayed just ahead of him, stripping as she went. By the time she was to the stairs, she was completely nude and he was rock hard. Following her example, he started shedding clothes, tossing them to one side as he stayed hot on her trail. "Damn, I'm glad you wanna play with me."

When they had arrived, he had shown her to his stateroom and she had been amazed at the size of the bed. All she could think about was being in Beau's arms again. Making love with him had been the most sublime experience imaginable. Laying her ever-present cell phone on the nightstand, she turned to see him come through the door. Swear to God, his cock got there a good few seconds before he did. Being bolder than she ever thought possible, Harley walked up and wrapped her hand around his manhood, marveling at the silk covered steel. "Can I be on top this time?"

His answer was a growl. With one powerful move, he clasped her close, cupped her ass and lifted her. "Kiss me," he demanded. She opened her lips, her thighs and her arms and wrapped herself around him. Lord, it felt like coming home.

God, she couldn't get close enough. Years of living on a starvation diet, void of affection and tenderness, never touching anyone, no on ever touching her had made Harley ravenous. She clung to him, making love to his mouth, all the while pushing her aching pussy against him. Feverishly, she kneaded the muscles of his back, rubbed her swollen nipples across his chest and hummed her relief to be allowed as much access to his body as she desired.

Tearing his mouth from hers, Beau took a harsh breath. "You're wet; I can feel your heat. Guide me in, sexpot." He couldn't believe what a little firecracker she was. If he wasn't so busy fucking her, he would get down on his knees and thank the good Lord above for this complete and utter answer to prayer.

Her hand shook as she encircled his thick rod. It was literally pulsing with life and she trembled as she opened herself to him. "I can't wait, I just can't wait. My pussy is so hungry for you." Beau supported her completely. So, all she had to do was just turn herself over to him, take him inside of her and let him do all the work...mostly. It seemed she would die if she didn't get him inside of her – there was an emptiness, a vacancy, a piece of herself missing. Harley held her breath as she placed the head of his cock to the opening of her vagina. He pushed in. "Ahhhhh."

Perfect. Tight. Hot. "God, nothing is better than this. Nothing." He sank the first inch into her hot pussy and thrilled as she nipped at his chest, her nails bit into his shoulders. His woman was losing control and he loved it. "Easy, Angel...I'll give you what you need." Unbelievable! Her pussy rippled around him, quivering in response every time he jabbed his cock deeper with short eager thrusts. Biting his cheek, he focused on making this last. Hell, he had so little control where she was concerned. Big Beau LeBlanc who always prided himself on his prowess with the women was totally at her mercy. But being inside Harley was as close to heaven as he would probably ever get. "I've got you now, I'm gonna move you up and down on my cock. Make us both feel good." He thrust deeper, in and out, enjoying the feel of her flesh as it drug up and down over his cock. Locking his gaze with hers, he stared down into amber eyes that held the secrets of the universe for him. Right now, those beautiful golden eyes shone with wonder. "Do you know how much I love this?" he asked.

"Not as much as me," she exhaled the words in a whoosh.

Pulling out, he surged back in, filling her to the brim, her little channel clasped him with a wonderful tightness, creating an agony of perfect pleasure that radiated throughout his whole body. Mine. Mine. Mine. His heartbeat out the litany of truth. Harley belonged to him. She always had belonged to him, since the days of Brownwood and their struggle for survival. Even during their days of separation, their souls had never given up hope. Even when their minds and hearts had moved on as best they could. "Look," she whispered. "Look at us, Beau." Through a haze of ecstasy he glanced to where she was pointing and realized they were framed in the mirror. An erotic display of decadent passion. The sight of her impaled on his cock, at his mercy, his total control, and the look of utter trust and joy on her face was almost his undoing. "We're beautiful," she breathed next to his skin.

Watching the dance of their rapture only enflamed him further. Leaning back against the door, he ground his cock deep inside of her, bucking his hips and making her moan and arch her back, almost pulling from his grasp. He tightened his hold on her, there was no way he would let her fall. "Cum for me, angel. Flutter that little pussy around me, let me know how much you enjoy my lovin'." She took his instructions to heart, the little noises she was making escalating to a scream that echoed over the waters as he erupted within her. The power of his ejaculation ripped a roar from his own throat as she milked him of every drop he had. He pulled her closer, letting the pounding of their hearts synchronize as they came down from the heights of bliss. The universe had become very small; there was only the two of them, all the rest had been burned up in the firestorm of their joining. But that was all right, he had everything he needed right here in his arms.

* * *

"It's peaceful here," Harley sighed with happiness. Sitting on the very back of the boat, on some steps leading off of the lowest deck, she dangled her feet near the water.

"You come back up here, Harley-mine, what are you

thinking? A big gator will come along and jerk you off there and I won't ever know what happened to you. It's almost dark, the buggers are stirring." Beau fussed as he stepped over Amos and pulled her back to a safe point. "I turn my back and you put yourself in danger like that. This isn't some regular swimming hole. This is the damn swamp, baby." She wrapped her arms around him, enjoying his discomfiture. "What's that hug for?" he grunted still trying to maintain his mad.

"Because I love you. And because you love me."

"Damn, straight." He returned her hug. "Come on and get you something to eat. I've made omelets, no onions…I plan on kissing you later."

"Damn, straight," she echoed him and he laughed. "I don't want to think about what happened today. By that I mean the prowler. Let's talk about something else. We've covered ghosts. You're always teasing me about Big Foot and the loup garou. Is the next thing voodoo zombie stories?"

"No zombies, I'll tell you about cannibals, instead. How's that?" He held her chair out for her and placed a plate of fried shrimp in front of her. "Want some red sauce? I made it myself."

"I thought we were just having omelets." She got her a spoonful of the fragrant egg concoction, too.

"I have to have meat, cher. I'm a big man."

"You're so talented," she was serious; he was talented in lots of areas.

"I know," he agreed resignedly. "It's a burden." The smile he gave her next made her cream. "Do you want to hear about the cannibals?"

"While we're eating?"

"We're not eating people... we're eating shrimp." When she rolled her eyes, he began his tale. "Very few know about the cannibalistic warmongers who lived in these swamps called the Attakapas. Their name in Choctaw meant 'maneaters'. The Opelousas and the Chitimacha tribes were enemies of the Attakapas and they knew that any battle lost with them would result in the Attakapas eating any warriors that they captured as prisoners."

The old-timers say that in the early 1700's these tribes had a battle near what is now St. Martinsville. The Attakapas lost the battle and were virtually wiped out, only a dozen or so survived. They escaped and went farther into the swamp; in an area we now called Indian Bend." He gave her a wicked little grin… "that's what they call the place we are sitting right now."

"You love to scare me," Harley swatted at him. "One of these days, I'm going to figure out how to scare you." She waved a half-eaten shrimp at him.

"I hope not, cher. It takes a lot to scare me. Anyway, the refugee Attakapas almost starved in these harsh swamplands. This is a veritable jungle; in fact, did you know they filmed the first Tarzan movie over by Morgan City?"

Harley was afraid he was going to change the subject. "Tell me about that later, get back to the maneaters."

"Blood thirsty little urchin," he kissed her on the nose. "The Attakapas became renegades, quarreling and fighting with everyone. They bore the brunt of the other tribe's wrath. Many were killed on the dark, narrow paths that wind through the swamps. Records of the local Spanish missions tell that starvation led to their becoming cannibals, but that wasn't the case. There were older tales that were much more mysterious. Not only about cannibalism but about the rugarou."

"Rugarou," Harley's eyes were wide with interest. "I thought you called him the loup garou?"

"Luop garou is a French term, ruagrou is native American. Same creature," Beau dismissed with a wave of his hand. "Many legends say that the Attakapas appealed to the Great Spirit and asked for help and he gave them the power to shapeshift, to become skinwalkers." Despite the warmth of the cabin, Harley shuddered. Either from fear or a thrill, Beau couldn't be certain. Either way, she would hold him tight tonight. So, he laid it on thick. "It was nights like tonight, when the damp chill would set in and the fish go to the bottoms of the bayou and the animals den up in their holes, the Attakapas would drop to all fours. And on long moonlit nights, they would search for human prey."

"Oh, that's an old wives' tale," Harley pooh-poohed his story.

"Nuh-uh," Beau insisted. "Just last winter there were sightings around Charenton. Many say that Hurricane Katrina woke them up. Anytime there is a disturbance in the eco-system, the rugarou seeks revenge."

"I'm ready to go to bed," Harley announced as she stood up and began clearing away the table. Beau joined her and they made short work of the dishes.

"You want to go hide under the covers?"

"No," Harley gave him a sultry wink. "I want to play on top of the covers." He lunged for her and she ran. Before he followed, he opened a cabinet door and took down a jar. Beau had a plan.

* * *

He looked bigger than life, leaning back against the headboard. His chest was a veritable playground of muscles, that dark hair hanging sexily down to his shoulders. A washboard of abs looked ready to be explored and she fully intended to make herself familiar with every ridge and rise. Especially the part that had rose to the occasion and was lying fully erect, just begging for attention.

"Come sit between my legs," he held out a hand. They

were both naked, a state she was fast coming to enjoy. As she started to straddle him, he directed – "No, turn around and lean back against me. I want to fulfill a fantasy."

"A fantasy?" Every moment they were together was a fantasy she had never even dared to dream.

He fitted her to him and began to run his hands up and down her body. "Something I have dreamed of doing to my woman. I had no idea it would turn out to be you, but I'm learning that miracles happen. You have the softest skin. I love to touch you." She laid her head on his shoulder, baring her neck to his kiss. "I have something that's going to make you feel tingly and sexy, but it will make me feel even better…cause I get to touch you." Taking a jar from the bed beside his hip, he unscrewed the lid. A sweet smell permeated the air. "White chocolate body cream."

"This is going to be delicious, isn't it?" she couldn't believe the difference in her days since she had walked back into Beau's life.

"Relax and enjoy." Dipping into the soft mixture, he brought his hands onto her breasts and began to rub. Softly. Gently. Concentric circles, round and around her tits. Soothing it around the swollen nipples – not touching, but almost. Her head pushed back against his shoulder, her wealth of dark hair spread out across his chest as Harley arched into his caress.

"Oh, God! Beau, this feels so good."

He kissed her neck, as he lifted her breasts in his hands, weighing them. Luxuriously, he kneaded them, molding and squeezing. Still he hadn't touched her nipples. He was making her wait. But not for long, she needed what he so desperately wanted to give her. Getting a bit more salve, he tended to her nipples, rubbing them gently. Harley's hips began to move, she couldn't be still. "I love these puffy nipples. They are so soft, yet they can get as hard as little jewels." In figure eights, he went round and round them, finally rewarding her by taking the nipples between his thumbs and forefingers and milking them.

"Jesus, Beau," she wailed, thrashing her head on his shoulder. His cock was already stiff with lust, but when she slipped her hand between her legs and began caressing herself, he felt his cock swell even more. She didn't know it, but he was helplessly in love with her. Having her in his arms like this was paradise. Harley was almost sobbing now, her body straining to achieve the climax she needed. Whispering in her ear, he told her how precious she was. "You are so sexy. What did I ever do to deserve you? Holding you like this, giving you pleasure, hearing you cum makes life worth living. Hmmmm, come on baby, fly for me." Her back arched almost double, and he had to tighten his grip on her to keep her in his arms. But she wasn't trying to get away, her body responded to every tweak and pull he applied to her delectable nipples. She was biting her lip and holding on to his leg for dear life, and when she reached her peak, her whole body vibrated. He just held on and fell deeper in love. "That's my baby, that's my sweetheart." He whispered to her, rubbing his face against her hair. Harley was totally lost in bliss, and by God she was his. All his.

"You are dangerous, Mr. LeBlanc," she panted, trying to catch her breath. "I can't believe what you do to me. You have turned me into a complete wanton."

"I'm not through, turn around." He helped her rearrange herself. "You don't know how pleased I am that you hunger for me – cause baby, I could just eat you up."

"Stop," she blushed. "You're going to go to my head."

"I want to be in your head, I want to be so much a part of you that you can't imagine life without me." His thumb tipped her chin up so he could claim her lips. She opened for him, and he sighed into her mouth, tangling their tongues together, he feasted on her kisses.

Sitting on top of him, she couldn't miss the evidence of his need. Like a moth to a flame, her hand sought his penis. "Can I?" One day she might be confident enough not to seek permission, but not yet. She couldn't believe she was here with this Greek god and he was hard for her – a girl whose very name labeled her as worthless. The harsh hitch of his breath gave her all the confidence she needed. "You really like me, don't you?"

"You think?" he teased. "Whatever gave you that idea?" He bit at her lips, smooching at their honeyed redness. "I can't keep my hands off of you and I stay hard twenty-four/seven."

With gentle strokes she enjoyed his size and shape. When he jumped in her hand, she smiled against his mouth. "Will you make love to me, now?"

"Soon, I want to do something else first, something I've been rehearsing in my mind."

"What?" She wanted to ask him if he responded like this to every woman he was attracted to, but she was afraid. She wanted to think she was special. "Show me."

Beau's focus returned to her tits. "I love the way your nipples plump up for me – they don't get all wrinkly and shriveled up – they get pouty and puffy." He lifted her and closed his mouth over one, sucking hard. When he sat her back down, he got on his knees before her. "I want to see how something feels." At first, she didn't know what he was up to and then she became mesmerized. He took his cock in hand and started nudging her tit with the head. She shivered as the very tip of her nipple slid into the tiny slit that leaked pearlescent pre-cum.

"We're beautiful together, aren't we?" Harley couldn't help but say what she thought.

"Push your tits together." She did and he slid in. They were still slick from the white chocolate cream. "God, yeah, that's so good."

"Harley got into the action, every time he pushed up she kissed and licked at the head and it didn't take but a few minutes till he growled loudly and shut his eyes as jets of hot cum began to bathe her tits. She watched his face, he was helpless in the ecstasy he was feeling. Wanting to be as close to him as possible; she slipped her lips over the head and sucked the last drops of his semen into her mouth. "Damn, that's hot! Let me clean you up," he grabbed a hand towel he had brought to bed to wipe the oil off his hands. Before he could remove his seed from her body, she placed her hands over her breasts and rubbed it in to her skin.

"This feels better than the massage oil."

"You don't know what you're doing to me, baby," he ground out, pushing her hands aside and doing it for her. She sighed – his hands were magic.

"When you pull on my nipples like that I feel it between my legs," she held perfectly still as he milked her nipples, rubbing his semen into her skin.

There was no way she could miss what stood before her so proudly. "You're hard again."

"No shit," he laughed, as he picked her up and flipped her on her back gently, as she laughed.

She had no fear in his hands; Beau would never let her fall. Lord, he was big and gorgeous. The moment froze as they looked at one another. Her vagina quivered in anticipation. "I've dreamed of this moment all day."

Holy Hell! She had no fuckin' idea how much he wanted her. Beneath him, he felt her open up and make a place for him between her thighs. Harley wanted him, too - there was no missing that. He loved the way she went all soft at the thought of his touch. Her body shivered like she was expecting a treat. So, he gave her one. All of him – all at once. With one perfect plunge, he buried himself balls deep. All the air whooshed out of her lungs at the shock of his sudden and complete possession. He felt her body conform and accept his cock, making a place for him – his own place. "Who do you belong to, Harley?" He pulled out, smoothly, then worked his way back in – in – out – in –out – in hard, jarring jabs. "Who do you belong to, Harley?" he repeated with words timed to the pistoning of his hips.

"You, Beau. I belong to you." After that, all she could do was hang on as he slammed into her repeatedly until they both cried out the other's name.

Beau rested his head in the crook of her neck, breathing in her scent. His cock pulsed the last drops deep inside of her. He wondered if she wanted children. Such an intimate act they shared, and how eternal could be the consequences. Suddenly, he wanted to see the evidence of their love. Sitting up, he pulled his cock out of her channel and watched as the creamy mix of their passion flowed from her body. "Beautiful."

"What are you doing?" Harley tried to see. "What's wrong?"

"Not a damn thing," he traced a finger through her slit, loving the way she looked. "Everything in my world is just right."

* * *

Something was wrong. Harley was instantly awake. She had been lying cradled in Beau's arms with her head on his shoulder, nestled close to his side. His breathing was even, he was in deep slumber. A scuffling noise sounded right over her head. Every nerve cell in her body went on high alert. Whomp! She set up, pulling away from Beau.

"What's wrong, baby?" Beau sat up. Then he heard it. The big gator was thrashing around. Something or someone was on the boat. "Wait here." With lithe grace he was up off the bed and pulling on his pants before she could scramble from the covers.

"I'm coming with you," she grabbed a robe and followed.

"Stay back, I can handle this," he insisted.

"No," she was insistent. Harley had a funny feeling. A sick, funny feeling. Up on deck they made their way in the early morning light to the old toothless gator only to find him writhing and twisting, an arrow like stick protruding from his mouth. "Oh no," she went to kneel down to help.

"Careful baby, he's hurt and that tail will hit you so hard it'll knock you into the middle of next week." Beau edged around to get in front of Amos in order to pull the cruel weapon from the soft inner flesh. "Amos opened his mouth to hiss at somebody and they shot him with a spear gun. I'm gonna have to try and get that out." Harley came closer to help.

"If you don't stand back and be safe, I'm gonna blister your butt," he warned her. Obviously unnerved.

A splash in the water drew Harley's attention and a spooky chill went down her spine. Somebody was in the water and all of a sudden, she knew. She could feel it. This was much worse than a wounded alligator. "Do you have diving equipment?"

Beau was taking the bull by the horns, or the gator by the snout, in this case. "In the equipment room, next to the generator."

He was occupied, and she was driven. She had no time to lose. Rushing to where he indicated, she found a tank and a mask. "I need my tools," she talked to herself as she went back in the cabin. Damn, she didn't have time for mistakes. Grabbing the small duffle that she never left home without, she extracted a small belt that would have what she needed. With shaking hands, she fastened it around her waist. "God, let me be wrong this time." She prayed that her imagination was working overtime, but she could feel it, a palatable evil that seemed to permeate the very air they breathed. "A flashlight, too," she reminded herself and after finding one, she was set. With determined steps, Harley went back on deck. "Beau, I have a sneaky feeling that something's wrong. I'll be right back. I'm going to check under and around the boat." With only that much warning, she walked to the side of the boat and jumped off into the murky waters.

As Beau extracted the sharp piece of metal from his gator's mouth, deftly avoiding the flailing reptile, he heard Harley's words and the splash. It took him a moment to comprehend what had happened. But when he did, he came unglued.

"What the fuck?" He ran to the side just in time to see his little darlin' disappearing into the alligator/snake infested waters of the Atchafalaya Basin. Panic washed over him. He couldn't think. What was she doing? Feeling like he was wasting precious seconds, he grabbed another tank, mask, light and the biggest knife in his equipment room and went in after her.

Holding his breath, he searched for her light. Shit! It was damn dark, but there she was, moving along underneath his boat. And then he saw it! At the same time she did. Holy Fuckin' Shit! There was a bomb on his boat. All he could think of was getting her out of the way. He began to pull on her, but she pushed back, glaring at him. He thought he would lose his mind! He tried again, but she slapped at him. Handing him the flashlight, she motioned for him to hold it. Beau was furious, totally pissed and scared shitless, for her and hell yeah, for himself, too. In a daze of pure panic, he watched her take some type of clippers and extricate a wire. There was no timer that he could see, but what the hell did he know?

Harley worked feverishly. Beau was right there! This wasn't a huge device, but from what she could see in this piss-poor light it was enough to blow them and the boat to kingdom come. And Beau was too close! Every time she had ever faced death, it had been her and the bomb. Of course, there was always the circumstances; the intended victims. The needless, useless risk of life and property. But never before had there been so much to lose! Beau could be killed! Because of her! There was no doubt about that. No doubt at all. Adrenaline was pumping through her body a mile a minute and waves of doubt and uncertainty were pounding in her brain. She had to do this, she had to do it. Forcing herself to calm down, she looked at the crude device. This wasn't what she had been seeing lately. What she was looking at appeared to be waterproof tubes filled with powder. Gunpowder perhaps and five cell batteries. A powerful, deadly combination. As she fumbled with the wires, she begged for insight. Hell, she couldn't think. Hate. She could feel hate emanate off the wires. This was Crocker and he hated her. He wanted her dead, and she would be, if she didn't get a grip. Closing her eyes, she made herself think. The batteries. That was the weak link. A touch on her shoulder reminded her that Beau was right beside her. Damn, how much time did she have? The water slowed her down, and she was breathing too fast. Too much concentrated oxygen was making her dizzy. Finding the lead wire to the batteries, she exhaled big, causing a myriad of bubbles to dance around her face, obscuring her view. There it was and this was it…she could feel it. If she could disconnect this - - - a jostle and whipping motion to her right caused her to look around. Beau had made some motion in the water. God, she hoped an alligator wasn't about to attack. She had to hurry! Taking the wire in hand, she felt it tingle. Yes, this was it. With stilted movements, she took the tool and bit down on the mouthpiece – hard. If she was wrong, it could all be over. With an even movement, she cut the wire and the green indicator light on the bomb went dead – it was over.

She was wrong.

* * *

"Do you know what the hell you just did?" He was wet and furious. A raging bull, but she understood his frustration. Maybe.

"I saved our lives," she stated flatly. "But, it's all my fault. I put you in danger. This wouldn't have happened, if I weren't here."

What she said seemed to change him. Moving toward her, he knelt at her feet. "I have to take care of you. It's engrained in me, bone-deep. Seeing you jump off into that water and tackle that shittin' bomb nearly killed me." Harley's heart melted when he laid his head in her lap. "Don't ever ask me to go through that again. I won't survive."

"Beau," she whispered his name. Smoothing his hair, she wished she knew what to say. There was no way she could make a promise like that. This wasn't over and it wouldn't be over until either she or Fox was dead.

He didn't let her go home. They returned to the dock and Beau called Indiana to bring his truck over for them to use. "I'm not taking any more chances with you. We're getting out of town. Hell, there might be a damn bomb on my truck or your Hummer." Harley watched helplessly as he made other phone calls, making sure all of his business was taken care of.

She was disrupting his life, plain and simple. Leaving her Hummer behind made her nervous. If she got a call, the delay would be costly. When he got off the phone, she tried to explain. "I'll go with you, but I need to take my vehicle. I can sweep it or your truck for a device; I can do that in my sleep."

Harley watched emotions play over his face. Strain was becoming apparent, his mouth was drawn and there were shadows under his eyes. Running a hand over her hair, she wondered what the mirror would tell her. "I don't want you putting yourself in danger again. Let somebody else handle it."

Not wanting to argue, she decided to give Waco a call at the earliest opportunity and get him to come after the Hummer. That way, if she was called, he could meet her at the location and they wouldn't lose any time. As soon as Beau calmed down, they needed to have a serious discussion. And she didn't have a good feeling about it either. Why was her life so complicated? Thankfully, she didn't have to respond, Indiana drove up followed by another vehicle.

"Hey, Boss, Harley," he greeted them, "the keys are in the truck and it's full of gas. What's up?"

"Too complicated to go into now, but you guys sweep that truck and my house and Willowbend for bombs and booby traps."

"No, it's too dangerous Call these guys," she gave Indiana a number. "They're in New Orleans and they're experts. This is their business; they have all the detection equipment that you don't."

"Harley," Beau began…then, he cursed. "Hell, you're right. Call them, Indy. No use putting you guys in danger, too."

She was putting him at risk, and she didn't like it. Knowing how Fox's mind worked, she knew Beau wasn't safe. Even if she walked away. He was marked now as being important to her, and that raised his value as a target.

"Sure, I'll get in touch with them." Indy stored the number in his phone. "I don't know where you two are headed, but there's a situation down at Avery Island that needs your attention."

Beau was almost relieved to have something else to think about. "What would that be? A rogue gator?"

Glancing over at Harley, he saw that she had stepped away to make a phone call. Damn, she was so little. He would never, as long as he lived, get the image of her struggling to disarm that bomb down in the dark dangerous waters of the Atchafalaya River out of his head. How was he going to survive this?

"No, it's not a gator," Indiana smirked. "It's a snake. A damn, big snake. One of the employees spotted a huge python down near the egret nests. They want you to come get it."

* * *

"I'd rather face a bomb any day than a snake," Harley grumbled as they headed south toward Avery Island.

Beau was calmer and in a better mood. In fact, he was hornier than hell. She was relaxed and had propped her little feet up on the dash and those mile long legs were making him sweat. "You won't have to get anywhere near the snake, I promise."

Out of the corner of his eye, he saw her move. So he looked over and found her staring at him. "When I was underneath your houseboat, who stayed by my side to keep the alligators and snakes off of me?"

He didn't answer right away, rather he sorta snarled at her, sweetly, but a snarl nonetheless. "This is going to sound totally arrogant and chauvinistic, but that's my job. I'm the man. That's what I do. I take care of what belongs to me." He lifted his head a bit, squaring his jaw, as if he was expecting her to challenge his right to claim her or defend her.

Harley knew what she had to say wouldn't go over well, so be it. "It thrills me; that you want to take care of me. I've been alone all my life, except for the short time we shared at Brownwood."

"Good, I'm glad we've got that straight." Beau

watched the road, deciding to pass a semi.

Harley smirked, her baby sounded like a dickhead. "All I ask is that you allow me the same privilege. I want to take care of you, too." Thunderclouds were no match for the darkness that marred his countenance. She sought to reinforce her argument. "We both have our strengths. If you were an electrician and I was a plumber, we would have a clearly defined purpose."

"My purpose is to keep you safe. Your purpose is to make me happy."

"You can't seriously be that old-fashioned," she didn't think she could let this pass. "If we are going to be together, you have to know that I want to share in all the responsibilities, all the decisions, and all the problems. I don't want to be put on a pedestal or wrapped up and put away somewhere safe until you get ready to take me out and play with me." Although she hadn't meant to, her voice rose the tiniest bit. He wasn't the only one that could get excited.

There was silence. She looked at him and he would glance at her, back at the road, and then at her again. Then he laughed. "I have never been more attracted to you, you sexy she-cat you."

Whew! "Good, I'm glad. Now, tell me about this python of yours." As soon as she said the words she realized he was going to take that the wrong way...and he did.

Typical male. He palmed his crotch and bragged. "My python is so big . . ."

"Beau," she laughed. "Be serious."

"Okay," he sobered. "The area police are making enquiries to see if the snake is somebody's lost pet or if it escaped from the zoo, or if it evidence that the big snakes in Florida are moving into Louisiana."

Her voice raised a little, again. "What big snakes in

Florida? I didn't know Florida had any big snakes."

She loved to watch him when he got like this, his whole demeanor changed; he became educated Beau, conservationist Beau. There were many layers to her man she loved every one of them. "Experts think it was a combination of factors. People disposing of snakes that grew larger than their owners could handle or pet stores, zoos, exotic animal warehouses and wildlife refuges like mine that were devastated by hurricanes. It's estimated that thousands of these animals are in Florida, perhaps hundreds of thousands."

By that time Harley's eyes were huge. "Hundreds of thousands? How can that be?"

"Big snakes reach sexual maturity in just a few years. They can produce thirty to eighty eggs at a time and reproduce annually. Do the math."

"So, you think this snake may have crawled from Florida?"

"Sounds farfetched, but people in residential neighborhoods are reporting seeing pythons cross their yards. They have been found crossing highways. One study estimated that eventually they would infest a third of the United States."

"I'm moving to Canada." Harley stated flatly, making Beau chuckle.

"No, you're not. You're staying right here with me. So I Can Take Care Of You." His slow and emphatic declaration made her happy.

* * *

It's a shame that we don't visit the places right under our noses. Harley knew this was a common ailment among people. They travel all over the world on vacations and don't appreciate the wonders right around them. Avery Island was new to her. "This isn't an island, is it?"

245

"Not in the traditional sense," Beau handed the man in the guardhouse a token for admittance. "Bayou Petit Anse surrounds it and marshlands beyond that. Avery Island is actually a huge salt dome. Imagine Mount Everest made out of salt and buried underground with just the tip sticking out – that's Avery Island."

Harley was impressed. "Tobasco Sauce is one of the most famous hot sauces in the world. I've always used it." She was talking, but she was also looking. It was as if they had left the mainland of the U.S. and drove onto the Hawaiian Islands. Lush, tropical plants were everywhere. Flowering trees and bushes abounded.

"Tobasco is shipped world-wide. The factory on the island produces 720,000 bottles of sauce a day. All of the seeds for the pepper plants originate here, and some of the pepper fields are here on Avery Island, but many are also in Central and South America." They by-passed the big brick factory, but Harley craned to see it. Turning down a small road they headed to the jungle gardens.

"It's all over the world. When I would be dispatched on missions, I was always surprised to see that familiar bottle on my table. Tiny bottles are even included in a lot of the MRE's they give members of the military." It didn't surprise Harley that she enjoyed being with Beau. He was smart, considerate, and so appealing that her body never truly came off of its aroused state. Even now, she could feel a whisper of desire making itself known.

"I'll tell you a funny story," Beau went on as he maneuvered down a smaller road into the swampier area of the island. "In the 1930's, the British government started this 'Buy British' campaign and their Parliament banned the purchase of Tobasco which had been available in England since the 1860's. It was even popular in the dining rooms of the House of Commons. This action started an uproar among the members of Parliament and they called it the 'tobasco tempest'. And the proponents of the hot sauce won."

"You know, you ought to be a teacher. You're so smart." She was proud of him.

As he pulled the truck to a stop, he winked at her. "The only thing I'm interested in teaching is sexual positions. To you."

As they exited the vehicle, Harley looked around cautiously. "I had almost forgot about that dang snake," she grumbled.

"Why do you think I sounded like a boring tourist guide," Beau came up and put an arm around her. "I was trying to take your mind off of it. Now before we get started, this is what you need to know." He tilted her face up to his with a finger under her chin. A gentle kiss was her reward for listening. "I want you to do exactly as I say and stand where I tell you to stand and move when I tell you to move. Got it?"

"Yes, sir." She felt a little mischievous. "Could we try that in the bedroom, sometimes?" That earned her a swat on the bottom.

The gardens were magnificent. Harley had never seen so many flowers. In the spring this place would be a Garden of Eden; and now, in late fall, it was a breathtaking tapestry of color and the odor of the many flowers was more heady than any expensive perfume could ever be. Beau held her hand, she knew she was safe but all the time they were walking, she was keeping an eye out for snakes. "Is there someone meeting us?" She knew he had talked to someone on the phone several times on the trip. Beau was armed with one stick with a hook on the end, very similar to his alligator stick and he had a large burlap bag. Harley thought they needed a cannon.

"Yes, one of the groundskeepers is watching our big girl. She's down by the egrets nesting ground."

"How do they know it's a girl?"

Stepping over a log, he held her hand while she did the same. "Same way I knew you were a girl the first time I saw you. By that sweet little tail of yours." At her disbelieving 'hmmmm', he explained. "A female Burmese's tail is longer and tapers slowly, while a male has a thick wide tail that quickly tapers."

They were headed down a steep hill and what Harley saw made her gasp in wonder. "What in the world is that?"

"That's Bird City." There were several men standing next to the swampy water. Waving Beau down, they pointed to an area near the shore that was completely covered over with green algae. He waved back at them, "this whole area was created by McIlhenny to give the White Egrets a place to nest. The old man was a self-trained naturalist, sorta like me, except he was wealthy. And he literally saved an entire species. Even though most of the birds fly to South America this time of year, a few old ones stay, who aren't able to make the trip. And that's what drew the python. Easy prey."

Harley shuddered, but marveled at the man-made nesting grounds built right into the swamp. From a distance it looked like a straw island, all contained on wooden docks. Thousands of egrets could nest in Bird City.

"She's right down here under these lilies, we think." The man sounded doubtful and a little nervous.

"How will you get her to come out?" she asked as they made their way down the steep hill to the water.

"I won't. I'll go in after her."

Growing up, she had watched shows on television about men who waded into water where they couldn't see the bottom and felt around for big snakes they couldn't see. Harley had thought they were nuts. And now she was watching the man she loved – yea, she could admit it; put himself in just such a dangerous position. She didn't like it.

At all. The fact that she took equal and greater risks just didn't seem to matter. "Be careful, Beau." She almost died when he took off his shoes and stepped in. Horrified she realized he was going to locate the snake by stepping on it. Ye gods! She couldn't watch, but she refused to look away. The other men just stood around like lunks and she wanted to rail at them that they should be the ones pussy-footing around in the muck trying to locate a monster.

"There you are." A lunge in the water made Harley jump.

"Step back, Harley. Way back.' In the midst of the mayhem, he took time to take care of her. The huge snake reared and its head came out of the water. Lord, it was as big as a football. Beau made a grab at it while the long, massive body lurched and flopped. "Help me! Grab her body." Beau instructed the men who, way too slowly for Harley's peace of mind, began to get in the water and attempt to grab ahold of what looked like an out-of-control, over-sized fire hose.

"Help him," she screamed. No one heard her. They were yelling, the water was churning and the snake was writhing and whipping around and she swore right then that if she ever got her hands on Beau again she would tie him to the bedpost. It took four grown men, plus Beau, to wrestle the python out of the water and onto the bank.

"Grab that sack, honey." Beau instructed as he subdued the snake and forced its body onto the ground. "Let's look at her before we bag her." He held the head while the other men attempted to straighten the big python out on the ground. "Inside the sack is a tape measure, Harley. Find it and give it to one of these fellows. There's a small scale in there, too." On unsteady legs, Harley dug out the tape and handed it over and laid the scale on the ground. It was the type that would hang over a tree limb and whatever needed to be weighed could hang from it. She had seen enough documentaries on this type of thing to recognize the tools. She just never thought she would be a part of one of the scenes. Lord, the things one did for love!

He was magnificent, truly he was. Harley didn't really see the other men, only Beau. With calm and sure movements, Beau managed the snake while one of the others stretched the tape measure down the long body. The snake was a little over fifteen feet long. "She's a big baby, let's get her bagged up and weigh her, then Harley and I will take her somewhere safe."

One hundred and eighty pounds. That was a lot of snake. Harley stood by the bag and watched it sort of pulse as the snake shifted around. The men huddled nearby discussing the situation. "So, there have been no reports of a lost pet or a zoo escape?" Beau examined the ground that led down to the water, searching for clues as to where the snake had been nesting.

"No sir," the tall man answered, tiredly. "But there has to be some explanation. Snakes like this don't just crawl out of the marsh."

Looking off into the distance, Beau surmised. "Actually, they do. They're in Florida and scientists speculate that they will spread. I'm not saying that's what has happened here, but I'm going to alert the Louisiana Department of Wild Game and Fisheries so they can be aware of the possibility."

"Have you looked at a map of the South? How could a snake crawl from the everglades to the bayous of Louisiana?" To say the man looked disturbed was putting it mildly.

"I didn't say she did, but we need to let them know, just in case. There have been estimates that these animals could survive as far north as Washington D. C. A severe cold snap can kill one, but if they have a place to bury up in and keep warm, like an armadillo hole, they could survive."

With that explanation, Beau picked up the big snake and threw it over his shoulder like it was an everyday thing. When he reached for Harley's hand she scooted to stand on the side away from the snake and Beau laughed at her move. "She's settled down now. We'll take her to the zoo over in Lafayette. They've agreed to take her and then we head to St. Martinsville. I'm gonna show you a really old oak tree, tell you about the world's saddest love story and make you orgasm five times before morning." Harley whirled around to see if the other men heard, but they were still standing at the water's edge as if they expected another serpent to rise up from the murky depths.

"Sounds good to me." And it did.

Chapter Ten

"The tale of Evangeline is one of the famous tales of Cajun history. There is a lot of debate, but most agree that Henry Wadsworth Longfellow heard the heartbreaking tale of Emmeline Labiche and Louis Arceneaux and retold it in his haunting poem."

"I've read Evangeline, but it's been a long time ago," Harley held Beau's hand as they sat under the huge oak. "I do remember that this tree is where the Acadian maiden, Evangeline, came to meet her lost love, Gabriel. Sadly, she missed him by only one day. They weren't united until the day that Gabriel died in Evangeline's arms. I can't imagine a sadder tale."

"No one really knows the truth. The story has become ingrained in our history. We accept it as fact, like Washington chopping down the cherry tree. Evangeline and Gabriel were part of the group forced out of Acadia in the 1700's. Acadia was the region that lies in present day Quebec, Prince Edward's Island and Maine. The British were afraid these French-speaking people would be treasonous, so they forced them from their homeland. During the confusion, they were separated and they spent a lifetime, apart. Searching for one another. They weren't reunited until it was too late."

Harley listened as Beau talked about a subject close to his heart. "Savannah's Patrick did more research on it than anybody I know. He was searching for family. I don't think he ever found a blood relative, but he did find Savannah. She became his home."

"How do you know this?"

"I took him out in the swamp one day, fishing. One of the crazy things he found out was that the United States wasn't just a haven for these people; my people. They were just as guilty as the British in expelling them from Acadia and pushing them south to where they are today. Cajun Country. It isn't a bright spot in our nation's history, I'm sorry to say."

"No, it isn't," Harley agreed. "It reminds me of the Trail of Tears. I had ancestors who were marched out of their home in Tennessee to Oklahoma."

"The Cherokee?"

"Yes, my mother's grandmother was Cherokee. I was interested enough to research it and found that they began their thousand mile march in the winter of 1838. Most marched on foot with very little clothing, and no moccasins or shoes. What was really pitiful was that the blankets they were given were from a hospital in Tennessee, left over from a small pox epidemic. Because of exposure to this disease, they were kept out of towns along the way. So many of them were starving, and when they came to Golconda Illinois, they were charged one dollar each to cross over on the ferry. The normal price was twelve cents, and the Indians didn't have the money – so they sat out in the freezing cold under Mantle Rock and many of them perished. Even the ones who had money weren't allowed to cross until everyone else who wanted to go was ferried over. It was a travesty"

Thinking of the injustice that so many had faced, they walked out into the cemetery where Emmiline was supposedly buried. "You know some think this grave may be empty."

Harley stood there and went completely still. "I don't think so," she muttered. "I hear a woman weeping. A man is walking away. Love is lost. I feel helpless, desolate, lonely, void of dreams, no hope for tomorrow."

Beau stood by, joining her in mourning the loss of love that this couple endured.

"If it's true, it's a tragedy."

"Yes, if it was true," Harley whispered. Her heart was pounding, her palms were sweating. The dividing line between the past and present had gone hazy. She didn't know if what she had felt were memories of the past or a glimpse into the future.

* * *

The Old Castillo Bed and Breakfast was absolutely beautiful. Harley enjoyed examining the antiques and the imported dishes and she loved walking the grounds down by the bayou. But what intrigued her the most was the big bed and what lay upon it like a powerful lion surveying his territory. That was it. He was a lion of a man. She felt her loins liquefy with excitement. "Come here, Harley." He held out his hand. They had gone shopping and he had bought her a negligee made of pure white lace. "You look like an angel. My angel."

As she moved toward him, she was overwhelmed by an uneasy feeling that seemed to vibrate through the air. It was almost like the distant rumbling of a coming earthquake or an approaching tsunami. Something evil was on its way. Perhaps it was because of the turmoil she had felt while standing at the grave of Evangeline. Looking at Beau, she was struck by how unfair all of this was. Their lives had been manipulated by Pell, and now Crocker. It wasn't fair, and Beau sure didn't deserve it. Pell was gone, but Crocker was still in the picture. And they were at his mercy. He could lure her back into his web of horror with just one phone call, and he knew it.

"What's wrong?" Beau rose from the bed and came to her, enveloping her in his embrace. "Your expression changed. Where did you go?"

"I just had a funny feeling in the pit of my stomach." She laid her head on his chest, wishing that Crocker was behind bars and nothing would ever threaten them again.

"Do you think you could be pregnant?" The words popped out of Beau's mouth before he thought. Images of Harley round with his babe came unbidden. He wanted it all with her, but that couldn't happen until she was safe from the snares of a madman.

"I don't think so, unless the birth control pill failed." It could happen, but she knew that wasn't the cause of her queasiness.

"Do you feel like making love with me?" He began nuzzling her face in a wordless seduction.

"Please, yes." She needed all of him that she could get.

Slowly, he drew back and held her hand, so he could gaze at her beauty. "You look like a bride on her wedding night."

"That's a sweet thought. We can pretend this is our honeymoon."

"Let's think of it as a dress rehearsal, cause I fully intend to have the real thing with you someday," he said softly, standing before her with his legs spread, the bulge behind his tight jeans drawing her eye.

Shivers of awareness coursed over her. Lord, he was hard and thick. Just looking at him made her ache. Harley wanted him so much. She wanted him now, and she wanted him forever. "You make me nervous," she confessed.

"Ah, cher," a flicker of sorrow passed through his eyes. "I thought we were past that."

"It's a good nervous," she assured him. He looked skeptical, so she decided to show him. Once, Beau had told her that he longed for the day when she would just take what she wanted like she did when she would grab his hand while they walked the streets of New Orleans. So, she moved to him, letting all the arousal and hunger and need that had been building up for a lifetime rise up and make itself known. Looking up through her lashes at him, she smiled and licked her lips. "I want you, Beau LeBlanc. More than anything."

A wild, hungry look lit up his eyes and he grabbed her hips, pulling her flush up against him. "Say that again."

"Hmmmm, I want you, Beau. I want you hard and fast and all night long," she purred, standing on tiptoe so she could nip at his lower lip, then lick the sting away.

"Why you little minx," he chuckled as he pulled her closer, burying his cock into her stomach. "You want me? Show me how much." He stepped back and unzipped his pants, releasing his swollen, thick cock. "Come on baby, I've got what you need." With one hand he stroked his rod from the base to the tip, a long, slow pump. The other hand tangled in her hair, pulling her close. "Kiss me, baby."

She needed no further encouragement. With a whimper of absolute surrender, she flung herself against him and burrowed her mouth against his; kissing him with a quiet desperation as if this were the last kiss they would ever share.

Beau held her fast, letting her feast, accepting and returning - lick for lick, sip for sip - knowing she was imprinting herself on his very soul. Precum was leaking from his cock. God, he needed to feel her skin. Without asking, he began pushing her sheer robe from her shoulders. She understood, dropping her arms and making it easier for him. Still they kissed. As soon as the robe hit the floor, he grasped the gown and began gathering it his fingers, lifting it up and over her head. She huffed a little protest when it became necessary to remove her mouth from his. Beau couldn't help but laugh. "Hungry, baby?"

"Starving."

Shit! Every time he saw her breasts he was struck anew with their beauty. Damn, they were cum-worthy. "You are so hot." He bent over and sucked hard on one nipple, drug his mouth over to the other and licked it, sensuously. "Are you wet for me?" Not waiting for an answer, he felt between her legs. "Hell yeah, I could drown in your juices." She pushed toward him, urging him to go deeper. "Touch me," he demanded, then hissed out a breath when her hand closed around his cock. Looking down, he noted with satisfaction that her fingers wouldn't meet. Raising his eyes to her, he grinned. "You might ought to use both hands, sugar."

So she did, and what she did took his breath away. Cock worship. He had heard of it, but he had never been lucky enough to experience it. With one hand she pumped, massaging his rod, letting her palm come up and over the head, rubbing the pearlescent drop of his seed into his skin. The other held him at the base and squeezed, driving him fuckin' crazy. "Damn, how did you know how to do that?"

"I researched it on the internet," she answered with a saucy little grin. "I'm a quick study."

"Show me what else you learned. Go down on me, Harley. Suck me; I need to feel your lips on my cock." With bated breath he waited as she kissed him on the neck and then began to lick her way south. She scraped his pecs, tongued his nipples and as she sank to her knees she nipped him on his belly, leaving a little mark of ownership. "God, you're good. The Lord loves me a lot, he does." Oh, she was making him wait, teasing him.

Having turned loose of his dick, she jerked on his pants. "Help me, Beau."

He didn't argue, but stripped his clothes off and prayed she would remember where she left off. Clasping him behind the ankles, she drug her hands up his legs, soothing, kneading, petting him. He decided not to take any chances. "Suck me, sweet baby."

"With pleasure."

Molten fire enveloped his cock as she fitted her lips over the head. Was there any more beautiful sight in the world than seeing your woman pleasuring you? Seeing her stretch her pink lips over your flesh? With heated concentration, Harley sucked. Beau hummed his satisfaction, "That's it baby. Suck me hard."

What was the best part? Harley couldn't decide. Was it watching his face? Seeing the emotion race across it, his lips curling in ecstasy? Or was it the very act, itself? She loved the closeness. Sucking him deeper, she eagerly gave him pleasure. He loved this she could tell. Sliding him out, drawing him back in, she fed their lust. He wove his hands in her hair and held her captive as his cock fucked her mouth in short, hard jabs. Little did he know, but she loved his dominance. It was a surprise to her as well. And she needed him, so much. Moisture was gathering between her thighs, saturating her pussy. More, she wanted more.

It was hard to be still and focus. Pressing her legs together, Harley fought the urge to rub her clit. Instead, she looked up at her man. His head was thrown back, his eyes were closed and his hair fell around his face giving him the look of a warrior. With swirls of her tongue she massaged the head. Groans of appreciation burst from his lips.

"Perfect...fuckin' perfect." Sensations so sharp and so intense arrowed through his body, making his balls draw up and his blood sizzle. Did any man deserve pleasure like this? Lord, he needed to cum. But he needed something else more. "Up, up...turn around." Helping her to her feet, he whirled her around. "Bend over."

Harley started to protest, but she was so turned on it was hard to think. Following his command, she bent over and felt him go down behind her. "Oh, Beau," she keened as he palmed her pussy, rubbing it sensuously, fingering her clit. "What are you doing?"

"This." Suddenly he spread her legs wider, and a big hand pressed down on her back. She felt his lips on her hips, his tongue tracing patterns on her skin. "You've got such a pretty little pussy," he groaned as he tongue speared into her opening. Clutching the bedspread, Harley held on. Pleasure her only reality.

"Oh, God," she moaned as he licked and sucked. She felt so helpless. Beau was tonguing her flesh, kissing and lapping, making her mindless with need. "Please?" she begged. His only answer was to take her farther, a little bite to her labia lips, his tongue working deeper in her channel, the pad of his thumb massaging her clit until she was bucking helplessly, pushing her bottom back against his face.

"Do you want to come, Harley?"

"Got to," she tried to reason with him. "Need to, please."

Beau chuckled at her desperation, but gifted her with exactly what she asked for. Closing his lips over her clit, he drew it his mouth and sucked. Harley shattered. Explosions of heat and color flashed through her. Arching her back, she ground against him. Her whole body trembled as the climax shook her to the very core. Still, she wanted more.

"I need you now." She felt him stand up, and she tried to turn over. Beau was going to take her and she was almost sobbing with relief. But, before she could move, she felt the stalk of his manhood probe at her opening. With one mighty thrust, he impaled her on his cock. Fiery pleasure scorched her pussy. He held her hips and pumped into her with grunts and groans of appreciation. "God, you are so tight. Your little box squeezes me like a vise." She held herself up on her arms, looking over her shoulder, needing to keep him in sight.

"Beau," she said his name. This was Beau. Her Beau. Over and over again, he rammed into her. Her whole body was at his mercy. His hands weren't still; they soothed her back or kneaded her hip. Biting her lip, she let herself feel his surging power. She could do this. All she needed to do was concentrate on how much she loved him and how good it felt.

How had he ever survived without her? Nothing or no one could compare. Beau was lost in Harley. Staring down he could see his cock emerge from her flesh, covered with her cream, only to sink back in to the sweetest, tightest little pussy he had ever known.

Shaking his head like the lion she had compared him to, he growled and pumped harder, deeper, faster, his balls slapping against her pussy. Harley held on to the bedspread and to her sanity. This was Beau. He loved her. "Beau, please!" she wailed.

He heard her as if at a distance. He couldn't think. He couldn't answer. The only thing he could do was feel. She tightened around him even more, her body undulating under his. God, he couldn't take anymore. He had to cum. Bearing down, he covered her, pressing her down into the mattress. His hand was on her back, her face in the mattress. "Milk me, baby! Fuck, yeah!" He rocked into her over and over again, until his cum boiled up and shot out, filling her up. She struggled beneath him. Her voice was ragged with emotion.

"Beau, please…I know it's you, but let me up. Please! I'm afraid!"

God, no. God, no. God, no. What had he done? Pulling out, he picked her up, holding her. "Harley? Harley, baby? God, I'm so sorry. What's wrong? Did I hurt you?"

Shit! Shit! Shit! She was shaking. How pathetic could she get? She had ruined it. "No, you didn't hurt me. It just got to be too much. I'm sorry, Beau." He sat down on the bed and cradled her to him. She threw her arms around his neck and sobbed. "I didn't mean to fall apart. It was just being held down like that. I couldn't help it, for a minute I was back in Brownwood with Pell. I'm so sorry!"

Beau felt like he was going to die. "You're sorry? I didn't think. I was too excited. God, forgive me, honey. Please!" He had known she didn't want to be taken like that and he had done it anyway. Fuck! Fuck! Fuck!

"There's nothing to forgive. It was my fault." Still, she shook in his arms.

"Never. Impossible." He set her aside and went to get a washcloth. "Sit still, I'll be right back." Returning, it hit him just how small and fragile she was. Damn, he ought to be taken out to the woodshed. She looked up at him, tremulously.

"I was okay till right at the last. You know I love to make love with you." He wiped her face, her hands and between her legs. But, he didn't say anything. She watched his face. All she could see was remorse.

Picking her robe up off the floor, he helped her get her arms in the sleeves and fastened a couple of buttons. Next he picked up his pants and pulled them on. "What kind of man am I? You entrusted yourself into my care and I failed to protect you. From me! Maybe, I'm not what you need."

"No. No…please, no. Let me show you." She reached for him, determined to prove that she trusted him, desired him, needed him above all other."

"Stop," he took her hands in his. Silling them. "Not now. I need to think." Beau was confused. He never thought that he would be the one to hurt Harley. But he had. What did that say about him? "Look," he framed her face with a tender grasp, "this isn't your fault. You are precious. But, I need to think. Just sit here and let me walk this off. You know how I am. I just need to clear my head."

He turned to go. Harley jumped up to stop him. "Don't go. It won't happen again. Please don't let this change anything between us."

"I'll be back, and then we'll talk. I promise. I won't be gone long. You know I'm not going far, not with that madman loose. Fresh air, that's what I need."

"Please don't reject me," she whispered, but he was already gone.

A frantic ring broke the silence. Three long. One short. "Oh, no. Not now." She went to the dresser, her whole body wound up like a tight spring. "Socorro."

"Harley, its Waco. I'm on my way to Baton Rouge with everything we need. In just a few minutes, a policeman will pick you up and take you to a helipad." She had kept him informed of their whereabouts and everything that had been going on – just in case. "You've got to get to Tiger stadium at LSU. It's bad. There's a beer truck parked next to the south side and the authorities say it's packed tight with C4."

"What else do we know?" She began to get ready as she talked.

"The stadium is filled to capacity. Ninety-two thousand people think they are at a normal football game. They have no idea they're sitting on a powder keg. We've received specific instructions that if the crowd is let go, the bomb will automatically detonate – no bargaining – no second chances. Emptying the stadium isn't really an option. There would be mass panic. Stampedes. People would get trampled and die in the confusion."

"I don't understand. This isn't my area of expertise. And I have no connections to LSU. This can't be Crocker." She had confided all of her fears to her employee.

"Oh, it's Crocker, he's identified himself and he wants to talk to you. He says if anybody else gets within a hundred feet of that truck he'll detonate the mercury switch and blow the whole place sky high. The death toll would be tremendous. That asshole is holding all those people hostage, and they don't even know it."

"What do we know? How much time do I have?"

"He's says it'll be a fourth quarter surprise. We're

running out of time."

"I'll be ready. You wait outside for me, keep me informed and be careful. And Waco," she cleared her throat fighting back tears. "I'm going to need you this time. I'm not in the best frame of mind."

"What do you mean? Has something happened with Crocker that I'm not aware of?"

"No, it's not about Crocker. It's Beau, I've messed up and let him down. I think it's over."

"Hell, baby. I'm so sorry. There's no way you could let anybody down. But don't you worry,

I'll be there. You won't be alone."

She closed the phone. Beau hadn't returned, but that really wasn't a surprise. She didn't have time to look for him. He had said he wasn't leaving, but he might have changed his mind. Grabbing a piece of paper, she hastily wrote him a note. How to say what she wanted to say in only a few lines?

Dearest Beau-ray:

I am so sorry for running off like this without saying good-bye. What happened this morning was not your fault. And I understand completely why you would think twice about being with someone like me.

I received an emergency phone call a few moments ago. I have to go Baton Rouge. There is a bomb at the LSU football stadium and it's filled to capacity. Pray for me, all of those people's lives are in jeopardy and we can't even warn them.

Whatever happens, remember that I loved you with all my heart. And I would have given anything in this world to have had forever with you.

Harley

She left it propped up on the dresser for him to find – then she made the longest walk of her life. Away from Beau.

* * *

Beau had never been angrier with himself. He had walked around the grounds for a bit, trying to calm down. Now, he thought he'd just sit in Indy's truck and think. With more force than he intended, he almost ripped the truck door off its hinges. How could he have been so stupid? A harsh laugh, almost a sob, tore from his throat. Visions of the last hour or so scalded his memory. He had taken her so roughly, in the very way she had asked him not to. Still echoing in his ears were the little pleas she had made as she begged him. Damn! He hurt so bad, like razor blades were slicing gashes in his soul. Idiot! Harley hadn't been begging him for more of his cock; she had been begging him to stop!

Oh, he had to work it out. He didn't have a choice. Harley was his life. He loved her and God, help him he hoped she loved him, but he needed more help than he realized. This was one time he couldn't afford to fuck up.

Sitting in the Old Castillo parking lot, he could see the grounds and make sure no intruder came anywhere near her. This was really a beautiful place. Everything looked so normal, so peaceful. He watched a cop car pull out of the front drive. That made him feel better, it was good to know they were out and about in the neighborhood.

All he could think about was Harley. He wasn't seeing the sleepy side street in St. Martinsville, or the Evangeline oak. He was seeing Harley smiling as they walked at Cypress Bend. He wasn't hearing the noises of traffic. Instead, he heard her laughing on the boat at Caddo Lake. Every moment they had spent together echoed through his mind. If he closed his eyes he could still feel her body as she clung to him, her refuge, when she had been frightened by the specters of Willow Bend.

God, he had to fix this. She was his Nada. The bond

they shared was so tight and complete; he didn't feel like he could breathe away from her. Why did his life have to be so complicated? Lord, he needed to get this off his chest. Taking his phone, he placed a call to the good doctor. Maybe they needed to go see Dane again. Ole' Beau LeBlanc didn't have his act together nearly as well as he thought he did. Checking his watch, he realized the doc probably wasn't in his office. It was getting late. Oh well, the answering service might patch him through. He was wrong – the doctor was in.

"Wagner, here. Beau, is that you?"

"Caller ID? Or psychic?"

"Not psychic. So tell me. How is Harley? Did you make her a happy and fulfilled woman?"

"For a while," Lord, this was hard. "Our first time was perfect. And the second and the third. But tonight I fucked up."

"What happened?"

"Hell, I got carried away. She had told me how those bastards had controlled her by holding her face down on a surface." He paused, but when Dane didn't jump into the conversation, he went on. "I thought everything was okay. We were going at it hot and heavy and I had made her cum. Shit, I feel like a heel for telling you this. She doesn't like us to talk details."

"This is important. Be respectful, but go ahead."

"I had her bending over the bed and had kissed her from that angle and I just stood up and entered her from the back. I swear to God, I thought everything was fine. She was ready for me, she seemed receptive. But something went wrong. She was talking, begging me 'please', and fool that I was, I thought she was happy and wanting more. Damn, man." Beau's voice broke. "She was begging me to stop."

"Where is she now? Is she all right?"

"She says she's fine, told me everything was okay and that it was her fault."

"Don't leave her. Don't walk away from her. There's something you don't know." He hated to break patient/doctor confidentiality, but this was too important.

"What?" She wasn't suicidal, there was no way.

"Twice before, Harley has been rejected by a man because of the rapes. They felt she was tainted." Several words of vehement protest from Beau colored the air. "That's her greatest fear about you; you know."

"I don't understand."

"Harley's convinced that you'll suddenly realize being with a rape victim is more trouble than it's worth."

After talking to Dane, Beau quickly made his way back to their room. Harley's words kept coming back to him. *"Don't go. It won't happen again. Please don't let this change things between us."* Did she think he was about to turn his back on her over this? Hell, no. "Harley?"

She didn't answer. Walking quickly from room to room, he frantically searched the suite. Everything she had brought with her was gone. There was no feminine toiletries in the bathroom, no clothes in her side of the closet. His heart was hammering in his chest. Her purse was gone. Her cell phones were gone. His phone lay there, right along side his wallet and change. And then he saw it. A note. Grabbing it, he hastily read the words. At first he didn't understand, so he read them again. Terror washed over him like lava.

Once he had said there was no way she could scare him. He was wrong. Harley was on her way to face the work of a madman, again. And the worst part? She was convinced he didn't want her.

Like a caged lion, he paced back and forth across the room. God, he had to do something. She would be in no frame of mind to diffuse a bomb. Jesus! Why hadn't he stayed with her? Why hadn't he talked it through, instead of running off and pouting like some adolescent? Didn't she understand? It was him that had failed, not her. Beau's chest ached like somebody had ripped his heart from its moorings.

He had to go to her. That was the only answer. He wasn't ready to give her up to a misunderstanding much less a tragic, senseless death. Not going to happen. Running out to the truck, he started his pickup up and slammed it into gear. "Hold on baby. I'm coming. And once I get you back in my arms, I'm never going to let you go again.

* * *

Flying north, Harley tried to calm down. This was no time to fall apart. There was time enough for that later. In her bag, her phone rang. Beau!! Grabbing it up, she dug it out. Her whole body shaking. She didn't even look at the number. "Beau?"

"No, someone else from your past. Hello, Nada Montoya. I've missed you."

A voice from the grave. "Why are you doing this?"

"To get to you. Am I succeeding?" Icy. Cold. Deadly.

"If you want me, why not come after me? Why put innocent people in jeopardy?" She was squeezing the phone so hard; she expected it to break in two. "I can make it easy on you. I'll come to you." After all, she had nothing to lose now. Nothing.

"What would be the fun in that? You just come on to Baton Rouge. And keep the phone on. I have some special information. . . . just for you." His venomous whisper caused her skin to crawl. Then he was gone.

* * *

Beau was driving at break-neck speed. He didn't know what he would do if he were stopped. A trip that should

267

take an hour was going to be a lot less. When his phone buzzed, he almost didn't answer it. But what if it were Harley? He didn't take time to look. "Harley?"

"No, it's Dandi. What's going on? Where are you?"

Knowing he couldn't tell her the truth, he struggled for words. "I'm on my way to Baton Rouge. I don't have time to talk."

"I know something is up. You just got a strange phone call from a man named Waco. He said he was Harley's partner and he told me to give you this message. He said that if you were half the man Harley thought you were, you'd come where she is. And when you get there to call this number." She called it out to him. "Care to tell me why you and Harley aren't together?"

"No, not now." He entered the number in his phone.

"Indiana has filled me in on the man that's after Harley. I couldn't believe when he brought in that bomb detection squad, I thought I was going to faint."

"Sweetie, I love you. But, I'm not in a talking mood right now."

"All right. I understand. Whatever's up. Be careful. Please. You're all I have."

"I'll do my best."

After he laid the phone down, he muttered. "I may owe Waco an apology, after all."

This was a trip he could make in the dark. LSU was his alma mater. He didn't know if Crocker had made it his target because of him, but he had a funny feeling that was exactly what was going on. Because he was prime in Harley's life, everything he valued would be threatened. There were a number of people and things Beau loved, but Harley was his prize possession. Fox Crocker's days were numbered; there was no doubt about it. Beau would see to that himself.

As he neared the college, there was no obvious

indication that something was wrong. Maybe a few extra cop cars were milling around, but they were keeping it low key. Still, he wanted to get where he was going as quickly as possible. So, he made the call. "Waco." It wasn't Waco who answered, but the man seemed to understand his request and in a few minutes an escort came to lead him to a delivery entrance. Apparently he was now an honorary member of Socorro. Damn straight. He should have thought of that himself.

Driving down through campus, following a motorcycle cop, he could see the football stadium ahead of him. Clemson's stadium was called Death Valley, but today that term might best apply to the home of the LSU Tigers. Some called this structure Deaf Valley because of the noise level achieved every Saturday night that a home game was played. It was considered to be the one stadium most unfriendly to a visiting team. Tiger Stadium held over 92,000 people and renovations were underway to take that up another eight thousand. When full to capacity, population wise, it was the sixth largest 'city' in Louisiana.

In a few minutes, he was parked and led inside. "My God," he breathed as he looked up into the stands. They were packed, and the roar of happy, excited people struck him as the saddest thing he ever saw. They had no idea what was going on. A cold dread swept over his body. It was the most damn eerie sensation, he ever felt. The lives of this huge crowd rested in the small, soft hands of the woman he loved and Beau wanted to bellow his anguish.

"Walk this way, sir; it'll be closer to cut through." The cop got his attention. "They told me to take you to Socorro's van." They turned and went into the belly of the stadium, a web of halls and room. Infamous Governor Huey P. Long had been allocated money by the state to build dormitories, but none for stadium seating. So, he had fooled the system and ordered dorms be built in the stadium walls with seating above them. Later, the living quarters were changed to offices and storage. As they walked through the halls, there were footsteps echoing. Beau heard an unmistakable sound he would recognize anywhere. It was muffled, but he knew what it was, a gunshot.

He didn't walk. He ran.

* * *

"Listen to me, bitch." Crocker's voice snarled into the phone. "I told you no one was allowed to help you."

"You shot him!" Harley screamed.

"Yes, I did. And I'd shoot you and let all these people die, but it's more fun to watch you sweat."

She shook, she quaked. What if Waco were dead? God, this was a nightmare. She put the phone on speaker and laid it down. Crocker was manic, but he might say something she could use. When she had first walked around the corner and seen this huge panel truck, she knew there were enough explosives in it to take down half the stadium. The Oklahoma City bombing instantly came to mind. Her first order of business had been to disable the mercury switch. She remembered where Crocker had said he would put it, if he were the one designing a car bomb. And it was right where he had mentioned, under the right fender, over the back tire. She had also found and destroyed the cell phone apparatus that cut off Crocker's remote control of the bomb. He didn't know that, though. And she wasn't going to mention that to him – not yet anyway. She'd wait till she thought the time was right. He was as susceptible to mind games as she was. More so, hopefully. If he thought he still had the option to set off the bomb early, he wouldn't be as reckless. Knowing their calls were being monitored, she longed to give the Baton Rouge Bomb Squad that info, just in case. Her main concern was that no one else get shot down like Waco, either. Crocker had her between a rock and a hard place…just the way he intended.

Opening the side panel, what she saw almost took her to her knees. Pallets of plastic explosives and bags of fertilizer were arranged in stacks that reached the ceiling and a control panel of wires and switches, designed to intimidate and overwhelm her stretched across the floor like a huge mixer board.

"How do you like my handiwork? It's beautiful isn't it?"

"It's the work of a madman," she answered. God, where did she start?

Her nerves were frazzled and whatever psychic ability she had seemed to be shorted-out by the turmoil of her sorrow over Beau and Waco.

"I'll tell you a secret. Something you need to know before you go farther."

"I'm waiting." She was listening, as she examined the intricate mass of electronics.

"This is the simplest bomb you could ever diffuse. In fact, I have colored the wires red that you need to cut."

Harley didn't understand his statement; it couldn't be that easy. "Okay, thank you."

"Not so fast. There are two of them, one on each end. Listen carefully, this is important." Harley's skin crawled just from having to listen to his voice.

"Crocker, damn you. Tell me!"

He chuckled. "You have a choice, sweet Nada. I always loved your body, by the way. It's a shame you're a frigid bitch. How are you able to satisfy that Cajun of yours? I can't imagine he finds any pleasure in your bed."

"Shut-up, Crocker," she snarled.

"Are you nervous, Nada? You should be. There's a wire on your right side that will stop the detonation of the bomb." She walked toward it. "Uh-uh – not so fast."

It was obvious he was watching her. Harley looked up and around, trying to see him. "Where are you?"

"I've been living in your head for years. Haven't I?" He laughed again. "Now, look all the way to the other end of the board." Crocker's voice took on a sick, sing-song quality. But, her eyes followed his direction. "All the way over there, where you can't possibly reach them at the same time – is another switch. That one belongs solely to you."

"I don't understand," she said that, but an image of herself choking and gasping for air was pulsing in her mind like a neon sign.

"You have a choice, Nada. Not a good choice, but a choice." A sly snicker told of his enjoyment at her unbelievable predicament. "If you clip the wire that saves the stadium full of people, a vial of poisonous gas will be released right in your face. You will die in seconds."

She had been right on the money. At least she knew her psychic abilities weren't out of commission. "You're a sick bastard, aren't you?"

"Maybe." He seemed to hesitate, just to play with her. "If you choose to cut the other wire on the left side, you save yourself – but everybody else may die. Thousands will be crushed by the falling stands and hundreds more will perish in the panic. You can't be in two places at once. It's impossible and I'll shoot anyone who approaches to help you. So what's it going to be? Will you pick yourself or everyone else? If you could only be two places at once, but you can't."

What did he mean by that? Shaking her head, she tried to clear her mind. Harley chose to say nothing more to Crocker. She had the information she needed. Her heart was pounding and she felt desolate, alone and hopeless. More than anything she wanted to hold Beau one more time. She'd never see him again. Because Crocker knew how she would choose. There really was no alternative. Today, Nada Montoya would die.

* * *

"Tell me what's going on," Beau demanded. Several uniformed SWAT teams and Bomb Squad techs stood around listening to the transmitted conversations of Harley and Crocker. He had walked up at the end of their exchange and he wanted to know everything.

One burly man with a crew cut glanced at him. "She's up shit creek without a paddle. This nut-job has built the perfect trap for her. Ms. Montoya can either save herself or everybody else, but not both." Sweat was beading on the man's forehead, clearly he was scared shitless. Beau glanced down at his pants, looking for a wet spot. Surely, the coward had pissed on himself.

Rage filled Beau. "Well, why in the hell aren't you doing something about it? Why don't you help her?" That these trained apes were standing there in relative safety while his little darling was fighting their battles for them absolutely infuriated him.

"She's trained. She'll make the right choice. Crocker has issued kill orders for anyone that tries to go to her aid. We're afraid he'll detonate the bomb early if we make a move."

"Where's her partner?" Maybe Waco could help him understand what was going on.

"Over there," another man pointed to where an EMT was working on the fallen man.

Beau walked over and got as close as he could. "Waco, I'm Beau. I'm here to help. What do I need to know? What can I do?"

Waco opened pain filled eyes. "You can stop hurting Harley for one thing."

"You don't have to tell me that. I know I fucked up.

273

What else?"

"I can promise you that she's killed the mercury switch. Get out there and help her. I don't know what's going on. They're not telling me everything, but she may need two hands." Waco pinned him with a stare. "But what she needs most of all, so she can concentrate to do her job, is to know that you still want her in your life."

"Can you tell these idiots to let me go to her? Will they listen to you?"

And then he heard her again; his baby's voice was coming over the cop's speakers. He hurried back to hear what she had to say. She was talking to Crocker. *"Let me ask you something, just out of curiosity."*

"What do you want to know? I'll tell you most anything now; consider it to be equivalent to your last meal."

"Why didn't you detonate the bomb when Waco walked out here, why did you choose to just shoot him?"

"Easy, I didn't want our game to be over so soon."

"I'm going over there to help her." Beau announced flatly. "She belongs to me."

"We can't let you do that. Crocker will end this thing before we have a chance in hell to stop him."

Beau had to hold himself back. "I don't see WE doing anything but standing here while a little bit of a female charges into hell for you fuckin' bloody morons."

"Now, Mr. LeBlanc. . . there's no need. . ."

Harley's voice cut into their conversation as if she was addressing their concerns.

"I hate to tell you this, Crocker. But your mercury switch is dead. You are officially out of the loop. It's in my hands now."

"I still have the gun."

"You won't need that. No one is coming out to help me…it's just me and you."

"That's where you're wrong, baby." Beau glared at the policeman and one of them nodded his head and Beau took off. She didn't know it, but the Calvary was officially on the way.

Chapter Eleven

Harley prayed. Her prayers probably didn't go any higher than the ceiling, but she didn't figure it would hurt to try. She prayed for a miracle. There was no way she would ever ask any of the others to come to her aid. They all had families and they might die getting to her. A Kevlor vest wouldn't be a deterrent to Crocker. He would take a headshot. Still, she hoped – for a few more seconds, she hoped. And she prayed for Beau…that her death wouldn't devastate him. She wanted him to be happy.

There was nothing else to do. She had examined everything. Crocker had won. She had to kill this bomb before it exploded and killed too many innocent lives to count. Rising, she went to stand by the wire that would shut this monstrosity down and end her life. "I love you, Beau." She raised her clippers…and another shot rang out…and another. She jumped when somebody touched her.

"I love you, too, Harley." Strong arms wrapped around her and hauled her back against his chest. "I'm here. What can I do?"

Turning in his arms, she hugged him hard. "You shouldn't be here. It's too dangerous."

"I play with fire all the time, baby. Just tell me what to do. I can follow orders. Let me save you."

"You're an answer to prayer. Did you know that?" She handed him some clippers and pointed for him to stand at the kill switch that would disable the panel truck bomb and she stayed next to the one that would release the gas. Maybe, if the noxious substance was released, he would be far enough away to escape harm. "And don't breathe in when I clip this wire. Hold your breath. On the count of three - - on the word three – cut the wire."

276

It worked.

"It's over," she announced to the men who were listening. They swarmed the place hunting for Crocker, and she breathed a sigh of relief. She had had doubts about surviving this time. Serious doubts. Her life had been turned topsy-turvy and nothing had made any sense. But in the next moment, she was swept up in Beau's arms and her world righted itself.

"I love you, I love you, I love you. I was wrong."

He spread kisses all over her face and squeezed her so tight she could barely breathe. Her feet weren't even touching the ground, he held her up in his arms and all she could do was cling to him and cry. "I can't believe you came," she marveled.

"You should have known I would," he whispered. "I can't live without you - - if I lose you, my world ends."

"What about my panic attacks?"

"Shhhhh," he kissed her cheek. "Stop worrying. Let's go home."

* * *

"I love your house." She couldn't say it enough. Blending into the lush landscape, his home sat on piers. Made of cypress, it was stained a dark golden oak. Decks and stairs and pathways wound down from the second story to end like magical paths at the edge of the bayou where a dock jutted out into the deeper water.

"Thank-you, doll." He kissed her. "I had hoped you would like it here. Won't we be a lucky couple with three places to call home?" A splash off to one side drew their attention. "Look, there's the Cuban crocs. We had to move them over here till Indy could get their area free of fire-ants. So, don't you go sleep-walking and fall of the deck or you'll end up a midnight snack." He grabbed her and hugged her close and this time, she didn't squeal or jump or flinch. She just held on like she would never let him go.

He carried her in. Like a bride over the threshold. She couldn't be still in his arms for looking at her surroundings. "You have a gorgeous kitchen, and fireplace, and couch and . . ." he never slowed down until he got to his room. "And bed," she finished as he sat her down on it. When he knelt down and laid his head in her lap, she began to cry. "Beau-ray, it's okay. Everything turned out okay."

"I know," he kissed her stomach. "But it could have so easily gone horribly wrong."

She rubbed his hair, soothing him. "You saved me."

"Hell, honey. You saved us all. You're amazing – so brave. You run toward what everyone else is running from. How many other people can say that?"

"I don't know about that. Look how I acted when you were making love to me." She kissed his head. "I love how you make me feel. You have given me a reason to live. Making love with you is the culmination of a lifetime of dreams. So, how could I fall apart like that? I'm so ashamed."

Beau got up and joined her on the bed. "Listen to me," he took her chin in his hand, so she couldn't turn away. "There is nothing that we can't conquer together. We can wrangle alligators, diffuse bombs, capture snakes and chase ghosts. Making love is going to be a piece of cake." She smiled and he kissed her tenderly. "We'll work it out. What happened before was not your fault. You had told me what would trigger an attack; and me in my lust-struck condition – I forgot."

"It's okay. We'll try again. Maybe, it won't happen anymore. It felt really, really good – until..."

"Until I held you down and reminded you of the past," Beau leaned his forehead against hers. "When you were saying 'please', I thought you were wanting more of me, not asking for me to stop. I'm so sorry."

She placed a palm on his cheek. "I always want more of you. We'll get past this, I promise. I'll go see Dane, again. I want to be perfect for you."

"You are perfect. It was me that messed it all up by walking away. If we had talked about it then like we're talking about it now, there would have been no misunderstanding. Just remember this, you never have to worry that I am going to leave you or reject you. We can work through your memories of being violated and they will disappear with time."

"But you said that you might not be what I needed."

Beau sighed, "Yea, I said that. But I never intended to leave. What I intended to do was change for you. Whatever it took."

"Will you make love to me now? In your home and in your bed?"

"Over and over again," he promised. Standing up, he pulled her to her feet. "Kiss me, cher." He shifted a heartbeat closer until nothing separated them but a whisper of heat. "I want to enflame your desires hotter than they've ever burned."

This man was heady, Harley quivered at the dark flame of desire she saw blazing in his eyes. "You are making me wet and achy," she whimpered.

"Good, I like you wet and achy."

Wrapping an arm around her waist, he pulled her close, and she couldn't help it. She rubbed her body against his, sensuously from side to side. "Oh God help me, I want you." Her nipples were hard, his cock was hard and every place their bodies touched detonated hot sparks of passion.

"You got me babe, now and forever." Without further ado, he claimed her lips in a savage kiss and Harley moaned her surrender. This man was her fierce protector. He was her best friend and if every prayer she ever uttered in her life was answered. He would be her's forever. Want gnawed at her clit, she needed him so much. Maybe it was the danger they had been through today, but she was ravenous for him. Harley was hungry to prove they were both still alive and had a lifetime of tomorrows. "God, I love you." He drug his mouth from hers and rained kisses all over her face from her forehead to her neck. "Look at me," he commanded. With the backs of his fingers he traced a warm trail down her neck to her collarbone, causing Harley to thrust her breasts out toward him wanting more.

"Touch me, please," she nipped him on the chin and a surprised laugh erupted from his lips.

"Oh my baby is getting brave," he bit her back, a gentle scraping of his teeth on her neck. But he rewarded her by tweaking an erect nipple through the thin barrier of her dress and camisole.

"Brave? No, I'm fearless," she tossed back at him as she rubbed the flat of her hand over his bulging erection. The gesture was meant to arouse him, but when it jumped in her hand hot tingles of excitement radiated out from her clit and made her hips pump in jealousy.

"Yes, you are, my Nada. You are my little warrior." Giving her what she needed, he put both hands between them and rubbed her nipples, tormenting them with milking motions that drove her wild.

"If you don't put your mouth on me, I'm going to hurt you."

Beau leaned back and looked at her, unable to contain his mirth. "Who are you?" he laughed. "Hold up your arms? Let me see those luscious nipples of yours." Dutifully, she raised her arms over her head and let him skim off her dress and her camisole, leaving her only in a pair of lacy pink underwear. "Damn!" Would he ever tire of looking at her?

Longing bubbled up within her from a wellspring of

dreams. This man was her fantasy, her dream lover, her destiny. He cupped her bottom, sliding his hand down into her panties. "You have fun teasing me, don't you?" Her breathing hitched when he stroked her rump and flirted with her crease.

"More than you'll ever know." Before she could blink, he picked her up, "Wrap your legs around my waist." When she did, he slid his palms under her ass and lifted her up – up – so, his mouth could close over a swollen nipple. Harley's head lolled back and she arched, giving him total access. "Hmmmm," Beau hummed his enjoyment as he consumed, devoured and ravished her tits. Total possession, that's what it was. This was more than lovemaking, this was more than sex. This was a total claiming. Beaureguarde LeBlanc wanted Harley Montoya…for better, for worse, for richer, for poorer…as long as they both shall live. The missing marriage license and ceremony was a mere technicality. As far as he was concerned they would become one flesh tonight.

A haze of pleasure enveloped her as he went from breasts to breast searing them with hot suction and a swirling tongue. "I want you inside me, Beau. I need you inside me."

Granting her wish, he laid her on the bed and tore off his clothes. He couldn't help but let his eyes feast on the picture she made laying there all rosy from his loving. Her nipples were wet from his mouth and her pussy was wet from excitement. And that face. God, her face was beautiful. Damn, he was hard. He fisted his cock, pumping it a couple of times, priming the pump. "Spread those legs, baby." And when she did, he groaned at the sight. Open, vulnerable, soft, totally feminine. Harley was a picture of what a desirable woman should be.

Lowering his big body, he fitted himself to her and at last she got the privilege of touching him. Greedily, she ran her hands over his chest and shoulders. It amazed her how hard his muscles were, the ridges and valleys were designed to be explored by touch and taste. Harley longed to map his body, to drive him as wild as she was. "Hold up, Beau. I need to feel your cock." He lifted himself up, giving her room to reach between them. And when her hand closed over his steel rod, they both groaned.

"Are you ready for me to fuck you, Harley?"

He hadn't known her intentions, but Harley had plans. Closing her hand around his hard, thick erection, she guided it to her opening. Only he could give her what her body craved. "Yea, I need it as hard and fast as you can give it to me." She didn't really know what demon possessed her tonight, but for the first time she felt free. Gone were the doubts and fears of rejection. Beau wanted her. He desired her. Beau loved her just the way she was.

"Hold on baby," he warned. "I've got to have you, now."

Holding her breath, she waited. With a dip of his hips, he entered her. Just the tip of his cock nudged inside. "Just that little bit feels so good," she encouraged. "I need more." Harley knew she was being demanding, but she couldn't help it. Her whole being felt desperate for him. She needed Beau to put out the fire that was threatening to burn her alive.

"Tell me what you want, Harley. Say the words." He needed to hear them. He hungered to hear them. "Tell me what you want and I'll give it to you."

It never crossed her mind to deny either one of them. "Take me, Beau. Fuck me. Please fuck me!" He didn't make her wait another moment. As she lifted her hips, he thrust in and both of them shut their eyes in rapture. Her pussy opened and separated, her soft flesh made room for him. "It feels so good!" she raised her hips, loving the drag of the big head of his cock over nerve-endings that screamed for more. Just hours before, she had thought it was over; just hours before, it had seemed they had no future. And now she was in his bed, in his arms and he was buried as deep inside of her as a man could be. She was aware of every inch – every vein – every slip and slide of his flesh against hers.

Stroke after stroke drove her higher and higher. Harley held on to his shoulders, fingernails digging in. If she didn't hang on, she would be swept away in the waves of ecstasy that were bombarding her soul. "More!" Her cries of encouragement echoed around the room. Shadows on the walls showed a dance of desire as they gave one another pleasure. Harley tried to hold out, she wanted to cum at the same time as Beau. But she couldn't. He pistoned into her, driving her right off the edge of the world…it didn't surprise her at all to learn she could fly. "Beau!"

As Harley screamed his name, he let go. The sensation of her pussy closing around him over and over again was all it took to trigger his own orgasm. Rolling up from his balls, his climax rocketed through his cock and exploded out in a rush of pleasure. But he couldn't stop bucking into her. It just felt too good. And her little body was still caressing him, massaging him. Milking him with exquisite convulsions. He bent his head to her neck and "I'll never get enough of you, and I'm never letting you go."

* * *

Early morning in the swamp was a sight to behold. Mist rose from the waters and birds took to the skies in colorful clouds of motion. Sounds of nature filled the air while Harley stood on the deck and surveyed the picturesque scene with more peace in her heart than she could ever remember having. The need for coffee drew her back into the house. She made it the way Beau liked it and the smell was so strong, she almost expected the paint to peel from the walls.

Pouring a mug full, she stirred in sugar and cream – a lot of sugar and cream. An omelet sounded good. The sound of the shower told her that Beau was up, so she took a sip, sat her cup down and took out eggs, cheese, ham and vegetables from the refrigerator. As if on cue, her stomach growled. Their nocturnal activities had given her an appetite. Twice before dawn he had reached for her, their need for one another almost insatiable.

A dull hissing roar almost made her jump. It was the bull croc. She recognized the sound and wondered what he found to bellow about so early in the morning. Harley had left the deck door open to catch the morning breeze, so the sounds of the bayou were drifting up to her ears. Peering into the cabinets, she located a bowl and other tools she would need to make them breakfast. She was anxious to make a place for herself in his home. The dinging of her cell phone broke her reverie. "I'm tempted to not even check," she muttered to herself. It was her regular phone and she didn't feel the need to hear from anybody. But habits were hard to break – so she looked. There were three texts and a voice mail. When she opened one of them up, she had to catch the cabinet to keep from falling. The words made her blood run cold. CROCKER WAS NOT APPREHENDED, BE CAREFUL.

"Is that about me?"

Harley whirled around and saw Fox Crocker standing in the open door. She couldn't even scream.

"Are you glad to see me?" The insane gleam in his eyes went along perfectly with his words.

"Beau will kill you." She knew he would if he got the chance, but Beau was in another part of the house. Whether he would find her in time was the question. There was no doubt in Harley's mind that Crocker had come to kill her.

"Today we all die, Nada." Fox announced

conversationally. "I'm trying out one of those new bombs, you've heard about them – a body bomb?"

For a moment, she didn't understand. Then it hit her. This was the newest weapon in the world of terrorism. "You've made yourself into a bomb, haven't you?" She had read about this. He had either ingested it or pushed it up into himself from his rectum. It would be plastic, undetectable by x-ray and detonated by a substance injected by syringe. The question was – had he already injected himself? How much time did she have and could she get Beau out of the house before it blew? That was the critical question. Either way, there was no way he could save himself if he didn't know it was happening. "Beau!" she screamed.

"What's the use to call the Cajun? Wouldn't it be more merciful to let his death be a surprise?" He stuck his hand in his pocket and Harley bit the inside of her jaw, hard. Trying to keep from screaming. If he pulled out the syringe, she was going to run at him and try to push him outside the house. That was a foolish and ineffectual choice, but she couldn't think of anything else to do. But it wasn't a syringe he extracted from the pocket, it was a knife.

"Why have you always hated me so much?" It was a question that she had always struggled with. How could one human being despise another to the extent that their every waking moment was devoted to giving the object of their loathing hell on earth?

"That's simple. Like the name your father gave you at birth, you are nothing. You are worthless. No man in his right mind would ever want you. I had you, and there was nothing special about you at all."

Harley tried not to listen. Beau loved her. Crocker was wrong. He was insane.

"You're ruined, desecrated, used up and disgusting." As he denigrated her, he moved toward her – knife raised.

"If you put one scratch on her silky-smooth skin, I'll gut you like a catfish," Beau ground out the words. When Harley had called, he knew something was wrong. Raising a 350 Mag, he pointed it straight at the black bastard's heart.

"Don't move a muscle, LeBlanc. You shoot me and we all die instantly, in a blaze of glory." He held up both arms as he yelled, triumphantly.

"What's he talking about, baby?" Beau addressed Harley.

"Crocker has made himself into a bomb. He has plastic explosives inside his body. I don't think a bullet would detonate it, but I can't be sure."

"Then, we won't take the chance. Is it like nitro?"

Harley knew what he was asking. If Beau fought with him, would it explode? "No, it's not that volatile of a substance."

"Enough said."

"How do you fuck her, LeBlanc?" Crocker snarled. "Does the bile rise in your throat every time you sink into her dirty pussy?"

"Hell, no. Don't you listen to him, Harley. Those were your last words asshole." Beau lunged at him, knocking him to the ground.

"Be careful, Beau," Harley begged. Crocker was nowhere near Beau's size, but he had a knife. Plus, he was insane and insanity is an incredible source of strength. She watched them struggle. The knife clattered to the floor, but still they fought. Crocker tried to gouge Beau's eyes and grab him by the throat, but Beau managed to wrestle him out toward the deck. Harley picked up the knife and followed, if she got the chance, she'd gut him herself.

Out on the deck, they struggled, moving first one way and then the other. Beau was backed up to the railing and Crocker had his back to her. This was her chance. She was just about to make her move and attack him, when Crocker broke away. With a horrendous yell, he charged Beau. Time seemed to freeze and Beau met Harley's eyes for a moment as Crocker barreled at him. And with the precise timing of an athlete, at the last moment – he simply stepped to one side. The force and momentum Fox had put into his attack carried him over the side of the deck. Harley screamed and Beau made a lunge to catch him. He managed to catch Crocker by one leg. Crocker struggled wildly, but Beau hung on. As he was lifting him, there was a splash, a sick scream and a horrible gnashing sound. The Cuban Croc, so used to accepting handouts, had sprang up and crushed Crocker's skull like a tomato.

The authorities came and took Crocker's body away. Harley warned them of what they would find inside of him and the precautions that needed to be taken. The syringe was still in his pocket and Harley was weak with relief. It was over.

After everyone was gone, Beau wrapped his arms around her. "I know I won't ever be comfortable with you putting yourself in danger. But what I do know is that I can't live apart from you and as long as we're both in this world, I want us to be together." He sank to one knee and took her hand. "Will you marry me, Harley Montoya?"

Seeing Beau on his knees before her, asking for her hand in marriage was almost too much. Harley couldn't stay on her feet. She knelt with him. "Yes, I'll marry you. I would be honored to be your wife. As far as Socorro is concerned, I'm through defusing bombs. I plan on letting Waco take over, I'll only consult."

"Thank God," Beau whispered against her skin as he placed a reverent kiss on her cheek. "I want you to know something. You are my world. You are my Nada. Your name may mean 'nothing', but that's the farthest thing from the truth there is. In my eyes, you could never be 'nothing' to me. You are my everything."

Epilogue

"Beau! There's an alligator in my bathtub!" Harley stood with a towel wrapped around her body staring at the small, scaly creature dog paddling around in her beloved claw foot tub.

"Talk to your son!" was Beau's amused reply from the bedroom.

"Mama! Don't disturb Madeline; she's having her morning swim!" A whirlwind in disguise, four year old Landry LeBlanc came rushing into the bathroom. He threw his arms around his mother's knees, almost knocking them both in on top of poor unsuspecting Madeline who was happily taking laps around her pool.

"Okay, I guess I can wait for my bath," she ruffled her baby boy's dark hair that was so like his papa's.

"Come back to bed. I'm lonely," Beau spoke with such a suggestive tone in his voice that she immediately went wet for him.

Dragging Landry along, who refused to give up his hold on her leg, Harley leaned against the door facing and gazed at the love of her life. Against the white sheets, he looked as sexy as sin. His body was tanned and perfectly proportioned, wide shoulders and that hair - - she refused to let him cut that sexy mane of hair. "Don't you think it's a bit crowded in here for playing house, what with Landry and Madeline keeping us company?"

"Beau! Harley! I'm here to pick up Landry" Dandi yelled up the stairs. That's all it took. Landry took off like a ruptured redbug. "Oh boy, we're going to the movies!"

"Thank you, Dandi! Close the door on your way out, Harley and I are busy up here."

Dandi's laugh told them she understood perfectly.

"Don't do anything I wouldn't do."

Harley blushed. "Don't you have any shame?"

"Not where you're concerned. Come here." He wiggled one finger and he might as well have been rubbing her clit with it, because her whole body went soft with need.

Harley shut the door and dropped the towel.

"Hot Damn!" Beau groaned in appreciation of his wife's beauty. As she walked to him, he thanked God for every blessing in his life. His business was doing well. The game preserve was expanding, thanks to a grant he had received from the state, and the rodeo foundation for disabled children he had founded with Joseph McCoy was proving to be a great success. Socorro still belonged to Harley, but she had turned day to day operations over to Waco and they had hired another talented EOD expert, Douglas Wayne. They divided their living time between weekends on the boathouse, summers at Beau's treehouse (as Landry called it), and the rest here at Willowbend where they coexisted peacefully with its spirits. The LeBlanc family had it all.

"Give me some sugar, cher," Beau pulled her down on top of him and they kissed. As soon as their lips touched, a spark flashed and their passion blazed bright and hot. Burning love…that's what they shared and neither one of them ever intended for the flames to go out.

"I love you, Beau-ray," Harley's voice caught in her throat as she gave thanks for what they shared and how very lucky they were.

"I love you, too," he assured her, "you are my everything."

"You are *my* everything," she emphasized the same sweet truth that he never failed to remind her of.

"Now, let's get down to some serious sex."

"What about Madeline?" she asked as Beau cupped

her bottom and pulled her up close enough so he could make himself at home playing with her tits. One of his favorite past-times.

"I'll take her back to the preserve later. Right now, your man needs attention."

"How much attention?"

"Beau-coup attention, baby. Beau-coup."

Harley smiled. "I'll give you all the attention you can handle." And she kept her word.

From the bathroom, the lilting laugh of a little girl made them smile. Madeline wasn't alone. None of them were. They had each other.

Sign up for Sable Hunter's newsletter
http://eepurl.com/qRvyn

Enjoy another Sable Hunter steamy romance!

Forget Me Never
Hell Yeah! Cajun Style

The TV was on, the food was spread out and she had on as close to something sexy as she owned. Savannah had more on her mind than football. "Wow, this looks great!" Patrick was a big eater, so she had fixed plenty.

"Did you have a good conversation with your friend?"

"Yes, I did. We talked about you, mostly." He settled down on the couch – just stretched out and left her a little spot in the corner. "Come here, I want to cuddle."

"What did you say about me?" She sat on her legs and looked him in the eye.

"You're a nosy little thing, aren't you?" Patrick teased.

"A little bit."

She fed him a bite of pizza. He took the bite, captured her hand and licked the remaining spot of sauce off her fingers. "I just told him how I felt about you. And we discussed some business, that's all." There was more to it than that, but he wasn't ready to tell her everything – not yet. "Look, the game's starting."

Typical male, he got into the game. Savannah had a good time watching him. He yelled at the quarterback. He snarled at the referees, but mostly he looked disturbed because the first half was almost over and the Colts were ahead of the Saints. "It's okay."

Patrick knew it was okay. But this game had come to mean more to him than just his favorite team winning the big prize. It might be silly, but he had wound this all up with his chances of being with Savannah. "The game's not over."

"No, it's not." There were a few minutes left until halftime and then The Who were going to sing. Savannah was still hungry – but not for food.

"Come on Brees!" Patrick yelled at the Saints quarterback. "Do something!"

Savannah decided to make her own play. He was sitting about a foot away from her. He had been closer, but he was eating and getting into the game and somehow he'd moved away from her. That would never do. He wasn't paying any attention to her at all, so when she let her hand inch his way – she waited to see what he would do.

Patrick knew Savannah thought he was oblivious to her advances. She was letting her fingers do the walking – literally. Her little hand was inching toward him, and he couldn't wait to see what she was up to. He leaned forward just like he was engrossed in the game. Right now he was more interested in her, but he wasn't going to let on.

She let her fingers touch his hard thigh – just barely. First, she pushed her hand under his legs just a little bit, like it was cold and she was trying to get warm. He just grunted – he wasn't taking the hint. Next, she let her fingers walk up his leg, like a little spider – still, nothing. Damn! Getting a mite bolder, she curled her hand over the top of his leg and rubbed her thumb up and down on the strong muscle. He had the audacity to pat her hand and say, "Hey, Baby. How's it going?"

Patrick bit back a smile when she huffed and muttered under her breath. It was the same little voice she'd used the day they met in the memorial when her friend had been embarrassing the heck out of her.

Before Patrick, she would never have attempted something like this. But he had given her confidence in her attraction that no one ever had. So, she let her hand – slide upward – upward toward his crotch, until she bumped into something rather large and hard.

"Uh-Oh," She looked up at Patrick.

"I'm kinda trying to watch the game here, Baby," he said with a smirk, trying not to laugh.

The feel of Patrick's bulge had caused a stir in her sex which made her feel naughty. She fixed Patrick with a vexed glare, but he ignored her eyes. She huffed, and withdrew her hand from the firm bulge that she'd wanted to explore further and folded her arms defensively across her chest. Her first attempt at seduction, and Patrick had rejected her; this didn't sit well with Savannah.

Savannah sat on the couch as halftime drew closer and the Saints marched down the field. Beside her, Patrick watched her out of the corner of his eye. The brazen way she'd grabbed for his package had turned him on, but he wanted to see how she would handle his rejection, see if she wanted him bad enough to make another move.

Savannah was doing a horrible job of masking her displeasure and when she innocently moved her hands up over her head for a stretch, something in the way her head tilted to the side filled Patrick with a need to kiss her neck.

Patrick shimmied a few inches closer to his Savannah and now it was her turn to pretend she didn't notice what he was doing.

When Patrick shimmied a few more inches, Savannah picked up a magazine from the end table beside her; she wasn't going to make this easy on him.

A few more inches and Patrick was close enough that his essence made her legs squirm.

"Hey," Patrick said.

He was right beside her now, his thickly muscled arm pressed against hers, their thighs touching.

Savannah ignored him.

"Whatcha readin'?" He inquired, snatching the magazine from her hands.

"Patrick!"

Patrick held the magazine just out of Savannah's reach. She made one grab for it, but gave up, not wanting to give him the satisfaction.

Savannah looked away from him. Not her best move if she hoped to remain cross with Patrick. That small patch of bare skin on Savannahs neck that had caused the tightness in Patrick's jeans was now fully exposed and with Savannah looking the other way, he seized the opportunity and leaned in to kiss it softly.

Savannah flinched when she felt Patrick's gentle lips on her neck, then her shoulder. "Pa...trick," she said, forgetting almost all of the annoyance he'd inspired in her so recently. "Stop," she offered weakly, but tilted her neck further to the side to grant him even greater access.

"Stop?" Patrick kissed her neck. "Stop what?"

He licked up to Savannah's ear, nibbling on the lobe lightly before moving back down to her collarbone.

Savannah whimpered with appreciation. Gone now was any semblance of the frustration and rejection she'd felt, in its place was nothing but bliss. The skin on her neck was dimpled with goosebumps; her chest beginning to flush.

"You want me to go?" Patrick asked between kisses.

His hand had found its way around to the front of her shirt, undoing first the top button of her blouse and then the next one.

Savannah placed her hand behind Patrick's head as he kissed her collarbone and shoulder. "I thought you wanted to watch the game?" The words barely came out of her mouth in an audible tone.

"I'd rather watch you," Patrick whispered in her ear.

Savannah's round bottom levitated from the couch when Patrick hit that magic spot just behind her ear. "I have to tell you, this is one of my favorite fantasies in the whole world."

Patrick's hand stilled. "What's that, Baby?" If she had a fantasy, he would do his damnedest to fulfill it.

myBook.to/ForgetMeNever

Burning Love

About the Author:

Sable Hunter is a New York Times, USA Today bestselling author of nearly 50 books in 7 series. She writes sexy contemporary stories full of emotion and suspense. Her focus is mainly cowboy and novels set in Louisiana with a hint of the supernatural. Sable writes what she likes to read and enjoys putting her fantasies on paper. Her books are emotional tales where the heroine is faced with challenges. Her aim is to write a story that will make you laugh, cry and swoon. If she can wring those emotions from a reader, she has done her job. Sable resides in Austin, Texas with her two dogs. Passionate about all animals, she has been known to charm creatures from a one ton bull to a family of raccoons. For fun, Sable haunts cemeteries and battlefields armed with night-vision cameras and digital recorders hunting proof that love survives beyond the grave. Welcome to her world of magic, alpha heroes, sexy cowboys and hot, steamy to-die-for sex. Step into the shoes of her heroines and escape to places where right prevails, love conquers all and holding out for a hero is not an impossible dream.

Visit Sable:

Website:

http://www.sablehunter.com

Facebook

https://www.facebook.com/authorsablehunter

Amazon:

http://www.amazon.com/author/sablehunter

Pinterest

https://www.pinterest.com/AuthorSableH/

Twitter

https://twitter.com/huntersable

Sign up for Sable Hunter's newsletter

http://eepurl.com/qRvyn

SABLE'S BOOKS
Get hot and bothered!!!

Hell Yeah!

Cowboy Heat

Hot on Her Trail

Her Magic Touch

Brown Eyed Handsome Man

Badass

Burning Love

Forget Me Never
With Ryan O'Leary & Jess Hunter

I'll See You In My Dreams
With Ryan O'Leary

Finding Dandi

Skye Blue

I'll Remember You

True Love's Fire

Thunderbird
With Ryan O'Leary

Welcome To My World

How to Rope a McCoy

One Man's Treasure
With Ryan O'Leary

You Are Always on My Mind

If I Can Dream

Head over Spurs

The Key to Micah's Heart
With Ryan O'Leary

Love Me, I Dare you!

Hell Yeah! Sweeter Versions

Cowboy Heat

Hot on Her Trail

Her Magic Touch

Brown Eyed Handsome Man

Badass

Burning Love

Finding Dandi

Forget Me Never

I'll See You In My Dreams

Moon Magic Series
A Wishing Moon

Sweet Evangeline

Hill Country Heart Series
Unchained Melody

Scarlet Fever

Bobby Does Dallas

Dixie Dreaming
Come With Me

Pretty Face: A Red Hot Cajun Nights Story

Texas Heat Series
T-R-O-U-B-L-E

My Aliyah

El Camino Real Series
A Breath of Heaven

Loving Justice

Texas Heroes Series
Texas Wildfire

Texas CHAOS

Texas Lonestar

Texas Maverick

Other Titles from Sable Hunter:

For A Hero

Green With Envy (It's Just Sex Book 1)
with Ryan O'Leary

Hell Yeah! Box Set With Bonus Cookbook

Love's Magic Spell: A Red Hot Treats Story

Wolf Call

Cowboy 12 Pack: Twelve-Novel Boxed Set

Rogue (The Sons of Dusty Walker)

Kit and Rogue

Be My Love Song

Audio
Cowboy Heat - Sweeter Version: Hell Yeah! Sweeter
Version

Hot on Her Trail - Sweeter Version: Hell Yeah! Sweeter Version, Book 2

<u>Spanish Edition</u>
Vaquero Ardiente *(*Cowboy Heat)
Su Rastro Caliente (Hot On Her Trail)

20142112R00168

Printed in Great Britain
by Amazon